To Gen
From June

W9-BIL-647

Fisher of Men

FISHER OF MEN

A Novel of Simon Peter

By

KURT FRIEBERGER

APPLETON-CENTURY-CROFTS, INC.

New York

PRINTED IN THE UNITED STATES OF AMERICA

Respectfully dedicated
TO HIS HOLINESS
POPE
PIUS XII
in grateful remembrance of the words of
the Papal Secretary of State, Cardinal
EUGENIO PACELLI
on May 18th, 1930
when he became Protector
of the
German Foundation
S. MARIA DELL' ANIMA
where the plan of this work was conceived.

Fisher of Men

VEN AS CHILDREN JAMES AND JOHN, the gentle sons of Zebedee, looked to Simon as their leader. Whether they were playing some boy's game in the streets of Bethsaida or fishing on Lake Galilee, Simon, son of Jonah, was always captain.

Strange that neither they nor Simon's brother, Andrew, ever questioned this. For Zebedee was rich and Jonah poor—poor to the point of being in debt to Zebedee for the very boat from which he and his sons eked their precarious living. Moreover, James and John, as well as Andrew, could read and write. Simon could do neither. Yet, even at fifteen, he was the leader.

For it was when Simon was fifteen that he held his dying father in his arms, sobbing, comforting him, caressing his neck and shoulder where, to his horror, his hand encountered the open blood-wet lips of a deep wound. It was then he knew for certain that Jonah had secretly been a member of the Gaulonites, the band of men who lurked in the woods and on the desert's edge, their short-swords hidden in their sleeves, and

I

killed any of the people's oppressors—Roman, priest, or wealthy heathen—who strayed their way. It was then he vowed to help set his people free, as his father had tried to do, no matter the danger.

After the murder of Jonah by the Romans and their Sebastene hirelings, James, the quiet one, realized why they all looked up to Simon: "We three think deliverance from Rome will come eventually," he told his brother; "Simon knows it."

And it was true that from the dreadful night of his vigil over his dying father Simon was convinced that freedom from the hated yoke would come in their lifetime. Often he repeated to the others the last words Jonah uttered: "Go with him when he comes. He will descend from the mountains, the king with his armed men, like the great Alexander, the ruler of the world." And those words, heard in his fifteenth summer, never left his mind.

NOTHER TWELVE HUNDRED DAYS and the new Kingdom begins!" Secretly, pilgrims carried this prophecy to Simon, now a bearded man, sturdy and forthright, and through blood and sorrow a staunch rebel of the Lord. He could hardly bear to stay at home with his wife Rahab. Men were resisting the Romans, resisting Herod, resisting the Temple priests in Jerusalem. By night, the rebel swordsmen met secretly in Simon's house, to hear the news and to plan fresh attacks. Had not Rahab's mother, stricken with the holy malady, foretold the coming of the Messiah in twelve hundred days?

In turns, muffled men kept watch in the darkness around the house, in case any Sebastene rode up, or any informer was lurking at hand. Today they had to choose by lots, for none wanted to miss a word of Simon's report. He had just returned from Caesarea with news of the challenge to the governor, Lucius Pontius Pilate. The new procurator had dared to set up a golden portrait of Caesar on the citadel of Antonia on

Mount Moriah, though no conqueror had ever carried an image of God or man through the city of the invisible Jahveh. The dense crowd of believers had burst into tears and howls of fury. "And did the high priests not have the shofar sounded?"

"The priests?" Simon laughed ironically. "They lick the Romans' shoes. But the people rose. Peasants and shepherds joined the townsfolk, all, all of them flocked to Caesarea, to the sea."

Impatiently, one of the sons of Zebedee asked: "Who won?"

"Without weapons?" Simon reflected a while. "And yet, it might be called a victory. Every street and square in the city was thronged till the house walls threatened to give way. The legionaries had their lances at the ready, around Pilate's palace. All troops were standing alerted in the barracks. Many of us had the short-sword tucked in the folds of our garments. On the roofs, the women had prepared boiling oil and scalding water. The little boys were gathering stones. Then the gate opened. And who should come along in her cushioned litter? You all knew her when she was but a child. Mary of Migdal. Just at that moment, a knot of Pharisees, the nine times righteous, were arguing in front of her house. They shrank back before the paramour of Pilate the unbeliever, as if she were a leper."

James, proud and pale, spat. "Whose paramour is she not?"

But Simon and his brother, Andrew, glared so furiously at the son of Zebedee that the desperate men began to suspect some secret, especially when Andrew indignantly declared: "Paramour or no paramour, is not Rahab the fallen woman mentioned in the Scriptures?"

Simon's wife winced. It was bad enough to hear them speak of Mary of Migdal; now her own name was being brought in. But her husband laughed. "Oh, you learned men! Did not eight priests and prophets stem from Rahab the harlot? But do you know whom Mary has supplanted? The noble Roman lady Claudia Procula. The Procurator's wife is obliged to be jealous of a little Judaean whore, because Pilate is infatuated with her.—They all shrank back from her. She looked like a Deborah, pale as death. The crowd parted before her and she

4

slid down from her litter and stood alone before the wall of spears. She glanced up to Pilate, who was standing on the balustraded roof with a couple of guards, bows at the ready, on either side of him, each bowman aiming at one of us. Well, the Roman smiled and waved to his mistress. He must have recognized his gifts, all the jewelry she wore. The Procurator could not make out what everyone was shouting down below, till a chorus of thousands, beat by beat, word by word, begged and implored him, over and again: 'Take away the Emperor's portrait from the citadel. Take it out of Jerusalem. Hear us, sire!' "

"Oh, miserable! That they should beg for it!"

"So I said too. I was all for attacking the legionaries. But when Pontius Pilate only laughed at their prayer, Mary took off her jewelry, piece by piece, from her neck, her hair, her ears, her arms, and threw the lot on the ground and trampled it underfoot. Then she threw herself full-length in the dust, and with her, everyone—men, women, children, and I as well—fell prostrate. For five days and nights we lay stretched out as if dead. Eventually the Procurator ordered the heathen emblem to be taken out, beyond the pale of the Temple."

"So it was a victory after all," conceded James, and he began to tell them of a mighty master of the Word, reputedly sent from God. John was his name. He was preaching to countless thousands by the Jordan that the time was at hand. Already the Sanhedrin had sent from Jerusalem to ask him who he was, that he should baptize and yet declare that he was neither Christ nor Elias nor the prophet. His answer was: "I baptize with water. Amongst you stands one you know not, who comes after me. Prepare the path of the Lord."

Simon and his comrades could not hear enough of the mighty preacher, John the Baptist, he of the camel-hair robe, the leather girdle, and his food nothing but locust beans and wild honey.

Next day Simon and Andrew, John the son of Zebedee, Philip and Nathanael made their way to the Jordan to seek him out and found him preaching to the multitude, urging them to repent before it was too late. They heard him speaking of the Pharisees and the Sadducees. "A brood of vipers," he called them, and advised them to flee from the wrath to come. They would all be chaff for the winnowing fan of Christ, who would burn them in the unquenchable fire.

Many of the comrades, and Simon first, reached for their short-swords, feeling that the day of deliverance was already at hand. Only one man, full of oaths and warnings, rose in opposition. It was the old centurion Aulus Cuspius, a Judaean who had served his time in the Imperial Army. On his discharge, he had been granted the fallow land neighboring on Zebedee's garden, and year by year he gathered a good harvest of oil and wine. Coarse and good-natured, for all his Roman officer's manner he had preserved a strong sense of solidarity with his fellow countrymen. He had taught his friends Roman tactics and the use of the sword in close combat. Had they not learned from bitter experience during the guerrilla campaign that audacity alone is unavailing against that evil monster— metal-clad, shield-protected and javelin-armed—the Roman legion?

"What can an army of starvelings and locust-hunters do? And that Christ of yours—did not the prophet Daniel foretell his death?" But they were not to be dissuaded. However hard their patience might be tested there on the banks of the Jordan, they knew the time was coming when, led by the new Messiah, they would march against Herod and the Romans.

Precious time was spent in waiting. Each day, they stood with the lean fanatical preacher beside the yellow, lazy-flowing river. High above the valley, where the spring pastures began and the bees hummed over the blossoms in the wind, the Baptist had pitched his camp. There they waited, all those with neither land nor work nor money to their name. Many of them called for a hunger march on Jerusalem. The most furious in their impatience were the men from Bethsaida. Nathanael had wandered away some distance, to a clearing where a fig tree spread its branches. Peasantwise, he had touched each branch to see if it was soft, and if the leaves were coming. But the summer's fulfillment was far off yet, and he drew his short-sword and hacked at the tree so that the chips flew.

Simon was squatting on the steep bank high above the

6

valley, staring down at the muddy Jordan, homesick for the clear water of the lake and for his boat. He saw hundreds of people crowding together by the Jordan ford. Probably the preacher from the wilderness was coming with his disciples. Ecstatic cries caught the fisherman's attention. He turned, and recognized his namesake Simon Magus who, with his strange following of twenty-nine chosen disciples and his mistress, Helena, was going towards the Jordan from the camp of reed huts and rag tents. How they aped the Baptist, with their skins, and their unkempt hair and their beards grown wild!

Simon, son of Jonah, sprang to his feet and laughed sardonically. "Why do you only carry cockleshells on your staves? Why not spearheads? Why do you not rise up against Herod?"

Simon Magus raised his eyebrows. "What is the Greek infidel—as the Baptist calls him—what is the Greek infidel to us?"

"You innocents! John calls him and those shameful women of his more heartening names than that. All Judaea and Israel calls them that much. And the Law says a foreigner cannot be King. Herod's cruelty is unbounded, and still more so that of his women, Herodias and her daughter Salome. Salome! That good Hebrew name avails her nothing. But you, you apes of your master—but there, in Egypt where you come from, they worship apes!"

The Magus shot him a malevolent glance as if he would bewitch him into silence. "What do you know of the mystery? The great light comes from us, the sun which is now inevitably passing into the sign of the Fishes."

"Fish—that is my work, catching fish. But the Baptist should hear your heathenish babble!"

Complacently and meaningfully Simon Magus answered: "He knows many things, does he not? He knows why we follow him. And according to his word, the Son will be here soon, He of whom the Master says that he is not worthy to unloose the latchet of his shoes." He gazed smiling at his namesake. "Perhaps you?" He drew himself up to his full height. "Perhaps—me?"

"Blasphemer!" roared Simon, and drew his short-sword. Before his onslaught, the twenty-nine staggered back; then

7

they too produced keen bright swords. The shouts of rage and the clash of weapons were so deafening that at first they did not hear the storm of eager voices from the Jordan, the shouts of joy that gradually changed to mass singing. Not till Andrew flung himself with a cry between the combatants did they stop and become aware of the singing. Andrew had so overtaxed his strength in hurling himself among them that his brown face was darker than ever with the rush of blood. Sweat dripped from his lips, and he had only breath enough to utter three words: "It is He!"

Andrew, gasping for breath, softly and devoutly panted: "He whom John was expecting has just come to be baptized."

Disappointment sounded in the Magus's words: "Whom do you speak of?"

But Simon the son of Jonah drew himself up and shouted with joy: "Weapons out! No more twelve hundred days! Rome—here is an end to you! The march is about to begin!"

Down on the Jordan bank, people were running and pushing. The vast crowd of the Baptist's followers stretched far up into the spring pastures. John walked among the multitude, smiling, radiant with happiness, utterly unself-conscious. Surrounded at a respectful distance by a wide arc of reverent followers, with all eyes upon him, one man in a simple blue garment walked alone.

Enormously excited, Andrew clutched his brother's arm. As if a storm had caught them both up and was impelling them towards him, they went leaping down the steep bank, joyously shouting the words of the second psalm: "Ask of me and I will give thee the nations for thine inheritance and the uttermost parts of the earth for thy possession."

Once at the foot of the slope, for all their jubilation, they were overcome by a desperate unease. For was not his gaze already turned on them? Simon hid his short-sword as if he had no further need of it.

The man came closer and closer, his gaze fixed straight on the fisherman as if he had known him for a long time. Eyes full of such compassion as only a man of might is capable of, held the fisherman under their tremendous spell. With a kindly smile that seemed to plumb every thought, in front of all those thousands, he called out to the greatly confused, profoundly happy man: "You are Simon, the son of Jonah; Kephas is your name."

"Kephas? A Rock?"

On a sultry spring evening many days later, one of Zebedee's fishing boats was slowly sailing along when Aulus Cuspius, a guest on board, waved excitedly to James at the tiller. Five travelers were resting on the bank. "It is your brother John! Jonah's sons are with him. That is Philip and Nathanael, squatting on their heels. Coming home again, full of disappointment, I'll be bound. A good few of their twelve hundred days are gone by already."

But this time, nobody took any notice of the old centurion's coarse barrack-room humor.

Andrew had hardly stepped on board than, unable to keep quiet any longer, he burst out: "James, he is here! All five of us saw him! He spoke to us!"

The master of the boat relinquished sail and rudder to his servants, and joined the narrow circle. In their hasty narrative, the newcomers constantly interrupted each other. They had been standing beside the Baptist when he saw him pass by and cried: "Behold the Lamb of God!" They had followed him, and asked him where he was staying. Andrew had fetched his brother at once: "We have found him!" He himself had then called Philip and Nathanael to him.

The Baptist had come down to the Jordan bank, thousands around him, hundreds ahead of him, people from everywhere, trembling before his wrath, standing meekly in line ready to submit to baptism as their last hope before final judgment and damnation. Suddenly the prophet of the thundering curses had grown quite humble, had timidly approached one among the multitude, and shyly said: "I have need to be baptized by you, and yet do you come to me?" But he wanted to fulfill the prophecy, he insisted on being baptized. And then as he came out of the waters of the Jordan—everybody had heard it, Philip and Andrew among them—a voice like the hurricane breath of God had announced: "This is my well-beloved son in whom I am well pleased."

James was sunk in meditation; silently he moved his narrow austere lips. At last, his gaze came back from infinity and wandered from one to the other. His question to Simon touched on the destiny of them all: "Tell me, in all the sleepless nights you spent in struggling and hoping, in hiding and in flight, was this your dream, this man you saw baptized?"

"No," came the honest answer. "God strike me, but it was not."

Philip the peasant pushed his lips forward and said: "Simon, you old fisherman, you have been looking aft for your rudder all this time and suddenly it is for'ard of you."

Simon answered with a half-relieved, half-rueful laugh: "To be a man, to be strong, to wield a sword, was the right thing to do, till now. There were more than enough Goliaths. Only the David was lacking. Of course, he was just a shepherd boy, but one who could use a sling. The one who has come now is a lamb, 'Lamb of God,' John called him. . . ."

"And is that what I have been teaching you right turn and left turn, and swordplay and close combat for?" mocked Aulus Cuspius.

"We were expecting a commander and conqueror," admitted Simon, "against Herod in Tiberias and the Emperor in Rome. You will not betray us, Captain, will you, you Jew of Jews?"

"Of course not. But it is laughable that the smartest lads in John's starveling army have to be lambs. God's lambs!"

Disapprovingly, James remarked: "You are disappointed in the blessing of the Lord?"

Nathanael made a gesture of dissent. "No. Just as you were speaking, James, it became clear to me where we have always gone astray. . . ."

Simon laughed. "Up gets my mother-in-law and prophesies: 'Only twelve hundred days more!' Everyone starts to rack his brains: Who is this Messiah, against whom neither Augustus nor Antony, the Romans nor the Parthians nor Aulus's Germans dare to march? We dream we are centurions and legates, knights and horsemen and generals, hoping that our great

10

coming Alexander will be a fellow like Moses or Samson, a true pious bull-horned giant."

James insisted: "Who is it? Where is he?"

Nathanael answered with a shake of the head: "He knew all about me and the fig tree that I hacked with my sword when not a soul was near." Breathing heavily, he stared into the darkness, in which the water shone like mother-of-pearl about the boat as it glided along. "We did not see him again. But since we did not understand him when he spoke to us, it may be that we cannot see him even when he is here by us."

They became aware of the cold wind and timorously followed the direction of his glance. But Simon turned to him. "Is that fit on you again? Just because you were sure nobody was watching you by that fig tree, it flattened you out, did it? Particularly as you had still been doubtful up to then. And how miserably you fell on your knees and stammered: 'You are the Son of God.' And the new King gave a kind smile and said: 'Just because I said I saw you under the fig tree, do you believe?'"

"And you, you old Gaulonite, you scourge of the Sebastenes, you great rebel! Did you not surrender like a lamb when he called you Kephas, the Rock?"

The experienced centurion nodded. "Every third Judaean is a Simon. A leader must take a name of some weight. My old friend Titus Pontius thought so too. When his son, our Procurator, wrote to him: 'In the course of my studies in the humanities in Subura, I have acquired an abominable keepsake, and my hair is falling out; in a little while I shall be bald,' the old man laughed. 'Bald? That's *pilatus*. Call yourself Pilatus, Lucius Pontius Pilatus. Everyone will laugh and remember it.' Simon, you do well to be called by a name that gives everyone shivers down the spine when you are mentioned as an opponent. Kephas... you know and I know what a mighty thing a rock is. The Greeks say Petra. And the Romans? Petrus is better, Peter, that has a stony sound, it hits hard. *Ave Petrus!*"

Trembling with impatience, James asked once more: "Who is he?"

11

"Jesus of Nazareth. We took him for the son of Joseph, the carpenter. His mother is of the house of David."

Aulus Cuspius shook his bald head. "He smiled? He is a lamb? Who can pray to a God who does not make you tremble?"

The others fell silent. Darkness spread over the lake.

Simon the fisherman had led a life of unrest, ambush, flight and wandering. And now, as Peter, whether with the five men of Bethsaida or without them, with new disciples or all alone, he was to travel on in search of Him whom John had greeted as the greater one, and against whom he bore a grudge, for it was said that he had declined the offer of the mastery of the world with the words: "Get behind me, Satan." This was the one whom he had cheered, when he cried to the staunch old Gaulonite fighters: "Do you think I come to bring peace on earth? I say unto you: No! I bring not peace, but the sword!"

Jesus took Simon and Andrew to his native town of Nazareth. Philip and Nathanael had joined them. The Plain of Jezreel shone around them, green and gold with the growing crops. To the south towered Carmel with its dark forests.

In Nazareth, they found the little white house of Joseph the carpenter locked up. Against the workshop wall leaned a number of untrimmed logs and a few half-worked beams. The five of them were standing amid the scent of the drying wood when neighbors came to tell them that Joseph and Mary had set out early that morning for Cana, to a relative's wedding. Their son had been invited too; he might bring guests; the bride's parents were rich and very hospitable.

While Jesus walked on at his steady, tireless pace, as if it did not in the least matter where in the world he spent the night, the disciples were racked with impatience. It occurred to Philip that now was the time to weed his fields, and Nathanael regretted his untilled vineyard, but they went on towards Galilee. Soon, however, they forgot their troubles in an argument about the Messiah. They recited scriptural texts about how he would destroy the enemy and sit on the throne of David. And here Jesus added: "The heathen shall worship him and his tomb shall be magnificent."

"Master, nobody likes to hear talk of the tomb when he is just setting out with a weapon handy in his sleeve, and the wish to carve out for himself a better life on earth." But the disciples fell silent and hardly dared to look up as, in the still night that lay bright and shadowless under the full moon, they heard the mild voice of Jesus say: "You will see the heavens open and the angels ascending and descending about the Son of Man." It would be some time before they realized that by "Son of Man" he meant himself.

"This is going to be a cheerful wedding, with tombs and heavens," whispered Simon to Andrew, as they stopped in Cana by a lonely gate, with long walls stretching on either side. But when it was opened for them, and black servants lit their way towards the night's festivities, they were astonished at the respect with which the rich folk here greeted the carpenter's son. Costly garments were put on them and the four disciples had great trouble in concealing their short-swords.

Simon said in an undertone: "If the carpenter's mate has a few more friends like the bride's father here, he could equip and maintain a good little troop of partisans." The servants were offering the strangers broad two-handled earthenware bowls, into which the cupbearer poured welcome wine out of a black goatskin. But there was only wine enough for three. The embarrassed servants whispered among themselves. There had been too many thirsty folk here today. Nathanael thought unhappily how much he could have supplied from his cellar.

Mary, the carpenter's wife, came by in her festive clothes. For all the amount of material used for her dress, the fabric was so fine that the slender woman seemed to be without any weight of her own. In the gleam of the many lanterns that shone through the garden foliage like the stars of heaven, a radiant blue light streamed about her figure. A broad white streak ran through her dark hair, but her complexion was young and delicate through much traveling in the open air, and her bearing was noble and upright from constantly being

13

in the saddle. A gentle sympathy sounded in her voice as she whispered to her son: "Look, they have no more wine."

All at once, Jesus seemed much taller, and like a prince and master beside the daughter of kings; and with a grave and curious smile he said mysteriously: "What have I to do with you? My hour is not yet come."

With a sigh, the mother laid her right hand soothingly on his arm and turned to the servants with the admonition: "Whatever he asks you, do it."

Full of curiosity, the servants and the four disciples followed Jesus into the house, where in the room beside the entrance, six enormous man-high earthenware jars, such as the Romans had introduced, had been let into the sand up to their wide necks. On the arrival of Jesus and his four companions, the diligent slaves dipped water out of these gigantic jars and assisted the late-comers in their ritual washing.

Now Jesus commanded: "Fill the jars with water."

The servants were surprised. "Master, almost all are full to the brim with pure water, our supply for the coming weeks of drought."

Nathanael looked in each of the jars, and declared: "Good, clear and cool. Just a few more buckets are needed." He followed the servants; the bucket was heard splashing on the surface of the well water. Laboriously, the servants filled the earthenware jars.

The guest's voice came out of the darkness. "Now draw some out and take it to the steward." But the steward had already arrived with the master, for they had heard of Jesus's strange instructions. Half-laughing, half-astonished, the cup-bearers took a sample from each jar. The corpulent steward filled his mouth, puffed out his cheeks expertly, and then gargled for a moment. At this, Nathanael burst out laughing. "Just look, will you, how he lets his tongue play about in the wet! Now he's spitting it out and trying again. By that red nose of his, he looks as if he'd never had good pure water in his mouth before in all his life, nothing but wine and more wine. It seems to taste strange to him, he's sampling jar after jar. He's tried all six!"

"Now his master is toasting him."

But all their laughter died away as the bride's father turned to the winegrower and invited him, as an expert, to sample the drink. Nathanael tasted and swallowed. He began to tremble, his eyes widened, his mouth fell open, he breathed heavily. The earthenware cup fell from his fingers and broke into fragments on the tiled floor of the entrance.

In the bowls a golden-green liquid glowed, like that from muscadine grapes. Those who had finished their drink proffered their cups again. The steward was most perplexed of all, for he could not imagine where the delicious wine had come from. He looked from the bride's father to the bridegroom and said: "Everyone serves the good wine first and then, when the people are drunk, the lesser. You have saved the best till last."

Word was soon passed around among the guests that a new and still more delicious wine was being served. The laughing guests crowded from all sides, the youngsters from their dancing, the old folk from gossiping. Those who had fallen asleep straightened themselves up and pretended they had been deep in thought, and now with empty bowls in their hands they made their way with the others.

The bridal couple led along the rabbi who had married them. The learned man pursed his thick lips in a superior fashion. He felt himself above such transitory pleasures, and it was only out of politeness that he took the precious silver goblet, the largest one, which the bride smilingly offered him. Then his glance fell on the earthenware jars. He set the goblet down with a frown. "A heathenish Roman custom! Wine in stone jars! Is this good Judaean wine, prepared by Judaean hands?"

The host was startled at the menacing look of his venerable guest. The company drew back in vexation, and those who had already tasted the wine were full of regret.

Only now did they realize what had happened. Certainly, the cupbearers were orthodox, the jars the work of orthodox men and bought from orthodox dealers. No unbeliever had touched either jar or contents. But the wine, the grapes, the grower?

The servants looked embarrassed and confessed: "It's water. Just . . . pure water from the cistern."

"I can swear to it," said Nathanael, gravely. Beside him, Philip had been looking on all the time, his sly peasant face deep in thought. He said slowly: "I should think, when a man does a thing like that for the first time, a miracle, I mean, he must have a very strange feeling. I mean, he must be astonished at himself to think: Look! an hour ago I was a man like any other. And now I am like no other. . . ."

"Now he knows who he is," murmured Peter to himself.

Though the cupbearers described what had happened over and again, no one was willing to acknowledge it as a miracle. Like a true servant of the Temple, the rabbi turned to the chief witness of the strange event. "Simon, son of Jonah, can you swear on your father's head that no one has been playing an unseemly joke on us?"

"As sure as my name is Rock."

"What's the meaning of that? Why should a man be called Rock?"

"The one who did this thing, which none of you understands —nor I, for that matter—he gave me that name."

"I have never seen anyone work miracles in all my life! We in Jerusalem are categorically opposed to miracles. They are tricks for Persian magicians and Egyptian idolaters. A righteous Israelite does not dabble in miracles."

"Sire!" The fisherman stepped forcefully before the rabbi. "He who gave a deeper meaning to this good clear water is the Lord's own son, like David."

"For such blasphemy, the Sanhedrin has the right to pass a sentence of stoning. For witchcraft, the Procurator can order crucifixion!"

"He is a poor fool who only sees jugglery in this!" Now that Simon had interceded for Jesus, his understanding suddenly quickened. "Only he who is pure water will become good wine for the One above."

"It is beneath my dignity to hold discussions of dogma with those who are not of my kind. You say the water is kosher. So the wine is kosher too. Let us pass as permissible this thing

16

you call a miracle." His conscience clear at last, the rabbi cautiously tasted the wine.

"Look well at him," whispered Philip to Nathanael. "First he threatens us with stone and cross, and everybody's knees are shaking—mine too, I confess, for they're quick on the flint heaps in Jerusalem. A very painful death, and not at all soldierly. But now he's put himself among those jars as if he's ready to drink them down to the bottom."

"He's trembling and trying not to show it. Such a thing has never happened before. I wonder what still remains as we believe it to be?"

"I should think Jesus himself must be trembling now. Trembling at his own power, his own work, trembling for himself. . . ."

The rabbi was deeply shaken. He murmured into his beard: "It cannot be. Is it a miracle? Are these miracles, then? Why should a carpenter's mate be capable of this, and not I? I am a scholar, I know how to pronounce properly the name of the All-Highest. I am a righteous man and keep the Law. Almighty One! You owe me this, you must grant me the same power! Make everything as it used to be—clear, self-evident, logical, and according to the Law. Lord, change this wine back into water! They are all looking at me. I'll have this cup filled once more, right to the brim. Lord, it must be! When I take the seventh sip—water, Lord, water!"

Fear of the Law, which the rabbi's first question had aroused, still held the guests in its power. Apprehensively, they counted each gulp. He prayed again: "The seventh sip, Lord? Be merciful!"

But Simon broke in, handing a silver goblet to the cupbearer. "For him who changed the water into wine. And this for his mother." He held out a second cup.

With a forced smile, the rabbi shot a glance in the direction of the speaker. He could suppress his indignation no longer. Once more he tried to reassert his power, the power of the rabbunim, the power of negation, the power of the curse. But when he opened his mouth, his seven hearty gulps assumed the mastery, and an irrepressible belch marred his first words. The master of the house suppressed a smile and said kindly:

"Rabbi, you've been a bit too hasty with that strong wine. A holy man is a sober man. Now, take a little mouthful, and let it trickle down gently, then another, and another, and your hiccups will be gone."

When the scribe set his cup to his lip for the second time, the spell that lay on everyone seemed to break. The guests all proffered their cups, and drank again and again, and the power of the miraculous wine began quickly to take effect. But the rabbi still had not dared to swallow for the eighth time. Let it be water, water!

Simon could no longer contain himself and, touching cups with his companions, he cried jubilantly: "This is what I call a miracle! What was Moses's water compared to this? Three good swigs for every man and we would overrun one legion after another!"

Unexpectedly, Jesus and his mother stepped out from the shadow of the old cedars. The fisherman quickly drew himself up to a ceremonious speech. "My Lord and King, and you, O daughter of David . . . Descendant of the Kings of Zion, whom the voice out of the cloud called Son! You have shown your power here before the weak, the kindly, the weaponless. . . ."

Andrew, still bright-eyed and alert, said: "What about the rabbi? He'll have his revenge. He'll not forgive this."

"What can he do against a miracle-worker?" answered his brother. "We were the sword, we were the courage. We were the faith. The Baptist prophesied and nothing else, but you must lead us! We'll storm Moriah! We'll storm Caesarea! Let the sun and the moon stand still, till your people are revenged on their enemies!"

As Jesus remained silent, Nathanael plucked up his courage and said, almost reproachfully: "It would be better, Lord, if you were to change pebbles into soldiers and priests into scapegoats to be driven out into the wilderness. I beg you not to work another miracle like this one. I've all last year's wine, skin after skin of it, still in my cellar, the whole vintage unsold. What's to become of us poor tax-harassed winegrowers if no more wine becomes money and all water, wine?"

Mary had not been able to take her eyes off the rabbi. She saw danger there. She knew she should not have asked this of

18

her son. "One man's happiness is always another's grief," she said with a sad smile and shook her head sympathetically at the winegrower.

As if he had felt the woman watching him, the rabbi turned and motioned to Jesus: "A word with you, sir." To his chagrin, a little hiccup again disturbed his dignity.

Jesus looked down at his robe, on which the purple fringes were hanging no less long than on that of the rabbi. Then he turned his gaze on him. "I share no secret with you."

The rabbi drew a deep breath, raised the silver cup to his lips, and closed his eyes in the prodigious effort of exerting his will. His right hand gripped the cup tight, and he clenched his left hand till the nails clawed into his flesh. Desperately, he wished: "Wine in the jars, be water again! Be my old world again!"

So he took the eighth gulp.

A horrible sight! The silver cup fell crashing to the floor from his trembling hand. The wine bled onto the sand of the pathway. The rabbi spat. His face was transformed into a dreadful gaping mask of rage and desperation. The eighth sip and it was still wine! The Lord had forsaken his faithful servant. The heathen god of his adversary was the stronger. The Promised Land was defiled! He intended to utter a curse, but the wine rose up in him again, and the men of Bethsaida laughed in his face. He turned away, burning with vindictive rage. Without looking back, he left the garden and walked on and on in impotent fury. Quaking with anger and hatred, he belched curses on all in the house, on the bride's father, the young couple, their children and their children's children.

But Jesus lifted his hands in prayer. The guests had not even noticed the rabbi's absence. There was laughter and gaiety under the trees, and a quiet happy serenity, while the lanterns swaying in the night breeze went out one by one, and far away, above the eastern heights, daylight began to spread.

The men from Bethsaida saw the lips of the miracle-worker moving in benediction. Shyly, the disciples followed him, with hope and victory in their hearts. Arm in arm they walked along the broad road towards the sun, which surrounded Jesus with its golden rays. Full of wine and joy, they sang:

19

"He who dwelleth in heaven hath put them to scorn, and the Lord mocketh them. . . ."

NAZARETH is a quiet town. Its narrow streets run steeply up from the spring at the mountain's foot. Many of its white houses have orchards about them, or hurdle fences, so as not to be too close to other buildings. The alleys are lined with walls, windowless and silent. Miserable pieces of washing hang out to dry on lines that stretch across the streets. High above the plain and the mountains, towers Mount Tabor.

It was Sabbath. The tangle of streets on the mountain slope lay quiet, quieter than usual. Not the slightest sound of human activity was to be heard. In a long wall which hid an extensive property from the eyes of the traveler, a little door opened in a mighty gate.

Father Halephai emerged, followed, one after the other, by the sons of his wife Maria, the elder sister of Jesus's mother. First came Jacob the Tsaddik, as he was respectfully known in the neighborhood—a lean man with a noble aquiline nose and a long, carefully kept beard, graying already, his head thrown back, looking as if his every word was law. His brother Simon the Zealot, a thickset man, looked younger than he was, since an almost hilarious fanaticism shone in his eyes. At each lively step he took, a bushy lock of dark hair fell across his forehead. When he pushed it back, a deep scar was revealed. When he had been with the Gaulonites, a Sebastene sword had given him an ugly wound. It had been Simon son of Jonah who dragged him away from the fight and out of danger. Jose, who appeared behind him, wore his fox-red beard parted. With restless fingers, he stroked first one, then the other of its strands. An utterly matter-of-fact man, even today, on this holy day, he seemed as if he was unable to shake off his preoccupation with household affairs, and work and servants. The youngest of them, Judas Thaddeus, was quite different. The happiness of this evening so near to God urged him ahead of the others, and he was obliged to stop now and then, in order not to walk in front of his father. It delighted him to go to the meetinghouse to pray, to sing and

20

to hear the Law, and quite involuntarily he began to swing round in a circle the two prayer thongs in his right hand. This earned him a disapproving glance from his eldest brother. "Don't you know there are holy texts wrapped in the little knots at the end of those thongs? How can you whirl the Law about you like a child's game?"

"Is it not beautiful to be surrounded by the Law? Didn't our Jesus say: You know not what the Law is? It should not be a matter of fear and dread, but of strength!"

Halephai spun round. "What do you know of my nephew?"

"They say he was here with four companions. He found his father's house locked and followed his parents to Cana."

"So long as he does not go back to Jerusalem! They would stone him there."

The sensible Jose calmed his father. "But you heard—they are on their way to Cana."

"He is like a son to me, like one of you. But his strange talk . . ."

Jacob said severely: "He ought to be watched. He often speaks as if he's out of his mind."

The Zealot protested: "He has orthodox folk about him—the sons of Zebedee and of Jonah, my friends."

"You are the only one of us who believes in him, because you won't abandon that notion of yours about a Messiah. Jesus was old enough—eleven, he was—when from Nazareth we saw Sepphoris burning. Two thousand crosses showed up black in front of the red flames. Judas the Galilean, another who called himself Messiah, perished on them with his followers."

Halephai clapped his hands to his ears. "Quarreling on the Sabbath, children!"

They had arrived at the top of the mountain, where the view from the synagogue doorway stretched far over the countryside. The Nazarenes stood crowded expectantly together. Suddenly one or two among the crowd shouted: "He is coming, look, over there!" They started to run, cheering as they went. Like sand in a storm they swirled down onto the road leading from Cana, where in the distance, a small group of men were making their way towards them. Nobody could say how the news had preceded them that a miracle had happened. At first it had been a cup of wine, then a dozen jars, then a score of skins. "It was raining wine! Enough to wash all your crockery out of the house and through the gate. Drunkenness without end!"

The four men from Bethsaida linked their strong arms. Behind them walked Jesus, smiling at the happy folk of his native town.

"Into the house of prayer! He must read our fortune and tell us what's going to happen to us." In the throng, Simon the Zealot unexpectedly jostled against Simon son of Jonah. The two friends embraced each other, stammering a greeting, but immediately they were parted again. The crowd's joy changed to impatience. Let the miracle-worker speak!

Long-bearded old men already filled the benches of the synagogue, while on the raised step, the venerable rabbi had unrolled the Torah, to find Isaiah's words about the coming of the Messiah. The old man had to put his bleary eyes so close to the writing, and he was so immersed in his sense of aloneness with the Almighty, that he only looked up when the expectant crowd surged towards him. Many people were thronging around him, some not from the neighborhood at all. He had never seen Andrew or Philip or Nathanael before, but Jesus he recognized. The withered old man was looking forward to hearing him interpret the scriptures. On many a Sabbath, he had been relieved in his weariness by the wisdom of this young man who foretold the coming of the Messiah. As Jesus entered, he handed him the scroll like a scepter, and gave up his place to him.

Jesus towered above them all in the dusk. He did not so much as glance down at the ornate letters, but looked over the heads of the sweating, shoving crowd, out of the doorway into the glow of the sunset. Neighbors, relatives, his parents, and even outside the synagogue, faces and faces.

His eyes were wide open, the pupils so dark and enormous, giving no reflection of the light, that everyone felt that the mild nocturnal depth of his gaze must surely be directed inwards on himself. His domed scholarly forehead was framed by the light-brown hair that hung down to his shoulders. His beard, which gradually came to a point, was rather darker, and darker still, the hair on his upper lip. His lean cheeks and noble narrow nose were tanned a deep brown from wandering in the sun and wind. Judaeans, who were not permitted to kneel to any man, stood reverently before him. They knew that his ancestor had worn the crown of the Promised Land a thousand years ago.

Powerfully, his voice carried the words of Isaiah above the dying whisper: "The spirit of the Lord is upon me for the Lord has anointed me to bring good tidings to the meek, to give liberty to the captives, to proclaim the year of reconciliation with God."

Simon Peter had remained outside, pressed against the sons of Halephai. He heard Jose call out: "Reconciliation!" That was the honest man of affairs speaking, the merchant who longed for peace. "Slavery is ended! Liberty!" both Simons cried. Beside them, Mary quietly bowed her head. But when the crowd shouted: "Lead us! A message!" the rabbi anxiously clutched at Jesus's garment and said: " 'I,' did you say? 'I'? As if you were He? Isaiah said that, and he was speaking of Jahveh. You must read on." He had a foreboding of danger.

Outside, around the two Simons, a number of sturdy young men were standing. Raising their fists, they broke into a shout of: "The Kingdom of Heaven on earth!" The crowd inside the synagogue and out could not bear to wait any longer. "We did not come to hear texts. We want miracles! Miracles of weapons, miracles of war!"

At the same time, the envious ones, the jealous ones, his kinsmen, began to mutter: "Is this not Joseph's son? One we grew up with, a carpenter's son, working miracles?"

A smile played around the lips of the heir of kings. "A miracle? For your sake?"

Here and there, people laughed sardonically. A few insolent lads whistled. "Stones here!" cried some old men. "Wine, here! Wine, here!" howled a group of young bullies.

They heard Jesus say: "A prophet is not without honor save in his own country. But such a country is nothing to the prophet."

"Down with him! Stone him!" The chosen people felt their

23

dignity deeply wounded. Under the assault of the furious crowd, the benches of the synagogue gave way. Old men rolled on the floor with cries of fear. A wave of angry people surged forward. Simon and Andrew set themselves in front of Jesus to stem the assault, but the mob surrounded them and thrust them out of the synagogue. They were swept along, across the wide square, to the edge of the steep slope above the valley of Esdrelon. Far below waved the cornfields of the plain. Those in front cried: "Stop! You are pushing the righteous into the abyss with them! The precipice! Help!" They broke away on either side."

Now there was a space around Jesus and his companions. One or two of them would still have liked to throw stones, but none dared to.

Jesus looked around at his disciples. In their apprehensive looks, he read the question: "Why did you say that, Master? Why did you not meet force with greater force? The miracle, son of the Voice from Above . . . ?" But he merely straightened his garment. Then he began to walk calmly towards the crowd of Nazarenes. His disciples fell in as if in line of battle behind him. The Zealot looked at the miracle-worker. Would it come to a fight? Those facing them stood their ground, angry and defiant.

Jesus approached them. His glance encountered one after the other of the men of Nazareth. The crowd began to stir. One of them said in an undertone: "The spirit of the Lord is upon him."

But he passed right through the hostile mob.

Only the four from Bethsaida walked beside him. Behind them came Jacob the Tsaddik and Simon the Zealot, and with his brother Thaddeus, the Master's mother. Later, when they looked up the steep rock face from the valley, they saw, high up on the edge of the cliff, closely crowded together, the men of their own country, of the native town that no longer meant anything to them.

THE few disciples who accompanied Jesus from Nazareth were still at a loss to discover the meaning of his words. When all those people who had grown up with him had run to meet him full of expectation, why should he first of all have told them about his mission? "The spirit of the Lord is upon me. He has anointed me to preach good tidings to the meek, a promise of freedom to the captive, of sight to the blind, and to prophesy the Year of Grace of the Lord." But why then refuse to work miracles in his native town? Was it merely because the old people and the companions of his youth had been astonished that he, whom they had known since he was small, should have been greater than them all? Seeing that his prophecy was as bitter as Daniel's concerning the death of the Messiah, how could he wonder that nobody really wanted to believe in him, and that only a few sufferers had been cured by the laying-on of his hands? "Physician, heal thyself," he had cried, before the others could say it. He had mentioned mighty prophets, none of whom had worked miracles in Israel, but rather on Syrians or Sidonian women, for no prophet has honor in his own land.

They wandered eastward, through wretched hamlets. More and more friends joined them. Thaddeus obtained an ass for Mary from one of Jose's servants. As soon as they entered a village, the children jumped up from the doorsteps and called into the houses. Men and women hurried out from the hearth, the stable, from meadow and plowland, from the reeds and the olive groves. "Miracle-worker!" they shouted. "Are there more of you coming?" asked the very small children.

"Which is He?" To most of them, the estimable Jacob seemed the most likely. Others had heard how youthful the Messiah was, and shyly stroked Thaddeus's hand. To the young lads, Simon looked the strongest. But at the sight of Jesus, all the others were forgotten.

"Give me a miracle!" begged the children, and ran beside them, holding out their dirty little hands.

The crowd around Jesus was so dense that the disciples felt the breath was being crushed out of them.

Roughly, the adults, hurrying to join the throng, drove the children away. "Get out of it! Chase those little brutes away! Master, my neighbor's cow, the wicked beast, has gored my heifer to death! A miracle, Master! Put the plague on his cow!

25

—they are putting me out of my house tomorrow because I could not pay my taxes. A little miracle, Master, just a little one, a ten-dinar one! I do not need more. —Master, can you kill by miracles? Then kill . . ."

The Tsaddik's face went dark. "You hundred thousand devils! You are possessed by hatred and greed! First purify yourselves, before you dare to step into the path of righteous men!"

Countless people still swarmed after the Redeemer from earthly sorrows, the blind with flies swarming in their purulent eye sockets, the deaf, the lame supported by mothers or children. They crowded round so closely that Jesus had hardly room to move. Then came the sound of leper rattles. A ghastly procession was dragging along the road, men and women clad in rags. The noise of their warning rattles was like the laughter of skeletons. Each of them carried in one hand a wooden bowl, in the other the restless rattle. Even at a distance the whitish scabs could be discerned on their faces, arms and legs. An evil odor of decay rose from them. The warm breeze that blew from the valley of Lake Genesareth smelled as if it came from a heap of rotting carrion.

Those in front shrank back, terrified. In horror, the unbidden followers turned aside. No pleading was necessary now, they all gave way. The men from Nazareth and Bethsaida were able to walk on unhindered.

Jesus himself had not forbidden any of the sick or crippled people to follow him. He seemed to pay them no heed. The lepers did not cry out, nor beg, they uttered no word. But as the miracle-worker approached, they silently formed up at the side of the road and stood in a long row to the left and to the right, worn out from their aimless wandering, crippled and bent. They made no mistake, they looked straight at Jesus himself. A silence fell upon their monstrous pain, and now that the rattles had ceased, only the chirping of the crickets was to be heard.

The Master's companions huddled together in order not to touch any of the lepers, nor breathe their stench. Only now did Jesus turn his gaze on them. He had not deigned to glance

26

at those who importuned him. Now with a heavy heart, he looked from one to the other of the scabby faces. Here, the eyes were gone, there the disease had eaten holes in flesh and bone. Others had mutilated fingers or toes. Couples were holding each other up; they had children with them, and these too were white and sick already.

"Master! Do you look at them?"

Jesus did not listen to the disciples' horrified question, who were aware that behind them was the army of sick, lamed and crippled folk, ready to follow them even if it cost them their last strength. These, in their desperation, were thinking: Those who don't give up, those who follow him, the mighty one, on his way to eternity, who march in step with him, will be made healthy and well. But the fishermen and peasants, hale and strong, and longing for some tremendous victory of a Messiah of action, were so full of horror and disgust that they were at a loss what to do next. Who would not be afraid of leprosy?

"Master! Do you beckon to them?"

"Master! Do you ask them to come with us?"

AFTER two nights, Simon the son of Jonah could stand it no longer. Late at night he got up from his straw bed in the colonnades of the caravanserai in Tiberias, and left Jesus and his comrades and the horde of sick people. He groped his way in the dark among the baggage and the unharnessed camels, who slept with their long necks stretched on the ground. If he tripped over a dozing ass, or a squatting caravan guide, that was of no account; more dangerous was the sudden snap of a white riding-dromedary. The fisherman had to leap back to escape it. The old watchman started and hastily threw some dried camel dung on the dying campfire. He stared at Simon and warned him. "There are some hundred lepers out there. See that you do not touch any of them. Not content with the Gaulonites robbing honest merchants, death comes in person now and sits waiting outside our gates."

Simon did not reply, but passed him with a growl. Over and again, he had left hearth and home, his wife and little girl

Petronilla, his boat and nets, to hurry off to the Jordan, to Caesarea, to Cana, to Nazareth. But now the one he had sought was traveling with a host of cripples, a legion of lepers. Were the Chosen People to be eaten up by leprosy?

When he arrived at Bethsaida, late at night and exhausted, he found his mother-in-law's house locked, the windows and door boarded up. The noise of his knocking echoed hollowly. Bitterly, he groped about in the dark. No net, no boat. His hands felt along the houses. They were as silent as box-shaped tombs. A few more steps, and he was touching the ruins of his father's hut. The Sebastenes had destroyed it long since. Had they taken off his people and his property too? He, who could never bear to stay at home, was dying with longing for his Rahab. He sat down by the last remnants of the mud wall by which, as a boy, he had so often squatted to sleep. Nothing was left to him. His father dead, himself a homeless wanderer . . . The door barricaded against him . . . A fisherman without a net . . . A man without a wife . . . A general without an army. With his cloak pulled over his head, he stared across the lake, which he could not see in the darkness, though he could hear the sound of it.

Next morning, his boat crew found him there, asleep. They had come ashore to collect what remained of the furniture. They had hurried suspiciously past the muffled sleeper, but when they had looked closer, they recognized their master, and carefully shook him awake. "Sebastenes?" "Yes, again. A house-to-house search. They threw all the household goods out on the beach. The women looked on from a distance, in despair. Later on, they picked out of the sand whatever was still unbroken. The next day, they went to Zebedee, and transferred the house and the fishing rights to him."

"I see. So now my home is under the sky?"

"You're neither peasant nor fisherman now. You're a town gentleman," they laughed. "Yes, your house is at the market place in Capernaum, opposite the synagogue; a grand house with a stairway and a loft."

An uncle of Rahab's had left them this handsome house. Simon's mother-in-law had kept the legacy a secret. She felt safe there from Gaulonites or wandering robbers. Simon's old swordsman comrades did not dare to go there; the Roman barracks were too near at hand.

Peter could hardly wait for the ropes to be cast off, so anxious was he to reach Capernaum. The sons of Zebedee joined him. Each had a great deal to tell. Everybody was looking for Jesus. Conspirators were going in and out of Mary of Migdal's house. One Saul of Tarsus, a pupil of the wise Gamaliel, was preaching reconciliation between the Pharisees and Sadducees, who were jointly to choose Herod as lord of all the four tetrarchies. After him had come a wild rebellious fellow named Gesmas. He had been with Jesus, and had mutinied against him. He preached horrifying things. Ever since Melchizedek, he said, the priests had been drugging the people with incense and prayer. The treasures of the whole world had flowed together in Rome. One had only to stretch out a hand! Bold lads were lurking on the other side of the Tiber, runaway slaves, who knew just where their masters had hidden their gold. These were to be the ringleaders. In league with him was one Judas Iscariot, who also fancied himself as a Messiah, a Messiah of money. According to him, the Temple was weaving a golden net over the whole inhabited earth, particularly since Augustus had ordered all Israelite believers, no matter how far away they lived, to pay a double drachma annually to the high priest as tax. Eventually, this net would succeed in overgrowing and overrunning Rome itself.

The sons of Zebedee had disagreed with him, and how furiously Judas had pounced on them! He had argued vehemently with them: "If you do not promise prosperity to the multitude, to each his due, and to each as much as the other, how do you expect to catch them?" When James called him a silver-piece Messiah, he slavered with indignation. Nobody had succeeded yet in mastering the Romans with weapons, but with money—yes! With the taxes of all the Jews in the world, he could buy Rome over.

Blissfully surrendering himself to the task of sailing and steering and feeling the direction of the wind, and concentrating all his thoughts on his destination, Peter held the tiller and the rope of the three-cornered canvas. The boat had heeled so far over in the morning breeze that James and John, who were leaning well backward, could see the ruffled surface of the lake right under their shoe soles. "Passover in Jerusalem!" On all sides they had heard this password whispered. Men on ass or camel carried the signal further. From the slopes of the Hermon down to Machairus, every able-bodied man was sharpening his dreaded short-sword. Throughout the trip across the lake, the sons of Zebedee and the son of Jonah the rebel talked with growing hope of angels and victory, of prophecies and, humbly, of the carpenter's mate of Nazareth, the miracle-worker of Cana. Jesus's intention was quite clear to the fisherman. Indeed, the Son of Man could do nothing else. As soon as all the patriots gathered overnight into a rebel army about the Temple, they would sweep away the hordes of the halt and the lame. "Strength will be about you, Jesus, and I as your Rock beneath you. King Herod? Never! King Jesus? And if you do not wish for that, perhaps—King Peter!"

ON THEIR way across, they had cast their nets in a good fishing ground. The catch was worth while. As they landed in Capernaum, the cool evening breeze was enticing everyone out of doors. The men stood talking in the market place, women crowded around the sellers, droves of yelling children raced about, now and then colliding with the scholars and synagogue officials as they gravely walked to and fro. The only person they seemed to fight shy of was the legionary, who marched up and down with his spear on his shoulder in front of the barracks opposite Rahab's house.

The fresh breeze agitated the curtain in the upper room, driving off the humming flies. Rahab looked round at little Petronilla, who was reaching up at the fluttering curtain, astonished at the movements of her own tiny fingers. Wearily, the woman got to her feet. She was famished. No money in the house. Her mother ill and delirious. Suddenly, she listened carefully. "Fresh fish! Lovely fish! Crucians fit for the high priests' table! Pike, speedy pike, greedy pike, good enough for bold Herod himself! Whitebait for the thrifty taxpayer! Come buy! I have had a good catch, so you will get no cheaper anywhere! Set your teeth in this, my fine folk! In the sea, too, the big ones eat their little brothers!"

That voice! She could not believe her ears. That was her husband calling out so jauntily that the whole market place echoed with laughter. Incredulous, she went to the window and peered through the lattice. There stood her Simon on an upturned fish tub. Shadows were already falling over the catch at his feet, and over the jostling crowd. He seemed to be reeling off some kind of double-edged talk, to judge by the people's laughter.

Now somebody was reaching up to speak in Simon's ear. She recognized old Aulus Cuspius, who threw down a gold piece and handed his friend, the cohort commander Cornelius, a sheatfish.

"For your sick servant," said the old man. The fisherman's face reddened. "Do not talk about sick people! My fish are sound and healthy! To me, you hardy ones! Into my net!" He went on talking, and to Rahab's surprise he did not seem to notice that the crowd was dispersing. Already his crew had impatiently collected up the empty fish boxes and hurried to the boat. Rahab came down to him, across the darkening, almost deserted square. She balanced on her head the wooden sled with the rest of the catch, and was about to say, "Come!" when a strange and enormous figure whisked past her. Huge and hairy, with a filthy cloth about his loins, the stranger cowered in front of Simon, among the fish scales, the vegetable refuse and rotting garbage, like a bit of garbage himself. A disgusting animal odor arose from the crouching figure, who began to scratch like a dog at the vermin torturing him under the matted hair on his head, his face and his body. Rahab was sure that this was the dreaded madman of whom the women had been warned. The devils who harried him were afraid of light and sunshine, and only pursued their victim in the dusk and darkness. Trembling, she threw him a fish. He bit off the head, spat it out and, grunting with pleasure, ate the still-wriggling body. Now that the possessed creature was occupied, she hastily took her husband by the arm and led him towards the house. Peter saw the madman grin mockingly at him, as if to say: "You are possessed, I am possessed, who is not possessed?"

As Rahab entered the house with Simon, she heard her mother moaning.

"What is that?" Peter was startled.

Rahab answered, sobbing: "It is mother. She is sick and dying."

"Sick people here too?" Peter raved, and tore his hair and cried: "I cannot stand any more sickness!"

"Simon." Her voice came sadly out of the darkness, but Peter had turned away. He thought he heard, in the distance but rapidly approaching, the clamor of a thousand voices. The tumult grew into singing, clear, holy and victorious. Peter and Rahab went out on the balcony, into the night. The thousands of stars above the Holy Land seemed to be reflected on the mountainside that sloped down towards the city in the south. Torches and lanterns were weaving and circling in the darkness. Faces were illuminated in the glow of the warm light, which lit up the happy eyes of many already close at hand. None of the multitude had been wearied by the daylong journey in the sun. They came like conquerors. Those who carried no lights waved palm leaves and olive branches. No more sticks or crutches were to be seen. Somewhere on the roadside, far away, lay the abandoned rattles of the lepers. Peter watched them striding by, rank upon rank, proud and erect, walking in time to the sacred songs, as if they were legion and invincible.

The sentry outside the barracks, the only man to stand his ground, called out the guard. Baying hoarsely, the misshapen figure of the possessed man darted by him once again. Had he disappeared into the synagogue? The legionaries, accustomed to springing to arms in this unruly land of Judaea, formed up beside their comrade with sword, spear and shield.

Momentarily, Peter recoiled. In the gleam of the festive torches as they passed the house, he saw a woman holding up her child with both arms. She seemed unable to stop looking into the shining eyes of the boy who could see his mother for the first time. She was telling all around her: "My child came out of the house this morning blind as he's been all his life.

There were a whole lot of blind people coming along the road. They found Jesus, and now my boy can see, he can see!"

The fisherman hurried down and stood on the steps outside the gate. Here and there he recognized somebody. "Simon!" A cousin called to him, a cripple who had begged his way about the country on a little cart. "Simon!" Now he stood out in the crowd like a legionary. "Simon!" Someone fell happily about his neck. It was an old battle comrade of the Barjonim, who years ago had his thigh sinew cut when a fallen Sebastene had slashed at him from the ground.

Silence fell over the wide square. Everyone, though forbidden by the Law to kneel before anyone other than God, sank on their knees. The starry night echoed with singing: "Lord, have mercy on me! Make me whole!"

Simon felt as if he were an outcast. He, too, should have been among this multitude of healed folk, with Philip, and Nathanael, and Andrew, who hardly seemed to notice his brother from the edge of the crowd. Cana, and the joy of that evening at the wedding, seemed merely an experiment in making people happy. Now Jesus came, the Master, his head held high. He seemed thinner to his disciple, and a head taller than all the others, though Simon knew that he himself was taller and broader, and that his brother was no less in stature than he. The disciples kept at a respectful distance from the Master. Among them, Peter recognized Jesus's cousins, Jacob the Tsaddik, his friend Simon the Zealot, and young Thaddeus. The sons of Halephai were carefully leading by the bridle the white ass that bore Mary, the Master's mother. Today, the crowd was kneeling before her son.

Rahab thought her heart would stop. Her husband had found his way home, was here in the house with her, she had dared to hope for domestic happiness at last. But now the stranger, with whose mission Simon was obsessed, had come again. With heavy step, she turned to her mother's sickbed, as if wishing that she too could lie down and die. As she did, she became terrified at the harsh and rasping breathing of the sick woman. In the light of the miserable oil lamp, the sunken eyes and pointed nose seemed strange to her. The chin, with the sparse hairs of age upon it, had sunk to her breast, which heaved laboriously as if she were choking. When she breathed out, great bubbles of whitish foam formed on her lips. Rahab found her mother so dreadfully changed that she fell on her knees with a cry and, half repelled, half yearning, she grasped the sick woman's hand, but the cold, thin, sweaty fingers only frightened her still more. "Simon!" she screamed.

He did not hear her voice. Simon the Zealot had joined him. They looked on as the square emptied, and the healed folk were taken home, and only a gloomy group were left standing by the line of soldiers—those who deemed themselves the worthies of Capernaum: the synagogue officials, elders, rabbis, and the horrified doctor.

With trembling lips, Peter asked: "Are they the same? The same ones who were around the caravanserai yesterday and the day before?"

"I can swear to it. I nearly turned deserter like you. I wanted to be a fighter for the Lord, but to frighten the enemy with a sharp sword, not a leper rattle. But now there are no more sick folk around us or him."

Contritely, Peter was joining the group about Jesus when he felt himself pushed aside. His angry gesture was arrested by Aulus Cuspius, making way for an armored man who sank to one knee with a clatter. It was Cornelius, the captain of the cohort of Capernaum.

Immediately, a space was made around Jesus, the Roman, Simon and Aulus, for the Judaeans feared contact with the unclean pagan. Even those who had been blind till now, saw enough to avoid the stranger. He knew of the inexorable laws of this race of haters. He would have liked to touch the hyacinth-colored fringes of Jesus's overgarment, but he dared not attempt anything that might hinder the fulfillment of his wish. In halting Aramaic, he stammered that his most faithful servant who, though wounded himself, had dragged him out of the thick of a hand-to-hand battle when he was wounded— this young friend of his, only a servant, but by his faithfulness a true proven comrade, lay crippled and in dreadful agony, with an incurable complaint.

With a smile, Jesus bent over him, a Roman. The elders

34

of Capernaum looked on darkly. The two Simons were bewildered.

The captain was conscious of the hostility about him. He had his legionaries to protect him, but what of his helper, the Saviour? He whispered devoutly: "Lord, I am not worthy that you should come under my roof; but only say the word and my servant will be healed. I, too, am a man under authority, having under myself soldiers, and I say to this one: Go, and he goes; and to another: Come, and he comes; and to my servant: Do this, and he does it."

Jesus turned his head to the hostile guardians of the Law who stood together in the entrance of the synagogue. They, and the disciples, were touched to the quick by his words: "I have not found so great faith, no, not in Israel. Go your way. As you have believed, so be it done to you."

One of the elders struck his forehead with his fist, but no one dared to utter a word aloud against the Roman officer. Only one cursed under his breath, and Peter heard him say: "How many wishes do the orthodox carry unfulfilled in their hearts, and a heathen, who burns incense to images in his house, is granted fulfillment. And is it not only a short while since he was cutting down the Jews of Capernaum?"

In a helpless rage, they began to run here and there. The doctor, trembling with fury, was shouting the names of the healed men whom he had recognized in the procession. "Is that charity, to heal the rich?" For he had recognized patients whose houses he had been constantly visiting for years, tending their incurability, and counting on them as on a fat rent.

"Stone him! Crucify him!" gasped the rabbi, under his breath.

Aulus had helped the deeply affected centurion to his feet. Gratefully, solemnly, he took his leave of Jesus with a Roman salute. He was so overcome with emotion and reverence that, not wishing to turn away from Jesus, he returned home walking backwards, as if leaving the presence of his Imperial master.

Mary had slid out of the saddle and put her arm about her son's shoulders as if he was in need of the protection of her love. With an anxious turn of her narrow face she indicated the elder, and to hold Jesus back, whispered: "Remember

35

Nazareth." For he was about to follow those who were entering the synagogue, to say the Prayer of Thanksgiving for the healing of leprosy.

Jesus listened. Soft distant music sounded from the synagogue. All of them recognized the age-old chant prescribed by the Law for the eve of the Sabbath. The very old men in the synagogue, wearing their prayer shawls and rocking themselves to and fro as they prayed, noticed nothing. They were not aware that the possessed man was hiding behind one of the massive pillars, humming and droning and singing their words with them. Placidly smiling, he identified himself with the community, and like the others, he too rocked his scratched and hairy body to and fro.

Then he started up in dismay. The singing seemed to break off.

Those who were not too deep in prayer fell silent. Disturbed by footsteps, they looked around. By the long hyacinth-colored tassels and fringes of his overgarment, the younger ones among them recognized the man who strode towards the shrine where the scrolls of the Torah were kept. Dusty travelers thronged after him into the synagogue. As Simon Peter and Simon the Zealot sought to follow their Master, a barefoot man, with the headcloth of the desert rider pulled low over his face, stepped up to them. He was about to put a question to them, when a shrill uproar reached the square from the north.

A swarming, grunting herd of swine tumbled against each other amid the barking of dogs and the shouts of the swineherds, squealing in terror as the dogs' sharp teeth sank into the ear of any who sought to break away.

One of the elders had been about to venture an obscene joke about the day's strange guests. But as he cautiously glanced around, he caught sight of the muffled figure beside the two Simons. Fearfully, he whispered to his neighbor: "Bar Abbas is here." His neighbor recognized the dreaded robber and gang leader. "Does he want to drive off the Gadarenes' pigs? It would be as well to double-bar the town gates tonight."

"It is high time that old privilege was taken away from the men of Gadara, by which they are granted safe convoy for their beasts, and allowed to overnight them in our market place."

"Do not vex yourself. You do not have to eat the unclean brutes. Let them drive their swine down into the heathen country by the sea. It brings us money. The swineherds have to pay for every single beast that overnights here."

The two Simons had recognized the mysterious man also, and would have liked to be rid of him. But he persisted: "Is it true? I know the password of Judas Iscariot: Passover in Jerusalem."

"What is it to you?"

"Oh, of course, you are a hanger-on of that Davidite. We have no need of anyone who vies with us at robbery, no Roman, no tetrarch, no high priest, no Jahveh, nor Jahveh's son."

Those at the entrance of the synagogue called for silence. Jesus was speaking. His mighty words came through the doorway: "The floods came, the torrents of rain, the wind howled and beat mightily against the house." The red-lit doorway glowed like a flaming mouth that threatened. "They shall be cast out into the depths of the darkness!"

Simon Peter bit his knuckle till the blood came. He heard someone say: "Jesus speaks like a man of authority." And now he prayed to himself: "I want a miracle for myself, a warlike miracle! Warrior after warrior! I, Peter, your prince and leader, will avenge my father, avenge Israel, avenge myself! Let no one ask for any other miracle till Jesus grants me mine!"

THE night brought no coolness. Matthew Levi, the corpulent tax collector of Capernaum, suffered most in the sweltering atmosphere. He was still standing at the other end of the market place near Simon Peter's house, wiping the sweat off his forehead. He knew he would be guilty of a grievous sin if he walked more than two thousand paces—a Sabbath journey— after dark. He ought to go home, but an uncontrollable desire to be the eyewitness of a miracle compelled him to stay. He, poor sinner, had planted himself close to the house of Rahab and Simon, so as to observe the Master's power from nearby. But what he heard and saw was far from all things miraculous —a woman who behaved as if she were insane and implored her husband to ask Jesus to restore her mother to health.

The people of Capernaum were afraid. The orthodox believers, each and all of them, had seen the army of the healed. If they did not get together now, to stone the Nazarene—but they were too cowardly. They were frightened of those strange reckless fellows, the Barjonim.

A scream, such as no human or animal utters, except in monstrous fear of death, issued from the synagogue. The crowd pressed in the doorway, swayed. In terror, those inside the synagogue swarmed towards the narrow doorway where the fugitives, painfully crushed together, were checked for a moment before being hurtled out into the open by the impulse of those behind.

The pigs jumped to their feet in terror before them, squealing and grunting, jostling together and scattering again as they were kicked away. Cries of fear, human fear and animal fear, were heard on all sides. Stumbling, the two Simons, Bar Abbas, the women and the tax collector were borne along with the others. Two legionaries came running with pitch torches, whose restless light flickered on the masklike faces like the reflection of a great fire. Out of the synagogue, now almost empty, another maniacal scream followed on their heels: "Jesus of Nazareth!"

In the torchlight, looming up like some strange gigantic monster, stood a naked figure with filthy matted hair, his shaggy fists menacingly clenched.

The storm of uncontrollable terror had driven the men and women of Capernaum off the square. Those lucky enough to reach an open door locked it in haste and set against it as many beams and as much furniture as they could lay hands on. Breathing heavily, they peered from the windows and the roofs, watching the devil-possessed man as he staggered backwards out of the synagogue. The Roman soldiers had lowered their spears, but the madman did not see them. Trembling, he stared towards the entrance to the brightly lit synagogue and shrieked: "Leave us in peace! What have we to do with you, Jesus of Nazareth! Have you come to destroy us?"

Jesus stepped slowly from the doorway, into the torchlight. He did not hurry, nor did his heart beat faster. With unmoving eyes and motionless arms he came nearer and nearer. Before him the possessed man rose once again to an inhuman height, and there came a roar, his roar: "I know who you are: the chosen of the Lord!"

Thereupon, he pitched headlong, and writhed convulsively, blood on his head, foam on his lips; breathing hoarsely, he threw himself about as if he were being whipped. Invisible beings seemed to be dragging him this way and that. His eyes rolled in agony till only the bloodshot whites were visible, and then, like a terrified animal, he stared sidelong at Jesus again. He was no longer crying out, but whimpering in a high voice: "What have I to do with you, Son of God the Almighty?"

Then he lay like a log.

Around him, the Gadarene pigs shrank back and hustled each other as they scampered off, snorting in fear.

Jesus bent sympathetically over the unfortunate man and commanded: "Unclean spirit, depart from this man!"

Again the madman thrashed about. Again he called on the name that no pious Jew would dare to pronounce: "By God, I implore you, torture me no more!" He reared himself high. "Legion—my name is Legion, for we are many!"

Jesus had straightened up. "Legion?" he repeated, with a smile that Simon Peter recognized but, in his bitter earnestness, had never fully understood.

"Leave us alone!" Again it seemed as if many voices at once were issuing out of the sick man's mouth. "Leave us here! Don't drive us out of this neighborhood, don't drive us away! Let us enter the swine, we want to go into the swine!"

Jesus merely nodded. And at that moment, it seemed to the hidden onlookers as if lightning struck the great herd of swine. Their hundredfold outcry was like that of an army of maniacs. They rose up on their short legs and reared over each other's backs, biting and snapping, then they raced across the market place with incredible speed, as if chased by hounds and huntsmen, between the houses, down the lanes leading

39

to the lake, so that the dust rose like smoke in the moonlight and the flicker of the torches.

Lamenting, the swineherds ran across the square after them, but the screams of the swine faded in the distant sound of the waters of the lake.

The sick man sat quite still at the Saviour's feet, exhausted from the enormous emotional stress. Jesus took off his garment with its purple fringe, and put it with a pitying smile around the poor, naked, filthy body. Soothingly he stroked the man's unkempt hair.

"Go home," he said, as if to a child.

IN THE pitch-darkness, under the few steps leading up from the market square to Simon Peter's door, Levi the tax collector crouched in hiding. Spasmodically his breath struggled against the stench of market rubbish, of rotting fish scales, of pig filth and vegetable refuse. Some unclean hundred-legged insect was creeping across his shuddering neck, and he dared not lift a hand to knock it off. So much effort in vain! The town elders would not want to repay the taxes levied on the pigs and collected by his men. But had not the pigs remained in the town only a few hours, instead of the whole night as had been paid for? Had not the swineherds and their masters suffered a terrible loss? Should it not be the duty of the town to prevent miracles being worked on those possessed by devils? Everyone's rage would fall on him, the tax collector.

By straining his eyes, Levi could discern the former lunatic being helped up by his parents, who were still nervous for fear that he might bite or assault them. More clearly now, the tax gatherer saw the couple lovingly lead away their son, grown strangely mild, whom till now they had disowned. Furtively, the old people looked about them, to see whether anyone was noticing that their child, their big strong healthy child, was wearing the scholar's robe.

In his hiding place, Levi knocked his head against the stone step as he shook it, thinking sadly of his Sabbath meal at home. He echoed the words of Job: "Do I not lie here as in a pit of filth, disgusting to myself?"

"Are you one of the legion too?" Paralyzed with fear, he heard a growling voice above him. With his powerful arms Simon heaved him to his feet.

"It's the Sabbath," protested the half-strangled Levi. "You wouldn't commit the sin of manslaughter on the Sabbath?"

"My Rahab is lying here, and her mother inside. Take them both in pawn, you scourge over us. Or was it you who prompted my wife to ask the Nazarene to perform another miracle?"

"Are you mad too? Tell me, were you there in Cana when he changed the water into wine? And did you say he is from Nazareth?"

"Born on a journey, in Bethlehem."

"Bethlehem? Bethlehem!"

"Don't get so excited. Why do you act like that?"

"Because it's he! It's he!"

Simon laughed scornfully. "You are just the fellow we needed to confirm it, Levi. Every evening for years I've been praying to myself, and every time I hauled the nets in, my song was:

> *"Bethlehem Ephrata, Bethlehem Ephrata,*
> *Small and apart you lie,*
> *Great through the Son!*
> *Yours is the ruler's throne.*
> *He shall be King,*
> *Grazing for evermore,*
> *In pastures near and far,*
> *Strong in the Lord.*

"I wanted to help him be the Master. Our brothers should never plod along under the yoke. The Romans should never plant their eagles on Moriah. He—he has his legions. And for what? So that he can cast them into a herd of Gadarene swine!" The fisherman beat his forehead in rage. His wife, whom he had carried to the house when she fainted, awoke from her deep unconsciousness and clasped his knees, sobbing. The tax collector availed himself of this moment to break free and run hastily across the square.

Simon bent over the weeping Rahab and clumsily stroked

her hair. "Don't you be possessed as well. There are no pigs left to miracle your follies into. Don't I count at all? Instead of me, he takes lepers, instead of staunch Gaulonites, crutch-riders! He hangs his sacred garment on a filthy madman. Instead of legions, he gives me pigs to feed my fish in the lake!"

With a heavy heart he lifted his poor Rahab, and helped her up the steps, one by one, as far as the door. He pushed it open, and carried her into the stifling darkness. All the lights had gone out. In the heavy, sultry night, his wife, all that was left to him, clung to him, sobbing.

ALL that Sabbath, the streets of Capernaum remained empty. Only at evening did the inhabitants dare to emerge. Had not Satan been in their town only the evening before, and not one merely, but a whole legion of Satans? Gradually the couples became groups, till the market place was filled with a crying, hand-wringing crowd. Among the townsmen stood a few perplexed swineherds, chosen by lot to carry the news of their terrible loss to the unfortunate owners in Gadara. Dourly, they listened to the rabbi's furious outbursts. He was a gloomy man. The black curly hair grew thickly on his cheeks and temples, round his lips and chin. Even from his nostrils and ears grew tufts of hair. His fear of God turned to a raging hatred. "He" had blasphemed, had defiled the Sabbath. He had dared to heal the sick after sunset. He practiced his magic on men and swine. The evil spirits knew him. Did you hear them? Death stood behind all his actions. Death and death again!

As Simon Peter came out of his house, he could only vaguely hear the rabbi's threatening talk. But he was recognized by some of the crowd who had set out before the end of the Sabbath in search of the miracle-worker, and who were now shrinking before the rabbi's wrath. Some of those who had been cured were there with their relatives, carrying presents for the miraculous healer. Others knew of sick people in the houses of their acquaintances, and were determined that the wonder-worker should not evade them. They crowded round the fisherman, asking where he was hiding Jesus. He angrily repulsed those who tried to get into his house, and almost pushed his brother away with them. But Andrew threw his arms round Peter and shook him to his senses. "Simon, can't you rejoice with us?"

"Rejoice, when there is a dying woman in the house, perhaps a corpse already? Rejoice, when your wife has gone crazy? Rejoice, over pig miracles and lunatic miracles? Rejoice, when you see yourself forsaken by him for whose sake you gave up everything, and who throws himself away on any leprous beggar or herd of swine that happens to come along?"

Andrew scratched his head in embarrassment. "I know where Jesus is. I could hardly believe it myself. He went to Levi the taxgatherer's house for the Sabbath meal, and we with him, seeing he wished it."

Simon clenched his fists. "Say that again, if you dare! At the taxgatherer's, the one who extorts money for them in Jerusalem and Rome? Did you get your own sweat to drink there?"

No time was left for the two to talk. As though they stood in the warm waters of Lake Genesareth, the human wave benignly swirled about them on the way to meet the miracle-worker. With horn lanterns in their hands, Jacob the Tsaddik, Nathanael and Philip walked arm in arm, making their way through the crowd. The multitude bowed like ripening corn before the wind, for now the one they were waiting for had entered the square. His outer garment was new. The hyacinth-colored tassels and fringes hung even longer than before. Secretly, the taxgatherer had bought the costly material for himself, but he had never dared to put on such splendor. He had kept it hidden against the day when he would at last be so good and just that everyone would deem him worthy of it. Now it had become a gift for Jesus, out of gratitude for the happy stroke of fortune that made it possible for him to shelter the miracle-worker.

Halephai's sons accompanied Mary. Levi, who was timidly attempting to follow, was pushed against the wall. Terrified, he mopped his forehead with the prayer shawl which he had thrown over his head and shoulders as he heard the rabbi's booming voice: "No human being shall be idolized!" The proud sons of Zebedee were driving back those who pushed forward, out of gratitude or eagerness for more miracles.

A hundred voices at once were shouting disjointed phrases of love and gratitude, but across their enthusiasm, the rabbi's bass voice growled: "Let the blasphemer be driven out of this place, and all who have heard him beat their fists on his head, and let the whole community stone him!"

Mary anxiously raised her hands as if to protect her child.

"Did you hear that?" said Simon the Zealot. A few wild beggars, who had been caught in the shower of salvation along with the others, brandished their crutches angrily. While they traveled here, they had been racking their brains what they should do now. They had only wanted to beg for alms and instead they had been healed. Among the people of Capernaum too, there were those who sided with the rabbi. There was the doctor, who had seen his most profitable patients cured. There were the elders, who feared a new massacre. Already Bar Abbas had bent down and seized a stone. He was only waiting for the word. He heard the furious rabbi cry: "Protect my Sabbath! Only so is the Covenant kept!" The Covenant ... Many of those with no relatives or friends who had been healed, tremulously prayed with him.

Those who had been healed stood about in bewilderment. They wanted to be happy. They wanted to tell everyone the story of their good fortune again! The Sabbath evening should have been a universal feast, brimming over with joy. There should be wine, food, the music of psalteries!

Rahab alone was not diverted from her purpose. "Only a few steps up, Master! To my mother who is sick and dying. You were all her hope, while she had life. You have healed so many, heal her too."

At that, Peter forgot everything, the rabbi, Bar Abbas, and all; he implored Jesus not to squander his strength. "They are agitating for your murder. Call me a stupid fool, but I and all of us were hoping for legions. And how did you fulfill our hopes? Legions into pigs! Is that a lesson for us? We beg for miracles, yes, but for our whole people!"

But Jesus walked unheedingly past his Rock and into the

44

house. The disciples followed anxiously. Jacob the Tsaddik could not stifle his pangs of conscience concerning the Sabbath, miracles, and the Law. Mary looked to her brother-in-law Halephai for support. To everyone's dismay, the door of the barracks opened suddenly. The commander Cornelius came out, followed by Aulus Cuspius and two soldiers, supporting a pale youth who walked with difficulty. Confronted by this crowd of people the officer turned back. He shouted an order. His clear Latin rang across the square, and echoed harshly in the barrack yard. Armored men ran out. Shouldering their spears, they lined up in wedge formation. Then they set their shields one beside the other, and began to advance down the street, through the crowd of Judaeans. Mary began to tremble violently. Were these soldiers going to support the followers of the high priests? Jesus whispered consolingly to his mother: "The Sabbath is ended. Now I can make people happy once more."

"You are tired," Peter warned him, still grieved over the waste of his miraculous powers, but Thaddeus nudged him and reproachfully asked: "Can anyone ever do too much good?"

The black-bearded rabbi shouted over the anxiously bowed heads of his flock: "You heal an unbeliever on the Lord's day!"

Bar Abbas gave a piercing whistle; at the same moment a stone whizzed from his sinewy fist past Jesus's cheek, and struck the curtain across the entrance to the room where Rahab's mother lay dying. Others bent down to pick up stones and gravel. Shrill whistles answered the robber chieftain. But the blare of the cohort's trumpets sounded their warning signal like the wrath of God. The legionaries lined up in double column. Shield bosses and spear handles struck out at the crowd, till a way was made wide enough for Cornelius and the healed servant to reach the foot of the steps on which Jesus stood with his disciples. "Master," said the soldier gratefully to the Nazarene, "what have we done to deserve this kindness?"

"None has such faith as the heathen," said Jesus, so softly that only those beside him caught his whisper.

"I know I may not give you anything," continued the Roman. "Whatever I touch is unclean to you. But if you need anything of me, I shall be there."

Jesus thanked the captain with his own Roman salute, and Cornelius, delighted, went back with his soldiers, after detailing two men to stand guard over the house on the steps of which Jesus was standing.

Peter was still hesitating two steps below when he felt the Master's hand on his hair. His hot and stubborn head was gently shaken. "Why are you so resentful when I heal?" Jesus drew aside the curtain. Rahab lit the way with a lamp which a neighbor had handed to her. With the guest and the sons of Zebedee, Peter stared into the strange emaciated face of his old mother-in-law. How sharp her nose was! Her glassy eyes stared at them all from between half-open lids.

Jesus sat down on the edge of her bed. He looked only at her, his men only at him. Rahab could see nothing for tears. To hide his embarrassment, Peter sought to brush away a fly that was wandering about on the bare foot of the recumbent woman. He was overcome with remorse. The old woman had always been good to him. Jesus took her limp hand, and Peter began to sob as the sick woman suddenly sat up. She stared in bewilderment at the men around her bed, and began to scold loudly: "Daughter, what's the meaning of this? Letting everybody into my bedroom! Such distinguished gentlemen as Zebedee's sons! And a scholar too! He's taken me by the hand, such an honor! A scholar, but he has kind eyes. And you, how did you get here, Simon? Found your way home, have you? Well, that's what I call a miracle! And Rahab, don't stand there like that, with the lamp! You should offer seats to such distinguished visitors—not come to see me, of course. I only have to doze off for a moment and everything's upside down!"

"Mother," stammered Rahab, half crying, half laughing.

"Mother," implored Simon, with his hands raised.

"Mother," said Jesus with a smile, as he stood up.

"Mother, mother, mother!" repeated the woman, embarrassed and vexed, but smiling too, nevertheless. "Be quiet, Rahab. Take the gentlemen away for a moment, so that I can

46

get up and set things to rights. Give me my overgarment. If you gentlemen would be so good as to retire, I'll be up in a moment. I'll have everything in order immediately. I'll wash the visitors' feet as is proper. Why is the fire out? Go and get a burning faggot from next door, immediately. And Simon, you run down to the lake and get a couple of fat crucians out of the fishpool, and a big pike. Nobody's going to say he left my house hungry, as long as I live."

The followers of the Nazarene, and particularly those who had been healed and were now all creeping back, saw Rahab stumble out of the door, so beside herself with happiness that she could not utter a word. They saw Simon hurry out, and then, suddenly, the mettlesome old woman herself appeared in the doorway. Her stout, familiar outline showed against the dim-lit interior of the house. Any who might have doubted that she was restored to life, recognized her by her strong voice, and the old woman, who was well liked for her kindliness, was greeted with shouts of joy. "What a riot!" she cried in amazement. "What's happened? Why are soldiers standing guard by my door? Do they take me for Milady Empress?" Her neighbors shrieked. The street urchins laughed. Here and there hands were lifted in prayer. "Miracle upon miracle!"

The mother-in-law stood on the steps above them all, arms akimbo, utterly bewildered. Tears came to her eyes. That she should be a miracle was something she could not understand. For all her garrulousness, she could find no words, as she heard such rejoicing about her as never before. In the light of the rising moon, the people of the whole town were looking up at her and at her house. Hundreds of them shouted: "Hallelujah!"

As she turned round, the faces of the sons of Zebedee flickered before her in the torchlight, and another face which she recognized. Did that glow come merely from the fire on the hearth? Did that light in Rahab's eyes—and she had never looked so beautiful—spring only from love and gratitude?

"Mother," she heard her daughter's faltering voice. "You've come back to me."

47

ANDREW had hurried after his brother to the fishpool. They came back, loaded with pike and crucians, and when they reached the market place, they stopped in wonder at the sight of the festive lights. Torches were shining above the shouting, laughing people. Women and girls were bringing sheets, table-cloths and cushions out of the houses and spreading them on the ground. They set out crockery for the men who were squatting around on their heels, while from every hearth sounded the clatter of pots and pans. The fumes of boiling oil, the fragrance of herbs and the smell of fruits were wafted around the waiting men, who were letting garnet-colored streams of wine fall into their open mouths from the wineskins. Peter and Andrew could hardly get to their house for the swarms of people about it. At last they had managed to push themselves far enough forward to be able to see the two legionaries, who had mounted the steps, and with crossed spears were laughingly keeping the crowd back. Between them stood Simon's mother-in-law, accepting all kinds of gifts from the hands of those who were pressing forward. She did not seem to be able to reach out and say "God bless you" quickly enough. It was very flattering that her recovery had made people so happy, but she would have preferred to refuse the gifts. However, impatiently they made her understand that all these presents, food and drink, crockery and household goods, silver bowls and jugs, and purses of money, were not for her, but for the great miracle-worker from Nazareth. Rahab was helping her mother and in the red torchlight, Peter noticed another helper who had forced his way through and was eagerly carrying the gifts into the house, and stacking them in neat piles.

When the fisherman had handed his mother-in-law the pikes, he wanted to ask Jesus to remove the intruder. But with a dreamy smile, the Master was watching the sprightly old woman as, beaming with happiness, she began to prepare the meal for all of them. Her friendly neighbors had contributed some glowing charcoal for the dead hearth. Rahab was fanning the fire with a feather duster, and the fish began to splutter in the pan. Nothing was left for the host to do but take down-stairs the cushions and blankets that shortly before had served

48

as his mother-in-law's deathbed, to push the benches together cornerwise, and finally to stammer an invitation to the guests who were standing about. Humbly the fisherman washed the miracle-worker's feet. In that festive atmosphere, it caused him no pain that the sons of Zebedee had already sat down on the right and left of the Master.

Then Rahab came to him. The great light in her eyes and the happy glow of her cheeks astonished him. She seemed at that moment more attractive to him than ever Mary of Migdal had, whose carefully groomed appearance had given the clumsy man of nets, ropes and sails an idea of what the heathens worshiped and the Jews did not understand of beauty. Smiling he watched her as she hurried to and fro. With wide intelligent eyes, little Petronilla peeped now over her mother's shoulder, now, when she turned, into the lights and the many strange faces. A little startled, she clung closer against the arm that carried her, for her mother had bent down with one of the silver jugs at Jesus's feet. The young woman looked about timidly to see who would take the child from her. Then Mary held out her arms. Rahab was not sure whether the slender fingers and small wrists were not too delicate to hold her baby, who was already thrashing like a little fish to get to Mary.

When Rahab's hands were free at last, she knelt before Jesus and begged him softly: "Baptize me, as you baptized the others."

"What shall her name be, Simon Peter?"

Simon wanted to remind Jesus of that day when he had been baptized in the Jordan, to remind him of his great and noble mission; his voice, hoarse from rain and wind, growled from his rough fisherman's throat: "Name her after John."

Jesus nodded and said: "I name you Joanna," and poured water over her head. She was no longer Rahab, no longer rebellion and opposition. Now she was Joanna, and would answer to that name till the end of time. Humbly, according to the old custom, she washed the feet of the other guests, the sons of Zebedee and Halephai, and lastly the narrow feet of the Lord's mother, which she dried with her unbraided hair.

Peter's mother-in-law was insisting that they should hurry. Nothing went quickly enough for her. The heavy cedar table

49

was pushed into the angle of the benches, a bright new table-cloth—a gift—was thrown over it, the earthenware drinking vessels and clay spoons were rapidly set out. Joanna distributed the fine wheaten bread, endlessly scolded by her mother, who was busy cooking with more heart than she had ever done since Rahab's wedding. Already the room smelled of browned onions and garlic. Soon the fish were ready. Grapes and figs, dates and melons were piled up in silver bowls, there were beans and cucumbers to be eaten with the fish, cow's milk and fresh cheese! A more splendid meal could not have been served in rich Levi's house. With a hearty laugh the old woman cried: "Here I am, feeding you with my own funeral supper."

"Don't, mother," begged Joanna.

"Isn't it so? A little more, and my all-fours would have been sticking out stiff like an upturned coffin trestle. But now I can reach into the bowl with the rest of you. Pikes—that long! Only Herod and the high priests should eat them! But, Lord, you're more to me than all the tetrarchs!"

"And to me too," stammered Joanna.

"To all of us," insisted James, and everyone agreed. Only Peter sat silent and thoughtful. He, the son of the poorest fisherman of Bethsaida, whose father had been murdered as an outlaw, he who had always been on the move because of the ceaseless unrest first of his body and now of his soul, he, who was at home in every ditch, now sat like a rich master, like a host at a royal banquet, eating fine wheaten bread, which he did not like, and drinking wine that was much too heavy for him. Facing him, beside the mighty miracle-worker, sat the sons of the richest man in his home village and a woman of David's blood. He was happy that instead of a wearisome Rahab he could call a joyfully blushing Joanna and a little laughing Petronilla his own. He had been searching everywhere for the miracle. Had it not come into his house?

Then he heard Jesus ask: "Where is our good host of yesterday?"

"The taxgatherer?" asked Jacob the Tsaddik, frowning.

"In my house?" Simon Peter laughed sardonically. "To put his seal on everything, to pawn and auction them all?"

50

More quietly he said: "We have one unbidden guest already—Judas Iscariot."

Judas, in his corner among the piled-up treasure, started up in the middle of counting the money. "Who else should administer these gifts for the miracle-worker? Who else should give account of this blessing to the twelve tribes?"

"And to Herod, eh? And the Sanhedrin? And to Pilate?" said Simon bluntly. But Judas was not to be silenced. "Of course. Let them know who is working miracles in Israel. I'll say it to their faces, not like you, you plotter, you traitor!"

Meanwhile, many sick people and cripples had gathered and were trying to get into the house. Two weary men who had come a great distance, carrying on a stretcher a man with a broken back, were shouting that the Nazarene must heal him. But the Roman soldiers stood with their spears at the ready, calling for silence. They only let the tax collector through. He had obeyed the summons with the hesitancy of one who is always being hoaxed, and he was quite ready to turn back. There, he knew it! Between him and the table stood the dreaded fisherman, his fists clenched, who growled through his teeth: "Get out!"

"Now, Peter," young Thaddeus restrained him with a smile. He took the angry man with one hand and the taxgatherer with the other, and led them to the table, with Peter still persisting: "This is my house, these are my brothers, as dear to me as my life—"

Then they heard Jesus speak. What should have been a benediction shook them all like a curse: "If any man comes to me and does not hate his own father and mother and wife and children, nor his brothers and sisters, yes, and his own life even, he cannot be my follower."

Simon stared at Jesus, who seemed to be looking right past him and far into eternity. His eyes wandered over the new possessions, over the vessel in his hand, over his own little girl, over Joanna's pale face. "Master," he groaned, "I always hated, and my mouth was bitter. Only for your sake I rejoice today, that it is good to be here. I want to take nothing from you—from you or anyone else. I've followed you everywhere, as poor as a beggar, and had nothing to rest my head on.

Today, you've given us a foretaste of what you can do. Already once before it was said that kings came to do homage to you with gold, incense and precious spices. . . ." Mary motioned him to be silent but he paid no heed. "Take it all. Take me too. Away with all possessions!" Beside himself, he flung the precious crystal cup behind him, and Judas Iscariot screamed as it smashed into fragments. "I, your Peter, stand with you. According to your will! I'll break my house into splinters too! Crash down! Break! Fall in ruins!"

At that moment, they raised their eyes terrified to the ceiling. They heard noises above, and saw a wide crack appearing between the rafters.

"An earthquake!" cried Rahab's mother, quickly pulling her smock over her head and dragging her daughter and grandchild from the table into the nearest doorway. Those around the table sought to escape, but the calmness with which Jesus looked at the ceiling, which was already splintering amid clouds of dust, made them feel ashamed and restrained them. For all that, Judas Iscariot rushed to the corner where the gifts were piled and tried to spread his garment over them as a hen spreads its wings. He was powerless to ward off the wood splinters and mortar dust that fell on him. A piece of rough-cast struck Peter's head. They heard a crashing noise like the sound of ax strokes, the beams trembled, chips and fragments showered down in a yellowish cloud. Suddenly the beams and the ceiling rose. The starry night arched over the room. Below it the faces of two men, dripping with sweat, appeared at the edge of the opening. They were too exhausted to utter a sound. They merely waved their hands and pleaded for patience in dumb show. As if to cover the great hole once again, a wooden structure moved across it, then it began slowly to sink into the room, let down on ropes to Jesus's feet. A stretcher lay before him.

"Have they come for me?" thought Peter, as it hung before him. But to his relief he saw that someone was already lying on it. From the roof, a man with an ax hesitantly explained that however many had tried to get in, the guards would let no one pass. They hadn't known what to do with this cripple of theirs, so they had clambered over the neighboring roofs with him, to let him down from above.

The paralyzed man turned his imploring eyes from one to the other; he was looking for the miracle-worker, who now bent over him, smiling, and said: "Your sins are forgiven, my child."

The onlookers stared at each other in astonishment. The man on the stretcher, with an expression in which boundless happiness was mingled with intense anxiety, began carefully to move his fingers, joint by joint, then his hands, then with a soft cry of joy his arms and finally his whole emaciated body. Now he was tossing about happily, while, with moist eyes and trembling lips, he stammered his thanks. Peter helped him to sit up, and laid a pewter plate of figs and dates on the cover. He looked up. There was no roof above him, nothing but glittering stars and the dark depths of midnight.

He felt again as he had so often felt on his travels, as if the sky were his house.

ROME's mightiest amphitheater was never packed with such a tense and breathless multitude as had gathered on the western shore of the Sea of Galilee. The ranks of listeners stretched right up to the surrounding mountaintops. Longing, hope, hatred, curiosity, faith and fear were embodied in these throngs of followers and opponents. Whole towns were setting out, whole landscapes began to move.

In deadly fear, the high priests sent messenger after messenger to the rabbis of Naphthali and Zebulon, and not least to Judas Iscariot, threatening to hand him over to the Romans on a charge of high treason, if he did not deliver up the Sabbath-breaker to be stoned. On the insistence of the high priests, Pontius Pilate had ordered the Sebastenes to parade in readiness, but their dispatch riders returned with the information that no attack on unarmed people would be carried out, and that already a number of pagans, untouchable Roman citizens, were joining the throng. Priests and magicians had lost all their power; they admitted that a new era had begun; at the time of the spring equinox, the sun would be moving from the sign of the Ram into that of the Fishes. The Lamb was about to be slaughtered, the fishermen were at work. All this, Judas Iscariot reported to the Sanhedrin. He promised that the Nazarene would show himself in the Temple in Jerusalem at Passover time. He insisted that he was fulfilling the Law, so he would be obliged to make the pilgrimage.

Meanwhile, day after day, Peter and Andrew diligently went out fishing in their boat. Joanna's mother urged them on. With such an influx of wealthy strangers, there was a good dowry to be obtained for her little grandchild. The catches were hardly large enough to satisfy the hunger of the masses, and the sons of Jonah were afraid of exhausting the lake. Besides, the big merchants were complaining that there was not enough salt fish for the Rome trade. If the consignments were delayed much longer, the new delicacy would lose its customers. But his worries over Jesus weighed heaviest on Simon's mind, particularly since Nathanael had returned from Fort Machairus on the Dead Sea. "It's a country to make you fainthearted, out there," he lamented. "Rock and sand and the emptiness of the scorching valley that has been a desert since the cursing of Sodom and Gomorrah. The rock face rises up sheer out of the shimmering heat above the pale-blue sea. Herod's stronghold, where the Sebastenes delivered the Baptist, is of naked black stone. When we got there, we found a number of our people at the mouth of the Jordan—some of the braver disciples, and a few spies of the high priests, as well. A man whom you all know was praying beside us on the shore, goodhearted old Rabbi Hillel. He was staring out at a head that was floating on the water. It was bloody and going black already. John the Baptist was dead, beheaded. There was a good bit of water between his head and his body."

Judas Iscariot leered maliciously up at Peter. "And where were your miraculous powers? Didn't Jesus send you out? There was your aim and purpose, out there. But you stayed here fishing in the lake."

Peter felt as if he had murdered John himself because he had not come to his aid. Nathanael continued, in a horrified

54

voice. "In that heat, within a few hours, what was left of the Baptist was already decomposed."

But Judas persisted: "Where was your faith, Simon the Rock?"

He defended himself: "John had completed his work. He called himself the Forerunner." The sweat was dripping from his forehead.

But as soon as Judas saw that he was weakening, he went on: "I suppose it was the same here on Lake Genesareth, when the Master walked on the water and called out to his Peter. You climbed overboard onto the choppy waves. At first everything went well and you were smiling like a child. But perhaps the surface was too rough. Your confidence gave out, and you sank down and down, till the Master caught hold of you and saved you with his strong hand. It was like that again by the Dead Sea. The corpse did not sink in that thick water, but you all foundered in your impatience and your doubts. It's easier to catch carp and crucians for your mother-in-law's moneybags!"

"Go and make a fool of someone else! You know full well we have caught nothing for three nights past!"

"You did, you did! A renegade from the Temple," whined Judas. He had come upon the others one moonless night, as the fishermen, still swaying and reeling, had stepped ashore. The fear of death was in them, as overpowering as the darkness on the lake. They were still shivering from the sudden cold of the north wind blowing from Mount Hermon, which had caught their boats in the middle of the lake. Coldest of all were Peter and Thaddeus in their dripping-wet undergarments. In their two cloaks, they carried a lad, trembling and delirious in a raging fever. They had picked him up by the harbor. His name was John Mark, and he came of a rich family in Jerusalem. He had joined Jesus once before, but had found it too difficult to renounce all his worldly goods, as the Master ordered. But when he was about to enter the service of the Temple, he had returned to Galilee and shown his mutilated thumb. He had inflicted the injury on himself, so that he could not be admitted among the Levites. Still

55

afraid of the wrath of the priesthood, the fugitive flushed darkly when he heard Iscariot's malicious words.

Simon's trade left no time for idle talk. He and his crew lit torches and rowed out with the lights to lure the fish into their outspread nets. When they hauled in their nets, the catch was poor. Their torches had burned down to stumps. They hauled the nets in again. Nothing. There was no blessing on their work that night. When the gray light of dawn began to show, the cold, exhausted men cowered on deck, muffled in their burnouses. Only Peter held himself wearily upright, and steered for home.

The mountains by the shore rose out of the morning mist. A light wind drove the boats towards the slope of the western beach. A heavier vessel, manned by the sons of Zebedee, who had expressed their disgust at the smallness of the catch by gestures and shouts, followed in the wake of Peter's slenderer craft. A bright golden ray shone over the eastern beach. In the huge light of the quickly rising run, the shore around Capernaum became suddenly brilliant. Far off under the olive trees, along the edge of the reeds, and in the shadow of the fig tree, the fishermen saw the slopes covered with the vivid tents of the God-seekers. They saw many who had no covering save a cloak drawn up over their heads, squatting together or leaning against the tree trunks.

"Is it he?" John and Peter called out the question almost simultaneously, from boat to boat, and both answered, "Yes." Without quite being able to distinguish his figure, they knew that he was standing among the sleepers, the only one awake. In the rising wind, the boats ran up on the beach to right and left of him.

Peter was trembling with jealousy. Would he board his boat or that of the richer folk? And now he was coming aboard his. As the two boats put out again, there came a ripple of movement on the mountain to the west. The sleepers were waking, they felt him, became aware of him, recognized him also, for a roar of disappointment rose, until a few folk who knew his ways motioned for silence. The Master was about to speak.

Once again, those on the shore and in the boat heard that

ringing voice, neither high nor deep, fraternal yet masterly, kindly yet compelling. Often the sense of the words seemed to come from the depth of the listeners' own consciousness, like the age-old sayings of the prophets, repeated, heard and believed for thousands of years.

I shall never escape him, thought Simon Peter, as he listened to the portentous sermon. He breathed a little easier when he heard: "Unless your righteousness is given more generously than that of the Pharisees you will not enter the kingdom of heaven." Why the kingdom of heaven and not of Judah? The preacher's last words were still echoing over the water in the stillness: "Heaven and earth shall pass away, but my words shall remain."

Hundreds of thousands of people called to him, shouting against each other, stamping on the ground, waving arms, shawls, cloaks: "Hosanna to our King!"

He turned to his boatmen and in the bright sunlight he said to Simon: "Put out to the deep part of the lake, and spread your nets."

Simon bristled, a man who knew his trade and had no intention of allowing an outsider to interfere. Were they not all tired and drowsy after their fruitlessly wakeful night? He had hardly been overjoyed at the sermon, with its riddles and threats and its maxims which the mob would not follow in any case, and now the absurdity of laying the nets in broad daylight, when they had not even been able to catch anything by torchlight, infuriated him. He protested: "Master, we caught nothing all night long, but—if you say it, we will lay our nets." He looked round at the sons of Zebedee, who had not heard Jesus's command, and who were only following in the wake because they thought he was going home. James and John, expert fishermen, were watching with a puzzled smile. But the nets had scarcely drifted below the surface before the listless crew found themselves hard put to manage the ropes. They were nearly dragged overboard. Terrified, Peter, Andrew, Nathanael, Simon the Zealot, and Mark leapt to give a hand, for the boat was heeling over as if some invisible army were dragging it down into the deep. Untended, the sail flapped to and fro. "The net is tearing!" cried Andrew.

In mingled fear and joy, they called to James and John to lend a hand, and these ran their boat alongside and jumped aboard Simon's craft. Everyone was on the ropes now and they pulled with all their might. With the bilge buckets they scooped the wriggling, leaping, glittering fish into the boats. Soon they were wading knee-deep in crucians, carp, pike and eels, and still the net was not empty and the boats were so full that they began to sink. Jesus stood high above them at the helm, looking down on the miraculous draught.

Simon fell on his knees and slithered over the scaly fish, full of guilt for his insubordinate thoughts. He cried: "Begone from me, Lord. I am a sinful man!"

The fishermen stared with bulging eyes at the catch, and at the water that was now splashing and gurgling over the gunwale in quick, leaping waves. A catch at the wrong time, a catch contrary to all experience, a catch too big to handle! In their terror they thought they were doomed to drown. But Jesus bent over Peter and grasped his thick hair, as he loved to do, and said softly: "Do not be afraid. From now on you shall be a fisher of men."

The disciple shuddered with terror. He saw a net and a catch—men of all colors, more and more of them, living and dead. The net was dragging him into a sea, a sea so huge that the sky could not contain it, a sea of humanity.

Gasping, they rowed for the shore. They made the boats fast and for hour after hour they carried the catch ashore. Then, leaving everything behind, they silently followed Jesus.

NEW moon had come for the second time since the twelve had last met together. Jesus had sent them all out, the sons of Jonah as well as those of Zebedee and Halephai, Nathanael and Bartholomew, Thomas, Matthew Levi the taxgatherer, and Judas of Kerioth. He had sent them to teach what he had taught them, to heal, to perform miracles. Before they set out, they had been terrified, terrified of failing when the lepers groaned before them, or the rattle sounded in the throat of the dying, or devils uttered their threats in the ravings of madmen. Over and again, they repeated the instructions given them by the Master as they set out: "You have received the power freely, use it freely. Take no gold nor silver in your girdle, nor a sack on the way, nor even a staff."

From all corners of the Promised Land came the news: Miracles are happening! A new doctrine is spreading! The enemy were thrown into confusion—Herod, Pilate, the high priests, the Sebastenes. They hounded the twelve messengers like wolf and jackal. It would have suited them well to show Thomas slain, to report that Jesus was no more, and that he who was going about the countryside was an impostor. The returned wanderers were full of pride as they reported on their work, but James stared resentfully at the despised taxgatherer. The question almost stuck in the throat of the haughty son of Zebedee: "And you—did you work miracles too?"

Somewhat confused, Levi nodded, but immediately he shrank under the indignant glare of those about him. "Well, not I, of course. He . . . it was he who performed them through me, his poor instrument." He clasped his hands. "Do not hold it against me!" Contritely, Thaddeus embraced him. "It is we who must beg your forgiveness."

"And I swear I took nothing for it." Levi solemnly raised his hand.

Judas Iscariot looked askance and growled: "God's believers will be the death of him." And Thomas asked in a dry voice: "One thing I cannot understand: Why squander so much strength on us and through us? So that someone may live a year or two longer? Or a sick woman lose no more sleep, or a devil leave a lunatic in peace? Was it for that that we studied the Holy Writ?"

Judas Iscariot seemed to agree. "Why does Ezekiel say: The Lord shall destroy the enemy and for ever? And Judas Aggaeus: I make all peoples tremble and costly gifts arrive from the heathen. Mine is the silver and mine the gold."

They all laughed, but there was grimness in the Zealot's smile as he said: "When I was in the middle of my holy work, as proud as the high priest standing with the cherub in the room of the covenant, we came, Thomas and I, into the district of the Gadarenes. Do you remember how the Master drove the legion of evil spirits into that herd of swine? Why

59

should not I reverse the miracle? I thought. There was the herd of swine, good for nothing save for heathens to eat. Why not make legions out of them? So I went and stood in a high place and took three deep breaths and fervently prayed. I pictured the mighty prospect to myself: The twelve of us at the head of an army bristling with weapons, chariots in front like those of the Pharaohs, a hundred times a hundred Sebastenes, legionaries stretching from one sea to the other, more than the Emperor in Rome can command. I willed it, I willed it!" He broke off.

Thomas nudged him: "Well, confess..."

"What happened? Wish remained wish and pigs, pigs."

SIMON Peter gazed thoughtfully from face to face, and then looked round the room of his own house. The household in Bethsaida had been wretchedly poor, but since the healing of his mother-in-law and the shower of gifts that had followed, prosperity had moved in. As the old lady's business expanded, she had been obliged to buy the houses on either side of her. Judas of Kerioth and Aulus Cuspius had given her valuable advice there. Of course, the place smelled rather strongly of pickle brine. On weekdays, workmen made barrels of Lebanon wood in the workshop. Nimble girls packed the fish in them and salted them down. Then camels took the salt fish over the western mountains towards the sea, where heathen ships transported it to the market in Rome. Judas bought up bread, he bought up fish. He sent his peddler after the multitude that followed Jesus everywhere, thronging the streets and cities.

The tiled floor was softly covered now, and cushions were piled along the walls. While the old woman worked and scolded and drove her servants on, her daughter Joanna went in silks from faraway lands, and her granddaughter Petronilla sported long earrings of filigree gold. Necklaces of gold coins jingled on the little girl's chest when she took her first steps.

Now, with her lamp held high, the old woman peered at them, one after the other. It was some time before she recognized her son-in-law. Then the light began to bob up and down as she made her deep obeisances. All twelve rose uneasily to their feet. He who had walked past their boat in the storm over the night-black waves and had called to them: "Fear not!" was leaning against the wall, paying heed to no one. A little offended, the old woman withdrew, and in doing so she knocked against some of the men who were timidly drifting into the next room. She whispered anxiously to Andrew: "Somebody should warn him." She jerked her thumb over her shoulder towards the open door. "Captain Cornelius asked Joanna to call on him, and just between the two of them he told her that Pilate is on the lookout for Jesus."

"Have we shaken off Bar Abbas?" asked Thaddeus, as if in a deep dream; he breathed again as Andrew quietly answered "Yes." "I feel as if death was on our heels. Five thousand joined us and would not leave our tracks. Bar Abbas had raised them to follow Jesus into Jerusalem. Passover is near; we were to have gone up, but the Master turned away from the Temple, northwards. For days the multitude went hungry. People like us are used to fasting, but not they."

Philip growled: "I asked where we were to get bread from. Only one of Judas's peddlers had followed us."

"How was I to know," protested Iscariot, "that Jesus would not eat the Passover lamb on Moriah, as he did every year? My people were waiting on the pilgrims' road. The bread and fish are going mouldy there."

"Who was waiting?" As Peter received no answer, he snatched the lamp so violently out of the old woman's hand that hot drops of oil spattered on the forehead of the startled Judas. "You were with us. So who was waiting?"

"What are you doing, spilling grease on me? Who do you think was waiting?"

"Was it Herod's men, or Pilate's, or the high priests?"

Judas behaved as if he did not hear.

Thaddeus voiced his fears: "Yes, Bar Abbas and his Bar-jonim. The cursed robbers started to shout. 'Jesus is the prophet! Into the royal city!' they howled. If the Sanhedrin get to hear of it . . . and they hear of everything . . ."

Judas muttered darkly: "They have their ways of finding out." And louder: "Where is the need for supplies and bag-gage trains if Jesus makes manna rain down on his army?"

61

Thaddeus went on: "Mary of Migdal, Pilate's paramour, sent word to her brother Lazarus in Bethany: Warn your friend Jesus! But Lazarus is sick and dying. The only man our Master listens to, cannot speak to him."

Judas made himself heard once more: "You must intervene, by force if necessary. Jesus should rest a little—in Nazareth would be best. Nobody asks miracles of him there; they do not believe in his powers."

Peter cried angrily: "They wanted to stone him there!" Thaddeus added: "His mother wants him by her, for she is afraid for his life. My father and my brother Jose are lying in wait, to bring him into safekeeping." Jacob the Tsaddik agreed: "He is without honor in his own home. . . ."

Simon Peter could contain himself no longer: "Traitors, the lot of you!" He rushed up the stairs, the flickering light streaking as he went. He hurried through the family bedroom and in the frame of the loft door he saw Jesus, silhouetted against the fiery red of the eastern sky, looming huge and massive as a pillar, as a monument. The Master continued to stare straight ahead.

When Peter turned his tear-filled eyes in the same direction, the lamp fell from his trembling hand. Far across the sloping rooftops of the town, they saw Lake Genesareth still blue and dark, for the sun's rays had not yet reached down from the mountains in the east. Over the vast stretch of water, something like an enormous swarm of gulls was approaching. As the sun came down, they saw that the surface of the lake was dotted with sail after sail, where a fleet of boats were scudding. At first they were driving before the morning breeze, keel by keel from east to west, but now they fanned out and swung into Capernaum harbor. The sun swept from gunwale to gunwale. The boats lay deep in the water, crowded with men from stem to stern. In every right hand, an upraised sword glittered in the morning sunlight.

From below came a muffled sound of quarreling. Judas's shrill voice could be heard: "You do not believe in him! You do not want me with you! The curse of Deuteronomy on all those against me! The stranger who dwells in your land will stand above you, and you shall come lower and lower! He shall be the head and you the tail, the tail!"

But from the shore, the cry of five thousand men rolled like thunder: "Jesus of Nazareth!"

Peter swung himself sailor-fashion down the wooden stairs. To the dumfounded group, who had heard the roar of the host and could not imagine what it meant, he thundered: "Lights out! Bar the door! Bar Abbas has come! The multitude fed by the miracle are here!"

Five thousand men were already crowded together in the market place of Capernaum. Ten thousand eyes stared at the barred door. All around, the windows were opening. Only one house remained dumb, blind, deaf. Inside it, the twelve bewildered apostles were silent. Then they heard the rattle of a bolt, and, terrified, they watched the door open. Almost blinded by the sunlight, they saw the figure of Jesus surrounded by golden rays. He went out, and they followed humbly through a lane of silent men. A narrow way opened immediately before the Master, and closed again behind the twelve disciples. The vast crowd moved towards the Temple.

Everyone had shrunk back from the quiet slender man with the ceremonial purple fringes on his garment. Then at last, someone at the back of the crowd, safe from scrutiny, called out: "Master, how did you get here?" For in the previous night's storm, no one would dare to cross the lake. Yet he was there.

Jesus did not look round. His gaze was directed straight ahead as if into infinity as he said, more in contempt than reproach: "Have you sought me out? I will tell you why. You have eaten of the bread and been satisfied, satisfied! Do not concern yourself with transitory food, but with food that remains till eternal life."

Some stood openmouthed. Others thought they had not heard aright. A half-grown lad laughed impudently, then immediately ducked away in fear, before Peter's threatening fist.

Nathanael hurried forward impatiently to fetch the door-keeper of the Temple. But words were not enough for the waiting crowd, they wanted deeds. Irritated at the delay, Bar

Abbas's men squatted on their heels, yawning and disappointed. Like the low shrubbery of the burnt-out southern landscape they surrounded him they had so eagerly sought, who towered above them like a noble cypress. Now, during this enforced rest before the Temple door, he turned to his faithful. The sturdy fishermen and peasants stood a few paces behind him, and in their shadow, the nervous but inquisitive tax collector, Matthew Levi. Judas, who had remained behind, beside Bar Abbas, seemed the only one who was unconcerned. Peter's mother-in-law had hurried after them. Ever since Jesus had cured her, she had been living in constant fear for him. Now she found herself in the middle of the crowd, frightened, unable to move forward or back, and she bitterly regretted having left the shelter of her home.

Jesus turned to the Twelve. "What were you speaking of?"

The disciples looked uneasily at each other. Did he not know their thoughts? But Peter laughed grimly. "They were quarreling because each of them wants to be more than his brother. But not I, Lord! I understand too little of what the Son of Man wants, and nothing about eternal life. Existence is hard enough for me as it is, I never want it to be eternal. But perhaps these fellows are right, who all want to be great kings and emperors."

"You will get us all crucified!" Judas hissed to him.

"Is it my fault the master spoiled your business with that miracle of the loaves?"

"Help me, Master," Judas appealed to Jesus. "There's no moving this stumbling block, this rock of ignorance you call the Rock." He turned to Peter and said bitterly: "That is your name, is it not? And you would like to be called the first among the disciples, you, who cannot even read or write...."

Peter burst out laughing and slapped his thigh with his broad hand. "But I am helped by an excellent memory, like most people who cannot write things down. Shall I recite all your wishes, you lords of the world, you leaders of the hosts? And I suppose my old mother-in-law would like to be the mistress of the fortress in Machairus, eh?"

"You slander me, Simon. Do I deserve to be mocked at, after all I have done for you?"

64

She was profoundly shocked to hear Judas splutter: "Jesus, you promised us all that we would sit on golden thrones. But you are the stone, Simon, you are our footrest!"

Such an insult to her son-in-law was more than she could bear. Her nerves began to twitch. She reared herself up, the whites of her eyes showed, and foam dripped from her lips. The strange horrible voice of prophecy burst from her like thunder from the clouds. What she saw, what she screamed, made them rigid with terror: "You the chosen ones? You, the exalted? Yes! I see you ascending through the clouds to heaven. They kneel before you as before the All-Highest, they crown you all, they swing their censers and sing before you! But under your damask robes is blood! Bloody wounds are festering beneath your diadems! Exalted you are, but on crosses, slanting crosses, crosses upside down, and you head downwards, Simon, my Simon! And this one they are sawing in two, and you, they are winding the entrails out of your belly, and you, they are peeling the bloody skin off your body, and you will be clubbed, and you, Judas, your guts are bursting out of your hanging carcass, and ... Jesus! Lord Jesus, what is happening to you? You are dying the death of all mankind. Every death is on your face and the angels are sobbing...."

She fell headlong. The squatting men had got to their feet and fearfully drawn back, staring at her from a distance as she lay writhing in the holy malady. But Jesus bent over her and lifted her up as if she weighed nothing, and held her till she breathed easily and freely, in unbounded happiness. Humbly, the women took her home. Bar Abbas's men kept their distance. Only a tiny curly-haired boy, brown-skinned and dark-eyed, remained by Jesus and the disciples. His mother called anxiously from the doorway of the house: "Ignatius! Ignatius!"

The boy looked around, and Jesus—who alone remained unmoved by the dreadful prophecy—took the child with a gentle hand, and drew the wet little finger out of his mouth, which was screwed up in terror. Nathanael had just returned, and the doorkeeper was unlocking the door of the synagogue. With his mysterious smile, Jesus said to the Twelve: "He who takes in such a child as this in my name, takes me in too, and He who sent me." And then he became very serious. "He who seems the least among you, he shall be the greatest."

To Peter, these words sounded like some delightful benediction. He would have liked to dwell on them, but Jesus had already stepped out of the bright sunlight into the shadow of the synagogue. However, the fisherman had to give vent to the fullness of his heart, and a half-stifled laugh escaped from him. Involuntarily, he raised his right hand and let it fall heavily on the plump shoulder of Judas, who staggered under the blow. "Your footrest! Then I am the least one, thank you!" Then he hurried up the steps behind Jesus, but he could only see his beloved Master from behind a pillar, so many had thronged into the synagogue. For the first time, the faithful disciples were not around Jesus. They had been pushed aside by Bar Abbas's cutthroats. Outside, the sun beat down on the multitude. They whispered to each other the questions they would like to put to Jesus, and a few courageous ones with beating heart cried out: "A miracle! A sign! You have given us bread, give it to us day by day!"

Those standing shoulder to shoulder in front of the synagogue took every noise amiss, because they wanted to listen. The synagogue had been a gift from Captain Cornelius, built on the plans of Greek architects who knew all there was to know about sound and echo. If anyone spoke in front of the shrine where the scrolls of the Torah were kept, his voice rang clearly and thunderously in the ears of all outside. The marble door became a speaking mouth which all could hear.

Now, like a desert storm from Sodom and Gomorrah, the words struck the listeners in the face: "I am the bread of life!"

"Blasphemer!" screamed the rabbi. "He insults the Lord! Hear it, Israel!"

Shrill whistling rose from the crowd, mocking laughter and a rebellious murmur. "Stone him!" shouted an old man's voice in the synagogue. As Peter shoved the old man back with his elbow, he heard Jesus utter the terrible words: "I am the bread of life. Whoever eats of this bread shall never die. Whoever eats of my flesh and drinks my blood . . ."

66

Peter forced his way through the crowd and embraced Jesus's knees in unutterable terror, imploring him: "Do not say it! Nobody will do that! I will not allow it!"

"He is giving us his flesh to eat!" Those at the back of the crowd shouted furiously: "Are we heathen devils? Away beyond Mizraim, where the Pharaohs dared not go, they eat human flesh."

But Jesus intoned like a song of victory over the horrified and indignant crowd: "Whoever shall eat my flesh and drink my blood, his shall be everlasting life."

Those listening began to howl with rage. They could not distinguish the words that came after. With vile oaths and insults they fought their way out into the open, in mortal fear of the powers of hell. In a short time the square lay deserted, as if their enormous terror had devoured them entirely. Only the thirteen remained in the synagogue. The preacher had fallen silent, and was counting. Twelve disciples, and not a single one more. Peter was still cowering at his feet. Jesus bent down and quietly consoled him. The architect's secret made it possible for the others to hear every word: "What I was speaking of was life in the hereafter, in which many of you refuse to believe...."

Jesus's pitying smile had changed into one of bitterness. A man in danger, misunderstood and betrayed, he looked from one to the other: "Do you not want to leave me also?"

Peter stammered: "Master, to whom should we go? Only you know about eternal life." With a great effort, he persuaded himself of what he was saying: "We believe and we know that you are the Christ, the Son of God...." He will not even look at me, he thought sadly, but all the others heard was: "Have I not chosen you, all twelve? Yet one among you will become a devil...."

They understood nothing further. Between the millstones of horror, their thoughts were ground into fragmentary phrases: "Drink my blood ... eat my flesh ... stoning ... crosses." Ever since Simon Peter had clutched his dying father to himself, death had been at his heels, so he was not disturbed by fear. He did not let his Master out of his eyes; but he reproachfully

67

murmured to himself: "A devil? Well, well, if it comes to that, I am but a poor, poor devil myself...."

THEY did not travel by day, only by night. Nobody was ever put more rigorously to the test than the few disciples whom Jesus kept with him: Simon the son of Jonah and the sons of Zebedee. He led them in all directions as if he wanted to shake off the last of them. Once, like a king at the head of an army he had surveyed the multitude on the desolate heights sloping down to the wilderness eastward of Lake Genesareth, where thousands camped, replete and happy after the miraculous feast. Now, after many weeks without pause or rest, their shelter was a mountain cave beside the young, steeply rushing Jordan, hidden away in the shadows of the undergrowth. Jesus had sent Simon up with his pack ass by the ancient tracks to Panias, the old heathen town of the great Pan, which the other tetrarch, Philippus, of the northeastern district, called his Caesarea: Caesarea Philippi, to spite his hated brother Herod. The Jordan had its source in the grotto of Pan.

As Simon returned, driving his big gray ass before him, he looked back on the past, and laughed bitterly. "You're a donkey. I'm a donkey. Do we bring bread from Caesarea for the life everlasting? No. We bring bread from Manasseh the baker in a heathen town." Meanwhile, Joanna was watching for her husband. With little Petronilla on her arm, she had stepped out of the thickets onto the side of the track. Wearily, she sat down on a fallen tree and held her daughter closer to her. The child wriggled happily in its mother's safe arms and groped with its tiny fingers towards the sorrowing woman's dark, deep-set eyes.

Suddenly the child's happy cries ceased. Nothing could be heard but the rushing of the Jordan in the ravine. Joanna looked up to see what had frightened her baby. John was standing by them. Under his penetrating look, the child's mouth began to turn downwards, and tears came to her eyes. She sobbed and pressed her wet little face between Joanna's soft breasts, back into the safe familiar darkness.

68

"Your little girl was laughing for joy, but you were weeping, and now you are both weeping together."

"The One above must surely weep too, every time he sees us laughing down here on earth."

"Especially we, who are wandering in misery like exiles. . . ."

"Why did my Simon have to go up to Caesarea, into such danger?"

"To get food, and news."

"Food? Did not Jesus feed the multitude? News? Does he not know more than all the rest?"

John shrugged his shoulders and looked round warily. Some way below them, at the river's edge, his brother James was sitting on a smooth-worn rock. Bathing his travel-weary feet in the cool mountain water, he was talking and gesticulating to himself. In the rush and echo of the river, his words could not be distinguished. John whispered: "Have you not noticed, the Master does not want to work miracles any more. One does not even hear about his healing powers now. I sometimes think he is fleeing from himself."

"Like everyone else. Who stayed, but you two and my Simon?"

"And you, a frail woman, who followed us secretly."

"I never wish to live through such another night as that last one in Capernaum, while you were locked in the synagogue, with Roman legionaries guarding you. If Captain Cornelius had handed you over, the Sebastenes would have driven you all to Caesarea to be crucified, or to Jerusalem to be stoned."

"If Cornelius had not locked us in, who knows? Perhaps we would all have left him on the spot. It sounded like heathen talk to us, that dreadful 'Whoever eats my flesh and drinks my blood. . . .' I seemed to see a sacrificial victim, just as its throat was cut, its eyes rolled up, its lips drawn back painfully from the glistening teeth, its legs threshing in the empty air as if in flight from the cruelty of the slaughterer. . . . And are we to imagine him like that? Our King Messiah?"

"In my time, I have spent many nights sleepless with terror, but none was worse than that. In the first gray of morning I sat on the house step, my child in my arms, watching for you.

My child was crying, and I gave her suck so that she should not disturb my listening. The people of Capernaum had locked themselves indoors. It became brighter and still quieter. At last the captain ordered the legionaries to return to barracks. His servant, the one the Master healed, unlocked the synagogue door and went away without looking back. . . . The door opened cautiously. The cousins of Jesus looked this way and that, to see if the coast was clear. Then, with their faces muffled, they crept away, hesitating at every street corner, towards Nazareth. Bartholomew and Nathanael followed. They turned off in the direction of Bethsaida. The tax gatherer went miserably home, then Thomas came out. He no longer resembled the Master, so dejected and desperate he seemed. Judas Iscariot came out with Andrew, who was so exhausted that he only got as far as my steps before he sank down. Judas was staring moodily ahead. . . . But you, where were you?"

"We stayed," said John.

"How and from whence you came I do not know. Petronilla had drunk her fill and suddenly she stretched out her arms. Her father was passing by, with Jesus, James and yourself. I could hardly hold the child, she was struggling so to get to her father. I had to go with you. I had not the heart to let you go alone."

"And now we are wandering as if in search of the promised life everlasting. Is it everywhere but in the temple of the Lord?"

"I gave my necklaces and coins and earrings so that we might have enough to live on."

"An endless road," sighed John. "We may not go to Judaea. Everyone is after our lives. In Nazareth they laugh at us. In Bethsaida they tested the Master with a blind man. Jesus took him furtively out of the village and healed him secretly. Were you there?"

"I can still see the man with his wide-open eyes, staring at us in terror. I can hear him stammering: 'I see something moving before me. It must be people. I see them walking about like trees!' Jesus warned him not to go back in the village, and to say nothing to anybody."

"We found no more disciples, only Pharisees everywhere, a supercilious and sarcastic lot. It has become their custom to invite him to a meal and to put barbed questions to him. They no longer take him seriously, but he despises them, however many violations of the Law they may prove us guilty of. We may not wash our hands any more, when we gather at table with the Pharisees. He talks of filthy and disgusting things just as they are taking their biggest bite."

James came climbing up the steep scree. While he tied his sandals, he was listening to his brother. "Are they not right to say we no longer keep to the doctrine of our forefathers? Where were we at Passover? Not in Jerusalem."

A man's voice rang powerfully from the upper part of the bare rock where the path from Caesarea came curving downwards. It was Simon. He turned past a boulder with his heavily laden ass, swung his stick, and sang loud and clear: "If I were Jehovah's son."

"Simon!" cried Joanna happily, and she held out the little girl to him. Simon swung the child high into the air like a wriggling fish. "... You would be the Almighty's grandchild, and be able to play with the Behemoth as happily as I with you."

Anxiously his wife admonished him: "The Almighty commanded: Thou shalt not take My name in vain! Do you not remember how the evil spirits were driven out and shouted to Jesus? 'You are the Son of God!' Beware!"

"Take Petronilla, and go and ask His rightful son why he had to send me up to Caesarea. He is the one they are waiting for. Does he not know that even away up there the Temple whore of Jewish freedom has been spinning her web, Pilate's whore, Mary of Migdal?"

Joanna snatched the child to her. She covered it with her veil, and covered her face as well. But Peter went on with his reproaches, shouting them into the forest. "They are all lying in wait for him—Judas, Bar Abbas, Gesmas, Saul. I had difficulty in getting away. They want to settle accounts with him for leaving them in the lurch at Passover time. Everything was prepared. It was to be a most serious affair. We cannot wait any longer. Our Galileans, the bandits, the short-sword

71

men, the old Barjonim, they had all marched up there. It was no longer safe in the forecourt of the Temple. The hucksters began to pack their wares away. It was the Messiah they were praying for so impatiently. Mary, 'the Magdalene' as Pilate calls her, had prepared a feast for him. Like Judith, she had laid her plans for the Roman governor's death. Meanwhile, we were to storm the Antonia, set fire to the Archive, lock the Sanhedrin in David's Tower and start the holy war. With Jesus—our Messiah."

James murmured to himself: "Passover—that is long past. The pond at the Jaffa Gate is dried up already, and the dust of summer's heat is blowing out of it. It is drought time, and the cattle are getting lean. The Feast of Tabernacles is not far off."

"Mark that—the Feast of Tabernacles, the last chance! Everything will be got ready once more. We must all rise up together!"

"But we are traveling northward...."

"No farther, surely," laughed Peter sardonically. "They are all at him—Saul is abusing Mary of Migdal and our Master, saying he is nothing but a magician. Bar Abbas says mockingly: 'He feeds devils because he himself is fed by devils.' And Judas of Kerioth complains: 'Who asks him to save souls? He ought to destroy souls! What is the use of my getting money together to finance a war? If we wait any longer, the Romans, the Sanhedrin and Herod will take it all from me again.' They wanted me to be commander. They still prefer me to Bar Abbas, of whom they are frightened. The Judas before me and the Judas within me were pressing me to become the leader of the host. Jesus had called me a rock, they said, and I should be a boulder rolling before them all. Oh, it was a great temptation in Caesarea!"

They had wandered along the narrow path through the thickets towards the cave, in front of which the sons of Zebedee had already heaped brushwood. While they unharnessed the ass and carried the sack of food into the hiding place, Joanna fetched the fire stick, to prepare a fire. "Are you sure no one followed you?" she asked anxiously.

"I got away from their rage as if they were after me with a whip. They would like to betray us to Pilate!"

The cold damp shades of evening made the men from the hot Jordan valley shiver. A night bird startled them as it flew above their heads with a mournful cry. Joanna had wrapped the sleeping child in her cloak. Tirelessly, she twirled the fire stick, and the men stared at the glimmer which was just beginning to show. Simon got up and stood guard. In the shadowless stillness, under the full moon, he watched the smoke drifting northward towards Hermon, which, in the clear brightness, loomed unnaturally close. The mountain was tiger-striped with snow, and as if perched on a gigantic claw of rock, the marble city of Panias glittered in the moonlight. One by one the lights went out in the windows. Only the watch fires occasionally flared up on the towers, when a freezing guard threw a log into the glow. Suddenly, they all started. Out of the darkness came the voice of the Master: "In sixty-two weeks Christ will be slain."

Jesus was standing in the darkness by Joanna's ass, scratching the patient animal's shaggy coat. Simon held out his short-sword towards Panias, and to hearten them, he cried: "They are ready to rise up in your protection. Thousands in Caesarea, thousands in Judah, tens of thousands in Israel, a countless host in the Diaspora, and everyone, everyone in Galilee."

"To bring about my death."

"Did you not cry woe to Korazim, woe to Bethsaida, woe to Jerusalem, the city that stones its prophets, and to Rome, that crucifies? Everyone's hatred has been roused," said James.

But Peter laughingly shook his head. "Jesus and hatred? All he does is to heal."

Jesus came quite close to the fire. He towered up as if angels held him, and none of them dared to remain sitting. They all rose to their feet and looked at him silently. With his next words they realized shamefacedly that none of their thoughts were hidden from him. For in the midst of their doubts, he asked: "Who do men say that the Son of Man is?"

While the others were staring silently at the ground, great drops of sweat broke out on Peter's forehead with the sheer strain of thinking. The bookish sons of Zebedee would surely

73

find some fitting text among all that learning they had stored up. But he had learned nothing parrotwise from the rabbis, he had looked and lived, had fished and quarreled and sought. By the Jordan, at Jesus's baptism, he had thought he saw the streaming light of Godhead, beside which the sun is black. He had stood by his mother-in-law's sickbed, and had seen Jairus's daughter, and heard the word *Talitha kumi,* and the girl, believed dead, had stood up. They called him the Rock, and he was to be a fisher of men. In fear and longing, Peter thought: "Everything depends on the answer—now!"

John stammered: "Some take you for John the Baptist. Herod himself believes the man he beheaded is risen again in you. Others say that you are Elijah...." James had nothing better to offer: "I have heard you named Jeremiah...."

The painful smile began to play about the Master's lips once more, the smile which Simon so feared and loved, for it held mild irony and reproach, and yet was full of kindness: "But who do you say I am?"

Before the others could speak, Peter, his voice jubilant, had answered. He did not know how it happened; something came over him. Just as he had so often leaped from his boat onto the shore, now he sprang across the blazing fire; with his right arm outstretched as if he were taking an oath, and his left thrust behind him, he cried in an impetuous rush of devotion: "You are the Christ, the Son of the Living God!"

At once the strong man became weak, and sank on one knee and waited for the touch of his Master's hand. The strong slender hand of Jesus of Nazareth tugged lightly at his curly hair, affectionately, soothingly, perhaps even gratefully. That mighty voice which had called the disciple a rock, now sounded gentle and full of promise. The kneeling man thrilled with happiness as he heard: "Hail, Simon son of Jonah, for this has been revealed to you not by flesh and blood but by my Father who is in Heaven...." The Master was not looking at his disciple, but had fixed his gaze on the distant fortress, lit by the moon, rising up indomitably, rock on growing rock. Then the stars of his eyes moved and he looked down on Peter's head. "And I say to you, you are Peter, and upon this

74

rock I will build my Church, and the powers of hell will not prevail against it."

Through the veil of his tears, Peter saw his Master as if unreal and transfigured. Rapturously he heard him say: "I will give you the keys to the Kingdom of Heaven. Whatever you bind on earth shall be bound in heaven, and whatever you"—and here the wonder-worker's voice became mysterious as if he spoke from the eternal stars, and deep and black as night—"loosen on earth shall be loosened in heaven."

A deathly silence had fallen on the breathless listeners round the campfire. Joanna glanced timidly at her husband. Carefully she carried her belongings—food, crockery, her sleeping child—into the depth of the cave, for the night's rest. The sons of Zebedee followed her, as if rebuked. Simon, whom Jesus had helped to his feet, looked around, proud to have such witnesses to his elevation. But he was alone. The others had gone.

But when Jesus spoke, they stopped and listened. His voice was once again that of the man of might, stern and peremptory: "Tell no one that I am Christ."

Over the whole land from Lake Merom to the Dead Sea, arose a shout of fear, a shout of joy: Jesus of Nazareth is coming south again!

As before, the multitudes streamed to him. But now it was only the most careworn, the beggars, the sufferers. All the Twelve, penitently, were with him again. In a cloud of scorching dust the weary procession dragged on southward, yet not by the shortest route. Before them, Mount Tabor lay like a monstrous beast in wait. The burning heat of late summer, and the gritty dust in their faces, their ears and the corners of their eyes, seemed to wear away all their hope. Like the rear guard of a battle which everyone knew was lost, they trudged on towards the battlefield.

A dried-up cistern lay by the desolate way. Dusty sun-baked steps led down into its bricked depth. Jesus sat down on a half-ruined wall. Slowly the circle round him thickened. The new arrivals pressed forward, and Simon and a few other strong men had to hold them back. The crowd looked down into the parched depths and longed for the miracle of a sparkling fountain, but Jesus only murmured to himself, clearly enough to disappoint and disturb them all: "I must go to Jerusalem. My cousins demand it. You all hope for it. Everyone impatiently awaits it. The Son of Man will be obliged to suffer much. The scribes and high priests will reject him. They will put him to death...."

Even the weakest of them cried out in fear, their thirst and weariness forgotten. Many threw themselves before him in the dust. Joanna knelt by him and entreatingly held up her child, parched with thirst. "Must we not all die your death?"

But Jesus looked past them all. Now came a new and somber riddle: "Crucified, dead and buried, on the third day he will rise again from the dead."

They stared at him wide-eyed. Instead of cries and lamentations, a silence fell on them as if a tombstone had been set between themselves and life. Then the Master straightened up and said: "If any man wishes to follow me, he must renounce himself."

This talk of renunciation grieved Peter far more than the prospect of a bloody future. What was the good of being the Rock and the Keeper of the Keys? Did his keys only fit the gates of death?

"Day after day he must take up his cross and follow me. For he who wishes to save his life must lose it. But he who loses his life for my sake will..."

"Master!" Simon protested, but the sons of Zebedee cried: "Silence!"

"... will save his soul."

The faithful were about to shout: "Christ! Messiah! For your Kingdom and ours!" but Jesus continued: "What shall it profit a man if he gains the whole world and forfeits his life?"

Like the others, Peter took this as a reprimand, but his feeling changed to one of gratification when he heard: "Whosoever among the adulterers and sinners is ashamed of me and my word, the Son of Man will shame him, when he comes in his glory, in the glory of his Father with holy angels." And

76

with a last consolation the prophecy ended: "Truly I tell you, there are some standing here who will never taste death till they see the Kingdom of God in all its might."

Simon the fisherman rushed impetuously to the speaker, and took him in his powerful hands as if he were some holy object to be protected at all cost. Hardly conscious of his own boldness, he pleaded: "Thank you, Master, for the Kingdom, but why did you give me the Keys if you believe someone is going to harm you? I would slam the door, even if Caiaphas himself stood there and it shattered the jewels on his breast. I would fasten the lock! I would not let it happen. I forbid you to allow it! Say no more of that rubbish about suffering and rejection and being bound to die. You have not the right to die. You are His well-beloved son, and He has not died from Adam's time till now. You must live! You are the King, I tell you!" Laughing and crying at once, he raised his fist as if menacingly. "Heaven have mercy on you, Master, it must not be!"

But the others saw Jesus turn sharply from Simon and face them. They clearly heard the Master's words to the fisherman who had wanted a King Messiah, so that he could be his victorious general: "Get behind me, Satan! You are an annoyance to me, for you do not think of what is God's but of what is man's."

Levi the taxgatherer recalled the fisherman's powerful hands about his throat. Tired as he was, he quickly drew stylus and tablet out of his satchel, and scribbled: "Satan! You are an annoyance to me!" so that it might be remembered forever.

EVER since Jesus had chided him, Peter kept apart from the others, gloomily going his own way. Joanna followed timidly with the pack mule, which carried her child in one of the panniers. Now that it was evening, Peter squatted, his legs tucked under him, and holding Petronilla in his lap, he played with the happy child, who thrust its little hand into his stiff fisherman's beard and tugged. Joanna tried to check the child, but Peter would not allow it. The more it pained him, the

77

easier he felt. Did he not watch Jesus suffering, the Son of Man, poor as a beggar, who seemed to compel himself to experience everything that could be crammed into the span of his earthly life, every distress, every torment; and bitterest of all: "Do you not understand me? Not even you?"

"You are to come with me," John whispered peremptorily in his ear. Peter was startled, so noiselessly the messenger had stepped up to him.

"I am tired."

"Jesus orders you to come. And the others are not to know."

"I suppose he is ashamed to be seen with me, with Satan?"

"He is taking just the three of us, you, my brother and me, up the mountain with him. Be silent and follow so that nobody notices."

Joanna took the child. "Go, Simon. You had better go."

Her husband wearily rose to his feet, stretched his arms and yawned. "I am dead-tired and heavy with sleep—" Surreptitiously, he peered around to see where John had disappeared. Then, grateful for her encouragement, he caressed Joanna, stroked her hair, grumbled again for a moment, and stole away among the sleepers who lay huddled in their cloaks. When he reached James and John, they were furious at his delay. They hurried to catch up with the Master. Soon, the weary climbers had entered the wood at the foot of Mount Tabor. By the light of the waning moon, they saw Jesus, well ahead of them, climbing the steep path with his steady tireless stride.

Gasping for breath, the three fishermen followed him up out of the hot Jordan valley. It occurred to them, one after the other: "Did he not once say: 'I am come here to go into the towns and villages.' But there are no towns and villages here. The moon will soon be down. The way and the return lie in darkness."

"As we climb, the mist is climbing with us," warned John.

More and more often, they were obliged to stop, to steady the beating of their hearts. The soles of their sandals, worn thin by long traveling over sandy roads, were poor protection against the rough stones and sharp pebbles. The next time they paused for breath, Simon sat down on a boulder and

78

leaned back, exhausted. "A fisher of men, am I? I suppose he did not tell you what we are to catch up here? He has just thrown the stars of his heaven over our heads like a golden net. But it has not been cared for properly, it is full of holes. On the thickest knots of stars sit heathen gods, thinking they direct our fate. But their power is finished now. In the mist, we can see no stars, no gods. There is nothing but white clouds around us, cold damp clouds. . . ."

Full of dread and desolation, they collected themselves and hurried after their Master. Simon's voice sounded strange in the damp mist: "My net is gone. . . . I cannot find my keys. . . . Master, drive me out of myself, drive the devil out of Peter!" Then with a cry of fear he reeled back and clutched his two companions. "I nearly ran into him," he stammered. Jesus stood in the mist before them. His voice sounded unfamiliar and reproachful. "Did I not think it was given to you to understand the secrets of the Kingdom of Heaven? And you, Kephas, do you think I am chiding you when bitter words are forced from me?" Compassionately, he added: "Sit down and rest. You have earned it."

STARTLED and desperate cries sounded through the early morning mist. One voice had started, and the others joined in. None of them, James, John or Peter, would have confessed that he had uttered the first cry.

"Has he not gone down to the valley, great and proud as a king?" Like drowning men the brothers groped for each other and for Peter who had already risen, ready to follow his Master. But immediately they drew back before the thick gray mist that spread about them, damp and ice-cold, a mist so strange, so living, that they almost expected it to speak. They were long accustomed to seeing things become quite other than what their fathers' experience might lead them to expect. Water became wine, the lame got up and walked, the blind looked knowingly about them, the ears of the deaf and the mouths of the dumb were unsealed, and terrifying devils tortured the possessed with incredible cruelty till at last they tossed the witless, foam-covered, blood-spattered bodies at the feet of the Mighty One.

"Why did you not take Andrew instead of me?" Peter whispered to John. He pointed ahead, into the obscurity. James answered: "Your brother, whom we call the Protoclete, sees and hears things in advance. . . . Each of us knows things which Andrew was the first to utter, the first to confide to us, things we have often repeated, as bemused in waking as in dream."

Peter asked suspiciously: "Do you think we dreamed this night?"

"Do we know it for sure?"

"I will not be lied to. You all saw the same as I did."

"Do we know what you saw?" James's mouth twitched. "How absurd our drowsiness and your dream-talk must have seemed to the Master."

"And do you insist that we were dreaming?"

"It was no dream," said John.

"Of course not." The words rushed from Peter's mouth. "We were lying on our faces. Nobody sleeps with his forehead on the rocks and stones. A bold sleeper turns his face faithfully heavenwards. My eyelids became so heavy that I was afraid I would fall asleep there and then. As I stared over to the spot where I knew Jesus was standing, my eyeballs were rolling with weariness. I did not know what I was saying, whether 'Your heaven endures for ever, Lord, in the Word,' or 'Your Word endures for ever, Lord, in heaven'—and suddenly heaven itself came upon me, and the everlasting glory and the eternal word. Deny me, if it is not the truth. On the summit like the rising sun, Jesus stood in a brightness beyond that of all the stars. His clothes were white; where is the fuller who could bleach cloth so dazzling white? And because you had taken him for Elijah, who came but Elijah himself! And more exalted than all the prophets and soothsayers, the bull-horned one, our hero and leader through tribulation and death and plague and the Red Sea, through forty years of desert: Moses! They towered up into the starry sky before us. The red glow of his fiery chariot was around Elijah and the flames about Moses were like the fiery pillar in the night before the ark of the covenant. But Jesus stood in snowy white among the choir of the angels. They spoke together, while we watched, dumb, trembling, enraptured, yet full of fear. I rallied all my strength to stay awake and more than awake. . . ."

The brothers interrupted him, their voices half stifled. Word for word was the same, as if they had been learning the sentence all their lives: "Moses spoke and Elijah spoke of Jerusalem, Alleluia, and of the King of the Jews, of palm branches, of the cross and the Ascension. . . ."

"I wanted to call out: Why, Master?" Peter lamented. "Why, here in the loneliness? Why, just for us poor fisherfolk? Why not on Moriah? Before the fortress of Antonia, before the legions? Make them fall on their faces, on their thousand faces in front of you!"

"You called out nothing—nothing at all!" James harshly rebuked him.

"Because I was so frightened I had nothing left but a laugh, and a silent one at that."

"But when they were leaving, some miracle gave you back your speech and the rest of your nonsense. It was laughable to hear you stammering to the three giants of eternity, out of the coldness of the night, with your teeth chattering: 'Master, it is good for us to be here. . . .' " He could not continue for laughing.

"You may laugh! But I had to say what was weighing on my heart. 'Not to Jerusalem.' Death is lurking there. I know they all want to drag him down there for the Feast of Tabernacles, the Barjonim, Bar Abbas's men, the Galileans, the lot of them. I want to see him here in safety. In huts up here, watched over by the giants of eternity. But the clouds swallowed us as the mist does now. The prophecy sounded again as Andrew heard it by the Jordan, only closer this time, much closer."

Lightly, the pale mist dispersed, and the three men who had thought themselves unobserved saw Jesus standing near them in the early sunlight. At his words they trembled and began to pray. "Tell no man what you have seen or heard last night, until I am risen from the dead."

Every available man from all the twelve tribes was already on the way to the Feast of Tabernacles in Jerusalem. But as the disciples were traveling through Judaea, Jesus suddenly disappeared. His followers turned back in search of him, and singly they stole from the beach into the little town of Capernaum, either through the side gates, as if they came from the grape harvest, or else through a gap in the wall, known only to them. They made their way to the house of Simon's mother-in-law. Joanna arrived before them, riding her little ass past the guards at the Syrian Gate, who were just searching a band of pilgrims for weapons, and did not deign to glance at the muffled woman. The Roman soldiers had been hastily recalled to Jerusalem, and Syrian bowmen had replaced them. The inhabitants barricaded their doors and windows in fear of these new troops. The ass trotted briskly through the dark alleys towards its stable. At the steps of her house, the young mother dismounted. The old woman was beside herself with joy. She pressed her daughter and grandchild to her, and whispered to the astonished Joanna that the miracle-worker from Nazareth was inside, resting by her hearth. Jacob the Tsaddik was no less surprised to find his father Halephai and brother Jose standing before Jesus, and reproaching him bitterly. They had looked for him in the Temple at Passover time. Was he going to be absent again, at the Feast of Tabernacles?

From the doorway, Joanna's mother whispered for them to be quiet. There were voices outside. And as Simon looked out, someone held a lantern to his face, with a mocking laugh. The double-drachma collectors stood before him, malicious and delighted that one they had been looking for so long had fallen into their clutches just as they were on their way home. "Salaam. Does not your Master pay the double-drachma?"

The double-drachma—that is, half a shekel—was the hated poll tax levied by the Temple. Simon's father had bled to death fighting against it. If they were going to persecute Jesus on such an account, then all his darkest prophecies might well be fulfilled.

Angrily, Peter stammered: "Of course," and was about to go back into the house to get the money from his mother-in-law, but Jesus himself was already standing in the doorway. Smiling, he gazed at them all in the lanternlight. "What do you think, Peter? From whom do the kings of the earth take their taxes, from their sons or from strangers?"

Peter laughed. "From strangers."

"So the sons go free. But not to anger them, go down to Lake Galilee, and throw out your line. The first fish that comes up, open its mouth, and you will find a shekel. Give it to them from me and from you."

The door closed in the faces of the taxgatherers. Their dignity wounded, they determined to accompany Simon to the lake, ready for action in any event. If he caught nothing, they would take the whole lot in custody. If he paid them by a miracle, they would charge him with sorcery.

When Simon hurried back breathlessly to report on the catch and the new miracle, he found the quarrel still raging. Excited shadows were moving to and fro in front of the flickering fire, darting whispered reproaches at each other.

"I will send you about your business"—the fisherman turned on Halephai—"you and everyone else who tries to persuade the Master to take the pilgrimage. Did you protect him, when they were going to stone him in Nazareth?" Sullenly, the relatives turned to take their leave. Andrew and James went with them as they hesitantly descended the steps. John joined them and turned to Jesus. "Master, we saw an unknown man driving out devils in your name. We stopped him, because he is not one of your followers."

Jesus took little Petronilla on his arm, and his voice had a metallic ring: "Restrain no one! Nobody offends me who works miracles in my name. Who is not against us is with us. But whoever offends against even a little child who believes in me, it were better for him that a millstone were hung about his neck and he were thrown into the sea." With both hands he held the child out towards the Zealot and his somber companions. "If your eye offend you, pluck it out. Better to enter one-eyed into the Kingdom of God than to have both eyes and be cast into hell."

The disciples listened but this time Simon Peter did not allow them to thrust him forward. Indeed, they had not asked him to speak for them, as they usually did, for the Master was holding up the fisherman's little daughter as something particularly precious. The talk turned again on the Kingdom of Heaven. Immediately out of the dusk came the question—not outspoken, only in an undertone—the disciples' eternal question: "Who then is the greatest in the Kingdom of Heaven?"

Jesus's answer was harsh: "If there is one who would be first, he shall be last and the servant of all." Then he pressed Simon's child closer to him and his voice was all kindness. "See that none of you despises any of these little ones, for their guardian angels look at all times on my Father's face."

Simon listened in bewilderment. What did all this mean? He himself had just taken part in a miracle that had terrified the tax collectors, just the kind of miracle for him. And was he—the first among them, the Keeper of the Keys—was he to be the last, and the servant of them all? Am I a devil again? Yet he is holding in his arms my little devil-child, who is wriggling to get to its mother. How gently, how kindly the Master spoke of his sinful brethren! Simon looked helplessly from one to the other, then he hazarded a question: "Lord, how often must I forgive my brother if he sins against me?" He named a high figure to show that he was willing to learn. "Up to seven times?"

"Up to seventy times seven."

It was late at night when, against all expectation, Jesus set out for Jerusalem. Wearily, bitterly, the sons of Zebedee and Jonah panted after him through the sultry summer night, past the barricaded entrances to towns, past deserted villages. When would the Master's word be fulfilled? "I come to cast fire upon the earth." Wearily they thought of their homes, as some nights later they cowered in the undergrowth, hiding from the sentries on the wall of the Samaritan mountain town before them. Andrew, standing concealed in the shadow, motioned the others to him across the moonlight on the path. "No one wants to shelter us. Bows and spears threaten us

84

over the battlements. They would pour boiling oil on our heads."

Jesus had walked to within a stone's throw of the walls. He stumbled. Sleep seemed to be dragging his trembling, exhausted body downwards. He heard the sons of Zebedee whisper: "Master! Do you wish it? Shall we say it? 'Fire, come down from heaven on those who deny us hospitality, and flames devour them'?"

Cautiously, Peter crept over to them to hear the answer. Jesus stood alone, like a man of might, for all his weariness. His reproach was hurled in the faces of them all: "Do you not know of whose spirit you are? The Son of Man came not to curse men but to save them!" But next morning he looked back sadly on the little camp in the undergrowth and murmured to himself: "Foxes have holes, and the birds of the air have nests, but the Son of Man has nowhere to lay his head. . . ."

Already they met with rumors that the Feast of Tabernacles had begun with a terrible night of massacre. But Jesus hurried on to Jerusalem. Ten of his twelve disciples had joined him, young Mark among them. He had often spoken enthusiastically of his desire to contribute towards arming them for their campaign of holy vengeance. His father was dead now; he was rich and, but for his mother, alone in the world. Full of sadness and grief at the loss of his father, he earnestly begged his beloved Master to tell him how he might gain the gift of eternal life, the one mysterious possession that was worth having. He had answered every question calmly and wisely. There was no law of the rabbonim that he had not strictly kept. But now he was confronted with the inexorable command: "If you would be perfect, sell everything you have and give to the poor." Sadly the young man returned home to Jerusalem, for he was "one that had great possessions" as Matthew Levi, who was in a position to know, had noted with regret.

As usual, the disciples urged Peter to be their spokesman. "Go, ask what we are to do. Must you give away your house in Capernaum, too, and sell your wife and child into foreign slavery?" Thinking of his sad farewell, he laughed bitterly.

85

"I am a queer camel already, and must the eye of the needle open itself to let me through?" The next time they stopped for a rest, he came up to the Master, with the others behind him, their advocate.

"Lord, we have followed you. What is to be our lot?"

The Master looked kindly into his stubborn, rebellious face, took the Rock's clenched fist in his hand, and answered with a smile of deep understanding: "I tell you who are my companions: at the resurrection, when the Son of Man sits on the throne of his glory, you too will be sitting on twelve thrones. Whoever leaves home or brother or sister or father or mother for my sake, what he has given up will be returned to him many times over, and he will have eternal life as his heritage. But many of the first shall be last, and the last, first."

Just as Peter took new heart, a cry from Andrew made them all look towards the road. Supported by his youngest brother, Simon the Zealot was staggering towards them along the way from Jerusalem. His forehead was bound with bandages stained dark with dried blood. His face was bruised. He could scarcely see out of his black and swollen eyes. When he caught sight of Jesus, he broke into a wild sobbing. As they listened, his account of the massacre of the Feast of Tabernacles seemed like the raving of a man in delirium. The priest had come down to dip the golden pitcher into the Pool of Siloam. Suddenly, conspirators had dashed the vessel from his hands. The Levites had uttered a cry of woe—"From the crowded temple came the sound of wailing, of entreaties, lamentations, and the battle cry of Bar Abbas's men. And through it all, the Roman signals for attack. Heavily armored legionaries came clattering across the drawbridge from the fortress of Antonia. Soldiers swung themselves on ropes over the balustrades of the Temple. Like hailstones in the storm of God's wrath, they hurtled down on the mob. Muffled Sebastenes threw off their Jewish prayer shawls and rushed to the fray. Women and children, trampled underfoot, cried out in fear of death. Bones cracked. Blood spurted from severed veins. Jew trampled Jew to the ground, stumbled over corpses, and slipped in the red sweet-smelling pools on the tiles and the steps. . . . Down below, the axles of the storm chariots were creaking. Legionaries! Legionaries! They ran with their battering rams, blow after blow, against the Tower of Siloam. Stones began to break, gaps appeared in the masonry. With the dull noise of thunder the tower collapsed on the rebels. The dust! The dust!" The Zealot fought for breath. Thaddeus told them how he had picked him up unconscious. The cunning of the priests and Romans had prevailed. Bar Abbas lay in chains in the fortress of Antonia. A few days later the high priests were already consecrating the building anew.

Jesus had listened in silence, smiling sadly and nodding now and again. Then to his followers' bewilderment, he resumed the journey.

Next morning, the sun rose in splendor. They traveled southwards, over the richly cultivated plateau, through forests of sun-drenched pine, past oaks that arched majestically above them, till among the noble carob trees and sycamores they obtained a view of rosy peaks and, far to the south, backed by the bare mountains, the dark-blue mirror of the Dead Sea, sultry and still, like the mark of some primeval sin. The other survivors of the Jerusalem rising, those who had come down from the north, from Galilee to Moriah, were camped at the edge of the forest, full of sadness for the holy festival that was now branded with such terrible memories. Many of them were in deep mourning. When they saw Jesus, the long-awaited miracle-worker, they got to their feet with a cry of indignation and despair. "With the blood of beasts of sacrifice, Pilate has mingled the blood of our wives and children, our own blood!"

But Jesus's expression caused them all to fall silent, and his words made them tremble. Matthew, jostled by the crowd, tried to write them down: "If the servant is evil and thinks to himself: 'My master is delaying his return,' and begins to beat his fellow-servants and eats and drinks with drunkards, the master of that servant will return one day when he is not expected, at an unknown hour, and will strike him down, and appoint his portion with the hypocrites, and there will be wailing and gnashing of teeth. The Son of Man will come when you do not expect him."

They had been ready to reproach him with forsaking the

brave Galileans who had tried to rise against Rome and the high priests. Peter cried out helplessly: "Lord, is this parable aimed merely at us, or at everyone?" The answer seemed to roar in his ears: "From him who is entrusted with much, more will be asked. I have come to cast fire upon the earth; what else should I desire but that it burn? I have a baptism to be baptized with. How impatient I am till everything is accomplished!"

His closest disciples looked at each other in bewilderment. What baptism? "What of the blood-baptism of those who fell in Jerusalem?"

"Do you think those Galileans were more guilty than the rest of their countrymen, that they had to suffer so? I tell you, no. But except you all repent, you will perish likewise. The eighteen men on whom the Tower of Siloam fell, do you think they were guiltier than the other people of Jerusalem? No, I say again. But unless you repent, you will perish likewise."

Those about him, blood brothers of the fallen, the Gaulonites, the short-sword men, stared at him bitterly. On them all, Jesus pronounced the sentence: "All those who came before me were thieves and robbers!"

Simon Peter, the son of Jonah who bled to death, grimly reached for the haft of his short-sword. "Thieves and robbers?" He thrust his elbow into the sore ribs of Simon the Zealot. "Shall I ask him again? Thieves and robbers! Is that a parable for us...?"

THROUGH the closed doors of his innermost room, Pontius Pilate could hear the regular crash of the breakers against the mole of Caesarea. Outside, the rain was splashing into the water basin in the peristyle. The cold and damp made him shudder as he impatiently felt the wall behind his couch, to see whether the heat was rising yet through the hollow bricks. He had ordered the Judaean slaves, those arrested after the rising, to be whipped. There were plenty of them, but they would eat nothing the Syrian cooks set in front of them, and they would rather be mistreated than do hard labor. The

Roman drew one more blanket round him and consoled himself with the thought that there were rougher provinces, and more warlike folk. No riots and rebellions could be successful in these winter rains. His fierce counteraction had cowed the stubborn mob. The high priests, too, he held on the leash of their own cowardice. He could make it known at any moment that the high priests had begged him, a heathen, to crush the threatened rebellion of the Chosen People in time. The next festival, the consecration of the Temple, had passed off quietly. So he could justify himself, if Tiberius were to call him to account for his cruelty. Even the most dangerous of the lot, the mysterious wizard, exorciser and wonder-healer Jesus of Nazareth, had taken refuge far away in the country east of the Jordan, where John used to baptize. For the sake of his women, Herod had beheaded this rebellious preacher. For the sake of his women, Pilate delayed Jesus's fate, for both his wife and his mistress ardently took his part. The noble Claudia Procula never imagined that her husband had listened with the same dubious smile to his Judaean friend, Mary of Migdal, as she, too, gave her account of the wanderings and miracles of the Nazarene. Now that the government and the future of Jerusalem rested on the sharp spear points of his legionaries, he longed all the more for his fascinating Magdalene. This was the name, arbitrarily derived from her native town of Migdal, by which he fondly called this enemy of his. For indeed, all his reasoning obliged him inexorably to come to the conclusion that she was his deadliest enemy. He was never really her master, nor master of her people nor her homeland. He thought again of how she had made him shiver as she told him of the inescapable vengeance of Jahveh, and translated the somber curses into noble Greek. She used to practice her secret dance-gestures in front of him, her lovely arms writhing to right and left, like deadly snakes in some heathen temple, dancing to the flute music of the conjurers.

He had had to summon all his courage on that unforgettable night before she had finally disappeared. Spies had reported they had seen her since, in the house of her sick brother Lazarus, in Bethany. She was scarcely recognizable. The bride of the Song of Songs is bound to blossom early, the younger she begins her song of yearning. The once-beautiful woman was faded now. Her hair was gray, they said; prayer and penitence and the care of her sick brother were all her work. Her brothers and sisters had taken her in according to the teachings of Jesus, who had even protected an adulteress from the sternness of the scribes.

How often the Roman had surreptitiously groped under the pillow, to see whether a dagger was hidden there. He had the feeling that she wanted to rise high in her people's esteem, like Judith, with his severed head. She seemed to him more dangerous than all the men of Israel and Judah, those eternally excited and quarrelsome characters who bickered with each other every time he sat in court. Pilate's blood had pounded in his veins when he gathered from Mary's conversation that this yellow-skinned, black-bearded, hate-filled rabble dared to despise him, and that their every thought was like a bog of spittle in his path. With desperate wit, the beautiful woman had mimicked their crazy mockeries for her dangerous lover. Anything to delay him until the prophesied insurrection of her people should take place!

Daringly, she impersonated her secret visitors, the conspirators. All the seven devils in her, the devils of her people, took shape. Sometimes, of course, breath and voice failed her, when Pilate, with half-closed lids, named the visitors who had attended a secret meeting in her house the night before, one after the other as if he were reading from a register, and asked her to impersonate them.

She would try all the more humorously to divert him. Bending back from the hips, she would sway towards him, the red strands of her hair knotted under her chin like a great beard, and her nostrils dilated. With a bored dignity she hoarsely croaked: "Reach me the Ephod, and put on my breastplate. . . . When the fumes of the incense thicken, I can see far into the future. . . ."

"And what do you see, most reverend high priest?"

"Curses without number, the sacred curses of Moses. Better one should die than a whole people. . . ." With her arms spread in prayer, she sang the age-old chant of execration: "I sated my arrow with blood, and gorged my sword on the flesh of the stricken and the wounded, on the flesh of the leaders of my enemies."

Pilate laughed. "How many golden vessels of Judaean blood did the most reverend high priests pour behind the Temple curtain on the night of the Feast of Tabernacles? I gave them their wish."

"What do my ears hear?" With one tug at her hair, Magdalene had changed her mask. Her face looked complacently up at Pilate, with a broad and supercilious grin. She pushed her girdle lower and began a belly-dance, made still more grotesque by her apologetic gestures. "We are Pharisees, more faithful than the faithful. We spend all our time in tittle-tattle, in discussions of the Law. We are mild and pious, like Moses who slew the Egyptians. Mild as Phineas who slew the Canaanites, and as Matathias who annihilated the Syrians. . . ."

Suddenly she felt her wrist seized and she was drawn so close to him that she smelled his repulsive breath. His voice was hard: "How many devils are lying in wait for me here?"

"Seven in me, seventy times seven in Israel. Do you feel at ease in the house of your faithful Herod?" She bent down to his ear and whispered in Salome's cajoling voice: "Beautiful, mighty King Herod! Dream of my mother's and my lonely sinful nights! Beware! The queen is staring jealously across at me, her unhappy Salome. . . . She would like to strangle me in my own plaits—you have cut off one prophet's head for me, a bloody blossom. Cut me a still more splendid flower, please, please. Betray him, poison him first, but let his throat be cut for me—the throat of the mighty governor, Pilate."

How she enjoyed her game, sneering into the face of the enemy of her people. Negligently she leaned against a pillar by the Roman's couch. Her eyebrows raised, the corners of her mouth drawn down, she whined, like some superior being who no longer believes in anything. "Swine and sons of swine, dogs and sons of dogs rule over Israel. They are cowards, these Romans. However heavily armed they enter the Temple, they squint over their shoulders after a God they cannot see. We sacrifice to him, not to the Emperor-God. The Governor allows it. And one of these days, we shall let His Majesty in Rome know it. There were five judges in Sodom—the liespitter, the lie-master, the master of everything corrupt, the pettifogger and the perjurer—and all five bundled together do not equal one Roman."

"One day, the Roman judge will pronounce sentence; and on that day you will all be nailed on the cross." She was terrified, and still more terrified at his icy question: "What does your friend Bar Abbas say?"

She shrank back into the shadow of the pillar, and her voice trembled at the bitter choice between a Roman death sentence and the slash of a short-sword across her throat, with which the gang leader would certainly have her dispatched for her treachery. She began: "According to his followers he says: 'The day of Rome's destruction will be as great in our calendar as the day of the destruction of Samaria.' "

"And that Judas Iscariot of yours? Does he not want to become the Messiah-King himself?"

Shaken, Mary sank down into the squatting posture of the women of Bethsaida. It was as if she were a child again, and heard the clatter of the Sebastenes. How Pilate had her watched! So she impersonated Judas too, and slowly glided out into the light. The Roman burst out laughing, so perfectly did she mimic the stocky fat-bellied man, with his squinting treacherous eyes, which always seemed to look past one, sleepy and cunning: "Who would be future Master of the world?—Just let me look after the Judaean money."

"No artist has risen among you. He would be filled with horror at your ugliness. And one of you wants to be the God-Emperor of the world, the war lord, with Jupiter Optimus Maximus his father? Where else could he be begotten but in Rome?"

"No!" she cried impulsively. "Your power came from army and emperor, and with emperor and army it will go. The true King's mother was a poor maid, his country, poor country. A manger was his cradle. Only the poorest are unconquerable." She stood in her proud beauty, strangely possessed by the thousand-year-old will of her people.

"What is his name—Simon, son of Jonah?"

Violently, impatiently she shook her delicate little head. She was lost in the silence of a helpless longing for the days of her childhood, for games by the still lake, for purity and peace.

Pilate roused her from her absorption with his applause. "Now you could justifiably call out as the actors do in Rome at the end of their comedy: 'Clap and applaud, my friends!' Oh, yes," and he clapped his hands. "But a greater comedy is going to be played soon. You have imitated demon after demon. One seemed to hear them, see them, smell them." He counted them off on his fingers. "A noble priest; a Pharisee; the she-devil of Hasmona, Salome; a Sadducee; Iscariot; and the she-devil, Magdalene. A pity one cannot behead the lot with one slash at your beautiful throat. —But one is missing. There is a seventh in you still. I want to see him. Sing, preach, do miracles like him. Show me—Jesus of Nazareth."

Terrified, Mary stretched her arms beseechingly to the heathen. "They are all devils, but he is good beyond everyone. He is not in me!" She cast herself down on the tessellated floor, and, shaken with sobs, she moaned: "Not he—not he—not he. . . ."

As if he were drawing back before attempting his last and mightiest action, Jesus had returned to Jericho once again. On the way, he had cured the old beggar Bar Timeus of his blindness. The healed man had wavered uncertainly and staggered along the road. His relatives followed him. Involuntarily, everyone in the crowd had imitated his stopping and stumbling, and his smile. So they had traveled on as if they had only just awakened to the light. Away at the back, the little tax collector Zaccai stood on tiptoe, to peer over the crowd. Desperately, he climbed a sycamore with his last strength. Jesus noticed him there, and kindly he motioned the stout little dwarf to him. "Tonight I must rest in your house."

Poor Zaccai hardly knew what he was doing, and promised —a new miracle. "Lord, I will give half of my belongings to the poor," he stammered. "And if I have cheated anyone, I will repay him fourfold." With that, he hurried to prepare a festive meal. He listened to the disciples' mystified conversation over the strange words with which their Master had greeted the news that Lazarus, his dearest friend, was dead. "Lazarus is dead and I am glad for your sakes that I was not at his deathbed, so that you may believe."

Others knew through Joseph of Arimathea—who on account of his importance as a member of the Sanhedrin had only dared to seek Jesus out at night—that the members of the priestly High Court had been summoned to a special meeting, because of their alarm at the approach of the Nazarene, whom the priests only referred to, in their abhorrence, as "A Certain Man." Joseph Caiaphas, the acting high priest, had been the principal speaker, but the old high priest Annas, the power behind the scene, had been carried there too. Nearly a quarter of a century before, he had been raised to the highest honor by the governor Quirinus, but another Roman had deposed him. To Valerius Gratus, he had seemed too patriotic and dangerous. Despite that, the powerful old man had succeeded in raising four of his sons to the high priesthood, and, when they died or had to give way to Rome, his son-in-law Caiaphas. Caiaphas had angrily warned them: "Only one thing can lift the man of understanding into the realm of the supernatural—ecstasy as the handiwork of the Lord. Whoever knows that, what need has he of a Messiah?"

An old man had protested: "The dying rise up, evil spirits take flight, the blind see, the lame bound like deer!" So the prophets had foretold.

"Old wives' tales! The password of rebels! Bandit tricks!" Annas had said. The wise Gamaliel had answered him: "What concern of the Sanhedrin are miracles? Gold and sacrifices, yes! But miracles are for the weak. Annas Chananel, once a year you used to enter the Holy of Holies. Joseph Caiaphas, you enter it yearly, yourself. I do not ask which of you has seen the Archangel Michael on the right of the altar. . . ."

The two men frowned. After a short pause, Gamaliel continued: "You are strong, and you know about the archangels. Only to a weak person would the servant of God need to make himself known and visible."

At that the old man was beside himself. "Grandson of the wise Hillel! No mockery, there are still miracles!

94

"For years it has been my privilege to belong to the Sanhedrin, but it has never been granted to me to work a miracle, nor to any other member of this Council."

Jonathan, a brother-in-law of the high priest, said lightly, yet every word was a threat: "Is not the sword of the Sanhedrin as good as a miracle to you? Whoever acknowledges that Certain Man of Nazareth and his works should be banished from the community!"

A Levite reported that the Certain Man was in hiding in the Jordan meadowlands, and that the sisters of Lazarus had thrice sent messages to him. Smiling complacently, Caiaphas interjected: "I had it cried in every town and village: 'Lazarus is dead; the friend of Jesus is lying in his grave.'"

But now a great roar of voices spread about the building, the mountain and the town, like the waves of the stormy lake. Bolts and beams burst asunder and set the Sanhedrin trembling. Jostled and pushed by a crowd so dense that they had no room to use their weapons, the captain of the Temple Watch and his seven men fell back into the hallway, and behind them swarmed men, women and children, with one cry: "Lazarus lives! Lazarus is risen from the grave! Jesus has called him up!"

MUSTERING all their determination, the Sanhedrin awaited Jesus, who was traveling faster now along the steep winding road leading from Galilee and its gardens towards Jerusalem. The Passover pilgrimage had begun. Singly and in groups, here families, there whole communities, drifted towards the Temple, singing as they went, and the nearer they came to the city, the denser the crowds grew.

Peter had lost sight of the Master. New disciples had arrived already and joined the Twelve. These Galileans passed their time in interminable question and answer, and on the steep slope leading from the Oasis of Kerith, Peter called down to them with a mocking laugh: "None of you can keep in step!" Halfway up the slope he turned to gaze around, and the sun, already high in the cloudless sky after the long rain squalls of winter, blinded him. When he looked down he saw his companions climbing among iris, crocus, and colored ranunculus towards the upland pastures which were already beginning to be white with the stars of narcissi. Beside the mountain path the spring waters of the past months' rains rushed towards a springtime glory of innumerable flowers. Those below hardly took any heed of Peter. Only Luke, the doctor and painter whom Peter had met in Magdalene's house in Caesarea, looked appreciatively at the powerful figure of the fisherman. As he was used when at the tiller on the lake at home, he had pulled off his smock and wound it about his waist, for he had grown hot in his upward climb. Sweat glistened on his chest, tanned by sun and wind; he stood and gazed around over the flowery meadows, silhouetted against the spring sky like some bronze hero in the strength of the Lord. Those who came after were disputing an ominous phrase which Jesus had uttered before they set out. "We are going now to Jerusalem. The prophecy concerning the Son of Man is about to be fulfilled. He will be delivered to the heathen, will be mocked, reviled, and spat upon. Those who scourge him, will execute him." Then Jesus had been silent. A ray of light illuminated his face, and as if with a cry of joy he had declared: "On the third day he will rise again!"

"He will rise again!" The words had seared into their memory. Peter had stood by the Son of Man, tensely expectant, as if he himself were rooted in the soil of the Promised Land, and ready to bud and blossom with the spring. "Too long we have been cast down, mocked and spat upon. Rise up, holy land and holy people! Rise with us!" But the eyelids of the Son of Man had drooped in pain at such lack of understanding. Already he felt the torture, the blood running over his skin, lacerated by scourging, and the disgusting lukewarm spittle on his eyes and cheeks. He must die the death of all mankind, and none would know to what end. . . .

By now the others had caught up with Peter. Their dispute was still raging. Jesus could raise others from the dead; would he be able, once dead, to raise himself as he had raised the buried Lazarus? Peter would not listen to such lugubrious ideas. He scoffed at them: "What do the wise men know? They have always been wrong about Jesus. Does not every fisherman know that it is madness to cast a net after sunrise? And yet, at Jesus's behest, we caught so many fish in the morning that the boat threatened to capsize."

Spitefully, Judas Iscariot's voice interjected: "Do not put on airs. For a joke he called you the Rock. You have a head of stone."

And when the others protested to this companion whom they endured so unwillingly, he went red with rage, lifted both forefingers menacingly, and shrilled: "You Galileans! Do you dare to threaten me, a Judaean? Read the deeds of my forefathers in the Book of Kings! We were always within reach of the throne. When I was a child I could already recite how, at the command of the pious King Jehu, my people had put an end to Ochozia, King of Judah, and to the sons of Queen Athaliah, and the sons of King Joas on his couch, and to King Amon. . . . Your bastard blood is spilt on the military highways of the Syrians, the Persians, the men of Assur and Babylon. You had to be our slaves!"

Thaddeus tried to hold back those who swarmed forward. He begged his brothers not to give the new disciples and strangers such a show of dissension. Peter let his clenched fists fall. "All right, all right. The washed swine is wallowing in the mud again." As he turned back up the mountain again, to his surprise he saw Jesus standing on a stone at the entrance to the village of Bethfagga calling to the disciples to bring him a she-ass and its foal. The ass trotted stiffly before them from stone to stone, while the half-grown colt occasionally sprang to the roadside to sniff at a thistle before rejoining its mother. It would neither let itself be led, nor would it allow anyone to take it by the ears. But as the disciples brought the she-ass up and set her across the roadway, the young one took its accustomed place at her side, kept quite still, and hardly bothered to flick the flies away with its long ears. Peter knew how painful to a rider an ass's long sharp back could be. Though he had little liking for a triumphal procession of this kind, he drew off his overgarment, folded it carefully, and laid it on the beast's back in place of a saddle. Nathanael did the same. Then the two powerful men, the fisherman and the peasant, lifted their beloved Master onto his patient mount, which accepted her first rider docilely enough, though somewhat puzzled. Momentously, the she-ass took a step forward, and her foal trotted lightly beside her.

When the valley of Kedron and the gently sloping Mount of Olives lay at their feet, they saw the sides of the hills of Moriah, Bezetha and Ophel teeming with jubilant life. Everywhere arms waved, branches were brandished, a whole town and more had come out rejoicing to meet the one they had been waiting for for years. Gaulonites, Galileans, the wild mountain shepherds would have been only too glad to thrust a short-sword into his hand. The crowd became a single people, crying out in a thousandfold yell that echoed back from walls and rocks: "Hosanna!"

The Twelve took up the jubilant shout. Then Peter felt Andrew's elbow in his ribs and, following his glance, he saw Judas. The man from Kerioth had slunk away, surreptitiously acknowledging the greeting of a group of Pharisees, who stood by in lofty disdain, as if wrapped in the shroud of their sensibility. They had been hoping that the righteous would strike down this heretic and his followers with a shower of stones. Instead, pale with fury, they heard even the student priests, the "buds from the stem of Aaron," taking up the chorus of "Blessed is He who comes in the name of the Lord."

Thousands united in a single ardent cry of "King of Israel!" Peter had been reft by inward struggle. Downcast at first by his Master's terrible prophecy of insult, death and burial, now he consoled himself with the realization that the resurrected Jesus, the victor over death, would be always by him, and a thrill of joy went through him at the thought of final triumph. He broke from the ranks as if leaping ashore from a sea of happiness, and stood straddle-legged before the jealous scribes. From out of the tempest of his emotions, he shouted full into their faces: "King Jesus!"

The Pharisees could no longer contain themselves. They did not deign to answer the fisherman, but they called to Jesus over the heads of the jubilant crowd: "Teacher, restrain your disciples!"

The Son of Man stopped. From his she-ass, he overlooked the holy city from the north wall to the south. Peter had swung round so as not to miss a single word of the rebuke, when he noticed in amazement that enormous tears were gathering on the Master's eyelashes. Softly, sadly, Jesus addressed the beloved city as if it were a human being: "If only you, even you, knew the things which belong to peace. But the day shall come upon you when enemies will surround you with palisades, they will oppress you from all sides. They will dash you to the ground and your children within you, and not one stone will be left standing on another. . . ."

As if to jostle him awake, Peter clenched his fists. "Not one stone on another. When we are enthroned with you, the Resurrected King?"

As mysteriously as they had stopped, the two asses set off again and trotted down the mountain. Only when they reached the other side of the Kedron valley and were taking the steep path towards the golden portico of the Temple, did they slacken pace. They carefully set one hoof in front of the other, for many more people were crowding on the road, to spread their overgarments before the King. For every garment, poor or costly, that lay strewn along the way from the Mount of Olives to the walls of Moriah, a man dedicated himself to struggle and death. Each took up his garment again and wore it proudly with all its dust and hoofmarks.

A LEGIONARY peered out from the tower of Fort Antonia. He called to the officer of the guard. A threatening mob was coming up from the Kedron valley, but they were waving green branches. Was it a trick? But before the commander reached the observation post, he heard the sentry laugh and saw him lean over to look down into the Temple yard, and then slap his thigh with delight: "The cursed rabble are killing each other at last."

Below, a man could be seen riding an ass into the great forecourt. As he dismounted, he tore the girdle from his waist, and began to whirl the thong. A crowd of men ran before him, tumbling over each other in their flight. Beasts of sacrifice, lined up for sale, broke loose on all sides, bleating, bellowing, cackling and screaming. Cashboxes fell to the ground with a clatter of coins. Dealers, money-changers, merchants fled; but the fury of Jesus's followers was not less than the fear of those he was scourging. Blow by blow, kick by kick, they made their way through the huddle of booths. The mob's hatred of the extortioners, of those who made a business of religion, who raised the price of beasts of sacrifice whenever the fancy took them, and acted as pawnbrokers on behalf of the Temple treasury, made them hit hard. Jesus, the hitherto gentle preacher of neighborly love, ran ahead of them all with his whirling thong. About him, like a silver cloud, a swarm of white doves rose, and their snowy wings shone over the hatred of the men whom Christ had scourged, over the fury of the righteous, and over the happiness of Jesus's companions. The last of the speculators were huddled in a corner at the far end of the forecourt, and as Jesus drove them out through the western gate, a number of Temple servants rushed up to seize him from behind, but before the wild looks of his followers, these parasites, who lived off what they could filch of the Temple offerings, fell back. What could they do without the help of the legionaries? Jesus turned on them violently. His face was flushed and streaming with sweat, the strands of his hair and beard were wet. He whirled the thong round in his sinewy fist and cried: "My house should be a house of prayer; but you have turned it into a den of thieves!" The terrified guards felt themselves thrust aside. A crowd of suffering people were desperately making a way for themselves. The blind, in whose purulent eye sockets the flies had settled, the lame, who dragged themselves up by the strong legs of the fishermen and peasants, begged for help, thronging closer and closer to the one who could stroke away their infirmity with his merciful hands, and pardon their sins, so that for the first time they could rise unsteadily to their feet. Everything gave way before them as they surged forward, till Jesus, breathing heavily, came to a halt on the highest step before the entrance to the Holy of Holies. The exhausted man let his arm fall. Fondly, Thaddeus took the girdle from his trembling hand and fastened it around his waist once more.

In his impetuosity, Peter almost collided with Jesus. "Do not stop now!" he implored him. "The storm is raging. Only a few steps more and the power of the priests is overthrown. Break the door down! Away with the pledges! Throw the debtors' lists into the fire! All Israel will be grateful to you!"

"The Romans are letting us have our way!" cried the Zealot, astonished and jubilant. "Everybody from the lake to Damascus is with us!" Even sober Bartholomew was a warrior that day. "Wise man of Nazareth! Prophet of God! What are you stopping for? You woke Lazarus, now rouse yourself!"

But amid their enthusiasm, there came the somber blare of the rams' horns, sounding the priestly curse. Up on the flat roof of the inner Temple stood the chiefs of the Sanhedrin, surrounded by the Levite trumpeters. Caiaphas was playing his last card, the anathema.

The noisy youngsters of Jerusalem, who had hurried there to be the first to pick up the coins, to recapture the doves, to receive Christ's blessing, shrieked at the priests and shook their fists. In their shrill voices, they shouted: "Liberate us, Son of David!"

At their hoarse cry, Annas leaned far over the balustrade and called: "Do you hear what they are saying, Jesus?"

His answer was a jubilant "Yes!" and with his own weapon, the Scriptures, Jesus countered him: "Have you not read that out of the mouths of babes and sucklings you shall draw praise?"

Like a sacred winged bull from the temple of the distant Land of the Two Rivers, the high priest stood in the midst of his bowing and bobbing court. He was strongly tempted to arrest Jesus as the ringleader of the rioting on the Temple hill. He knew, of course, about the Gadarene swine, and the magical power of the mighty miracle-worker, but nevertheless, the white-robed priests and Levites were astonished at the uneasy ring in Caiaphas's voice, as he asked: "By whose authority do you incite your followers to do all this?" Jesus replied with a counterquestion: "Was John's baptism of God or of man?" For all his power of anathema, for all his thousand-year-old authority, the high priest could only give the feeble, evasive answer: "How can we tell . . ."

How differently the Master's speech sounded, with its gentle irony: "Then how can I tell you by whose authority I act?"

101

And now, to the thousands of listeners below Caiaphas's terrace, he began to tell parable after parable, till finally he called up to the priests on the terrace above, the most audacious words ever spoken on Moriah: "The taxgatherers and the harlots shall enter the Kingdom of God before you. The Kingdom of God shall be taken away from you and given to a people who bring forth the fruits of it. Out with you into the uttermost darkness! Whoever stumbles on this stone, he shall be broken, and he on whom it falls shall be crushed."

Matthew scratched busily on his wax tablet. . . . "Tax collectors"! That delighted him, but "whores" seemed rather offensive. He heard an old priest call down to the Nazarene: "What miracle will you show us, to prove what you have just said?"

Jesus's answer thundered against the marble walls like the waves of the sea, and aged Jews beat their foreheads till they bled: "Tear down this Temple, and in three days I will build it up again!"

Everyone cried: "It took six and forty years to build the Temple, and do you want to raise it again in three days?"

"Not one stone will remain on another!"

Furiously Caiaphas gave the signal, and again the ghastly blare of the horns made the godly tremble. But the man at whom the curse was leveled turned away with a contemptuous smile. His day's work completed, he quietly walked down the lane of disciples, who gave way before him. The pilgrims, their hopes dashed, stood mutely staring at the victorious priests, who were whispering a prayer of thanks. Even the Twelve only followed hesitantly, from a distance, Simon Peter last of all. They hung their heads as they went.

IT WAS already getting dark when Sister Martha extinguished the fire on her hearth. She heard footsteps, and a gentle knocking at her door. At so late an hour, she dared not open to anyone. She tried to go to sleep, but could not rest, because the knocking had agitated her. She listened at the door for a long time before she peered out. The moonlit land lay empty in the chirping of the crickets.

Reassured, she went out on the threshold, but immediately she was stricken with fear. Out in the road stood a figure: Jesus. Alone, he was staring down the street. His disciples had walked past him, blind, dumb and emptyhearted, into the darkness.

When, that night, Jesus climbed to the summit of the Mount of Olives, the disciples following him began to quarrel among themselves about the fall of the Temple. They were standing in groups around him, as he sat alone on a fallen turpentine tree, their faces turned towards Moriah, red with anger, and redder still from the bloody glow of the sinking sun. A golden aureole outlined the contours of the holy Temple, which, to Jesus and his followers, lay black in the shadow. They stared at it, blinded. Even those who tried to transfer their glance elsewhere could not escape the glitter, and saw suns, suns everywhere. . . . Peter was as incapable of getting Jesus's last words out of his stubborn skull as he was of getting the purple sun-discs out of his eyes. "Pull it down? The Temple of the Kings? The palace and fortress for the Son of Man? And build it up again in three days?"

Terrible were the prophecies they had to listen to on the mountain. People would rise against people, nation against nation. The disciples would be handed over to the judges and would be clubbed to death in the synagogues. Peter thought of his brother Andrew, at the words: "Brother will deliver up brother to death," and at: "The father will yield up his child. . . . Children will rise against parents and will deliver them up to death." He thought of his little Petronilla. Only at the end of all the terrors had the Son of Man walked in the clouds, in all his power and glory. Thrice he had called on them to keep a careful watch.

"Lord, do not risk staying in the house of your enemy!" The sons of Zebedee had begged Jesus not to accept the invitation of Simon, the wealthy Pharisee. The nearer the Feast of the Passover came, the more keenly they sensed hatred and malice in the air, and the more bitter grew the disappointment in their Master.

Now, before the house of the rich Simon, they reminded

him of their warning: "They will poison you. They will trip you with their questions. They will hand you over to the Romans for execution!" But Jesus only smiled.

In the rich Pharisee's palatial home, copied from a Roman villa, a lively conversation was in progress concerning the mistaken idea of a Messiah, with which the Nazarene was stirring up the people.

Everything was promising so well. Under the protection of the Roman eagle, their coreligionists had been able to expand in all directions. There was no region, no town, where families of the Jewish faith were not settled, and able to trade with the heathen, and to lead a life worth living. They bought up the produce of the land and sold it far away. Around the Mediterranean and the Pontus, along the amber route, through the whole of Gaul, down the Rhine, even as far away as the tin islands, the righteous were settled, and were sending gifts to the Temple, and enriching the land of their fathers.

If the Promised Land had to pay taxes to Rome, the whole of the Roman world had to pay taxes to Judah and Israel. Wherever any Hebrew set foot, his brothers and cousins came after him. No man or woman among them mixed with people of impure blood. The Law and the promise of God's reward made it possible to proselytize among the heathen. They flocked in masses to the faith of Moses. Not that they were regarded as full members, but they were allowed to worship with them, and to celebrate the feasts. "God-fearers," they called them. So the men of faith learned how to subdue the men of might, and the genial Philo of Alexandria began to put even the people of wisdom, the Greeks, in thrall, and presented the admiring pagan world with a new Plato.

The flower of the scribes and theologians were gathered in Simon's house. They stood together in the colonnades, and their host greeted them with a kiss. Slaves brought golden jugs and basins for them to wash their feet. Simon himself casually poured a little lukewarm water over the well-tended toes of his guests. Young slaves did the rest.

A dispute was already in progress, as to whether the followers of that Certain Man would be likely to resort to violence. The captain of the Temple guard curled his lip in scorn. "A general on a donkey foal? The conqueror of money-changers and dealers in beasts of sacrifice?"

"To a scribe those childish parables of his mean nothing at all," said a presumptuous Levite.

Their host tried to pacify them. "We are going to have the pleasure of hearing him explain his mysterious wisdom himself."

"Is the Nazarene coming, then?"

"He said he would. Just as, unfortunately, he does not observe the Sabbath, so too he seems to take little notice of mealtimes. As the Law is unimportant to him, I am sure it would not annoy him if we were to begin."

An old scribe, whose tongue was heavy with age, foresaw certain embarrassments. "I have been told that that Certain Man has been abusing us for hours on end to thousands of listeners." From a writing tablet he read off a string of insults: "Hypocrites, blind counselors, fools and dupes, whited sepulchers, descendants of the murderers of the prophets, a brood of vipers. . . ."

Simon calmed them: "Rabbi Zadok is going to honor us today by putting a question to Jesus that will make us split our sides with laughter, and will be worth talking over for years—a little smutty, perhaps; something for the connoisseur in matters of love, but very exciting." Their keen minds turned swiftly to sensuality. With a wink, a plump Sadducee had just started to tell an anecdote, when a slave drew back the curtain, and Jesus stood on the threshold. The storyteller did not want to abandon his tale before he had reaped his harvest of applause, nor did his host dare to interrupt his influential guest, though he felt embarrassed before the mysterious power of the great preacher, to whom the garrulous Sadducee paid no heed. His listeners were grinning and grimacing as Jesus entered the dining room. They were reclining at either side of the table, with all their attention centered on the point of the long-drawn joke.

Simon, the host, nicknamed the Leper on account of his white skin, was annoyed that the decaprot Nicodemus had got up to conduct Jesus and his followers into the room, which was really his duty. The captain of the Temple guard, Segan Malchus, knew quite well that the wealthy dignitary had more than once stolen out by night to the Nazarene, and he remembered how the Sanhedrin had shouted him down when he had openly sided with "that Certain Man" over the riot at the Feast of Tabernacles.

The host's embarrassment increased when he noticed that all the best places at the table were already taken. He had neglected to greet his guest and to wash his feet, and now he committed a third blunder by obliging him to sit at the foot of the festive table. To Rabbi Zadok's annoyance, the end of the doubtful story was lost in the disturbance caused by Jesus's arrival.

The Pharisees and Sadducees had to admit that by his bearing Jesus showed his royal blood. But they took offense at the long purple fringes on his overgarment. Did this carpenter imagine himself a scribe? His four companions hardly resembled the Sanhedrin's mocking description of clodhopping plowboys or stinking fisher-boat hands. They behaved calmly and with self-assurance, hard, sinewy men, with the clear gaze that comes from wind and weather. Unperturbed, they looked around the table. They recognized Segan Malchus. Was it on his behalf that Jesus had been enticed here?

Peter, Andrew and Simon the Zealot had settled themselves down beside their Master, but Judas of Kerioth, who had been furtively greeted by many of the guests, tried to find himself a place higher up the board. Jesus called to him: "Do not sit in the best place you can find. Perhaps some more important man than you will arrive, and he who invited you will come and say: Make room, and you will be obliged in shame to take the lowest place."

The bewildered host began a prayer, as if the meal had not yet started. Then he looked at the shimmering little fish which had just been served. "They are from the Sea of Galilee. They must have often heard your wise sermons, good Master." Jesus answered coldly: "Why do you call me 'good'? Only God is good. And have yourself called 'Master.'" And turning to Peter and Andrew, he continued, with a smile: "All these scribes think they are sitting in the seat of Moses. Whatever they order you to do, do it. But do not imitate their deeds. They preach magnificently, but act otherwise."

The "Leper," paler than ever, asked reproachfully: "Are you instructing your followers and reproving mine?"

"You are shutting mankind out of the Kingdom of Heaven. You cannot enter yourselves, and you will not allow others to enter either."

"It is not easy to enter," sneered the Rabbi Zadok, who bore the Galileans a grudge because the anecdote had misfired. And now he posed the eagerly awaited question: "Teach me, Master, and calm my sleeplessness— A married man dies childless. Now, the Law prescribes that his brother should marry the widow, in order to have children to honor his memory, is that not so? But the second brother also dies childless. And the same with the third and fourth, right down to the seventh brother. And in the end the sevenfold widow follows her husbands to the grave. —They say you believe in the resurrection. Then to which of the seven will this widow belong, when she is resurrected? All seven had possessed her. Will the eight of them dance a heavenly wedding-round in Paradise?"

But the rabbi's last mocking words died away like the smiles of those around him. He was told that he did not know the Scriptures. Heavenly angels do not perform worldly actions. "God is not God of the dead but of the living, since all live for Him."

Simon Peter would have liked to fling his arms round his Master's neck, as Nicodemus and the distinguished Joseph of Arimathea said reverently: "Master, you have answered well." But at that moment, the Rock saw the guests raise themselves indignantly from their cushions. Behind him, the curtain across the doorway was torn aside with a cry, and a slender figure entered and looked searchingly round the table. She was no longer a beautiful girl; her suffering face was a pale ivory color, and her huge eyes were dark with sorrow. Mary of Migdal looked from one guest to the other. She had not even waited to pin up her hair, in order not to arrive too late. With her left arm, she pressed an alabaster vase to her breast.

Weeping, the woman tottered towards Jesus, whom she had

at first looked for in the places of honor at the table. The lid of the vase fell and shattered on the marble floor. The perfume of costly spikenard filled the room as with her slender hands she lifted the noble vessel and let the balm trickle slowly onto Jesus's hair. Tenderly, the woman's fingers stroked his moistened head. Then Mary sank to her knees, unbound his sandals, and washed his tired feet with her tears.

Judas shook his head and indignantly whispered to his neighbors something about shameful waste, and the cost of the stuff, and a considerable sum of money for the poor. But Jesus smiled. "Why do you rebuke this woman? She has done good work for me. You have the poor always with you, but me you have not always. She has anointed me as if for burial. Wherever in the world the gospel is carried, everyone will hear tell of this woman."

The host felt obliged to make it clear that he had nothing to do with the presence of Mary of Migdal in such a respectable gathering. His reproof rang out: "If this individual were truly a prophet, he would know what kind of a woman this is—a sinner."

Peter could not take his eyes off the kneeling woman. Son of a people who allow no pictures, he knew nothing of beauty and nobility of appearance, and the sight of this woman, once so charming, moved him deeply. She seemed to be touched by a gentle breath of autumn, so that her face showed a few fine wrinkles and almost imperceptible lines. As if ashamed, she held her pale hands over her face, and took her blond hair, in which the silver of age was already beginning to shine, and dried the narrow blue-veined feet of Jesus as gently as if they were priceless jewels.

"Simon!" Peter started, as if he feared some rebuke, but it was his host who was being addressed. The Nazarene put him a question. "A creditor had two debtors. The one owed him five hundred denarii, and the other fifty. As they had nothing with which to pay their debt, he forgave them both. Which of the two, Simon, will love him most?"

"I suppose, the one to whom he gave most."

"Do you see this woman? I came in your house. And who gave me no water for my feet? You. But she washed my feet with her tears and dried them with her hair. Who gave me no welcoming kiss? You. But when she came, she did not cease to kiss my feet. Who did not anoint my head with oil? You. But she anointed me with precious ointment. Her sins will be forgiven for she has loved much."

Wide-eyed, Peter looked at him, ruefully aware that in his heart was far too much hatred and all too little love.

Wherever the last rays of the hot sun slanted down between the mats hung across the streets, and shone on the throng of natives and Passover pilgrims, it surrounded the vivid chaos of the multitude in a glitter of golden notes, blinding and transfiguring them at the same time.

Water carriers, ass drivers, mountain shepherds jostled this way and that, women with oil jars on their proudly erect heads, strangely dressed travelers from Alexandria and Antioch and even more distant places, moved forward step by step, amid a smell of animal skins and hot sweat. Right in their midst, children were shouting and chasing each other in play. The sultry smoke of boiling oil and of newly slaughtered lambs, sacrificed in hundreds for the Passover feast, rose from window holes and dark doorways, and tickled the dust-filled nostrils of the passers-by.

John was jostled aside in the crowd, and Peter looked back suspiciously, to see whether some spy was shadowing them in order to find out the house where they would celebrate the Passover—a destination as yet unknown to themselves. They were to follow a man with a water jar, Jesus had whispered to them, very quietly so that no eavesdroppers, not even Judas who was lurking by, could hear. For an hour they had been drifting around in the narrow streets of the upper town, till they had arrived in the dangerous neighborhood of the high priest's palace. John, younger, and of frailer build, was wearily supporting himself with his arm around the shoulder of the sturdy fisherman. "Am I good enough for you, Son of Zebedee? I am only a clumsy Rock, but today, as your mother always begged the Master, there are those thrones to right and left of him, eh?"

"Forgive her. You hardly saw your own mother, and you do not know how great a mother's ambition can be."

"Who would not despair, when Jesus enters with palms and hosannas, and then talks of nothing but death? Everyone will hate us. If we were their masters and governors I would not mind that. But they are going to drag us before the Sanhedrin and scourge us in the synagogues. Is that what we have been wandering about for, these last three years, from Hermon to the Dead Sea?"

"Do you not think that his Kingdom and ours is and will be greater? How did he send us out, once? We were to take nothing on our travels but a staff—no short-sword! Neither bread nor wallet nor coppers in our girdle. We were to tie no sandals on our feet, and had not to wear even two garments. Would Caesar or the Senate send their governors out into the provinces like that?"

"There, look!" Peter pointed excitedly towards the doorway of an imposing house. "The man with the water jar!" All their tiredness was forgotten. An old servant was hurrying in front of them, looking for something against which to rest his heavy earthenware jar, which came to a point at the bottom so that it could be driven into the cooling sand of the cellar. Peter went over to him and took his heavy burden with a laugh. The old man was thus permitted to unlock the courtyard door and as he did so, he glanced suspiciously at the two strangers, who said that they had been looking for him for hours. Anxiously he called to the people of the house, that he had been obliged to wait until the water from the pool of Siloah had started to bubble up, so that he could bring it for his mistress's cure. Meanwhile, a small window had opened above. When they looked up, they laughed in recognition. It was Mark, stubby-fingered Mark, who, to the astonishment of his old servant, hurried down and greeted his guests. He was beside himself with joy when he learned that his own room had been chosen for the love feast of Jesus and the Twelve. "Mother, set the table and prepare the food. Now you will be healed too. They are all coming, Peter, John . . . and the Lord himself!"

Peter felt a painful grip at the nape of his neck, and he was about to cry out furiously, but as he turned his head in the direction of Caiaphas's door, he gasped. Judas was just disappearing in the doorway. The son of Zebedee growled, "The devil, it was because of him that we had to go looking for the man with the water jar. Now he has seen us in front of the house and he is off to the high priests."

Peter laughed bitterly: "Do not curse Judas. He is driving the Son of God to action."

THE long table was festively decked. The servants laid pillow on pillow for the thirteen guests to recline on. They set out baskets of aromatic wheat cakes at regular intervals, and also *charoseth,* a sweet mold compounded of apples, nuts, figs and wine, whose savor was intended to take away the sharpness of the herbs with which the lamb was roasted. Its bricklike form was an age-old reminder of forced labor in the land of Pharaoh. A very old man distributed golden vessels about the table. The most beautiful goblet he set in the place of honor. Then the servants noiselessly left the room.

The city had grown quieter, and the streets and squares of Jerusalem were empty. The sacred meal in celebration of the exodus into freedom had caused all pious folk to gather in their homes. Even the poorest were looking forward to a good meal of roast lamb that evening.

As the sun went down, the dim light of the oil lamps in the candelabra began to flicker in the darkening room. The disciples had taken off their dusty sandals and were standing in silence, waiting for the Master, who was still with Mark and his mother, down in the kitchen, where she was supervising the servants, for the lamb was almost ready.

"Can it be that this old, old feast is about to take on a new meaning?" whispered Andrew. And Thomas answered: "Do the likes of us know what he is going to do?"

"I know, anyway," cried Judas. The Zealot felt his blood pounding, and even John could not contain himself. "Did you find it out in the house of Caiaphas?"

Judas answered, shrill with rage: "Someone has to pay the Temple taxes, do they not? The Master himself ordered me to."

"On this holiday?"

John walked over to the man from Kerioth. "For once you gave? You can do something else but take?"

"Hate me!" ranted Judas. "He who does not hate himself cannot be Jesus's disciple. Jesus himself said so. From time immemorial I have nursed a consuming hatred. Obedient to my Master's word, I hate my brother and my sister and"—he shuddered—"my own soul."

Silently, the curtain across the entrance was pulled aside, and Jesus entered between two boys with torches lighting his way. When Thaddeus saw the sad and loving expression on his Master's face in the flickering light, a sob rose in his throat. The Son of Man looked from one to the other, as if he wanted to press each one to him, to feel each heartbeat, to draw support before he stole away, only he knew where.

In their eyes, he read question after question. Jesus took the sons of Zebedee by the arm, James on the right, John on the left, and walked to the table with them, to the place of honor with its handsome cup. He set himself down among his companions to eat.

"So they are enthroned to the right and left of him," thought Peter as, not without a sense of grievance, he threw himself down beside John. Already they were singing the ancient chant of the exodus from Egypt, the reminder of an entire nation's will to freedom. The words rang powerfully across the street to Caiaphas's house:

> *"The Lord is a valiant hero,*
> *Almighty is his name!"*

The disciples' tempestuous breath made the little oil lamps over the table flicker. Simon urged John: "Ask him: What are you waiting for, Lord? Strike at last! Out there in Gethsemane our Galileans are camped in thousands. Tell us now what is going to happen!" But the favorite disciple shook him off. "In eternity, all time is alike. He knows what is going to be as surely as we know what has been. Past and future is one boundless present."

Peter felt giddy. How did he stand in Jesus's eyes, if Jesus saw him as a rough fisherman and a mighty fisher of men at one and the same time? He cried aloud: "Rise up, Lord! You come from God and must return to God. Your throne is on Zion!"

Amid a hail of questions—"All our thrones around yours?"—"Where, Master?"—"Which of us?"—Jesus stood up. Not a man among them remained seated. The Master drew off his overgarment with the purple fringes. He tucked his white undergarment into his girdle, then took a silver ewer and filled it with water.

The Rock looked on in amazement. The others began to sing the royal oath of the forty-fifth psalm: "Gird your sword upon your thigh, O mighty one!" The prophecy which each of them applied to himself rang out: "You shall make them princes in all the earth." Jesus came slowly nearer and set the heavy basin down in front of Peter, sank on one knee and, King over all and Son of God, he prepared to wash the feet of poor Simon, son of Jonah. Peter called out in desperation: "Lord, do you mean to wash my feet?"

"What I am doing, you do not know as yet. Later, you will understand."

"You shall never wash my feet! Not in all eternity!"

His answer sounded like a threat. "If I do not wash you, you shall have no part with me."

"Lord!" The tears sprang to his eyes. "Not my feet only, then, but my hands and head as well!" Let Jesus's strong slender fingers knead and press his head, that head that could never catch the deep meaning of things, till at last it took on the proper shape for a true apostle! But the Messiah was already lifting the fisherman's other foot into the warm bath. Peter's poor wits groped in the darkness for mysterious words about the bath of holiness that purifies whoever is washed in it. Only the foot that is always stumbling through the dust of error is in need of such a washing. After Jesus had performed the same service for all twelve, he said sorrowfully: "You are clean, but not all. In spite of everything—not all of you."

The Twelve looked at each other, dismayed and embarrassed. Jesus had dried his hands, and, as if in farewell, he was tenderly stroking the fringes of his outer garment, which he had resumed. With a shudder, the fisherman observed that

113

Jesus's eyes had stayed wide open, that as he spoke they never fleetingly closed as human eyes should, not even almost imperceptibly, like the flicker of a butterfly's wing.

"Do you know now what I have done to you? You call me Teacher and Master, and that I am. And if I, the lord and master, have washed your feet, you also must wash one another's feet. I have given you an example. The kings of the heathen enslave their subjects and those with authority call themselves benefactors. You shall not be so! But he that is the greater among you will become like the less, and he that is chief, like the servants." And now came the words they had been waiting for: "You have been persistent in my dangers, and so I appoint you my heirs, as my father appointed the Kingdom to me. Then you may eat and drink at my table in my Kingdom, and you shall sit on thrones judging the twelve tribes of Israel."

This was the prophecy they wanted to hear! They shouted jubilantly. Simon Peter trembled for joy: He is going to do what I want.

But Jesus shook his head. "The slave is not greater than his master, nor the messenger than he who sent him. When you have grasped these things, happiness will be yours. I do not say this of all of you. I know whom I have chosen."

They held their breath, eager to be among the chosen. But instead, he continued with the somber words of a fugitive king of old: "He who eats my bread has raised his heel against me."

Whenever Jesus looked up, his gaze fell on the bland face of Judas, who had insinuated himself directly opposite Jesus as if to challenge him: "Look into my thoughts! You know what I want. The promised world empire of Judah! If Jahveh took you for his adopted son, then be the triumphant Messiah! Cast down all the peoples who have brought sorrow on us, to atone for our agelong disgrace: our cities held in fee, our men mutilated, our women ravished. Let me remind you of Isaiah's words: I have determined on a day of revenge. The booty of the strong shall he divide, so that he gives his soul up in death. —If it must be, then die!"

"I tell you, one among you will betray me."

114

Eleven of the Twelve started up in confusion, and looked suspiciously at each other and at Judas.

"The hand of him who will betray me is lying on the table with mine."

John threw himself across the cushions and embraced Jesus, pressing his head against Christ's breast. He heard his heart beating like a fist on a locked door.

Just as impetuously, Peter was about to protest his innocence. But had he not been guilty of treasonable thoughts that very day? That impatience which could not wait for satisfaction though, according to all the prophecies, it meant Jesus's death? While the twenty-four hands flew up from the white tablecloth like fluttering wings, the fisherman timidly nudged his neighbor John to put the question; but already one of the others had cried, out of his indignation: "Is it I, Lord?" Only John felt strong enough in his love, and he put his arms about Jesus as if he would never let him go. "Who is it?"

"One among you twelve who have dipped your bread in the bowl with me. The Son of Man must die, of whom it is written, woe to the man who betrays him. Better for him he had never been born."

While they were all searching their consciences, John heard his trembling Master whisper: "This is the one, to whom I reach this bread."

Judas, who alone was staring mutely in front of himself, shrank from the hand of the Son of Man as he offered him the soaked piece of bread. "Is it I then, Lord?"

The answer came softly: "You say so. What must be done, do quickly."

Without a word, without a salutation, Judas got up and turned his back on the lights, on all light. In his boundless mortification, his underlids were twitching, and vertical folds appeared between his eyebrows. A deaf-mute might have read a wild curse on his lips. Could there be a more pious fulfillment of the divine command than the way in which he hurried to the Sanhedrin to report: "Jesus of Nazareth and his underlings are preparing their coup. He who made his entry with hosannas and palms, as King of the World, is rising against Rome, against the Temple, against Jahveh. You have pronounced sentence, Caiaphas: 'Better one should die than a whole people.' "

ANDREW had pulled aside the curtain over one of the windows. While his lips sang the Hallel with the others, his eyes were following Judas, who turned once more at Caiaphas's door to see whether Jesus had sent anyone to bring him back. Virulently he snarled his last warning: "I will crucify you, unless you bless me."

The apostle turned back into the light, pale and choking. He stammered: "Judas . . . has gone to Caiaphas . . ." But Jesus's voice overrode his: "Now the Son of Man will be raised to glory, and God will glorify himself in him. My children, I am with you but a little while yet. You will seek me. . . ." His voice fell, and only John caught the words and repeated them over and over as his command: "Love one another as I have loved you. By this, all men will recognize that you are my disciples, by the love you have for one another. . . ."

Then Jesus raised his voice as he spoke to God: "Father! I have given them the glory which you gave to me, so that they should be one as we are one, I in them and you in me." As if he were waking from sleep, he looked from one to the other. "I have looked forward to eating the Passover lamb with you before my time of sorrow. For I tell you, I shall not eat with you again till all is fulfilled in the Kingdom of God."

They stared at him miserably, and again Peter felt they were looking to him to put the question for all of them. Did he dare to beseech the Master: You have taken everything from us—house and home, wife and child, daily work and evening rest. And where is that earthly Kingdom, and the promised thrones? You were to destroy Jerusalem and the Temple. And now, are you taking yourself away from us? But Jesus had stood up, and his words and gesture were to remain unforgotten for thousands of years. He took the unleavened wheaten bread, blessed it, and broke it, and gave a fragment to each of the eleven. Reverently, like children, they took from his hand the gift of their fruitful earth.

116

They had hoped for crowns and thrones, and received a morsel of bread.

And to their bewilderment, the Master explained the meaning of his action. "This is my body, which will be surrendered for you. Do this in my memory."

The patriarchs had called it "eating a man's flesh" when one was slandered. Had this phrase, which had caused an uproar in the synagogue of Capernaum that had almost ended in stoning, acquired a new significance? The last dying lights flickered as if from a rush of wings.

As a sign for prayer, Jesus lifted his right hand to the light, which shone up from the candelabra on the deep and hallowed lines of his right palm, the lines of fate. At the same time he curved his left hand round the great golden cup, full of dark wine. "This drink is the new blood brotherhood—in my blood that is to pour out for so many. Do this, whenever you drink, in my honor."

As Jesus stood up, and the little group with him, the last lamp went out, and apart from him there was no more light in the room. The apostles stood around the candelabra in boundless night. Behind them they sensed the hopeful multitudes of centuries to come, kneeling in supplication; they passed from one to the other of them, to the end of space and time. The mouths of all were open, mute and expectant. The apostles proffered them the bread, the inexhaustible food that is never finished however many eat of it. And no hour was to pass but one among them should raise the glittering chalice as high as he could, somewhere before kneeling men. They sang the last hymn, and knew it was indeed the last.

JESUS strode on ahead. "Do not leave him alone," urged Peter. "He is not going to the Mount of Olives where our armed pilgrims from Galilee are camped, whom Caiaphas fears so much. Death is lurking on Moriah. That was no farewell, today. He has never been nearer us. If we hang back, will he not rightly complain: 'Those around me did not understand me'?"

They caught up with him at the south gate of the Temple,

which was open on this holy night. Terrified at Judas's behavior, about which Andrew had confided in him, Peter uttered the question that he was to ask once more, in deadly fear, the tortured question of his whole existence: "Master, where are you going?"

Without listening, Jesus walked through the women's yard to the entrance of the Court of the Israelites. There he stopped, as if the question had just reached him. Between the milk-white moonlit pillars, the warm red-gold glow of the burnt offerings could be seen, and before these aureoles, his warning sounded: "Where I go, you cannot follow me now. But later you will follow." With anguish in their wide eyes, they heard him say: "You will all be offended by me this night. It is written: I will strike down the shepherd and his flock shall be scattered."

Peter growled bitterly: "Always that disbelief in us." "And what of our disbelief in everything?" asked Thomas.

But Peter was so furious that he did not hear the Master's prediction: "As soon as I am risen from the dead I will go before you to Galilee," and he furiously shouted: "If all the others are offended by you, I shall never be!"

"Simon, Simon," warned Jesus, with a pitying smile.

Am I not a Rock any more? crossed the stubborn fisherman's mind, but the next words wounded him deeper. "Satan asked to have you, so that he might sift you like wheat. But I prayed for you that your faith should not fail and that one day you may be a support for your brothers."

"Master, I am ready to go with you to prison or to death!" But from the step on which he stood, the Son of Man gripped Peter's hair, and with a pitying smile he looked searchingly at him. "I tell you, Peter"—and even as he sadly reminded him of his cowardly failing, he called him his Rock, Peter, again—"that tonight, before the cock has twice crowed, you shall have denied me thrice."

"If I must die with you, I would never deny you!"

All eleven of them passionately protested their faithfulness, but Jesus looked long at them till they fell silent, then he said: "When I sent you out without money, without a bread sack, without sandals, did you lack for anything?"

"Never, Lord."

His bearded pupils shook their heads. Thomas, Philip, the sons of Zebedee and of Halephai shouted each other down with their questions. One wanted to know the way, another wanted to see the Father, but the youngest, Thaddeus, who was so proud of his Master, expressed the grief of them all: "How does it happen that you only reveal yourself to us, but not to the world?" and to these obscurities was added the most mysterious of all, the revelation of the Holy Spirit: "The Father will send him in my name. He will teach you everything, and bring to mind all that I have taught you."

Their hearts were set on liberating their people, on saving them from Roman rapacity, from Syrian cruelty, from Herod and his host of intolerable laws, yet they were to wander about as beggars. Was this freedom?

"Everyone who has a purse, let him take it, and his bread sack too. And if he has neither of these, let him sell his garment and buy a sword...."

The disciples flared up in wild enthusiasm, and both Simons showed the hilts of their short-swords tucked in their sleeves. "Look, Lord, here are two ..."

But their joy died away abruptly, for Jesus cried sharply: "Enough!" and turned and began to mount the fifteen steps into the Court of the Israelites, each step a psalm, or so it is to the orthodox. Stone inscriptions warned the Roman, the Syrian, the Greek: *No foreigner may enter the enclosure surrounding the Temple. Whoever is found here has only himself to blame for his death.* They were almost the only ones praying there. A few old men crouched between sleep and prayer by the parapet.

Some Temple guards eyed the handful of Galileans suspiciously, and a Levite looked up fearfully towards the Tower of Antonia. The moonlight was shining on the bright helmets of the Roman sentries, and the shimmering spear points gave spiritual comfort to those who were in the secret. Soon, with the help of the heathen, the high priests' swift attack on the heretical gang leader Jesus of Nazareth would succeed.

Jesus leaned against a white marble pillar whose shaft

twisted upward strangely like the slowly rising smoke of sacrifice. Huge grapes and sacred vessels were carved on it at regular intervals. High on the wall above the entrance to the
sanctuary and the Holy of Holies, a relief of gigantic vines
shone ruddy and golden. James whispered devoutly to himself at the thought of the secret in the innermost vault, whose
enormous brightly colored curtain was dimly lit by the flames
of the seven-branched candelabra: "What sacrifice must be
made before we see the tabernacle at last, and your Cherub
who rests and keeps vigil with his eight wings folded, before
God's ten commandments. Jesus—open the way!" But he compared himself to the vine. He pressed the grape harvester's
knife into God's hand, against himself and his followers. They
listened in consternation as Jesus uttered the terrible words:
"The hour is coming when those who put you to death will
think they are doing a service to God. . . ."

None of the disciples was able to follow what he said. Perplexed, they nudged each other and whispered: "What does
that mean: 'Just a little while and I shall be no more, and
just a while longer and you shall see me again'? What is this
about 'going to my father'? And what is 'a short time'?"

Then Jesus comforted them: "I shall see you again. And
your hearts will rejoice and no one shall take your joy from
you. On that day you will question me no more."

"There, now you are speaking openly, and no longer in
parables. Now we understand everything." And together with
Peter, they cried out: "There is no need for questions now.
We believe you come from God." Then Peter heard the quaver
in the voice of the Son of Man, and could not bring himself
to protest at the words: "The hour is come. You will disperse,
each to your own house, and leave me alone. Be comforted, I
have overcome the world."

Out of all this, they gathered only one thing: that their
wish was fulfilled. Master of the World! Their Master! Proudly
they walked back with him through the Temple courts, out
into the open country, down the Kedron valley and between
the garden walls of the Mount of Olives. Like a high priest,
mighty in the glory of his words, Jesus had cried out to his

Father: "Endow them with divine ways for I have given them the power, the power!"

THE eleven knew about seeds and nets, fig harvest and vine pruning, and a few of them also knew about the Law and the prophets. But on the previous night, Jesus had confided in them the secret of the Kingdom of God. He had described in terrifying terms the end of the world, and the Last Judgment. Yet now they were walking behind him, subdued but happy, devoted and expectant. Drowsy and exhausted as they were, one saying especially lingered in their minds: "You shall eat and drink at my table in my Kingdom, and shall judge the twelve tribes of Israel." Half-asleep, they reached their destination, where the olive trees raised their arms as if in terrified flight and spread their silvery leaves over a low wall in the night. A little further along the slope, tent after tent was pitched. The sons of Halephai knew that this was the camp of their partisans from Galilee. They were asleep. Jesus dismissed eight of his disciples, and took only the three witnesses of his transfiguration, the Rock and the sons of Zebedee, to his hiding place under the palm roof of an old oil press, after which the garden was called Gethsemane.

Again Peter forced his eyelids open and peered about to see whether anyone was spying on them, or if some muffled figure was creeping along the shadow of the silent wall. Quietly, they closed the garden gate behind them, and walked to the pressing shed. The landscape had lost all its colors. The Master's face shone ghostly and moon-pale before them. He was standing on the next slope of the terrace garden, in which every handsbreadth of fertile soil was walled in with painstakingly gathered stones, which held the soil firm about the olive trees, wet with night dew and already showing the green of spring.

Fear of being forsaken brought a tremor to Jesus's voice, as if he were being taken to his tomb already, and his disciples would not accompany him. "Sit down here while I pray."

Peter tried to say: "Look, now, you are dead-tired and so are we. I am ready to drop. Why do you not sleep too? Those

Passover crowds swarming in the streets make us dizzy—we are used to the sea, and the open spaces, and the quiet. And our poor pious bellies, punished by fasting and privation, are not used to being full of roast lamb. And my head is heavy with all you have taught us. I cannot stay awake." But his voice would not come, so he made a lying gesture of assent, and all three of them sank down on a bed of leaves. In the depth of his sleep, he looked at himself and felt he must wake that Simon Peter up, must shout to himself: "Do you not hear the clatter of marching warriors, and iron handcuffs?"

They felt themselves being shaken and stared up in alarm. The moon had gone down already. In the uncertain light of the stars, they sensed rather than saw the presence of the Master. His familiar voice sounded strange, as his quivering mouth formed the words with difficulty: "There is a deathly sorrow in my soul. Stay here and watch with me." They heard his step, barely a stone's throw away, then he fell on his knees with a cry: "Father! If you will it—and all things are possible to you—take this cup from me. Yet not what I will but what you will. . . ."

When Peter awoke, he felt as if an iron ring was growing and pressing inside his head. He tried desperately to stay awake. As if caught red-handed, he started up. Jesus stood tall before him and said bitterly: "Are you sleeping, Simon? Could you not stay awake for a single hour?" It was no command, but rather an entreaty that he addressed to the contrite Peter: "Watch and pray, lest you succumb to temptation. The spirit is willing but the flesh is weak."

"John thought he saw an angel," Peter told Mark afterwards. "If only the Master had not been so unspeakably sad. When he shook me awake for the third time, I thought he would be bound to see my blushes even in the dark, especially as he said: 'Sleep on now, and take your rest; the hour is at hand. Behold, the Son of Man is betrayed into the hands of sinners. Awake, let us be going. He who betrays me is here!' "

There was a rattle of weapons. Cries rang out. Torchlight shone on helmets, spear points, breastplates. Temple servants in their festival garments shook the railings. Legionaries swung athletically over the wall. The mob surged forward. There were dealers among them, whose faces still bore the weals from Jesus's strap, and money-changers who had promised handsome payment to a handful of tough Syrians, to work their revenge. Judaean bailiffs thrust their torches under the roof thatch of the oil press, fire for the wizard. All their hands were trembling.

The Romans advanced more boldly. A man, walking beside the golden-helmeted captain of the Temple guard, guided them straight to the pressing shed. The light of a torch lifted his face suddenly out of the darkness. It was Judas. "Master!" he cried in his shrill falsetto voice, and he rushed towards Jesus, who stood gravely by the oil press, looking straight at him all the time. The Son of Man felt two arms about his shoulders, and a protruding, thick-lipped mouth on his cheek.

Jesus went on gazing at the apostle as Judas stepped back, in trembling expectation of some dreadful miracle. If the Son of Man had now become the Messiah and King he desired to be, then his array of Romans and Temple guards would be of no more avail than reeds in the wind.

A detachment of legionaries, shields up and spears at the ready, were marching eastward to the Galileans' camp. But nobody stirred about the tents in the windless night. The torchbearers and Temple servants feared any moment to hear the war cry of Jesus's disciples: *"Maran atha! To arms!"* But their fears were groundless. Not even the eternal chirping of the cicadas was to be heard.

To the end of his life, Peter lamented the manner in which he failed his Master that night. " 'Are you not coming to help, you cursed Barjonim!' I wanted to shout, but where was my voice? Judas's squint eyes were sliding here and there in terror, and suddenly they met mine, and I understood him, and was ashamed. I, whom Jesus had called his Rock, felt my cheeks burning in secret complicity. The last hope of our centuries-old faith in the Messiah was at stake. For a whole lifetime and three years more I'd had no thought for anything but the coming of the liberator, revenge for my father, the fulfillment of countless prophecies. And here was Judas, looking to me as an accomplice for his desire: Jesus! There is no way out, you cannot walk over the stormy sea here. Do as we want! Our thrones, or you will be dethroned. —And yet, the greatest miracle of all was—not to work a miracle. Without any act of violence he won mastery over the world."

If Israel's kingdom of revenge failed to be established that night, the kingdom of their language, their faith, full of the thundering curses of their Jehovah from Sinai and of implacable justice, then—Judas of all the Jews shrieked it soundlessly in his desperate glances—then of the bold attempt to force God's son to a seizure of power, nothing was left but the pitiable treachery of a venal and damned soul.

Helpless, not knowing what to do next, Judas turned to Malchus, the Temple captain, who took off his golden helmet. And at the sign, his servants rushed towards the Galileans like hunting dogs, brandishing their cudgels.

"*Maran atha!*" roared Peter. His sword whistled down on the captain's head but as he struck, Jesus's sorrow made his arm falter. Instead of falling to the ground with a cleft skull, the terrified Malchus clutched at his bleeding wound and found his almost severed ear was hanging by a shred. The sons of Zebedee closed their eyes, certain that with Peter and Jesus they would be struck down before they could draw another breath.

"Put away that sword," they heard the Master say. "Those who take to the sword shall perish by the sword. Do you think I could not call to my Father in heaven, to send me twelve legions of angels? But how should the scriptures be fulfilled then, if it must be in this wise?" With the unfaltering gesture of the skilled doctor, his right hand set Malchus's ear gently and firmly in position. When he took his hand away, the blood was staunched.

Malchus gingerly felt the wound and he smiled perplexedly as he found his ear was back in its usual position.

"He can still work miracles," stammered Peter. And now the voice of the Son of Man sounded far over the tops of the olive trees: "You have come to take me with knives and cudgels, as if I were a bandit. I preached daily in the Temple and you did not take me. But let the scriptures be fulfilled. This hour belongs to you and to the power of darkness."

The armed men gaped in terror at Malchus's ear. And as

Jesus came towards them they shrank back, stumbling, and some sat down on their buttocks.

"Whom do you seek?" he asked.

"Jesus of Nazareth," one of them croaked, and his voice broke like a eunuch's with fear.

"I am he whom you seek. Let the others go." He looked up to the stars. "Of all those whom you gave me, I have not lost one."

Already some of the torches were burnt out. The stars disappeared. In the gray of that dreadful morning, the last three fled, ducking from tree to tree. The other eight already lay huddled in their tents, as if they had no part in what had happened. But Mark slipped out, wrapped in a blanket, to beg for one last glance from Jesus while he was still alive. He felt a hand clutch at his covering. Someone tore the blanket off him with savage force and struck at him with a burning torch.

"Everyone, get away from here!" warned a fearful voice, for at any moment the Galilean camp might spring to arms. So the cowards left Mark, who ran breathlessly, and fell, and sprang up again and ran on and on, a man to whom nothing was left, stark-naked and abandoned.

WHEN Peter arrived at Caiaphas's palace, the courtyard was lit by a fire, which the shivering guards had kindled in a huge metal brazier. A plump maidservant of the high priest's household held the high bronze doors open, ready to slam them if danger threatened. She looked longingly across to the fire, with the lively conversation going on around it, but her instructions were to stay at the door, for all the men, including the doorkeeper, had gone off to hunt the Galilean sorcerer who could even raise half-rotten corpses, like Lazarus of Bethany, to a semblance of life with his Chaldean magic. Fortunately the Roman legionaries were still camped at the gate. Without their help, nobody in Jerusalem would have dared go after the wizard. Everyone knew the West was immune to the sorceries of the East. Unfortunately!

The girl started, as someone spoke to her. She recognized a

respected guest, Joseph of Rama. Was he frightened too, that his voice failed him? Impatiently, he waved from the doorway to someone else who had hurried into the courtyard, and now the two of them, deep in conversation, walked towards the brazier. The servant girl stared steadily at the man who had come out of the night. Joseph of Rama had left him now, to hurry off to the Sanhedrin. She was sure she had seen that stranger with the shaggy forelock, when she herself, bewitched along with thousands of others, had shouted Hallelujah to the Galilean. She left the door, and went over to the fire; and in the midst of the circle of armed men, she suddenly remembered. "You were with him too!" she cried. Peter felt as if someone had pushed him headlong into the brazier fire and into the flames of hatred. He protested furiously: "Woman, I do not know him!"

At that moment, someone hissed for silence, and the chatter ceased round the fire. Caiaphas's ponderous bass voice was raised inside the hall, and they strained to hear what he was saying. With a sound like the blare of the rams' horns in the anathema, he bellowed at the mysterious and fettered magician: "By the living God! If you are the Christ, the Son of the Blessed One, say so!"

The night was so still that even the faint crackle of the burning wood made them suddenly shudder. At that moment someone nudged Peter. "You are one of them, too."

The cock crowed.

Peter turned, testily flung his arm across his face and protested: "I tell you I am nothing of the sort!" Then he felt as if a stake had pierced his heart, for he heard the familiar and beloved voice in the hall: "If I speak, you do not believe me. If I ask, you give no answer. Yet soon you shall see me sitting on the right hand of the Almighty and moving among the clouds of heaven."

There was an outburst of furious and indignant voices shouting: "Are you the Son of God?" And behind the majestic answer lurked a sublime smile: "You say that I am."

The uproar in the judgment hall was as if all the demons in a horde of possessed maniacs were howling at once. "Put him to death!" one of them shouted, and other voices, breaking with fury, took up the cry, till a cruel, implacable bass chorus was roaring harshly: "Put him to death! Put him to death!"

The man standing beside Peter would not be put off. To him, a faithful servant of Malchus, the arrest and punishment of this Galilean was a matter of great importance. "Did I not see you in the garden with him?" Peter's voice broke shrilly as he cried in fear: "No!" Both of them were too excited to notice that the trial was at an end, and the prisoner was already being hurried out towards the door of the prison.

"You were! This fellow was in Gethsemane with him! He's a Galilean!"

But Peter persisted: "I do not know what you mean, man."

Both of them were pushed aside by the spear shafts of the Temple servants. The impetuous questioner found himself wedged among a howling group of furious men, some distance from the fisherman who found himself confronted not by his enemy, but by Jesus. As he passed, had Jesus heard his disciple's lie? He gave him a scarcely perceptible nod, in order not to betray his follower. And a mocking cockcrow screeched all Peter's shame in his ear.

Day broke with a southern suddenness. Above the shouting and yelling of the excited crowd that streamed out of doorways and side streets, Peter heard the crowing of the cocks. Cock after cock crowed till their clamor drowned the cries of the Judaeans; every cockcrow a blaring accusation. The unhappy disciple felt as if every cock in Jerusalem, every cock in the world, were jumping at him with red swollen comb and angrily fluffed-out feathers. Their encircled eyes threatened, their hard beaks and pointed claws and sharp spurs hacked at his faithless heart.

The hurrying crowd pressed closer and closer, children screamed in terror, women fainted, and cries of woe rose on all sides. And amidst it all, Peter heard someone quietly, desperately murmur: "Betrayed! Forsaken!" He had not the courage to look round, to see who was the owner of this mournful voice. "Has a cock become a Judaean? Is he nudging me with his elbow and jeering at me? Surely I know that voice. . . ?" Surreptitiously, he glanced sideways. Beside him stood Judas Iscariot.

With a wild cry, Peter struggled to free his hands and set them about Judas's hated throat. But though the veins stood out on his forehead like blue cords, his hands remained fettered by the press of the multitude around him. "I forsook him, you betrayed him." And grinding his teeth, Peter realized that he was guilty again, and that this time he had denied the very teaching of Jesus. Matthew, the taxgatherer and sinner, had written down one of the most important precepts that the Master had given to the multitude from the mountaintop: Judge not that you be not judged.

"Simon Peter." The voice of his hated companion was so close to Peter's ear that he felt the spray of his spittle. "Do you know what the Sanhedrin has decided?"

"To put him to death. Are you glad?"

"Simon Peter, I am an apostle like you—" stammered the other, his jaw quivering.

"Like me? You do not know how true that is."

"It cannot be true. You were the only one to draw your sword, and the Master quickly made that good."

"Galilean sons of dogs!" screamed an excited youngster at the two of them. "Everyone who sides with the holy men of the Sanhedrin demands the cross!"

"Caiaphas said: Better one should die than all of us!" raved another. "The Romans are only waiting for a pretext to slaughter the lot of us, women and children and all." "At the Feast of Tabernacles, some Syrian pig-eater ripped my mother's belly open while she was alive, to see if she had swallowed any gold." "And all because of the Galilean bandits!" "There they are! Death to them! Crucify them!"

"Where are they taking him? One of Jesus's eyes is bloody. Where are they going?" moaned Judas. Someone boasted of his knowledge, just gathered from a Temple servant. "To the fortress. Pilate will have to execute him."

"Today? On the day before the feast?"

The Judaean laughed grimly: "This Passover will be a feast for all time."

With their clubs and spear hafts, the Temple servants had

made a lane for the procession of the Sanhedrin. The two disciples, jostled and trodden on, pummeled and pushed against the wall, watched Annas and Caiaphas go by between two Levite guards, dignified, not deigning to cast a glance at the crowd who were now cheering them. Behind came the old men of the High Council, and the decaprots Nicodemus and Joseph of Rama. Behind them, handcuffed between two muscular Benjaminites, fellows like butchers, walked Jesus of Nazareth. Hatred, cowardice, and the lust for murder howled around him. At the gateway out of the Temple, Syrian cohorts lowered their spears to drive back the raving Judaean hordes. The wise men of the Sanhedrin did not desire Jesus to be stoned. Rome had taken from them the right to carry out executions. Let Rome be the hangman.

Only when the priests had crossed the Temple courtyard and passed through the passageway at the northwestern corner, on to the terrace of Gabbatha, were the people allowed to follow. And now they swept forward in their thousands, filling the spacious square in a buzzing swarm that left not a handsbreadth of free space from the parapet of the outer fortifications, with their smooth unsurmountable walls, right across to the Temple hall itself. But here, fear stilled their outcries. Not one of them dared utter a word. From Lithostrotos, the mighty stone-paved forecourt to the fortress of Antonia, polished, helmeted, armored and harnessed, the Roman legionaries were peering up. And high above, on the roof of the fortress and in the watchtowers, loaded ballistas could be seen, and the bows of Syrian archers, raised ready to release a volley of arrows.

In front of the crowd, Simon Peter and Judas leaned wearily over the sloping parapet, looking despairingly down at Jesus, who stood before the sentries at the foot of the ramp. Their sorrow for him made them forget their own danger. Peter could hardly distinguish what Judas was feverishly muttering to himself: "The cursed usurers! How they mocked me! Jesus had more pity on me than they did. I was his treasurer. What did he, who needed nothing, want with money? It is in good hands. Matthew the taxgatherer will find it at the house of the Pharisee, Simon the Leper. It is accumulating interest

there, a lot of money! Use it to get to Galilee and save yourselves. Annas mocked me as if I wanted to sell the Master. I
only wanted to force his hand, like you."

"What lies are you telling now? Force his hand!"

"Do you deny it? We all wanted him to be King of the
World. We came to think him cowardly, when he is the bravest
of the brave. He wants to suffer." Judas turned and supporting
himself on one arm, he learned far over the parapet and called
down to Jesus: "I did not want to sell you! I wanted to challenge you. I wanted you to dash your enemy to the ground
with the lightning of your miracles, to breach the Antonia
with the battering-ram of your might, and to lead the hosts
of avenging angels! You could do it, you said so. Why do you
not want to? I kissed you, so that you would know it was not
treachery. No! I wanted your victory."

Out of the growing unrest, mocking laughter rose. "Listen
to him, the Galilean traitor!" But Judas was not listening. He
cried: "They tricked me. Thirty pieces of silver for a Jesus!
Thirty pieces of silver for the Son of God!"

Peter struck the foaming Judas in the chest with his hard
fist, so that he fell back against the parapet. A few onlookers
ironically cheered: Serve the fool right. A number of sturdy
men wearing the headdress of desert riders had gathered there.
The scars of old sword wounds showed through their beards.
They were partisans of Bar Abbas.

Like wind over the corn, a shudder ran through the multitude as Pilate stepped out onto the Praetorium steps, to greet
the Sanhedrin. He cast a fleeting glance over the mosaic of
brown and yellow faces, glittering with the hatred of a thousand
eyes. But as an ambitious youngster in Rome he had written
witty comedies, and had learned from the actor's art a great
deal for his career. So, gallant and distinguished, he walked
towards the oldest of the subjugated people, and let them
do homage much longer than necessary, their arms held up
in the Roman salute, while he gazed absently at the accused
man, whose name he had so often pronounced during the
last three years.

Too far away to hear what was said, the two disciples only
gathered that the Roman had ordered the prisoner to be

taken into the Praetorium. When Peter turned to see whether he could detect even a sign of indignation in the faces of the desert warriors and camel herders, he saw that Jesus would get no help from them. He found that even Judas had left him. And then he saw him a long way off, in front of the high priest, and heard him cry desperately: "I delivered an innocent man to you!" The priests stared at him stonily. Annas shrugged almost imperceptibly. "What is that to us? It is your affair."

At that, Peter saw Judas fumble in his robe, saw him hurl a purse at the priests' feet so that the leather burst and the money sprang out of it and rolled over the stones.

The crowd drew back in fear as Judas stormed right through them across the square and through the hall. Just once he bent down and picked up a rope which had fallen from some beast of sacrifice.

MARK had taken the disciples out of Jerusalem and its perils, and had brought them one by one to his mother's house. While the men were squatting on their heels, silent and grieving, the sound of helpless weeping came from the women's room. A hasty knock at the door made them all start up. The knock was repeated, more urgently still. Mark hesitantly opened the door, but before he could stammer a question, a woman stole out of the brightness of the square into the dark passage and hurried into the women's room. The eleven pressed after her full of curiosity.

"Mary, your son is alive! I come from Pilate." She had thrown off her veil. A slender shaft of sunlight struck her hair, which was bleached with sorrow. Pale and unadorned, Mary of Migdal told her story: "Pilate sent for me in the women's courtyard of the Temple. I had been avoiding him for a long time. He raised his eyebrows when he saw me. 'I did not send for Magdalene's mother.' " She did not add that she had wailed: "I have aged away from your heart." She told them of the governor's ill-humor. "He paced up and down restlessly, and then said: 'Caiaphas asks me to crucify Jesus. He says he calls himself King of the Jews. He is a Galilean, so

131

I am sending him to Herod.' —Startled, I cried: 'To John's murderer?' I threw myself at his feet and clasped his knees, and the steel of his greaves made me shudder. He laughed at me. 'You women always get so excited at a few solemn words. I should be jealous. My wife and you have both pleaded for the King of the Jews. Did you suffer for him in a dream too, like my wife?' Always, but when I am awake, I told him. Pilate knew of no way out: 'I wash my hands of him. He maintained he was a witness for the truth.—What is truth? Your King was silent.' "

Outside, shouting people were racing along the street. The air was full of threats against the Romans, against Herod, against Jesus. A howl rose above the guttural rumble of Hebrew sounds. It seemed to be a name, known to many, furiously repeated. Mark came back from the doorway. He was trembling. "Judas Iscariot—he has hanged himself. . . ."

Their murmured prayer for his departed soul was interrupted by a new bawling.

"They are bringing Jesus back!" Thaddeus, at the window, shouted for joy. "Herod's lancers are pushing the crowd back. Our Master is magnificently dressed; his outer garment is of pure gold. But why do they not set him free? Annas's servants are taking him to the Antonia again."

In vain, the high priests had reminded Herod that his great forebear, a generation ago, had butchered a whole year's harvest of living boys. Jesus had attacked the Temple by word and hand. But now they complained that the degenerate adulterer Antipas had nothing of the great Jewish severity. To him, the agitator seemed little more than a fairground juggler. For his women's sake, he had asked him to perform a miracle, just a little one. But Jesus did not deign to grant him a word, let alone a deed. However, the foxy Herod guessed that it was not convenient for the Roman governor to act as hangman in Caiaphas's service. Averse to shedding any more blood, he showed that as a diplomat he had seen through the other's diplomacy; instead of slaughtering the victim, he sent him back in costly robes, with a guard of honor.

Now a fourth trial was required. Stubbornly, the elders refused to budge from the Lithostrotos until Pilate went into the Praetorium again. Behind him a troop of legionaries came tramping out of the Antonia. In their midst stumbled Bar Abbas, pale and emaciated, in heavy chains. His followers hardly recognized him, so much had imprisonment affected him. Flies swarmed on his festering limbs, rubbed sore by the rusty chains. He paid them no heed.

When Pilate indicated that despite Herod's knowledge of Jewish law even he had been unable to find any guilt in Jesus, the elders of the Sanhedrin cried out in a holy frenzy. But the Roman continued in such a low, disdainful voice that they immediately fell silent, so as not to miss what he was saying. "To my knowledge, it is an old custom for the Jewish people to set a malefactor free at the Feast of the Passover. We have the choice of two: Jesus, and the murderous bandit Bar Abbas. I would extend my clemency to the innocent Jesus."

The behavior of the Temple elders, who were beside themselves with fury, disgusted him. Their garments hung in shreds, ripped by their own clawing fingers, and in their desperation they had scratched their foreheads till they bled. With a dull sound, they beat their breasts with their fists, and the multitude howled with them: "Give us Bar Abbas!"

The governor had turned his back on the mob, and was talking to one of his officers. A warning given him by his father, the experienced centurion, came to his mind: "There is no man so strong that he could be of real help to you; but no man is so wretched that he could not harm you." Bitterly he recalled the warning voices of the women. He cherished one last hope, as he thought how his compatriots, when they had seen enough of a gladiator's grave wounds, would have his life spared. With bitter irony, he ordered: "Scourge the King of the Jews." He took his place on the judgment seat and watched Jesus as the soldiers pushed him through the archway into the courtyard.

The sweating, stinking mob listened in anxious silence. Had they not been standing on sanctified ground, right by the Holy of Holies, they would have been overcome by horror and dread. The rumor had gone around that Jesus drove out devils with the aid of Baal Zebul. Uneasily they listened to a soldier's song from the fortress, a song whose wild rhythm was marked by a curious whistling. They were scourging Jesus's quailing body with rods, red with his blood. Three Syrian soldiers walked in a circle around the pillar to which Jesus was chained. They had dipped the hazel rods in water to make them more pliant. Watching from the Lithostrotos, Malchus, the Temple captain, called down to the waiting crowd: "The executioner's assistants have plaited a wreath of thorns. They are driving this crown into his forehead with sticks."

Huddled in a corner, the eleven disciples and the women listened. The mother of Jesus stood as if turned to stone. Anyone seeing her could only weep. "Physician, heal yourself . . ." Peter tried to whisper. On his right, he heard the scarred Zealot sobbing like a child. On his left, Luke, the doctor, whom he had met in Mary of Migdal's house, thrust himself forward, risking his life among the demented crowd of Judaeans. Quietly, he tried to console his distracted neighbor: "Now the heathen will have to honor Jesus of Nazareth, as the Greeks their Socrates. Just as he was forced by the Athenians, so the Galilean is forced by his people to the ultimate ethical act."

The eastern sun was already high over the heads of the impatient crowd when the screams of horrified women greeted the appearance of Jesus, but the screams were immediately drowned in the merciless howling of the Judaeans. In an ecstasy of joy, the members of the Sanhedrin linked arms and began to sway as if in a dance. Malchus cried jubilantly: "Do you smell the blood?" Breathing heavily, he roared: "Baal Zebul did not help him this time." And the Gaulonites of Bar Abbas shouted exultantly: "Strike him again!"

The legionaries led Jesus out like a prince of mockery and scorn. His breast, arms and face were a bluish hue. From his cruelly lacerated head, the blood ran steadily in fine red streams to the corners of his mouth, over his swollen lips, beneath the knotted rags of his cloak and down his agonized breast. Here and there, the thick drops halted, and their smell attracted the greedy flies. On the head of the stumbling man bristled a dreadful crown of long-pointed thorns. The fettered Messiah stood blind and helpless. He could not raise

134

his eyelids because the blood from his lacerated forehead was running over them.

Pilate listened in vain. Instead of the pity he had hoped for, he heard the old men of the Sanhedrin shouting: "Scourge him again! Flog him to death!" Only Nicodemus the decaprot stood apart and covered his face.

The governor turned to the mob. At a sign from him, the trumpeters blared a warning that made the bloodthirsty crowd fall silent. And into their silence, the Roman cried: "Behold, the man!" The answer was Caiaphas's furious cry: "Crucify him!" And a thousand voices repeated: "Crucify him!"

The noble Roman felt himself soiled by the hatred of the mob who—as he well knew from his spies—only a few days ago had greeted the luckless King with their cheers. A slave brought a silver basin and a silver ewer. Reflectively, Pilate let the cool water run over his hands, then, breathing heavily, he said: "I am innocent of the blood of this righteous man. Witness that."

At the same moment, an entire people pronounced the gravest of curses upon themselves: "His blood be on ourselves and on our children!" Peter and those around him saw the governor speak sharply to the high priest, whose answer seemed to disconcert the Roman. Caiaphas repeated his threat: "If you let him go, you are not loyal to your Emperor. Jesus called himself the Son of God, and King. Anyone who sets himself up as a king rebels against the Emperor."

The shout struck Pilate like an arrow whose shaft remains quivering in the flesh. He stared scornfully at the high priest, who played the part of an honest man in order to commit murder.

Pushed still further to the side, the weeping disciples saw the rough soldiers tear the scarlet cloak from their victim— it had adhered to his wounds—and throw his own garment over his head.

"He called himself King!" Disconcerted, Peter stammered the words of his lifelong hope. Beside him, Thaddeus moaned: "The cross!" The legionaries forced Jesus to shoulder an enormous cross, while behind him, two malefactors were whipped out of the town, each bearing the crossbeam of his gallows across his shoulders like a yoke, with his outspread arms already tied in position.

"How sadly we all failed him!" Mary of Migdal pressed her fists against her eyes. But a wild reproach broke from Peter: "And Jesus himself?"

A soldier took his position in front of the cross-bearer, and began to march ahead. High on the end of a spear shaft he carried a placard. "Read the placard! What does it say?" Peter tugged at Luke's garment.

"Jesus of Nazareth, King of the Jews. —It is in Greek, Latin and Hebrew." They could see the high priests were protesting against the inscription. Pilate was firmly shaking his head.

As if lamenting for the dead, the eleven covered their faces. Their hope was gone. Of what avail was all their ceaseless wandering, their toiling over the dark mysteries of the doctrine? Of what avail the miracles worked on the possessed, the lame? Those risen from the dead would soon be dead once more, and forever. Father Jonah bled to death, poor as a beggar. The Temple was victorious. Their King, the Messiah-King of Judah and Israel, was about to be executed before the mockery of the heathen. . . .

THE second night after the death of the Son of Man seemed as if it would never end. Poor Peter! They buried your sleep with your Master. He would not have had to warn you now to stay awake, as he did in Gethsemane. Something kept urging you to spring up and make good what was irretrievably done. But it was pitch-dark now, no sun was rising. This was the hour of the Mount of Olives, that returned night after night.

He crouched in a corner of Lazarus's house beside the sons of Zebedee, and tormented them into wakefulness with his despair. "The third day, and Jesus has not come."

"Wait, Peter. It is still night."

"Are they allowed to execute him on the Day of Preparation, on the very eve of Passover?"

James explained that the Sanhedrin had exhumed some old precept: "If a man has performed such and such a task on the Sabbath, whether from compulsion, oversight or error, then what he has done is done."

"And think how often they complained because the Master performed miracles of healing on the Sabbath."

"I saw Jesus suffer and die. Where were you then?" John asked.

"When I came to my senses, the forecourt of the Antonia was deserted. You had left me lying there like a bit of rubbish. By the way the clouds were coming up, tattered and heavy with weather, I foresaw storm. I heard thunder, and I wrangled with God for sending his storm too late. Then I, a blasphemer, was dashed to the ground so that my bones bounced on the flagstones, which seemed to be breathing, heaving to and fro. It was the eternal rock that was swaying there. The masonry was riven asunder. Walls collapsed in rubble. A flash of lightning tore into the Holy of Holies like a trumpet blast. The great tall curtain hanging in front of the unapproachable chamber of the Ark of the Covenant was rent from top to bottom as if by the enormous hands of furious cherubim. It hung like a torn sail, and the void lay open before me. The angel was keeping watch no longer. Death had fled out of the world and I saw the mighty ones of old come up out of the depths, the guardians of wisdom and the light." He whispered in fear. "Believe me, I saw the Kings, Solomon and Melchizedek. They laughed at my complaint that Jesus had begun the building but had not been allowed to finish it. Listen to what they said: 'Mount the seat of the mighty which is above the void of night. The Milky Way is the carpet that covers the steps of your throne over the depths of the firmament. Only when you can think in aeons, so that your forehead requires three bands in order to contain the wine of wisdom, only then have you earned the throne and the diadem.' And they laughed like the threat of thunder. And when, trembling, I dared to protest: 'I am his Rock. On me he built his Church,' I heard the mysterious words: 'A sad and wonderful lot is your inheritance: You must be all men, the conscience of those without a conscience, the remorse of those who are punished, the happiness of those who are pure. . . .' "

Silently, James groped for the clumsy hand of the fisherman, who continued as if shaking with fever: "I did not see Jesus dead, but ironically enough, I saw Judas. In the potter's field in the valley of Gehinnor, I smelt the decay of him from a long way off. He had rolled right across the path, with the broken rope still round his neck. Vultures flew up from his intestines. He always imagined himself the most important of the apostles, and now he has hanged himself."

"Only he and you were missing on Golgotha." There was no sound of reproach in James's voice. "All of us who had been with Jesus stood some distance off, even the women. But my brother John stood with our Lord's mother, right under the cross, in the drip of the blood."

"Where is his grave?"

"Joseph of Rama gave us his tomb. He came with Nicodemus. They brought myrrh and aloes. Pilate had given them permission to take the body down. With Mary Magdalene, we tended his limbs, lacerated by his cruel mishandling. She sobbed as she told us how grateful he had been for her nard ointment, in the house of Simon the Leper. The Master had warned us then: 'She is anointing me for my burial.' Joseph of Rama had brought a fine linen sheet, and on the half of it, we laid what had once been Jesus. The body hardly measured fifteen and a half handsbreadths. Then we wrapped the rest of the shroud over him and bound him firmly with beautifully woven bands, so that we men could carry him to the tomb and lay him on the resting place in the innermost vault. We kissed his shrouded forehead and his gentle hands for the last time. We went away, and no more tears were left to us."

"Nicodemus belonged to the Sanhedrin too."

"What can one voice do against so much hatred?"

"How we boasted, when Jesus washed our feet. Lord, I am with you in prison or in death! And I did not even help him to die."

"Only my brother John stood with the Marys beneath the cross. I am not lying . . . none of us dared go nearer."

"He prophesied that Satan would sift us like chaff. Me, the Stone, he has thrown out. Now the third day is dawning, the third day . . ."

"And that prophecy will be fulfilled, too. I can still hear his words in my ears: 'On the third day the Son of Man will rise again.'"

"And you left him alone? How will he get out of the bands, how will he not smother under the shroud?"

"Did he not say he would pray for you, so that you would remain strong?"

"I did not run away out of cowardice. When I stood in Caiaphas's courtyard, was I not risking my life? It tore my heart to see him beaten, to see him standing there, shaking from his hurts, crowned with thorns . . . and was I to watch him dying for hours? He was no King any longer, only the poorest, most sinful of all poor sinners. And we? Cheated of our thrones and of the mastery of the world. Forgive me, Jesus—then I will forgive you."

Outraged, John and James stumbled to their feet and pushed the door open. Outside, in the gray of morning, the remainder of the disciples stood around, singly, like beaten soldiers who do not even dare to make a campfire. The Zealot began to reproach the sons of Zebedee: "How could you let my mother go with Mary Magdalene to Jesus's grave?"

"They set out long before daybreak with his mother, to tend the body with balsam and spices."

"They will be driven away. Roman soldiers are guarding the tomb. Tell them what you know, tax collector."

"Annas and Caiaphas remembered the prophecy about the resurrection. They went to Pilate, full of fear. He heard them with a sardonic smile, but they called us thieves. They asked to have the grave guarded until the third day, so that we could not come to steal the body and declare that he was risen from the dead. They think us capable of their trickery. They complained that this final bit of witchcraft would be more serious than any before. So the governor granted them a guard. 'Go and make everything secure as best you know how.' I saw them go and seal the tomb with the seal of Solomon, that is stronger than all the spirits of the abyss, and before which even the angels bow; and they posted the guards all around."

"And if he rises again, I, Simon son of Jonah, tell you he

will have himself crucified a second time. When Jesus died, the stone floor of the Lithostrotos began to heave like the sea that time when Jesus came walking on the waves in the storm and called to me. I jumped overboard and came across the water to him; but in the surge of the waves, I lost my balance and began to sink. There was Jesus, close by, and he took my hand and lifted me up and held me. And on Friday? Where was the Father of his well-beloved son? What is a Son of Man, what is a man, to God?"

Stouthearted Thaddeus said in a ringing tone: "What he believes!"

Andrew pointed over the valley and the town. "It will soon be daylight over Golgotha. The women will be reaching the grave now."

"Reaching the legionaries," cried his brother bitterly. "Reaching the seven seals, and the Star of David on the wax. David himself keeps his grandson imprisoned behind stone." He stood up and stared into the rising sun. "Shame on us. Did not the Master send us out to work miracles in his name?"

Deep in thought, John shook his curly head. "To work a miracle on Jesus in the name of Jesus? There are deeper mysteries here than ever. Was his saying about the resurrection merely a parable? Why did he entrust his mother to me as he died?"

"And yet, John, let us be stronger now than the Son of Man himself. —I am standing here without a sword, without a purse, just as you commanded. If you are the new Messiah-King of eternity, stand up and come back again from death and from the grave, and go before us into the Temple, invincible, and we will be invincible too!"

Gravely the sons of Zebedee replied: "Invincible. . . . The gateway to eternal life is death."

But Peter would not allow himself to be diverted. "Son of David! You owe us the fulfillment of your prophecy. The third day! Lord Jesus, I take you at your word!"

"Simon!" shouted Andrew, and he pointed down to the valley towards the northeast. "Mary! She is running; she has fallen to her knees; she is waving to us!"

"What have those accursed men done to her?"

John reminded him: "Love your neighbor."

The men hurried down the hillside, springing from stone to stone, in the direction of the exhausted woman, who climbed towards them, breathing heavily, and seemed about to fall. Her left hand was pressed to her pounding heart, and she had raised her right arm, imploring them to hurry. Peter and John were just in time to catch her as she sank down. Her hair, wet with sweat, was clinging to her temples, and her cheeks and forehead were deeply flushed. "The grave is empty!" she gasped, and fainted away.

The two startled men carried her up the hill, calling to her sister Martha. After much effort, she was restored to consciousness. Weeping, she sought protection on her sister's breast, and could only report in a disjointed stammer: "They found the stone pushed aside. . . . Mary and Salome . . ."

"My mother?" urged the Zealot. "And mine?" asked John. "Yes, and Joanna." Her gaze wandered from one to the other. She spoke solemnly, now clutching at her sister, now at John. Disturbed at her terrible experience, none of them were able to make sense of what she was saying. Somebody— they could not determine whom she meant—had told the women to inform the disciples and Peter—yes, he had mentioned Peter by name—that Jesus of Nazareth had risen from the dead, that he was on his way to Galilee, and they were all to follow. They would see him again there. The women had hardly dared speak at all.

The disciples suspected a trick of the Sanhedrin, to get them in their clutches, and they asked after the legionaries. "They are not there any more."

Peter and John could hold back no longer. In furious haste they stormed along the valley, past Golgotha, where the cross still towered. From afar, they could already discern the open tomb. John, the younger, dashed ahead. As soon as he arrived, he bent down to peer into the interior. Gradually, he perceived in the darkness that the bands lay on the floor, the shroud crumpled and carelessly flung aside. He sought for a hold on the rock wall. He was so agitated that he could go no farther, and he fell at the threshold of the tomb. There he lay in Peter's way, who could not check himself as he came rushing up. In order not to harm his companion, Peter tried to jump over him, and to support himself in his leap, he reached out involuntarily at the great millstone which had been rolled aside in its deep furrow. At his sudden push, the stone began to sway.

"The stone! The stone is starting to roll!" cried Peter, wildly, and with one bound he was in darkness. Noisily the great stone rocked back and forth, two or three times. Before John could get to his feet, it had come trembling to rest again. Finding himself in pitch-darkness, Peter cried fearfully, "Jesus!" But the cave seemed to swallow up every sound in its terrifying stillness. However carefully the searcher ducked his head, he constantly knocked against cold hard stone. With trembling hands he groped along the walls, and gingerly touched the stone bench where the corpse should have been lying, but all he encountered was stone, smooth hewn stone, with the coolness of living subterranean rock, not that of a rigid corpse. Peter struck here and there with the flat of his right hand—emptiness, emptiness everywhere. At last, he threw himself full-length on the stone bench, where the corpse had lain. Pressing his burning forehead against its hard coolness, he lamented: "Now you are risen with your people, and those of time to come, and I am dead in your place. . . ." For a long time he lay there in meditation, till an icy shudder ran over him. Propping himself up heavily, he spoke to the one he sought as if he had wrestled him and was holding him down by both shoulders: "Are you up and gone from me again? Why do you do this to me?"

"Whom are you talking to, Simon?" The voice of John betrayed his fear, for he dared not enter the tomb.

Then Peter emerged out of the entrance to the grave, and drew a deep breath. "To my own grief. If I only could see him face to face!"

"That is no faith, that requires to see and to have things proved."

"Faith is a great leap in the dark. —What did Mary say? We were all to follow him to Galilee? Then what was all this for, death, the cross, the grave, the miracle?" Bending down, he drew out of the empty vault the bands and the winding sheet. They rolled up the bands. They spread the shroud out on the narcissus meadow in front of the dark opening and carefully set about folding it.

John stared at the length of linen as it lay in the sunlight. Suddenly, he seized his companion violently by the arm, and pointed without a word at the dark traces of the corpse that showed up as an image more and more clearly, the longer one looked. But everything dark, such as the hair and the eyes, looked light, and the body's pale skin remained shadowy. The darkness of his human existence lay before them, and most painful of all, the marks of his wounds. When Joseph of Rama and Nicodemus had taken the dead Jesus down from the cross, they had laid him on the shroud with his head halfway along the narrow length of the material, and had spread the remaining half over him. So that now his face, delineated in the center of the shroud, was turned towards his favorite disciple. With trembling lips and tear-filled eyes, they read all the torments which the mysterious image displayed: the long stripes of the rod on breast and back, the sharp scratches of the thorny crown, the cruelly long-drawn holes in the soles of the feet and the wrists, torn by the clumsy nails, and the broad gape-mouthed wound of the spear thrust.

"He always turned away from me," murmured Simon disconsolately, for he was standing at the other end of the shroud, which presented to him the image of the dead man's lacerated back. "Always away from me, never where I wanted him."

The two men carefully rolled up the winding sheet and carried it and the linen bands back towards the town. The Rock murmured sadly to himself: "Instead of marching at our head as the terror of all, the living dead, the invincible victor over death and the scourge of every enemy, he has us carry the dumb image of his wounds. As if that were all that was needed."

FROM the terrace of his villa on the shore of the Sea of Galilee, Cornelius the centurion stared across the dark evening blue of the water which was enlivened, in the distance, by the foam crests of little scurrying waves, surging forward in increasing

143

numbers, and with astonishing regularity. Deeply he breathed in the cool air of the first gentle breeze as it blew across the lake, refreshing his eyelids and his gray temples after the heat of the day. As he lay there, comfortably relaxed, all that reminded him of the blazing hours of daytime was the red sunset on the heights leading down towards the desert over in Transjordan. To right and left of him, the mountain ranges held Capernaum in their eternal embrace, and he watched them sinking gradually into the shadows of the night. Around him, the twilight swallowed up the redness of countless anemones, as they closed their petals.

Through the splash of the waves on the shore, and the lapping of the water against the fishing boats anchored on the restless lake, he could hardly distinguish the cries of the crowd in the market place behind his house, which was just coming to life again after the heat of the day. At last he said to the waiting slave, "Go, youngster, give the copyist from Antiochia this purse, with his payment. Tell him I do not know whether his version corresponds exactly to the account given by the taxgatherer Matthew Levi. But I am glad to pay, because I like his work."

Leisurely he took from the marble table a long parchment scroll, and unrolled it before the lad's astonished eyes. "Look, there is something about us two here. Do you remember? You were dying, and I went to the miracle-doctor Jesus of Nazareth."

"And I recovered!"

"The people of this country are full of insulting superstitions. If they enter my house, they are obliged to purify themselves, as if they were soiled from head to foot. Jesus scorned such ideas, and wanted to come to you himself. But I trusted his eyes and his strength, and told him so. And look how he praises me." In the still of the evening over the lake, Cornelius read aloud the beautiful Greek version of Jesus's words, in which the healer of bodies and souls declared he had never found such faith before; and he read of the table which has been set in the Kingdom of Heaven. "And his own people put this wonderful man to death like a runaway slave."

"But why, master?"

The Roman let his sword hand fall heavily on the table. "I have been stationed here for years with my cohort, and not a year without unrest, not a day without conspiracy. The Galileans are the most dangerous of all. Do you think I commissioned this account from Matthew Levi merely out of boredom? I want to know what the partisans are planning. You could threaten these fishermen and peasants with crucifixion ten times over, and they still would not stir out without their short-swords in their sleeves. It is three years now since I first heard of Jesus of Nazareth. More and more people were flocking to him; whole villages and towns set out to follow him. Priests and Pharisees, the Sanhedrin and the Sadducees all issued warnings that he was a wizard, an agitator. There were dangerous men around him, the most dangerous being the son of a certain Jonah, who had been killed by the Sebastenes. I was on my guard. I ordered a detailed report from Levi. This is his work. Only Jesus's death is lacking . . . and the treachery of his followers."

"And you let them do it, master? Have his disciples been crucified too?"

"They deserved to be. This book is full of their willfulness. Jesus could cure all possessed people except these, the most devil-possessed of all. Woe betide them, if they fall into my hands. The guards on every gate have their orders: As soon as Jesus's companions try to sneak back to their wives and children, arrest them and bring them to me."

"Did they learn nothing from him then? Except to betray him, to kill him?"

"You need not be ashamed of your tears. When once men understand this account of Matthew's, it may be they will become worthy of eternal life. . . ."

The young slave listened in astonishment. "Eternal life?"

"Whoever reads this book knows that only the good is eternal."

"Will you take me with you into eternity, master?"

The captain smiled at his faithful servant, who was still as pale as ivory from his illness. "It depends on you. Jesus pointed the way to his followers. He told them, reminded them, warned them, of his death, which he had known about all the time. And perhaps it is because of that knowledge that, in this account, he is called 'the Son of God.' "

"Did ever a people murder a God of their own blood?"

Cornelius knitted his brows. "My lord and emperor is the god of Rome. I have served two of these gods, the great Augustus and the terrible Tiberius. The one was often ill and suffered from those around him. The other was isolated in his own contempt for mankind. Both of them brought people from life to death, never from death to life."

"And the Judaeans had their God crucified?"

"He demanded something enormous: Love your neighbor as yourself, he said."

The young slave whispered: "I do."

His master laid a benevolent hand on his head. "Not only me, everybody."

The handsome young man stared at this master, whom all his life he had been accustomed to see walking about in helmet and harness, with his broadsword hanging from his belt. The centurion nodded and said with a bitter laugh: "That is the most difficult thing of all. How am I to obey this God, when I think of his followers as traitors, bandits, rebels?"

The blare of trumpet music approached and suddenly broke off, close at hand. The centurion stood up. "They are bringing the Galileans to me. Let them in!"

The slave took the purse and hurried away. The centurion made a pretense of concentrating all his attention on carefully rolling up the parchment and putting it away in its metal case, as the sergeant of the guard entered with seven weary, dust-covered men, who found it difficult to keep in step with the legionaries on either side of them.

Cornelius ordered the guard to return to their gate, then, leaning back on his couch, he surveyed each of his seven strange guests, while the young slave brought in a tall bronze lampstand, from whose chains little oil lamps swung to and fro, their weak ruddy flames more like friendly stars than givers of light.

The centurion recognized his neighbors from across the market place, the brothers Simon and Andrew. And he remembered the sons of Zebedee, too, by their proud bearing, and Nathanael and Thaddeus, whose youthful wide-eyed look reminded him agreeably of his favorite slave. Thomas's appearance moved him deeply, for he was as like the crucified man as a twin. The seven stood lined up by the wall; it was noticeable that they took great care not to touch anything in the heathen house. Cornelius lashed them with the scorn of his words: "You sold Jesus of Nazareth to the high priests and have stolen his corpse! Right?"

All seven shouted: "No!" He silenced them with a glance; uneasily, John answered the challenge of the soldier's outthrust chin, and described the last events which Matthew had not yet written down. In the meantime, word of the arrest had spread, and the superstitious men and women of Capernaum had anxiously gathered outside the heathen's house. Their murmured prayer for the "polluted" prisoners reached the lake terrace like a whisper of fear, and above it rose the horrible lamenting cries of Peter's mother-in-law. In disgust, Cornelius murmured to himself a line of Horace: "I hate you, O common people, and I try to fend you off." He shouted at the Galileans in Aramaic: "I only granted you respite from the gallows for Jesus's sake. I took a heavy responsibility. Your betrayal of the Nazarene has robbed you of the only grounds for clemency. Where do you keep his corpse?"

Thomas stepped forward. With his resemblance to the Master, it seemed as if Jesus himself was speaking for his disciples, and confessing his own disbelief. Breathing heavily, he gave an account of his ghastly meeting with him who had died on the cross before the eyes of all Jerusalem. His eyes were wide with terror, as if the risen Jesus stood before him again, and as if, on the Master's insistence, he had to lay his left hand, which was tremblingly raised as a witness to his words, on the wounds, on the right and left instep, on the wrists, and finally in that dreadful mark which the spear point had slit in the right side of his breast. With such power did the recollection grip the doubter, that he fell on his knees. As at the first encounter, his cry rang out: "My Master and my God!"

The gray-haired soldier shuddered, as if he felt the risen

Christ near at hand. "You all deserve the death sentence, you bandits."

"Sire!" The respectable Nathanael could not bear such an insult. "We have changed." While the sons of Jonah tended Thomas, who had fainted away, the Roman noticed they no longer had their short-swords hidden in their sleeves, but he mistrusted them nevertheless. "Do not deny it! I have obtained detailed reports about your intentions and your deeds. Your aim was to sit on thrones. You called Jesus 'the Son of the Living God'; nobody is to be your living god, on pain of death, except the Emperor in Rome! Pompeius has defeated your invisible god." Haughty as the victor of a battle, Cornelius turned away from the wretched, dusty travelers, and walked to the lakeside edge of the terrace. Leaning against the balustrade, he gazed into the boundless night, and saw star after star, however high he lifted his eyes, however low his gaze sank on the water. Pityingly, he asked his prisoners: "What do you know of this?"

"Nothing," answered John, humbly but proudly. "We believe. One hope is left to us, one promise and one prayer."

"One prayer? A single one?" Cornelius glanced with a sigh at the niche in the wall, with the little statuettes of his house gods. He was an obedient soldier, and made an offering each morning to his Emperor and to Jupiter Capitolinus. Behind all the enemies of his military life stood various gods, powerful ones, vanquished ones, perhaps even vengeful ones. To atone for the shame they had suffered, and to make them favorably disposed, was no easy matter. The most mysterious power of all appeared to be the invisible God of this race of fanatical haters, to whom a hundred different kinds of prayers did not seem enough. And now, were they to be satisfied with one? He knew the words by hearsay, and he spoke them in Greek: "Our Father . . . is that enough?" And he continued in Aramaic: "Of course, you pray day and night: Thy Kingdom come?"

"Yes, sire, day by day."

The Roman laughed. "Yet the kingdom is still ours, and so is its invincible army. The land is cultivated, we have made roads everywhere. The whole country is opened up

148

for trade. Wasteland has turned into gardens, forests into plowland. The sands of the desert bear fruit and the rocks grow grass. The drained marshes await the seed like rich fallow. All of it my country, everywhere my people, the universe my state, and flourishing life on every hand! What can be greater than Rome?"

"Our God," said Peter, defiantly.

"The one our God-emperor nailed to the cross? The Master of the World?" He surveyed the fisherman haughtily. "Imagine that you are young, handsome, bubbling over with life, and that you step out of the Holy of Holies as Emperor and God. Slaves of all colors are setting the festive table with the delights of distant lands piled on golden dishes. Hordes of girls more beautiful than ever your Mary of Migdal was, bow sighing to your every desire. The most celebrated gladiators fight to the death for your pleasure. The mightiest generals, the most distinguished poets, you appoint them, you play with their lives. The jewels of Asia, the gold of Ophir, the amber of the forests of ice, all is yours. The freest are unfree compared to you. Only you are free."

The seven Galileans stared at him uncomprehendingly. But the Roman's laughter was cruel. "And the end of all this intoxication of happiness is envy, hatred, murder, disgust and nausea. And is it for such glories that you long? Have you never listened to your Jesus?"

"For three years, sire, for three years."

"He has told you children a hundred fairy tales, allegory after allegory. But you only heard what you wanted to hear. Perhaps I too only derived from it what we orphans of God are longing for. But from us, the masters of the world, do you want Tiberius's misanthropy, our boundless melancholy and inner desolation? Did not the crucified one teach you: 'Blessed are the poor for theirs is the Kingdom of Heaven? Blessed are the peacemakers!' For the sake of that promise, I am letting you go."

Shaking his head, Peter said: "Now the Master is speaking out of your mouth. Were you the only one to interpret his sermons aright, and we the only ones to go astray?"

"Go to Rome with the faith of your Jesus and the wisdom

of the Greeks, and enter into its might—which is now perhaps no more than an empty gilded shell—and grow into it. Instead of the will to kill, have the will to do good. Only then will Rome become Rome." Smiling, he raised his hand. "And do not disappoint me, now that you are without your Lord and Master. . . ."

"We are not without him!" Nathanael stubbornly persisted, and the others protested: "He is alive!"

Cornelius, whose clear Latin mind had rejected Thomas's remarks as mere ravings, looked questioningly from one to the other. "Your old God is gone, as well. The curtain before the Holy of Holies was rent. The room was empty."

James could not endure such heretical talk. "Men die, God never. Jesus was a sacrifice to atone for all mankind."

The Roman nodded. "Your King of the Jews had to die, in order to become Master of the World. Now he has fulfilled himself. The unassailable one has emerged the victor."

Thomas did not understand. "I—I assailed him!"

The centurion laughed bitterly. "You assailed him? Poor Jesus. To be a God, the Messiah-King of a nation of quibblers, just so that in the end some childish fisherman thinks he can hold him back like a thief?"

They did not know how to withstand his mocking gaze. Then Peter thought of a convincing proof and he boldly cried: "He ate with us, ate with us!"

The seven of them all began to talk at once of the big piece of grilled fish, the honeycomb, the bread and wine with which the crucified one had stayed his hunger, till the centurion's angry and impatient gesture gave the welcome signal for them to quit his heathenish house.

"I AM going fishing," Peter shouted, next evening, as the surface of Lake Genesareth lay smooth and quiet across its whole extent. The sons of Jonah and Zebedee, Nathanael, Thomas and Thaddeus took deep breaths of the moist, warm lake air. The atmosphere of their home-coming had made them forget their longing for what had been the very meaning of their existence for the past few years. At Simon's shout, they all turned to, with the inherited skill of their fishermen fore-bears. The regular rhythm of the oars seemed to steady their souls. The net glided silently into the water. Alluring torches shone above it. In the silence, a secret regret rose in them, that all these years they had tempted God with their restless demands for great and new things, that God who had put so many fat fish into their nets, and their fathers', year in, year out. Now they were being punished with the anxiety of wait-ing. Jacob the Tsaddik and his brother Simon had gone home to their father, Halephai. Philip was tilling his fields. Matthew was torturing himself with his report on the last days of Jesus. All the six dozen disciples whom the Master had endowed with power before sending them out, had nervously dispersed be-fore the bloody cross. Only a few women still lingered in the house of Mark's mother.

For many hours they rowed the heavy boat about the lake. But however often they hauled in their gear, the nets remained empty. Occasionally, in the dying light of the torches, a tiny silver fish jumped overboard, back into the lake again.

Longer and longer they left their nets in the water, and squatted together, trying not to admit that their courage was failing. The stars had grown pale now, and only the snow-covered summit of Hermon shone in the north like their hope of the Messiah, till at last the sky and the eastern horizon began to brighten. Heave by heave, they pulled up their net for the last time, and mesh by mesh it rose empty in the gray light of day. Then a cold wet mist descended on them, and they had to row with great care. Out of the grayness came Simon's voice, and his grim laugh as he steered shorewards: "Did we catch nothing because the Master has left us, or because he is near?"

Thomas said mockingly: "Do not frighten away the fat crucians. The Master was right to send you home, so you could learn your trade at last, for you do not know it. Not yet."

An echo came back: "Not yet."

Andrew warned them: "The shore slope is to the right here. If we are going to cast the net again, it had better be on the other side. To starboard, it would get torn on the rocks."

A first tremulous ray of sunlight pricked through the veil

of mist. Then the golden-green of the shore showed, and ahead of the dark shadow of the boat, a bright figure. Through the damp twilight his voice called: "Children! Have you nothing to eat?"

Furious over their wasted night, the fishermen called back: "No!"

The figure seemed to fade, then it spoke again: "Cast your net to the right of the boat and you will find fish."

The experienced fishermen laughed. Too bad for their neatly folded net! But Nathanael and Thaddeus, who knew much less about fishing, had already begun carefully to do what the voice advised. It was too late to stop them, and the ill-humored fishermen could only watch their precious net sinking down towards the rocks below the gently heaving surface of the lake. As they waited, they peered anxiously towards their unbidden adviser. Then Simon's conscience stirred. Had not he, the expert, disbelieved a similar piece of advice once before, advice that all his experience had told him was senseless; and had not his nets been torn with the weight of the catch? On that occasion, he had fallen to his knees, a repentant sinner.

As he bent over the starboard side of the boat with the others, to try to make out the man on the shore, he lost his balance and almost fell into the lake, so violently did the boat begin to heel over.

The fishermen braced themselves straddle-legged against the side of the boat and heaved on the net ropes till the water fell back foaming from the twitching fish that leapt against each other in huge glittering abundance: plump crucians, barbel, and carp, snapping pike, and the broad-mouthed Galilean sheatfish that screams with fear.

The fishermen were frightened too, but they did not cry out. Instead, they gritted their teeth with the effort of pulling in the net. Their hands gripped the rope till their fingers bled. Gasping, John groaned to Peter what he had long since guessed: "The Master . . . !"

Just as he was, in only his undergarment, and that tucked about his hips, the Fisher of Men threw himself over the net and the catch, with a mighty spring into the lake. The boat was lighter. The others relaxed and steered for the shore, dragging the net behind them, even if some of the fish swam away.

With a few pulls at the oars, they had landed. A charcoal fire was glowing on the shore. Fish were cooking on pointed stakes. There was bread. High up on the steep rocky shore, a bright figure was resting, and a voice called: "Bring the fish that you have just caught."

Peter waded over the irregular stones on the beach, seized the net rope and dragged the catch ashore, step by step. "Over here!" called the voice once more.

Breathless from their heavy labors, and still more breathless with anticipation, the seven dared go neither forward nor back. Timidly, they picked the fattest crucians out of the catch, spitted the golden-scaled fish on the stakes and cooked them in the way they used when they were boys. The man who had called to them began to come down the slope, with the sure step of the mountain traveler, and they recognized him by his walk, though they scarcely dared look in his direction.... Mutely, with beating hearts, they took the bread that he offered them once more with his kind blessing.

All around them was the morning stillness of the lake and their own dear, bright landscape.

Thaddeus had dragged a wineskin out of the hold of the boat but he was ashamed to offer the earthenware bowl, which seemed too poor for the guest. However Jesus paid no heed and took it as if it were a most precious goblet. He saw beads of sweat gathering on the Rock's forehead as he painfully sought for the right words. "Lord—" They would need to be something like this: "Lord, I am taking you at your word. Fulfill yourself. Be the Son of God and the God-King...." But immediately the fear struck him that men might then crucify the miracle-worker a second time. Not only the Judaeans, as King of the Jews, but everyone, everyone, as King of the World. Crosses, and crucified men, to the very tops of the highest mountains, on the last cliffs of the shore, at every crossroads, over every bed, in the hand of every dying man, on every grave. Poor Lord Jesus!

Peter fearfully swallowed the last morsel, startled by the

shadow of the guest as he bent down to him. The blood mounted hotly to his cheeks as he heard the gentle question: "Simon son of Jonah, do you love me?" Peter looked him steadfastly in the eye. "Yes, Lord, you know that I love you."

"Then feed my goats."

Be a fisherman and a herdsman too? Peter was nonplused. Naturally, he knew how to look after animals. When he was too small to help in the boat, he used to drive the goats of the poorest folk in Bethsaida out to graze. How they stank in their cheerful malice! Bleating, they would bound higher and higher up the rocks, playfully teasing him in his weeping anger. The child had climbed after them, his legs scratched with thorns, and lashed out with his switch, half in rage, half in fear, at the monster that was so much bigger than himself, till the great he-goat on the highest rock lowered his horns and with a devilish glare in his wicked eyes, with their long rectangular pupils, challenged the little herdboy so that he stopped uncertainly, and slipped back in the loose rubble.

The whispered question came again: "Simon, do you love me more than all these others?" And the impatient fisherman answered: "Yes, Lord, you know I love you."

"Then feed"—his voice was full of compassion and of kindly irony at the mention of such a gentle vocation—"my sheep." Still the Rock did not assent. But he was sad and knew why the Master asked him for a third time. Was it from pity and forbearance that he avoided using the name Peter, the name "Rock," at which the cock had thrice crowed, as he called to his old companion, louder this time: "Simon, do you love me?" Grieved, Peter answered roughly: "Lord, you know everything. You know that I love you." The Master nodded sympathetically. "Very well, then. I tell you that when you were younger, you girded yourself and set out wherever you wished. But when you are an old man, you will reach out your hands and another will prepare you for the journey, and will guide you where you do not want to go." He stood up and ordered: "Follow me!"

They walked along the shore, and Peter turned the words over and over in his mind. Could he speak without being called a Satan again? Yet Jesus was taking him with him, the one who denied him, the one who always knew better and who failed every time, the man of all men.... "And still, Master," he cried jubilantly, "I am yours. I, the one the rooster mocked, the hero of the severed ear, I who cannot read or write, one among a thousand shepherds, fishermen, peasants. Yet you take me with you! I am so poor and so wicked that I understand the poorest and wickedest better than you in your goodness.... Forgive my sin! I am beside myself with happiness." He would have liked to kiss the hand of the figure walking in front of him, but he noticed that John had drawn near again, the favorite, learned in the Holy Scriptures, to whom Jesus had entrusted his mother. He had been allowed to lay his head on Jesus's breast at the Last Supper. He had not asked: "Lord, is it I?" but: "Who is it who will betray you?" Grieved, Peter whispered: "Master, what of this one?"

He did not ask out of his old ambition, nor with the jealousy of the past three years. He asked in perplexity, and with a guilty conscience. Jesus smiled to see how ashamed his faithful companion was because he had not stood beneath the cross, and how grieved because the sad, beautiful woman with the white streak in her hair had since become the mother of John. Half in reprimand, half in consolation, came the answer: "If I wish that this one should stay here, what is that to you?"

Simon was forgotten, Peter remained, who knew that he was a rock because his Jesus understood him and smilingly trusted him. "Yes, Lord, I am for you the weakness of mankind, on which your work is founded in eternity."

But the Lord spoke with enough trust to last a thousand years and more: "Follow me!"

Peter's heart leaped into his throat for joy, so that he could not utter his "Yes." He gazed at the Lord with eyes in which there was nothing but the sun-bright Jesus.

NOT to leave Jerusalem but to wait there for the Almighty's promise, was Jesus's last command before he vanished from the sight of his eleven disciples. They had gathered once more in the house of Mark's mother, though the women feared for their lives. They had come there from the Mount of Olives, to the indignation of the Sanhedrin who had met to discuss the extermination of Simon and his Barjonim. Towards midnight, the decaprot Nicodemus visited the disciples to tell them that the venerable rabbi Hillel had insisted on being carried to the meeting in the interests of truth and justice.

Caiaphas had hurled bitter reproaches at Nicodemus and Joseph of Rama. He said they were polluted by contact with the dead. "I was the first one on whom the blood of the Son of Man fell," interjected Nicodemus, and the others understood him, for they had brought down that innocent blood on themselves and their children.

"Move away from him!" The voice of old Annas shrilled. "He helped in that lie about the stolen corpse."

But the venerable Hillel, who all his life had insisted on the strictest truth, pronounced his judgment: "Throughout the centuries, you, the descendants of Aaron, shall be witnesses that the crucified Jesus of Nazareth on the third day rose from the dead." The Sadducees, the household of the high priest, Segan, the whole Sanhedrin, covered their ears as Hillel ceremoniously proclaimed: "Pilate gave you the bravest soldiers in the world to keep watch over the grave. With the holy seal of Solomon you guarded the tomb. But the sentries gave evidence here before us. They saw the cherub. In obedience to the new Law he rolled the stone aside and sat down upon it. The Roman soldiers lay as if dead; when they returned to their senses, they found the grave empty. But you gave them money and lied and incited them to lie. 'Say the Nazarene's disciples stole the corpse in the night while we were asleep.' And you had to reveal your deception to the heathen Pilate himself so that he would not punish the legionaries." The kindly Gamaliel added contemptuously: "There are Roman sentries all over the world, and they have to fall asleep just here! When the Syrians jeered at them, the Romans shouted the truth in their faces. From the Syrians it spread to the Galileans, from them the world has heard it. So you have made known the resurrection of Christ—you, of all people—for all time to come."

Nicodemus warned Segan Malchus, who wanted to arrest the apostles, that no miracle-worker would stick on the ear of the handsome Temple captain for a second time. Then he calmed down the Sanhedrin: "You can breathe easier! Jesus of Nazareth has ascended in his might to Jahveh, and is enthroned on his right hand. You will see him again when he comes to judge the living and you, the dead. But to those who believe in him he is eternal day to the end of the world." And old Hillel whispered before he died: "Ours is the Chosen People, for from them the Messiah has come."

The apostles had never entered again the room where the Last Supper had been held. But on the first day of the week following Easter, despite the barricaded door, Jesus stood among them there. "Peace be with you," he had said to his disconcerted disciples, and had breathed on them with all the warmth of his manly breath. "Receive the Holy Ghost."

Peter had brooded day and night over his mission as a shepherd. If, according to Christ's orders, he repeated the Supper, with the blessing of the bread and wine, would they not quarrel again about where they were to sit? Would not James, the learned heir of rich Zebedee, his former master, or John, the appointed son of Jesus's mother, demand precedence?

After some hesitation, Peter, at last master of his emotions, called the bond servant, Rhoda, who humbly peered in behind Mark's mother. His call for a pitcher and basin sounded rough and louder than he had intended. He asked the servant to bring him the slave apron of humility. Then he knelt before James. "When our Master washed our feet here, it was as an example to us to do to each other as he had done. I owe it you, to wash your feet."

None of them dared restrain him. Peace was with them, as Jesus's greeting had so often begged. One after another they bent over the humble Peter as he knelt before them in turn to pour the warm water on each instep. The first, his boyhood companion from Bethsaida, begged to be allowed to do him the same service. The other son of Zebedee, when his turn came, whispered, with a regretful smile at his own former ambition: "Those on whom the Almighty Father confers the right, shall sit on either side of our Lord. . . ."

Then all of them recalled sayings of the Lord, conferring honor and precedence on Peter. The tears came when he looked at Thomas, who resembled the Risen One like a twin, and who whispered with Jesus's knowing smile: "He who is our servant shall be the first among us. Did not the Master say so?"

Humbly Nathanael beat his breast. "Jesus called me a trusty Israelite, but he gently reminded me that I had first believed in him because he knew about the fig tree. Yet he only had to look at you and he said: 'Simon son of Jonah, you shall be called a Rock.'"

"Fishers of men, you and I!" cried Andrew, while the cautious peasant Bartholomew respectfully embraced his old friend from the Galilean homeland, saying: "On you, you Rock, he will build his church." Impetuously, the Zealot interjected: "And the gates of hell shall not prevail against you."

Jacob the Tsaddik, Thaddeus, and, last of all, the timid tax collector were still waiting for Peter to favor them. Jacob nodded at him solemnly and his words sounded like a prayer. "Bind yourself close to me. Then I know that we shall be bound together in Heaven too, you and I. I do not want to miss you in eternity." His younger brother had already flung his arms wide apart. "Feed me as God's lamb!" But Matthew unrolled his precious parchment and read aloud: "I will give you the key to the Kingdom of Heaven, thus said the Lord."

ON THE first day of his mission as a shepherd, Peter had to gather together all the disciples who had been begging for admission into their band ever since they heard of the apostles' return, for the ceremonial election of a successor to Judas Iscariot. In the place where he had been buried, everything remained desolate. For that bloody field, the words of the psalm are apt: "His habitation shall be made desolate, no one shall live there any more," and for him who found no mercy there: "His office shall belong to another." With a simple prayer the Rock began to cast lots to determine which disciple should take up his duties as one of the Twelve. The conditions were strict: He must have been with Jesus the whole time, from the baptism in the Jordan to the morning of the Ascension, a witness of the resurrection, and one who knew that, according to the ancient prophecies of Isaiah, Daniel and Ezekiel, the Son of Man would go from them, ahead of them all, "with his bones clad in flesh, to see God." The lot fell on Matthew. With three years of Jesus behind them, and thousands of years ahead of them, they waited now, and prayed. Peter's words strengthened them: "He who perseveres to the end, shall be saved." No more was necessary.

Till now, the group had not dared to leave the house of Mark's mother. Death was lurking around them. They sang softly at nights, they prayed in a whisper by day. They fasted and waited. "You will have the strength as soon as you are filled with the Holy Ghost." Then they would be Jesus's witnesses in Jerusalem and in all Judaea and Samaria and on to the end of the world, as the Son of Man had prophesied.

Now one of the most important feasts was at hand. Every day the bond servant Rhoda or the old man who came home with the water pitcher reported that Temple servants were lurking about on the corners, that hostile elements were gathering, and finally, on the morning of the feast of Moses's Lawgiving, armed men drew up by the gateway of the high priests' palace, amid the shouting of orders and the clatter of gear. Pilgrims from all over the Diaspora had gathered in the squares—believers of the twelve tribes and new "God-fearers," recently converted to Jahveh. They stood around the scribes and listened to the disputations of Pharisees and Sadducees, of doubters and die-hards, as they shouted and made threatening gestures at each other. However, all agreed on one thing: Today would prove whether the last of the Barjonim would dare to show themselves. It was known that orthodox believers were hidden in the constantly shuttered house, who kept all the observances and missed no holy festivals, men such as the sons of Zebedee, and Jacob the Righteous, who was said to have calluses on his knees from the Temple floor. And now the door would have to open to allow them to go to the Temple, as God had ordained. Then Segan Malchus would surround them and the Sanhedrin would stamp out the last sparks of hellish fire.

Unseen, Peter peered down at those lurking by the house. As this was a matter that concerned not only their lives, but

Jesus and eternity, they had asked Matthew that evening to read them the Master's sermons once more. Nicodemus had come late at night. He tried to warn them of the Sanhedrin's unshakable determination, but the listeners had waved him aside. "Woe unto you, you scribes and Pharisees, you hypocrites! A nest of serpents and a viper brood! ... how shall you escape damnation?" At the words "Jerusalem, that slays the prophets..." he looked up. Sadly he counted the few disciples. Thousands of enemies would be making the pilgrimage to the Temple that morning, among them a young scribe from Tarsus, Saul, the implacable hater among the pupils of the mild Gamaliel. The youth were flocking to him. And how they would rejoice at his furious cry of "Stone them!"

A Mount of Olives night, without sleep or rest, ensued for the Rock. His feverish pulse seemed to be hammering threats in his ears: "He who renounces me before mankind, him shall I renounce before the Father.... They would be locked out of the synagogue...scourged...Has the hour already come when those who kill you believe they are doing God a service?" —As if in a foundering boat, he felt like crying out: Help us, Lord, or we perish! But he knew the answer: "Man of little faith, why did you doubt?"

Silent and weary, the disciples got up for their ceremonial washing and their morning prayers. They put on the prayer shawls that were also shrouds. With trembling hands, the women adorned themselves for the festival. On the mouths of many of them were brave, mad smiles. And so they prepared for the sacrificial procession, with themselves as the sacrifice.

The serving maid, Rhoda, drew aside the curtains from the windows of the room where the Last Supper had taken place. The early sunlight streamed in, and the sounds of the street below—psalms of execration and revenge. No one in the house had dared to speak as yet, then Peter threw himself on his knees, his hands raised to heaven: "Son of God! I dare not say again: I would give my soul for you. See, how few of us have remained faithful! Where are they, whose sins you forgave, who can see now, and hear, and are risen from the dead? You chose us, but those who murdered you are triumphant. In Samaria, the magician Simon Magus is deluding the masses.

Saul and those round him are threatening murder. We are standing beneath our crosses already, a hail of stones is clouding the sky above us, but you told us you are the light of the world. You came to bring fire. What do you want? That it should burn? You said: 'The last shall be first.' The last of your followers, the handful in this room, are the very last of all—but the first in the world to come. Let heaven and earth be kindled by our fire!

"Fire!" the cry roared from the breast of the fisherman, who was used to shouting orders in the storm. "Fire!" The others sprang to their feet with a cry of alarm that changed immediately to one of jubilation.

In the sunny Whitsun morning such a gale arose that superstitious folk groaned: "An earthquake wind!" With trembling fingers they pulled the prayer shawls about them, while the followers of Caiaphas and Saul, and those who shouted "Crucify him!", beside themselves with terror, pointed up at the windows of the house where the apostles were staying.

It had stood there, a dead block, seemingly rigid with terror. But now the curtains blew out of the windows as if from some storm inside, and fluttered and cracked like sails torn loose in the wind. At the same time a light streamed from the house, a light so powerful that the sun seemed dull and tarnished. At the sight of that tremendous glow, the timid were seized with terror, and a murderous joy flashed through the hearts of those consumed by hatred.

But inside the house, the apostles were still more stirred, terrified at first, then all the more elated. It was inexplicable where this gale had sprung from that roared through the room and shook their hearts. Peter and his companions were amazed to find themselves surrounded with sparks. There was a crackling and sparkling, a rustling and flickering about them, such as surrounds a mountain traveler as he walks through the storm clouds on the highest rocks, lightning above him, lightning below him, hair and fingers and iron charged with sparks and death.

But here, it was hearts and souls that were afire. With ecstatic eyes they watched the fiery tongues that divided up and descended in gentle brightness about the heads that Jesus had blessed and John had baptized. They looked at each other in amazement as their heads blazed like jeweled lamps, glittering golden reliquaries for the Word that was God. Now they felt the tempest inside their brows and temples. With their tongues aflame, they began a chant that rang out clearer and clearer into the street.

The storm had died down as unexpectedly as it had arisen, and the hush of a nameless fear fell on the packed crowd in the square below and in the nearby streets. Would the earth open up as it had at the Nazarene's death cry? Yet out of the fiery glow within the room, no dreadful cries for help came, but the sound of rejoicing, of stammering happiness, of jubilant hymns, so that those below whispered to each other: "Are they not Galileans up there?" The crowd became more and more disconcerted, especially those who had come from far away, Parthians, Medes, Elamites, men from the land of the two rivers, and those from the Black Sea, and the God-fearers from Egypt, Libya, and Cyrenaica, proselytes from Rome, Cretans and Arabs, who could hardly understand each other's speech. In Greek, Latin, Aramaic, they cried to each other: "How is it that we hear them speaking of the great deeds of the Almighty in our own tongue? How long is it since I heard anyone speak like my father and mother and my playmates?"

But the men standing in Caiaphas's gateway shouted mockingly over the heads of the crowd: "They are drunk with sweet wine!"

Peter sprang up. The Twelve could not restrain themselves. They ran, or rather the storm within them carried them along, up the stairs onto the flat roof and across to its balustraded edge. They stood in a row, the target of the Temple soldiers, the target of hatred and mockery. And in the intoxication of their joy they were derided once more: "Look how they stagger, the drunkards!"

The Fisher of Men laughed aloud. Derision against derision, he shouted: "Drunk? We? Already? Three hours after sunrise?" Secretly he wondered where he got the courage from, he who could not bear to hear a cock crow, and who was full of shame that he had not struck harder at Malchus. But now that he had begun to speak, no one dared laugh. Dumbstruck, they realized they were confronted with the most mysterious, most improbable miracle of mortal man: To understand and to be understood.

Now that the apostles understood Jesus, they understood everyone. The high tower of Babel had collapsed before them, with the curse that had been laid upon it. Now each man in the crowd heard only words to which he had been accustomed as a child, but words which struck deeper at his heart than ever before. Every man's favorite prophet spoke to the unease of his heart and the hope of his days: Joel spoke of death and the final judgment, and David, who trusted God, sang: "My tongue rejoices . . ."

They were listening to a speaker entirely lacking in tricks of oratory, but from whose mouth issued the breath of God. After all their fear of earthquakes and curses they heard the blissful promise: "It shall come to pass that you shall call on the name of the Lord and shall be saved!"

Many of them began to fear the punishment of the Sanhedrin, when the bold man on the rooftop cried: "Jesus of Nazareth, proved by God through mighty deeds and signs and miracles which God has worked through him in your midst— and you know it!—Jesus of Nazareth you nailed up and killed, according to God's prophecy and decree." But none of the Sanhedrin dared contradict him now. The words of David were quoted against them: "His prophecy is fulfilled; on God's own throne sits Christ, the Son of David, whom you have crucified." What spirit spoke through this preacher and the eleven around him? With tongues of flame in their mouths, they sat in judgment over a whole people. Unnerved, those below called him "Brother," and cried imploringly: "What shall we do?"

As they stood there still blinded by the surge of fire from the Holy Ghost, they were answered with the mighty promise that they themselves might receive the Spirit. It was a promise extended to all, whether in Jerusalem or far away, as many as the Lord our God shall summon!

The twelve disciples had not water enough for that day's

baptisms. They went with the first believers to the pool of Beth-Hasda, of which it was said that an angel set it boiling every day with his wings. Three thousand of them knelt with the disciples in the Temple and offered up a prayer of thanks. It was a harvest-thanksgiving like those in the old days of the prophets, a harvest of souls. Caiaphas's palace lay in darkness, shuttered and bolted and as if dead. The torn curtain hung limp before the Holy of Holies.

Peter swung himself on the edge of the "Sea of Brass" in the joyous realization of how great was his power in heaven and on earth. Like a Rock, he had taken on himself the host of new believers, though they came from every part of the world. The glow of eternal Whitsun was about him.

TWELVE years had passed since Jesus's farewell on the Mount of Olives and his promise to return. Peter had started his travels in the fifth decade of his life. At first Mark and Thaddeus accompanied him, both of them now grown to manhood, the one eager to learn, and trying to keep the Master's every word in his memory, the other all love and devotion. According to divine command, they had set out without knapsack or shoes, with only the barest necessities tucked into their sleeves. But the youngest apostle had a leather bag hung about his neck on a long strap, which he never took off, even when he lay down to sleep. The bag contained his most precious possession, which he had begged from the pious Sister Veronica, she who had gently wiped the blood and sweat off Jesus's face with a fine cloth, while he was panting and struggling under the monstrous burden of the cross. When she went to fold up her kerchief again, it bore the features of the Saviour, distorted with pain. But Veronica could not bear to look at the agonized and loving eyes, and she gave the kerchief to Thaddeus, the favorite of them all. When critical decisions were to be made, the Twelve took heart and resolution from God's gaze.

Decisions must be taken for centuries to come. There were conflicts of words, conducted with wisdom and an unwonted display of love; conflicts of the soul, waged with implacable harshness against themselves, against the ancient Law, and against the prejudices of their own people. Most of the disciples, like Peter, were accustomed to work, to action, to the restlessness of the Son of Man. In the first few weeks they had a sense of being locked up within themselves in meditation and speculation whether and when the Lord would return; but following the Whitsun miracle the candidates for baptism began to flock to them in thousands. The faithful lived together and shared everything communally. "Like tending the herds of the erring stars..." murmured Thaddeus, as he brooded on the difficulties of keeping order among such a motley crowd as were attaching themselves day by day to the community of the apostles. The rich gave all they had, and the poor gave themselves, as they came to understand the wisdom of Jesus's words: "You are all brothers." They began to relive the life of Jesus as, one after another, the apostles related the Master's works, his words, his wonders.

MIRACLES! Because of them, the Sanhedrin had repeatedly summoned the Twelve before them, and especially Peter. They had thrown them all into jail, and despite guards and chains and iron portcullis, the apostles had made their way back to the Temple to preach the Word of Life. "God, not man, must be obeyed!" Only the intercession of the wise Gamaliel had saved them from being stoned. He had pleaded with the Temple priests: "Leave these men be and let them do their will. If it is but man's will and man's work, it will perish; if it comes from God, then you can never destroy it."

The mighty men of Jahveh did not dare to lay hands on Peter now, for they knew he had been given power over life and death. Anyone looking at him had to remember the fate of Ananias and Sapphira. This couple had sold all their belongings in order to take their place in the holy community, but the husband had laid only a part of the proceeds at Peter's feet. "How dare you deceive the Holy Ghost? It is not men you are cheating, but the Almighty!" When Ananias heard these words, he fell dead on the spot. Three hours later his wife Sapphira entered, knowing nothing of her husband's death. Peter asked her: "Did you truly sell your goods for this price?" "For that price exactly," she lied, and the words of judgment rang in her ears: "How could you conspire to cheat the Lord. Beware! The feet of those who buried your husband are at the door, ready to bear you away." Her throat rattled, and she fell at the feet of the Rock.

It was not only the believers and unbelievers who were frightened of his deathly power. Peter himself tried to keep his righteous anger in check. He could no longer fling himself at Jesus's feet with the confession: "Go away from me, for I am a man who errs, Lord!" All too often he found himself on the verge of flying into a passion as he had when he upbraided the Son of Man for prophesying his death. He forced himself to be mild when the baptized God-fearers from Antiochia and Alexandria, formerly pagans, then orthodox Jews, but now pious followers of the teachings of Jesus, complained that the widows of their people were being neglected in matters of daily welfare, compared with the baptized Hebrew women.

While the twelve disciples reserved for themselves the care of praying and preaching, they chose from the Hellenistic Antiochians and Alexandrians seven young men as deacons, fiery, well-educated scholars, whose task was to attend to the food and everyday requirements. Peter had to wrestle with himself not to work some dreadful miracle, when the boldest and most scholarly of the deacons, Stephen by name, was put to death because he had repeatedly leveled accusations at the Sanhedrin, based on his deep knowledge of the scriptures. On the evidence of false witnesses, they charged him with blasphemy, and he lashed out at them with the bitter truth: "You dash yourselves against the Holy Ghost, just as your fathers did!" The high priests ground their teeth in fury. When their prisoner cried out with shining eyes: "I see the heavens open and the Son of Man on the right hand of God," they pressed their fists over their ears, and screamed that he should be stoned, and dragged him to the wall.

The faithful ran to Peter for help. "Strike them to hell with your key! Save Stephen!" But Peter beat his breast and prayed: "Lord, you have forbidden me the sword. Lord, you have twelve hosts of angels. Lord, you prayed for mercy for your murderers; they know not what they do...."

In the meantime, those who were going to do the stoning had laid their garments at the feet of the apostles' fiercest enemy. Peter knew Saul of Tarsus only too well. How he despised him, that Pharisee who gave himself the airs of a Roman! He had been born of the people of faith, was imbued with the knowledge of the people of wisdom, and wore the toga of the people of power, and on that account he was not to be touched, under pain of the most rigorous punishment. "Master, are you going to allow Saul to look on while Stephen is stoned to death?" Only Stephen spoke. As the light went from his eyes, he prayed like Jesus on the cross: "Lord, do not lay this sin to their account."

The community dispersed. Peter sent his wife and child home. He told everyone to flee, for Saul had already begun searching the houses and dragging men and women off to jail, to the gratification of those up on Moriah. Only the twelve apostles remained. In the midst of their grief over the death of the beloved deacon, news came which gave rise to further anxiety. Philip, a deacon of Stephen's fiber, had gone to Samaria, a land of lawless heresies. "Pig's blood is purer than water in Samaria" was an old saying. The disciples themselves had hardly concealed their annoyance when they saw Jesus talking to a woman of this race at the well of Sichar.

In a storm of fury, Peter resolved to intervene, but he took John with him, to remind him that "he who loves not is of the hosts of death." It was rumored that before Philip had arrived, the magician Simon the Magus had made his appearance in Samaria, had seduced the people with his magic arts, and was calling himself the Power of God. "I wonder if Simon Magus will remember Simon son of Jonah of the Baptist's camp?" Peter laughed grimly. "Now he is admiring our Philip. They say he has had himself baptized by him. Because he is a Samaritan himself."

Through prayer and the laying on of hands, the two messengers from Jerusalem taught the Samaritans the meaning of the Word, of the Faith, of the Spirit of Life. It was a miracu-

167

lous transformation of a whole people from the outward to the inner forms of belief.

Peter hardly recognized Simon the Sorcerer, who had never appeared so humble as now, when he was imploring him to grant him the grace to be a bearer of the Holy Spirit. His request came hard to Peter, who knew of the magician's boundless pretensions. What would happen if he were able to boast that he was a bearer of the Holy Spirit? John reminded the Fisher of Men in a whisper how he had once complained to Jesus that someone, not a follower of the disciples, was driving out devils in his name. "Do not forbid him," Jesus had advised with a smile, "for he who is not against us is with us." Simon Magus grew impatient, for he could not understand the apostle's hesitation. He offered money if he too might be able to practice the laying on of hands and to impart the Holy Ghost to others.

"Money?" Peter could hardly control himself. In an access of fury he vented his horror of those who thought to buy the grace of God. "Your money perish with you! Your heart is insincere before God. Repent of your wickedness and pray God to forgive you for what is in your heart." The magician quailed before his threat and could only stammer: "Pray to the Lord for me, so that what you have said may not befall me."

Had the Rock became too hard? And did not harder tests of his charity lie ahead? The mere mention of the name of Saul was enough to make the veins stand out on his forehead. Yet the day came when the much-feared Zealot of Tarsus made his way to the house of Mark's mother. Above his superciliously arched eyebrows rose the dome of his massive head, the pale skin shining through the thin hair that hung down to his shoulders. His narrow, distinguished nose curved down above his mouth, which concealed its scornful mastery under a drooping mustache. He wanted to see the disciples. In vain! His whole being brought with it a sense of paralyzing terror, as if a merciless and bloodthirsty horde were lurking behind him. Might they not have sent him on ahead, so that he could secretly open the door to them? Would the blood-spattered fanatics cast the garments of the Twelve at his feet, would

168

they drive the sons of Jonah and Zebedee and all the Galileans out of the town, and spit on them, cuff them, club them, maim and kill them with sharp stones? Saul stood outside the locked door, at his back the hatred of the Temple dignitaries, who held him guilty of the capital offense of heresy, and before him, the ineradicable sorrow of his responsibility for the death of Stephen. In the stillness, the echo of his futile knocking terrified him more than any thought of vengeance for Stephen's blood.

It was a day of shocks. Barnabas, Mark's uncle, had taken pity on him, and implored the Rock to receive his erstwhile enemy. The room of the Last Supper was deserted. The Twelve had locked themselves away for prayers. Deathly pale, Saul listened uneasily as they sang the hundred-and-ninth psalm:

> *"He loved cursing. The curse upon him!*
> *He delighted not in blessing, let blessing abandon him.*
> *Clothe him, you curses, like a garment!"*

When the strains of the last verse of the Mantle of Shame had died away, Barnabas called Peter by name, repeating Jesus's words: "Lord, how often shall I forgive my brother when he sins against me? To the seventy-and-seventh time!"

At last the door opened. The sturdy fisherman and the slender thinker stood face to face. Peter felt like asking Stephen's forgiveness for such treachery. But the stoned man's last cry sounded again in his ears. The victim had forgiven his murderers. The chief apostle stood like a rock, staring past the conscience-stricken Saul into the depths of the unforgettable eyes of the dead deacon. In that way, he listened to the account of the journey Saul had made to Damascus, to seize men and women who believed in Jesus and to drag them to Jerusalem in chains. The penitent Pharisee told of the vision that had blinded him; was he the last man on earth that Jesus had spoken to? He had said to him: "I am Jesus, whom you are persecuting." Peter bowed his head and beat his breast and—difficult though it was—he forgave him.

The other put away his pride and listened to what the simple fisherman had to say. He asked question after question till James, the most pious of the pious, came to Peter's aid. The other apostles avoided the stranger. None of them showed himself. The "Pillars," Peter and James, sent the great pupil of Hillel home to Tarsus, to commune with himself and to meditate on the words of the two apostles.

Here was glory and salvation at the same time, for in Jerusalem, the Jews of the Temple were seeking to encompass his death; and now the mighty man of hate thought only of love, and was to teach that "it surrounds everything with silence, it believes everything, hopes everything, endures everything." But as yet he dared not tell mankind how much he loved it.

As HE lay resting at midday, Peter thought of the incredible speed at which the years in Jerusalem had passed. Here he was, several days' journey from the sacred soil of the city of David, in the former land of the Philistines, ready like Samson to tear down the heathen temple that towered up so resplendently. It was here that the noble Andromeda had been chained to the rock and Perseus had freed her. Guides had swarmed round the apostle as he walked out, trying to show him the basin in which the hero had washed his hands after killing the dragon.

He shuddered with the disgust which every true Jew, however poor and despised, felt in the presence of the unclean customs and beliefs of the heathen. However, Simon the tanner, who had received him so hospitably, was a godly man who followed the law of Moses. He had sent word to the apostle: "I am not poor, and after work, mine is a restful house. The old fig tree in the courtyard gives shade; there is a deep well directly in front of it. To right and left, stone steps lead up to the rooms. True, the tanning vats are beside the steps; some people think my work unclean, because of the smell of tan, but my good colored leather is praised everywhere."

Over the flat roof of his handsome house, the tanner had rigged up a worn sail on four poles, as a canopy against the sun. The densely woven material filtered the hot golden light of high noon, so that the couch and the meal table were in the shade. The lake, the sun, and the frolicsome wind that tugged at the poles, now lifting the sail into a tight vault, now rumpling it till it cracked—all this was very much after Peter's heart, who was at home on the sea. He could not get enough of the view over the lake, and when he gazed at it he almost forgot the enormous happiness of his success in Joppa. The fine purple overgarment spread over one of the taut guy ropes was a present from the city's generous benefactress, Tabitha. With tears, she had persuaded him to take it. The rough homespun robe he had worn till then seemed good enough to him, though it was threadbare from many sea trips and countless journeys, and had been patched and darned everywhere, not only by Joanna and her mother, but also by the mother of Jesus. When he had come in with the sweat from the sultry streets still on his brow, he had remembered to draw the purple robe over his head and hang it up before sinking down on the cushions.

Now for the first time Peter became aware that voices down in the street were repeatedly calling his name. The impatient clapping of innumerable hands accompanied the joyful cries. Peter shook his head angrily. He was not going to slip his garment on again for the sake of such cheering. Was the enthusiasm genuine? Did he deserve it?

Tabitha, the generous benefactress of Joppa, had died of a serious illness. Her body had already been laid out when the mourners sent for Peter, who was preaching at Lystra. With wild weeping and lamentation, they begged him to help as he stood by the deathbed. Mark and Thaddeus stayed unobtrusively in the background. When they looked at Peter, they folded their trembling hands with such ardor that their joints cracked. They prayed so hard, with every muscle tense, that the very core of their brain began to ache.

But in a calm voice, Peter had ordered: "Leave me alone!" Men, women and children drew shyly back. The two disciples were the last to leave. They drew the curtain over the doorway.

The Rock took three long breaths, then threw himself on his knees beside the bier on which the veiled woman lay. He closed his eyes and repeated the words he had learned from Jesus when his Master had cried out on the road to Gethsemane: "Father, now the hour is come! Glorify your son that your son may glorify you!" As if unseen hands were lifting him, he stood up, his eyes on the dead woman as he said in a powerful voice: "Tabitha, stand up!"

Over her gently curving breast, the veil seemed to lift as if she were sighing, then it sank, and lifted again. In a flood of joy, Peter saw her eyelids flutter. Her folded hands parted and groped for support; her slender left foot glided to the floor, the right followed. Slowly, still rather weak, she took the outstretched hands of the man before her, a man unknown and yet somehow familiar. He helped her to her feet. She was frightened at the power of his voice, as he called the others back into the room.

Impetuously, Thaddeus had drawn back the curtain, and the metal rings clashed together, as if to accompany his joyous cry: "She lives!"

Supported on the fisherman's arm, the weary, graceful woman became more and more awake. With a happy smile on her still youthful lips, she saw old and young rush towards her to cover her veil, her hands, her shoes with kisses. Maternally, she spread her arms to all her dependents.

But Peter had left the house, silently motioning his companions to follow him. As he went, he indicated with an almost imperceptible nod Simon the tanner, who was leaning against the wall near the doorway. His prayer shawl had fallen from his shoulders, unnoticed by him. He was gazing with enraptured eyes at the beautiful woman as her protégés rejoiced around her. Huge tears were running down his cheeks into his gray beard, and onto his trembling lips which softly stammered: "Tabitha. . . ."

PETER's memory was like a bronze tablet. Once he took in a thing, he retained it forever. Now, dozing in Joppa, strange figures appeared to him, of Greeks who had implored their fellow countryman Philip to make it possible for them to speak to Jesus after the triumphal procession of Palm Sunday. The disciple had not dared go alone to the Master with a request from the heathen, so Andrew had accompanied him.

Jesus's answer was unforgettable: "The hour is come when the Son of Man should be glorified." Had not Jahveh prophesied to the Messiah through the mouth of Isaiah: "See, I give you as a light to the heathen, so that you may be for salvation to the uttermost ends of the earth." And at his farewell, before he was taken from the disciples, Jesus had said that they should go out into the world as his heralds to bear the glad tidings to all creation.

Was it thunder that sounded out of a clear and cloudless sky? Or was it the voice of some mighty armed angel? The words of Jesus moved him greatly: "Now judgment is delivered on this world: now the prince of this world shall be cast out." Mysterious prophecies issued from his mouth: "As soon as I am carried up, I will gather everything to me...."

In his sleep, the Rock heard a rustling sound, as if some costly linen of vast dimensions were unrolling like a sail big enough to drive a whole island along against the wind and tide. It was tethered to the earth at all four corners.

While it bellied loosely above his head, it seemed to be agitated by a hundred fluttering movements, but before long, it sank down and lay before him like an immense table, spread in readiness for a feast. And only then did he realize what was crawling, creeping, flying, hopping about on this enormous tablecloth. He started back aghast, for every kind of beast swarmed in confusion there. Rosy young pigs squealed and jostled against calves, which tried to rear up over the backs of lambs and kids, but could get no foothold on the slack cloth. Ducks and geese bustled noisily towards the margins, and hens fluttered about wildly, in mortal fear of the bears and boars; and in the midst of everything, great shoals of shimmering silver fish of all colors and sizes darted hither and thither, while frogs, snakes and giant squids scurried in every direction. Crabs and lobsters tried to escape by running backwards on their eight long legs. The hunger of all Joppa could not have done away with such abundance.

Peter was nauseated, for the holy Law forbade the eating of these animals as a grievous sin, declaring them unclean. But like mighty laughter, a thundering voice sounded across the vast distances, saying: "Rise, Peter, kill and eat!"

173

It seemed to him that armored angels, as high as towers, were holding all four corners of the boundless sheet. They laughed at him, but he defiantly cried: "No, Lord. I will never eat anything that is prohibited and unclean!"

More solemnly than ever, the voice repeated the command. Paying no heed to his hunger, the fisherman ventured to answer: "Lead us not into temptation." When the order was threateningly repeated for the third time, he could only stare in horror at the hurly-burly in which he now seemed to see the fin-thrust of a gigantic shark, and worms a thousand feet long, crouching beasts of prey, and the whale-huge behemoth of the deep, the entire fifth and sixth days of creation. Again, full of revulsion, he dared to refuse, though he heard for the second time: "What God has declared clean, you shall not call forbidden!" At his third refusal, giant hands lifted the enormous cloth heavenward.

Shuddering, Peter stirred on his couch, at a loss as to the meaning of his dream. He heard his name called again. What bearded angels were these? A soldier stood before him, accompanied by two servants. He greeted him, and asked: "Is this the house of the tanner, Simon; and is Simon, called Peter, staying here?" Peter got up, and made himself known.

"My centurion, Cornelius, whom even the Judaeans call a righteous and God-fearing man, was advised by an angel in a dream to bring you to his house, and to hear from you what has been said." Respectfully, the soldier insisted that Peter must go with him to Caesarea on the following morning at the latest. The centurion's guard quarters were still in the palace of the late Herod the Great, though the return of his successor, Herod Agrippa, was expected. The Romans had held him for years as a hostage, along with other princes, but Caligula, a friend of the young Hasmonite, had released the noble prisoner immediately on the death of the Emperor Tiberius, and had presented him with a golden chain similar to the iron one which he had been obliged to wear as a hostage. Since Pilate had failed to pacify the Promised Land, they would have to try to do so with a native king. If he too failed, the legions would trample the country underfoot.

Sadly, Peter nodded: "That will not be long now." He repeated Jesus's words: "Then shall the dweller in Judaea flee into the mountains, and he who stands on the roof shall not go down to fetch his garment."

"Those who have power over the other world, like you, are fortunate. We have had more than enough of fighting and looting, and now we are thinking of things to come. The youngsters in our legion are the same. . . . Partisan warfare and Parthian battles both teach a man to think. What is waiting for us after death? Jupiter and Mars"—he pointed to the reliefs of the gods on his medals—"hardly scare the enemy any more. The more we soldiers travel in the world, the more gods we encounter. And we are obliged to come to terms even with the gods of those we conquer. And on top of that, with every new emperor a new god arises."

"Render to Caesar what is Caesar's and to God what is God's, was Jesus's answer to the Pharisees' question," replied Peter cautiously. The messenger from Cornelius looked at him in surprise, and said with a smile: "In the eastern part of the empire here, we are ordered to begin our prayers—if we are speaking Greek—with the formula: 'Kyrie Kaisar!' What are we to do?"

"Our prayer says: 'Kyrie eleison!' We have but the one master, our Kyrios. It is a battle cry also."

"Let us hope the Emperor Caligula does not kill you for it. Nor us either. We side with you. Not only those of us who are here, but the whole of our famous Twelfth Legion, the Thunder and Lightning Legion, as we are called."

A legion of the heathen army, gone over to Christ? Peter was obliged to close his eyes. Roman soldiers had put the purple garment on Jesus, had crowned him with thorns. Legionaries had divided up the robes of the Crucified One amongst themselves, and had diced for his seamless undergarment. The sail above the fisherman's head cracked violently in the wind; he looked up, as if the huge tablecloth were spread above him again, with all kinds of food upon it, food which he was forbidden to call unclean. . . . Go out and teach all peoples, had been the last instructions of the Son of Man. It required a great effort on his part to decide to follow the Roman. But had not Saul of Tarsus told of a similar task allotted to him by Jesus through a believer in Damascus—Saul, who used to boast that he was more zealous than anyone in upholding the traditions of his forefathers?

As Peter entered Herod's stronghold in Caesarea, the mighty Cornelius, lord of the cavalry and infantry, master of the city, sank on his knees before the son of the poor Bethsaida fisherman Jonah. But Peter helped him to his feet, and said kindly: "Rise up. I, too, am but a man."

Stone idols, set up by the Idumaeans so as to curry favor with the emperors, stood along the walls, staring blindly past the Roman's friends, his relatives and servants, and his warriors. The deacon Philip had baptized them also, and introduced them to the sacred customs of the community. From the copy of the notes of Matthew Levi which the Roman officer had bought in Capernaum, most of them were already well acquainted with the deeds and sayings of Jesus of Nazareth, but their great concern was that they might be excluded. "Why should the Judaeans, the murderers of the Son of Man, be permitted to join, and not us?" Who would dare to exclude them from the community of saints, as the original group in Jerusalem called itself, when the Son of Man himself held up Cornelius to his disciples as an example of the deepest faith? "He whose soul dies with him, lives without hope," the centurion lamented. Peter was unable to put the line of a Greek poet—one of the most cheerful, most serene, so it was said—out of his head: *Sorrow is sister to the life of man.* He took the Roman by both hands. "There can be no such thing as a melancholy saint." True, he had wept bitterly himself at the cruel death of Jesus, but since the Risen One had breathed on him, how could mortal man harm him now?

Cornelius wanted to test himself once more, whether he should cling to the old traditions, for he was being recalled to Rome to command the young emperor's guard. He still shuddered with disgust as he spoke of the capital city of the world. Peter listened attentively. He had been receiving letter after letter, asking him to visit the growing community in the Eternal City. "What is a man there?" cried Cornelius. "Something to be slaughtered in hundreds at the festival games, to be crucified in thousands after a victory. In that vast huddle of houses founded by the foster sons of the she-wolf, everyone lies in ambush for everyone else. A man who will not be bribed is persecuted as a spoilsport. Even the gods are for sale."

The Fisher of Men recalled the warning of the most righteous of the apostles, the Tsaddik. "When Jesus began to send us out, he ordered us: 'Tread not the path of the heathen.'" Anxiously, Cornelius watched the apostle, who was sunk in meditation, remembering the Redeemer's words. Bitterly, the Roman interjected: "Are you like Rome's most celebrated orator, who declared that, as a high priest, he knew nothing of his gods? Our Greek teachers are proud to have overthrown their gods by their wisdom. The best of them teach: Virtue is wisdom, ignorance is vice."

Peter smiled, and said soothingly: "As if all knowledge were not merely faith, and faith alone the true wisdom! Jesus never said: 'I have made you whole.' Never: 'I have raised you from the dead.' No, he merely said: 'Your faith has helped you.' The Song of Solomon refers to him alone, when it says: 'All the kings of the earth pray to him, all the peoples serve him.' The Son of Man was a relentless judge. Who of all will be cast into the everlasting fire, where the worm never dies and the flames are never quenched? Shall not the iniquitous sons of the Kingdom, from Abraham's time on, be cast into the darkness where there is wailing and gnashing of teeth?" The fisherman drew himself up and jubilantly repeated the words of Jesus: "To all peoples the Gospel shall be preached!" and he rejoiced to see the shining eyes about him, for he had given them eternity.

IT WAS twelve years to the day since Pilate had ordered the inscription *King of the Jews* to be lettered on a tablet in three languages, and set above the head of the crucified Jesus, to the indignation of the orthodox. And now the followers of that King were making their way to Jerusalem in mourning garments, to climb up the rock steps towards "his Father's house," as he called it, to commemorate the dreadful earth-shaking day of his death. At the same time, two men were entering the city, each unknown to the other, both of them awaited with burning impatience.

The one was poorly dressed in coarse linen, and walked barefoot. A silent woman and a slender girl accompanied him, dressed in the costume of peasants from Lake Genesareth. Their long head shawls hid their neck and shoulders and concealed the precious necklaces of gold coins that were at once ornament and dowry.

The other approached in splendor on a gold-bridled, dapple-gray horse of the finest blood, with two mounted spearmen ahead and on either side of him, and behind him a retinue on horse and on foot. The one was seeking power, the other merely the freedom to bestow spiritual life. The man on horseback presumed to be the Messiah of his people. Woe to all who are not of his persuasion! The other carried the Messiah of loving kindness in his heart, to free the peoples of the world from every kind of enmity, save that towards evil. The priests were awaiting the horseman, dressed in their ancient sacred robes which, at his intercession, Lucius Vitellius, the imperial legate from Syria, had given back after withholding them for years.

Herod Agrippa had left the harbor secretly. After Alexandria, any gathering of men made him uneasy. The huge community of orthodox Jews in Alexandria had greeted him with wild rejoicing when he arrived from Rome. Children had waved palms, and old folk had bowed to the ground. To celebrate the arrival of their long-awaited liberator, tens of thousands of Alexandrian Jews had formed themselves into an enormous procession. And suddenly another procession had surged along the splendid main street, right into the one around Agrippa, a procession that grotesquely aped his triumph, and erupted in a storm of Jewish hatred. Immediately, weapons flashed, stones flew through the air. With difficulty, the Roman guard—supplied as a precaution—had managed to get Caligula's friend out of his litter, and had brought him along narrow alleyways towards the harbor and into safety. Behind him, the homes and synagogues of the Jews were already being stormed, plundered and burned to the ground; their elders dragged to the amphitheater and flogged, women and children in boundless fear of rape and murder fleeing out of the town to the seashore.

At the harbor entrance, Agrippa had stared back in impotent fury at the beautiful, terrible city, whose fires cast a hideous reddish-purple glow over his abortive welcome. Oh, for the power of Herod the Great! How he would have liked to order a massacre of the children, not a modest Bethlehemite one, no, an Alexandrian one of enormous scale!

His nerves could not stand a similar experience in Caesarea. His eunuch had concealed him in a four-wheeled cart, drawn by two mules, the kind of cart found everywhere along the even, paved roads of the Roman empire. On account of the heat, the prince preferred to travel by night, for during the day, the atmosphere under the leather wagon cover was sweltering. Air and light could only enter sparsely through two small slits behind the driver's seat, These slits also served the passenger as a peephole.

Sunk in thought, Agrippa had not at first noticed that the rumble of the wheels had ceased. Through the spy hole he saw that, ahead of the mules, a vast crowd of men stood motionless along the broad highway that led to his great ancestor's stronghold. On the opposite side, a similar dense wall of men was drawn up in tense expectation. Everyone's gaze was turned towards the east. Was it the good people of Caesarea, wanting to do homage to their native ruler?

Nearer and nearer came the roar of singing. A new Sabbath hymn? What were his compatriots celebrating?

With their music master, the synagogue precentors passed by. Men, women and children followed, with hands raised devoutly, and heads humbly bowed. Their jubilant song rang out:

> "Our Lord sleeps not, our Lord slumbers not,
> To him alone our song is raised.
> Like the mighty surge of breakers, like the roar of the
>   waves,
> Our mouths praise him. Our hearts are lifted
> Even to the arch of heaven, and our hymns shall
>   glorify him.

179

You have set weapons in our hands and our foes are
*   downcast.*
You have struck off the chains that bound us;
You are the saviour from the sword and the healer of
*   sickness,*
A thousand thousandfold are your mercies.
Let everyone glorify, praise, laud and honor you.
Where is the mouth that does not profess you,
Where the tongue that does not name you in oath?

"None is so high that he bows not before you,
Nowhere a knee that bends not before you,
Nowhere a heart that trembles not before you.
From every side the worshipers come.
Who is so poor, who so wretched
That he turns not his face to you,
Trembling and praying to you the Redeemer.
Be then our King, for who is like you?"

The vast throng began excitedly to wave to a man they hailed as Simon Peter, the author of the new hymn. They clapped their hands, some wept, some cheered. Children were held in the air. Kerchiefs and palm branches waved overhead, till one single mighty song united all their voices in a sonorous hymn of thanksgiving.

Then Agrippa saw a column of heavily armed legionaries marching past in step, men of the "First Italian Augustus Cohort of Roman Citizens," whose headquarters were in his ancestral fortress. The soldiers were followed by a sturdy man of some forty years old. His grave, kindly face was framed in a thick and lightly graying beard, a fisherman's beard. His hair was shaggy above a forehead that bulged from much meditation. In his expensive purple robe, he gazed straight ahead, for despite all the rejoicing he did not find the way easy. A second column of Roman soldiers completed the procession. . . .

Now, in full splendor, the prince and his cavalcade, which had come through the Herod Gate, was finding it difficult to pass along the narrow streets of the old fortified city, for innumerable pilgrims from the great camp outside Jerusalem had been making their way towards Mount Moriah since early that morning. The three other travelers were just climbing the steps towards the Golden Gate. Peter sought to compose himself in prayer before he came into the presence of his companions to give them a report on his years of wandering.... From the women's courtyard, Joanna and Petronilla looked back at him. "What is written over that gateway where Father is standing?" asked the girl. "The Jesus Door," croaked an elderly goat-bearded man beside her. "It leads all who are not of pure blood as far back as Moses straight to the gallows. Anyone who is just a stray ape of our holy customs can read there, that he only need enter and he is among the dead."

Petronilla huddled close against her mother. With a heavy heart she saw her father embrace one of the marble pillars, which twisted upwards like the gently ascending smoke of a sacrifice, with reliefs of vintners' tools, pitchers, knives and grapes carved on it at regular intervals. "Is not that the pillar which Jesus leaned against when he preached to the disciples?" Joanna nodded in silence, too deeply affected by memories.

Today, the steps seemed lower to Petronilla, the pillars less high, for the tiny girl had now ripened into a beautiful, slender young woman. She would have liked to hurry across to Peter, despite all instructions to the contrary, so as not to leave him alone; for she could not help recalling in terror those early days of her childhood, when her beloved father, that strong and upright man, had been brought home after being flogged. Young disciples supported him and led him along. Blood and tears had mingled on his face. His beard was crusted and dark red, his body naked above the waist, for coarse linen would have been too rough against his swollen weals, which here and there had burst into open wounds. Loudly weeping, the terrified child had clung to Joanna as she hurried to help Peter. The Lord's mother had lovingly bent over the little girl, to take her to her heart. Mary had drawn out a fine kerchief—to Petronilla it seemed as if she could feel it now—and gently dried the child's tear-stained face, and the terrible sight of the scourged man seemed to fade a little into forgetfulness. She lay snugly against the heart of the most maternal of women, who was singing a lullaby under her breath. Just once she had sobbed, and drawn a deep breath, and whispered a few words over the child's head, words whose meaning she still did not grasp, but which she had never forgotten: "What they did to your father, they did to my son. . . ."

The high priest Theophilus emerged from the sanctuary. Young Levites swung the censers from which blue clouds of incense drifted about the descendant of Aaron, who now wore the curious two-horned headdress as proudly as his dead brother Jonathan a year ago. He too was a son of the old priest Annas, and, like Jonathan, he had a harder heart than Caiaphas, who had been dismissed by the Romans in order to check the cruelty of the high priests.

The girl became conscious that glances of deep hatred were being leveled at her father. The first to recognize Peter was Malchus, the Temple captain, who hurried to the mighty Theophilus with his news. Theophilus did not turn his proud head with its curious diadem, but nevertheless, from beneath half-closed lids, he fixed his gaze on his enemy. . . . Amid the fumes of incense and the intoning of hymns, the whole priesthood walked in procession past the Rock. Petronilla's heart contracted, as she watched each of them, one after the other, enemy after enemy, turn his head towards her father.

HEROD AGRIPPA had just entered the spacious men's courtyard. Silver trumpets blew fanfares. The choir struck up a song about the Messiah. Incense wafted towards him from golden censers. The new king stopped. For all his pride, he experienced a thrill of happiness and victory. At last he, the youngest Idumaean, was wearing the golden diadem of Herod the Great, the gold-embroidered royal cloak, the golden scepter in his right hand. Could he win over these stubborn people till he had the power of Solomon? Or would he remain a despised "God-fearer" in the eyes of his subjects? Would they shout at him, as they had to his mighty forebear: "You are unclean! You have sat at table with the Romans!" For that cry, Herod the Great had butchered six thousand Pharisees.

Suddenly in the crowd Agrippa caught sight of the man who had crossed his path soon after he landed in Caesarea.

Though Peter was not wearing the costly purple robe today in the Temple at Jerusalem, the prince recognized him immediately. So this was the dreaded bandit chief, at whose mere word his followers fell dead to the ground. The choir was silent now. Despite the resplendent ritual, despite the incense and the hymns, an icy silence had settled over the colonnades. The vast crowd waited, hushed and motionless. Did the high priest not dare to keep to the secret arrangement, and anoint Herod as Samuel once anointed the young David? Had not the seed of David blossomed again? In Theophilus's mind, the Davidite Jesus lived again in a dreadful vision: A cross stood on Golgotha; the earth trembled in an access of terror; in the dim gray twilight of an eclipse of the sun, an innocent man hung dying on bloody nails, above his head an inscription: *King of the Jews.*

How many of his followers would be filling the Temple hall today, their short-swords in their sleeves? What if they should dare to attack the Temple guard, and the legionaries have to come in to restore order, and the high priest suffer the fate of Caiaphas? Like Agrippa, Theophilus started as the voice of Segan Malchus—a little hoarse—bellowed the salutation: "Blessed be the King of the Jews...." Hardly had the words been uttered, before a roaring bass shouted across the forecourt of the Holy of Holies: "Jesus of Nazareth!"

A cry of joy went up over the whole city. Tens of thousands of voices burst into the new hymn, the hymn of the baptized, the creed of John, the son of Zebedee:

> *"In the beginning was the Word*
> *And the Word was with God*
> *And the Word was God!"*

Peter had drawn himself up to his full height and stood his ground against Malchus's furious glare. Then he became aware that bright eyes were all around him. He had thought he was standing among strangers, but all at once he recognized this face and that, many, many of them, and they recognized him. From right and left he suddenly felt himself seized. He stiffened his body. He tried to resist. Had they pounced on him at a gesture from the Temple captain? Was he to be dragged out and stoned like Stephen? Petronilla's cry of fear rang out from the women's courtyard. But those around him lifted him on their shoulders and carried him to the exit. The singing crowd waved to him and followed after. They formed up in their hundreds, and left the house of the ancient Jahveh. Singing the festive song of Jesus, and of the ages to come, they marched towards the future.

Past the crowned king they carried the uncrowned one. The voices of the girls and women rang out as clear as the sky. In their midst, Petronilla waved her scarf in the direction of her father. All around her, a single song resounded, a single rhythm of jubilant throats and beating hearts.

The Temple halls lay empty, the courtyards deserted, the marble flagstones bare. A few very old men hobbled about, utterly at a loss. The censers hung cold and extinguished from the hands of the Levites. Nobody dared look into Agrippa's bronzed face, now gray with fury. He did not deign to give the priests a word, a look. With the silent tread of a beast of prey he strode past the Sanhedrin, towards a bronze door. With a sudden gesture he tore from his shoulders the long golden chain, Caligula's gift and symbol of his imprisonment, and threw it with a clatter over the iron nails on which the festive wreaths were hung above the door of the Temple treasury. Wise old Gamaliel shuddered and sighed. He was the only one who understood the meaning of this gesture: The new king had freed himself from all his fetters—the fetters of gratitude, of duty, of morality and faith, of law; he had cast the chains of his own will about the Temple.

IN THE midst of Peter's triumphal procession, Joanna and Petronilla could not help feeling that there might be some trap, some trickery behind it all. Even among the twelve disciples, Peter had his rivals. When the Rock had gone out to ascertain how the work of the deacons was succeeding, they declared that his long absence was mere willfulness. But as soon as they learned that he had eaten in Caesarea with men who did not bear on their bodies the mark of the ancient covenant, they called him home. Whatever would he be up to next to strengthen and consolidate the faith of scarcely baptized heathens?

They were awaiting him now in the house of Mark's mother. They all rushèd to the window when they heard the songs and shouting of the crowd approaching the house. They had delayed their visit to the Temple, in order to make their accusations straightaway. But now he was making his entry like a conqueror.

His wife and daughter had hurried on ahead, through the arches and alleyways, and they were crouched in a corner of the anteroom when Rhoda, the serving maid, conducted the Fisher of Men upstairs. He strode on, his gaze so firmly fixed on the door of the sanctified room that he did not notice the two women. They listened in fear as excited voices sounded through the carpet that hung over the doorway. Peter's was the loudest and most resolute voice. He was telling them of his vision in Joppa, of the enormous tablecloth, and the "Take and eat!"

The others had lapsed into a puzzled silence. Only the skeptical voice of Thomas was heard: "How many cocks crowed that time?"

"Must you always put your hand on an open wound?" asked Peter. And Jacob the Tsaddik said appeasingly: "After all these years, and in the midst of our joy at seeing our brother Simon again, are we to quarrel for the first time?"

Joanna was whispering a blessing on the kindly Tsaddik, when heavy steps were heard ascending the creaking wooden stairs, and in the company of Thaddeus, the bearded Cypriot Barnabas entered. His head was held high. A lock of hair fell forward across his forehead. He looked as strong and beautiful as a pagan idol. He brought important news. As the youngest of the apostles lifted the curtain for him, the rigidly orthodox elder Tebuitis was angrily shouting: "Did not Jesus say he was only sent to the lost sheep of the house of Israel?" Peter laughed aloud. "Then he was probably sent to you, you sheep, who are so lost that you presume to teach us, who accompanied the Master through deadly perils and over the stormy waves, before ever you were reborn through baptism!"

The two newcomers laughed also. The excited elder protested in vain when Barnabas was allowed to speak as soon as he had been cordially greeted, whereas Tebuitis, who loved the sound of his own voice, would have liked to continue. In his powerful bass, the disciple excused himself for breaking in upon the holy circle in this manner. Thaddeus had urged him to do so; the earthly world was at stake: "Here you are living sublimely apart from mortal affairs. Only one of you knows anything about the great world: Jesus's Rock, our Peter. Did the Risen One die on the cross only for those of whom he said: 'This tribe is a wicked tribe? In Israel, the great, the scribes, the priests and their followers are hard and obdurate men. But out in the boundless world, wherever men live they are tormented by hunger and thirst for the Body and the Blood, the Bread and the Wine of the Redeemer. Can you guess at mankind's fear of the Last Judgment? The heathen make merry at their festivals with eating and drunken orgies, but deep in their hearts the voice of conscience tortures them inescapably. The wisest among them see their misfortune clearly."

As he had sided with Peter, so Peter now sided with him. "With my own ears I have heard the same. Let any of you, even if he is as wise as the sons of Zebedee, talk to Cornelius, the centurion! He knows all the writings of the Greek thinkers; a Stoic, he calls himself. What he told me of his teachers was good and beautiful, and the more beautiful it was, the nearer it came to Jesus's teaching. But their soul dies with their flesh. No human power is capable of fashioning the wise order which they long for. The grace was given me to open the door into eternity for him, that eternity which his much-prized Greek scholars speak of, but sadly consider beyond man's reach."

"You are right," Barnabas agreed. "Ask the heathen in Rome! Their life is unbearable! Death in the shape of greed, envy, trickery, tyranny, snatches at their every heartbeat! Beyond the frontiers of the Empire, starving hordes of murderous men are massing their countless wagon-trains. Germans and Parthians are forming themselves into cavalry armies. The earth is shaking more and more fearfully under their feet. Those with property are growing fewer and fewer in number, those with nothing, the slaves, grow more and more numerous. When will the ones in power be overthrown? When will vengeance be taken on them for the shame of the women, the misery of the children, the endless starvation? In the capital, hundreds of thousands are demanding bread and the cruel spectacles of the arena. Already our prophet Agabus is foretelling famine. When the power of numbers breaks loose against the power of property, everything will be submerged that the heathen prize as good and beautiful. How are we to shape these countless multitudes into the image of God? The sad condition of the world drives everyone into the arms of our evangelists. Our deacons are obliged to wander farther and farther afield. On all sides, new communities are blossoming for us. It is Christ they are waiting for, and his Last Judgment, when they can throw all their distress, all their shivering sorrow into the scales, for they imagine that is all that counts, all that carries weight. But we teach them that what carries most weight of all are Faith, Love, Charity." Meaningfully, he added: "I come from Antiochia."

Beside himself with rage, Tebuitis cried: "Shall salvation come from the mire? Would you waste the water of baptism on the scum of heathendom? Where the seven deadly sins dwell in marble palaces? How can a godly man set foot in the city of vice, where lewd women stand for sale on every stone?"

The Fisher of Men called to the taxgatherer: "Tell him what Jesus said to me in Caesarea Philippi. You must have written down that it was I who declared the Son of Man was the Son of the Living God." Trembling with pride, Matthew had to wait for a moment until he had mastered himself. He read: " 'You are blessed, Simon Peter, for flesh and blood did not reveal this to you, but my Father in Heaven.' "

With a motion of his hand, Peter modestly indicated that the scribe should not read about how he came to be called the Rock, but merely of his office as Keeper of the Keys: "What you shall bind together on earth shall not be put asunder in heaven."

Was not Barnabas's warning the continuation of his vision of Joppa? Peter asked himself. Being from childhood more at home on the heaving planks of his boat than on firm ground, Peter saw himself chosen for the sea journey to the Emperor's city. But Barnabas wanted to return to Antioch, the capital of the East. Before he left, he wanted to make it clear to the apostles how badly he needed a helper. "I know of one," he said, "who understands what is at stake. He commands a wider knowledge than the rabbonim. He has a deeper understanding of Greek wisdom than Cornelius. His parents, descendants of Benjamin, came from Gishala to a town with Greek schools. Through his grandfather, who did a service to General Pompeius, he has acquired Roman citizenship. No cross threatens him; the high priests dare not sit in judgment over him."

Peter knew what it meant to be a Roman citizen. The mistrust of all of them spoke in his question: "Jesus found us fisherfolk and peasants good enough. And this new man of yours ...?"

"He is a craftsman: a tentmaker."

By now their hesitation had turned to suspicion.

"Are we to send out people who are strangers to us?"

"Two of the Pillars know him, and you are one of them, Simon Peter."

Peter struck the table with his fist. Was it their deadly enemy, who had once come to him humbly with the request: "Teach me everything"? Did he presume to the Power of the Key? He remained silent as Barnabas passionately urged: "Give me the right to teach with Saul. Rome calls you, Peter. Divide up the world, grant Saul the East!"

The chief apostle thought sadly of Stephen. Might not the learned pupil of Hillel and the Greek sages surpass him? Were they always to cross his path, the all-too-spiritual Saul and the all-too-worldly Magus? Matthew guessed at his worries; he turned his scroll back and read, in a louder voice than usual, the words of Jesus: " 'When they deliver you up to judgment, do not be anxious how you will speak, for it will not be you

188

that speak, but the spirit of your Father speaking from your mouth.' "

"Your spirit, Father? How shall we show we confess our faith? Speak out of our mouths. Utter what only we know, but what all must know who are with us. Let us write it down as Jesus taught it to us. Let each one say what he believes to be most important." Ardently they called to the fiery-tongued kindler of the pentecostal flame. Matthew wrote down what each added to the eternal creed. James cried in a great voice: "I believe in God the Almighty Father." Peter immediately added: "And in Jesus Christ our Lord, his only begotten Son." Andrew raised his visionary eyes: "Conceived of the Holy Ghost..." "Son, behold your mother," John thought he heard the dying man say, and he whispered: "... born of the Virgin Mary." The Zealot groaned: "Suffered under Pontius Pilate..." A shudder ran through them all at the thought of the darkness of the earthquake, as Nathanael reflectively said under his breath: "Was crucified dead and buried. He descended into Hell..." But Thaddeus raised his voice in jubilation: "On the third day he rose again from the dead, and ascended into Heaven, where he sits at the right hand of the Father Almighty." The Tsaddik added the terrible phrase: "From whence he will come to judge the living and the dead." Matthew himself said devoutly: "I believe in the Holy Ghost, the Holy Church." Thomas nodded his handsome head as he spoke of the remission of sins, and Matthias, the youngest of them, of the resurrection of the body.

Even at such a time as this, the Fisher of Men recalled with a shudder one of the last utterances of the Master, foretelling his end: "When you are an old man..." He still felt himself to be powerful in his mission, and he envisaged a long and hard road ahead of him. He raised his head and spoke out of his iron determination: "Do you know what our Master said, the last time I took up my sword and used it? 'I could summon twelve hosts of angels to my aid.' —But he did not. How can the Scriptures be fulfilled, when such things have to happen? I am awaiting my fate. Let Herod and Caiaphas unite in their hatred."

Barnabas protested: "What of your work? Your journey? Your Rome?"

"If the Lord wills it, angels' wings will carry me across the seas."

A BLOODY Easter, like the one a dozen years before when Jesus died, threatened the Christian community in Jerusalem. Already, the more fainthearted pilgrims had folded their tents. Agrippa's Syrians roamed the streets and alleys on foot or on horseback, bold fellows with flowing white headdresses, fastened above their dark faces by a cord across the forehead. Their eyes flashed hatred, their smile was dangerous, and anxious mothers dragged their playing children into the houses. The nervous dealers in sacrificial beasts drove their goats and lambs home; money-changers hastily put away their money. Already hordes of followers of the Pharisees and Sadducees, from hired ruffians to orthodox fanatics, crowded before the king's palace. Worried at the growing number of Jesus's followers, they looked to the Idumaean governor for help. For the first time for many years, there were no legionaries within the city walls. The high priests maliciously kept their distance, behind locked doors.

Feted and feared as a guest, Agrippa had ascended the throne prepared for him in the house of Annas. The two highest dignitaries in Jahveh's land showed each other every respect, though inwardly they were consumed by hatred and suspicion. The worldly prince wanted his revenge on Peter, the spiritual prince could not tolerate that Jesus should remain the victor. His work had to be obliterated. The old man longed for one of his sons to be raised to the dignity not merely of high priest but of Messiah, of King. The young prince knew only too well that he meant little in the eyes of this nation of religious fanatics, inasmuch as he did not wear the holy garments of a high priest. In their mutual enmity, they found common ground. Again Caiaphas hinted to them, as he had to Pilate, that to tolerate Jesus's followers was not short of high treason.

"Yet those who believe in him fill every room in the Temple

with prayer," mocked Agrippa. "Did you not take the beautiful hymn of Simon Peter into your Sabbath service?"

The old man protested: "How are we to protect ourselves against the majority? How are we to make them suspicious of their leaders?"

"I have heard that one of their number, Stephen by name, was stoned as a second martyr after Jesus. Name me your martyrs!"

Wild cries penetrated the heavy tapestry across the doorway, oaths, the sound of blows, and suppressed wailing. The young high priest Theophilus burst in, red with anger. "Is there no law nowadays?" he stormed. "Can any youngster mock at us?"

Annas rose. His patriarchal beard jutted forward on his masterful chin. At his baleful expression, everyone fell silent. Theophilus recognized the new king. Ashamed of his own impetuosity, he glowered all the more because Agrippa had passed by him, the high priest, and had visited his long-since-deposed father.

Quickest to recover his composure was Segan Malchus, behind whom two Temple guards were trying to push a young lad into the room. From his black hair, a thin trickle of blood ran down his face. A great weal, of which the skin was broken here and there, ran right across his head. Though the indignant youngster's teeth were chattering with pain and agitation, the look which he turned on the priests was full of contempt. Prudently, Segan tried to hide him, and hastily let fall the curtain across the doorway. But the lad, already on the threshold, felt the heavy material fall on his sore back like a scourging rod, and he shrieked: "Strike me again, you coward!"

Agrippa enjoyed the discomfiture of the arrogant priest. "There is a guest at your door. If he is worthy, he is welcome. But if you wish to charge him—the law is the King's."

To the high priests, both the dismissed and the one in office, such an encroachment on their spiritual law-dealing was like whips and scorpions. Sweat broke out on Theophilus's forehead, but he was obliged to order Malchus to let the boy enter. A little giddy, the youngster stood in the room. By the red smear on his forehead, it could be seen that hasty hands had tried to remove the traces of his cruel punishment. But the blood began immediately to trickle down his childish face again.

Agrippa walked over to the youngster, took from his sleeve a costly kerchief of brilliant whiteness, folded it, and after a moment's hesitation, laid it like a bandage round the head of the bewildered boy. Questioned as to his name he answered, full of astonishment and gratitude: "Ignatius." His origin he gave as "Galilean," and to the question "What do you want to be?" he replied: "A priest."

Roughly Caiaphas shouted at him: "You? Are you of the stem of Aaron then?"

"Oh, not one of those. No, a priest of the Son of Man, according to the decree of Melchizedek. His name was 'King of Justice.' When will you be worthy of such a title?"

"How do you want to discharge your function as a priest?"

"Like Simon Peter who is just setting out to conquer Rome." Turning violently on the priests, he cried: "When are you going to stone me?"

The Idumaean prince shook his head.

"A pity!" cried the boy.

"Do you not enjoy your young life?"

"When you stoned Stephen, the seed sprang up magnificently. Our communities blossomed everywhere; our numbers grew and grew. Stone me! Then Rome will be ours!"

THAT week before Easter, fear lay like a nightmare over the house of Mark's mother. Soon after Peter had returned from the Temple in triumph, Herod Agrippa struck for the first time. He still avoided the leader of the apostles, of whom there were ominous rumors of his power over life and death. But Syrian spearmen seized James as he came home sunk in meditation after praying on Moriah. The young high priest Theophilus considered his office too precious to forfeit as Caiaphas had, after the stoning of Stephen. . . . He contented himself with leveling certain of the charges: a number of violations of the law. The godless did not accord due respect to either emperor or king. The priestly profession was going to the dogs since the apostles had taken to working for a mere "May God reward you." Moreover, they were lazy. To Monday and Thursday, they had added Wednesday and Friday as penitential days; they rested not only on the Sabbath but on the following day, till, in the end, only Monday was left for work. Hypocritically, they evaded the law concerning the freeing of the slaves by pretending that the slaves were as good as their masters. According to reports, their secret meetings were accompanied by unnatural orgies, and it was alleged that they slaughtered orthodox children and drank their blood. A certain Simon Peter was said to be about to set out for Rome, there to stir up rebellion amongst the slaves and the rabble of the metropolis. James did not deign to answer, since he knew he would find no justice.

The bondmaid Rhoda had arrived just as the death sentence was being carried out. Beside herself with terror, the girl watched the noblest of the apostles kneel helplessly on the leather execution sheet. She wanted to rush away, but her knees failed her. A wild hope that the ghastly thing might not take place, and a compelling curiosity kept her riveted there. The sword flashed. A dull thud caused everyone to shudder. The head rolled heavily on the leather. The body, so strong a moment before, collapsed. In place of the head that had been lifted heavenward, was now the red surface of the severed neck. A jet of blood gushed from the body onto the head, whose eyelids still seemed to be twitching. Rhoda staggered home. She could not drive the spectacle from her mind. She dared not leave the house again. Leaning against the doorpost, she sank to her knees, and her eyes closed.

Joanna, who had feared for her husband since the flogging of little Ignatius and the arrest of James, had urged Peter to get away quickly. When the spear hafts of Agrippa's soldiers hammered at the door, she collapsed in a flood of tears. The Fisher of Men appointed Jacob the Tsaddik to be bishop of the community. He embraced his companions, one after the other, and, bowing deeply, he kissed his unhappy wife's head. Then, without resistance, he let them fetter him. Courageously, the remaining ten apostles accompanied him to the ramp leading up to the paved forecourt of the Antonia.

Sadly they gazed after him as he disappeared under the echo-ing arches through which Jesus had once been led.

The Lord's mother and Petronilla tried to comfort Joanna in vain. Had not Caiaphas arrested the Fisher of Men once already, him and all the apostles, when the sick from every-where around had been laid out on beds and litters along the length of the Temple road, so that Peter's shadow might touch and heal them as he passed by? The Sanhedrin had met, and on the morning after the arrest, had sent to the prison to summon the disciples before the ecclesiastical court. But the Temple servants had returned and reported: "We found the cell door locked and bolted, the guards at every door and gate, yet when we unbolted, the cell of the twelve men was empty." But wise Gamaliel, who had been praying in the Temple on his way to the session, had come to them smil-ing, and reported: "The men you threw into prison are stand-ing in the sanctuary, teaching the people."

The community had lived through all the sorrow of Easter Friday, and now the Day of Resurrection should have caused them to rejoice. But theirs was a sad joy. As if her heart was his, Joanna felt for the prisoner. At this moment, her Simon was crouched in the Antonia, between his heathen guards, within those gloomy stinking walls, he who had been used to breathing the pure air of the lake ever since childhood. Perhaps his death sentence had been pronounced already. Trembling with impatience, she felt with him what was the bitterest thing of all, the fact that his life's work was not yet completed.

For all her preoccupation, she felt someone's gaze upon her. It was Thaddeus. His eyes seemed like suns to her, as if they could see all the better in the swiftly falling darkness. Noiselessly he came from the supper table to her and whis-pered: "Prepare with Petronilla whatever you need to take with you, and hold yourself in readiness." Her astonishment prevented her from obeying at first, but at his earnest "Go," which allowed no argument, she drew Petronilla to her and wakened Rhoda, who uttered a faint cry, for she had just been dreaming that James raised himself up from the leather, took up his head with both hands, and carried it like a light before

194

him. They calmed her with difficulty and, quietly sobbing, she helped the two women hastily to pack. They haltered the ass, led it into the yard, saddled and loaded it. Joanna and Petronilla, tired and shivering, returned to the room, to tell Thaddeus they were ready.

Meanwhile Rhoda was strewing another armful of hay before the ass, when she heard a knocking at the great gate giving out on to the square in front of Caiaphas's palace. Trembling, she softly crept towards it and listened. Her horrifying dream came back to her. Supposing James were standing out there, his head in his hand like a lantern?

But the one outside knocked louder still, and seemed in his fear and impatience to have divined a rustling noise in the passage. Insistently, he cried in a low voice: "Open up! Quickly! They may be on my heels already...." When the cry was repeated, louder this time, the maid thought she recognized the voice of Peter. Beside herself with joy, she forgot to unbolt the gate, and rushed back into the room, tearing the curtain aside, hardly able to utter the words: "Simon ... Peter ... outside! At the gate...."

Everyone sprang up. Confused, incredulous, some of them stammered: "You are mad!"

"No. Truly. It is he!"

Trembling, one of them whispered: "His angel perhaps."

Then they themselves heard the knocking at the gate. Some still hesitated, but Thaddeus hurtled down the stairs, Joanna hurrying after. She groped for the bolt, but could not find it at first. The gate was scarcely open before a man's figure pressed in amid a clatter of iron. He threw himself against the door and propped himself there, breathing heavily. The lamp, held high, shone on the face of Simon Peter. Despite the fetters on his hands and feet, he laid his right forefinger against his lips, and listened in the stillness. All was quiet; only the chirp of the cicadas persisted. Confusedly he began to stammer something about dreams and angels. "The Lord has delivered me out of prison; the name of the Lord be praised."

Bartholomew and Andrew hammered the chains off him, then Thaddeus and Mark accompanied the escaped prisoner to a secret way out through the city wall. They carefully guided Joanna and her daughter, while their donkey seemed to put its feet down almost soundlessly in the darkness.

The sun had scarcely risen from the Jordan on the morning of the high Easter festival than it lit up the whole sky with its blazing heat, like a golden background of holiness. It blinded the eyes of any traveler coming up from the lake towards Jerusalem. The patient ass, bearing Joanna, Petronilla and their little bundle of belongings, could hardly be discerned now, with Peter striding along powerfully in front of them. At their first halt, he tied a crosspiece to his traveling staff. This cross-staff was to be his weapon against the wordly-wise, against the gods, against Caesar himself. He would teach them and everyone else about the Man whom God became.

GRAY sky and a heavy sea. From the western horizon the Ligurian sea rolled blue-black towards the Etruscan beach, where, bordered with countless pearls of foam, it spilled itself on the sands. Far out the huge waves were crested with white manes. The nearer they came to the mountainous coast, now gradually growing brighter in the early sunlight, the more oily they became. Only where the Arno and the Serchio, at that time still united at the mouth, had deposited their sand, did the long swell rear up for the last time, before plashing wearily ahead and dissipating itself in a crackle of foam.

Around the hardly stirring deadwater of the harbor basin with its landing steps, and along the river mouth, stretched the ancient town of Pisa, famous among the twelve towns of the Etruscans. A dense array of masts swayed sleepily to and fro; swift, slender boats from the Roman war fleet lay moored beside squat coastal vessels, and among them, since the previous day, was a big merchant ship.

From the hold of this ship, for some hours now, slaves had been carrying down the gangplank barrel after barrel of Palestinian salt fish, bales of Oriental carpets, baskets full of dried figs and raisins. A clerk stood on the quay, marking off the goods, item by item, on his tablet. Finally, he reported to the captain that the unloading was complete. With a jovial smile, the captain turned to one of his passengers, a sturdy, sun-tanned man, gazed at him for a moment with eyes shining with wine and gratitude, then hugged him to his breast. He could not praise enough the navigational skill of the man whom he was embracing.

"My dear Simus Petron, or Praetus Sumon, you must know a damned powerful spell for exorcism. If you will write down the magic formula for me, I will pay you gladly and well. Imagine getting into port quicker by the longer route! Sailing against the wind! Fabulous! I hope your weather charm is in Greek or Latin, Aramaic is too much for my old head these days. So now, out with your abracadabra!"

Peter smiled to himself. Soon after the start of the voyage, adverse winds had beset the ship, and the crew had begun to mutiny, saying they wanted to lay up in some harbor over the winter months, like other seafarers of the time. The captain had fled to his cabin, partly in order to escape from the fury of his crew, partly out of superstitious fear of the elements. As the weather by then was so rough that the helmsman could not control the ship, the Galilean fisherman had offered to take over, provided that everyone would obey him implicitly. Of course, he was only used to handling small craft at home. He had first to bring the huge ship under his control. He tried out a number of commands and maneuvers with the Syrian sailors, to make sure they understood him fully, said a prayer to him who was able to walk the waters in the storm, and took the tiller himself. Gradually he brought the vessel into the wind, rejoiced to find her so obedient, and steered an oblique course, at which the anxious helmsman cried out that they would lose sight of the landmarks. No sailor on the high seas dared do that. Fortunately, the stars, so familiar to the fisherman, were appearing. The crew soon noticed that the ship had swung far over to port, for their bracing of the sails and his bold steering had caused the vessel to heel steeply. They laughed at such zigzag sailing, which they had never experienced before, but then they observed that despite the adverse winds, the ship was driving forward, and the landmarks they had believed lost were in fact looming unexpectedly close. Peter and Andrew had learned this style of navigation at home, in reaching the market with their catch ahead of the other boats. Because their course, which now lay to starboard, now to port, could be laid together like the beams of the cross, they called this secret of theirs "cross-sailing."

But hardly had the superstitious captain heard the word "cross" mentioned than he spat three times ahead of himself in fear. "Now you come to me too with that gallows-cross they are all whispering about. Decent people shudder at the thought of such torture, yet you calmly finger the sign of it on your forehead and your mouth. The rope off a hanged man brings luck, but the wood of a cross, what is the good of that?"

"It brings the purest happiness, far beyond all earthly kinds."

Suspiciously, the heathen screwed up his eyes and shook his head. "Do you think they are happy when they are slowly perishing away up in the air on the cross, tortured by flies, limbs twisted, sinews stretched, sweltering in the sun or whipped by the cold rain? —I can see you are not going to part with that magic of yours. A pity. You could have done good business with it."

"I am not concerned with business. My concern is with men."

"Are you a slave dealer then, who hangs his wares on the cross?"

"Perhaps one day I shall be nailed to the cross myself." Startled, the captain recoiled. "What is your trade then?"

"I am a fisher of men."

A shudder ran through the seaman. According to the custom of his kind, he had never learned to swim. The only men he ever saw fished out of the sea were always corpses. He stammered a hasty farewell and staggered towards the nearest tavern.

Peter stood for a long time on the steps waiting for his wife and daughter, who after the joy of washing in fresh water were putting on their best clothes and jewelry. Startled by a strident cockcrow, the fisherman began to examine his conscience, to determine whether he had not been guilty of some weakness again. In jokingly demonstrating to the captain his superiority in the captain's own domain, was he not guilty of vanity? The penalty for witchcraft was death. Anxiously, he began to look around, and soon ran the seaman to earth in a waterside tavern, sitting in the red glare of an open hearth, on a rough-hewn bench at a coarse table. Jug and cup at his elbow, he sat dozing; and did not look up until the fisherman stood before him, laughing into his glassy eyes. "You who are at home on all the seas, believe me, there is nothing mysterious about that affair. You can have my secret."

But in his cantankerous drunkenness, the captain stood up with an effort, supporting himself on his two fists, and thundered: "By Hercules! Are you trying to beguile me into your lawless wizardry? Do you want to fish my body up, too?"

"Rather your soul, but for that you need to breathe the breath of God first. What is blowing from your mouth just now is nothing holy. Let me sit down beside you, as one honest man by another. You will laugh to see how simple my secret is."

With that, he pulled the resisting man down on the bench beside him, and used the wine the drunkard had spilled to draw the direction of the wind and the ship's course on the table. At first the captain would not look, but familiar words caused him to listen. Eager to learn, he soon understood how one had to set the sails and the tiller. To his own delighted astonishment, he quickly solved the problems Peter set him. He learned too that his crew had been already drilled for every maneuver, in the course of the long voyage. Gratefully he drank his instructor's health over and again, as if he had been given a gold mine. From now on, the winter months would no longer be a dead time without income; he would earn twice as much in a year as his competitors. And as Peter refused any payment or share, and merely asked with a smile whether he still felt so hostile to him and to the cross, the emotional heathen fell on his neck and embraced him.

Outside the last breakers were ebbing away. The sun had struggled through and was shining warmly on the slender figure of a girl who sprang light-footed out of the hatch of the big merchant ship, spread her arms and took a deep breath of the salty air, then looked around for her father. The wind gently fondled the embroidered lace veil which was twisted into place by a wreath of long dark plaits. A headband interwoven with gold reached from her left to her right ear, and from it on either side, colored streamers hung down to her chin. The flowing purple garment which the grateful Tabitha had first given to Peter was now decorated with handsome embroidery.

Petronilla pouted with disappointment. Her father was not there. Her mother was still loading the ass. The harbor around her was deserted. But before her, looking landwards, lush green meadows stretched, which the mild winter could not harm, colored with flowering anemones. The girl danced across the crazy gangplank and ran towards the flowers. She hurried over the gentle lawns and bent here and there to pluck a blue, dark-red, an even more beautiful white anemone. They grew in such profusion that her nimble fingers quickly made wreath after wreath, a modest one for her head, two more showy ones to go round her neck. To her delight, she discovered on beds protected from the wind great long-stemmed marguerites, of which she gathered a huge bouquet. As she gazed around, she saw that she had wandered much farther than she had realized, and was standing in front of a handsome building surrounding a great open colonnade that looked out on the garden. She had never seen such a beautiful place. Inquisitively she hurried towards it. Everywhere were glittering stone mosaics. From the dark-red walls, handsome youths and dancing girls looked down in silence. In an open dining room, white marble tables surrounded a rectangular pool. Slices of fragrant bread had been set out instead of plates, costly knives were beside them, and before each diner's couch a shallow cup was laid, of baked red or black earthenware, beautifully painted. Enormous-bellied two-handled jars stood against the walls, ready for mixing the wine.

The fact that no one was to be seen made all this strange splendor appear as something ghostly, something out of a fairy tale. Uneasily, the garlanded child turned, intending to return to the ship. Suddenly, half frightened, half relieved, she heard voices, one of them high-pitched, the other deep, both cheerful and lively. Evidently they were young noblemen, for they spoke in Greek. Petronilla had learned this language thoroughly, from an Alexandrian deacon, on her grandmother's insistence. The wealthy old merchant-woman wished her handsome grandchild to make a good marriage, so the child had to learn the speech of well-bred folk.

"Wonderful!" cried the high voice. "Much better than my throw! And the force of it! Your javelin shaft is still whipping to and fro."

The heavier voice answered in Latin verse:

> *"Our father's time—unworthy of its elders—*
> *Created us, less worthy still. We beget children*
> *Still more debauched than we are ...*

Do you think your celebrated ancestor Horace's lament for the decline of Rome applies to us too?"

Petronilla was shocked. Such a pleasant voice from a vicious mouth? With exaggerated politeness the lighter voice replied: "Of course not, O noble offspring of the Egyptian Kings."

The other laughed, though had he been a child there would have been tears behind his laughter. "I take your homage as a joke, and not as mockery. You are the only Roman whom I like well enough to tease, rather than to insult, with that verse of Horace."

"The throne of the land of the Nile might well be worth hating us Romans for, seeing that we robbed you of it. Of course, my friendship conflicts with my sense of duty. If my heart wishes you the crown, my head condemns me for treason."

"Whatever good you wish me is bound to offend against something that is sacred to Rome. An ancient curse lies over my house."

Full of compassion, the girl made the sign of the cross with her bouquet in the direction of the sad voice. She heard the other say: "Since you so like to recite verses from my ancestor

Horace to tease me, here is something of his which you may find useful:

> *"You govern in the extent to which you submit*
> *to the gods,*
> *Here is the beginning, herein lies your end."*

The listening girl was shocked at the answer: "How shall I honor strange gods, who am myself a god to my people?" A god? There was but one God, and she, when she was small, had been allowed to see him herself. He had caressed her, had been crucified, had risen from the dead and gone up to Heaven. How could she help this unhappy young man to see the truth? In anguish, she heard what seemed sheer blasphemy to her: "I am a Ptolemy. In every king of this name, the Falcon-god Horus is made flesh."

"All your Nile gods seem to be beasts."

"Do not speak ill of animals, you do not know men yet."

"And what if the Emperor allowed you to return? Syrian princelings whom we held here like rare parrots in golden cages—Herod Agrippa was one—have been let back on to their little thrones; why not you, whose throne Alexander mounted?"

"I, master of your granaries? If I desired it, Rome would starve. And starving Romans would murder their emperor."

"Does such power tempt you?"

"No. Since I have known Rome, Egypt is too small for me. I dream of a kingdom of men who are good at last. But for that I would need to speak to every heart, to be a slave among slaves, a king among kings. Make the people good and you would have a kingdom worthy of a god."

"It is here already!" Petronilla wanted to cry, but she heard the other say: "Do you say that, who despise mankind so?"

"Not mankind as it is, but mankind as it is obliged to be because others force it to be so wretched. But I am a latecomer of a ruined dynasty, begotten in misery, grown up in servitude. Because I know every privation, I dream of helping everyone, I dream of being a ruler to whom every heart will belong."

Petronilla longed to call to him: "He whom you seek is everywhere, he is beside you, if only you wish it." She felt sorry for the owner of the deepest voice, but the lighter voice was dearer to her, and a sweet shudder ran through her body as she heard him cry in admiration: "God of the falcon-glance! You can see right through the world, and through all of us."

"And what do I see? You have founded a world empire. A forest of spears holds up the canopy of peace. Do you want to create peace with weapons? While the god of war rejoices, men tear each other to pieces like beasts. Who is your master? A Tiberius, a Caligula, beside the weakling Claudius his terrible wife Messalina. Informers, assassins, poisoners! The capital city of the world, in which the rich man is not worthy of his riches, nor the poor man of his poverty."

"You are right," said the higher voice, sadly. "What awaits us? A few summers still remain to me, and then according to Augustine law, I must pay a heavy penalty each year if I do not marry, if I do not put children into this ugly world. Would the children be mine? Go into any noble house: You will recline at table with the hostess and her young daughters. Players will act their filthiest comedies for you and them. Even the most innocent cannot help becoming possessed of evil thoughts. Noble girls practice boxing. Women fight as gladiators. Slaves are their lovers. They have nothing in their heads except who won the chariot race."

The other concluded sadly:

> *"Not to be born is the most desirable:*
> *But if you live, best is to return*
> *Speedily from whence you came . . ."*

The downturned corners of Petronilla's mouth trembled as if she must cry. The poetry which they so lightly tossed to each other seemed to her sad enough for tears. Now the high-voiced young man began to praise death too:

> *"What is of such value, O man,*
> *That out of all measure*
> *You grieve and groan for fear of death?*
> *Why do you weep?"*

203

And the other added soberly: "Yes. So sang our beloved Lucretius. He knew that the soul dies with the body."

The listening girl could contain herself no longer. She was on the point of crying "No." She stepped swiftly out of the laurel hedge before she had considered whether it was prudent to do so. She saw before her a carefully marked-out area, covered with light gravel, on the lawn. There stood the two young men. For their javelin-hurling, they were wearing only loincloths, and they resembled the images of heathen gods which her mother had always hurried past so squeamishly in Caesarea. Such things did not seem strange to her young eyes. Scarcely a year ago she had been splashing in the warm waters of Lake Genesareth with the crowds of happy boys and girls, all as God made them. But the manner in which the two young men greeted her made her stop, speechless.

"Sing praises to Diana, O gentle nymphs!" they recited together, and sank on their knees in front of her, both of them at that fortunate age when sadness can still change immediately to merriment. The girl uttered a startled cry and the young men, springing to their feet, begged her to be patient for a moment while they put on their tunics and togas.

Petronilla was just about to turn regretfully away, but they were already tucking the end of their overgarment girdlewise around their hips, as was the fashion of the young knights of the time. The high-voiced youth walked on her left side and the other on her right. The one was golden-haired; a fine down shone on his bronzed skin in the early sunlight. The other was dark-complexioned, and his hair was like black enameled metal.

To the young men, the strange, lovely creature in her curious costume, dressed in purple and garlanded with flowers, seemed to have sprouted out of the laurel bush like some nymph of spring. Flaccus's voice failed him as he invited her to be their guests, but the swarthy Ptolemy objected that today they were only guests themselves on the estate of Lucius Junius Bassus. For Flaccus's uncle had handed his estate over to his slaves and freemen for the few days of his absence in Rome, so that they might worthily entertain some guests from the East.

Flaccus suggested that the servants on the estate were sociable people, and would probably welcome such a lovely creature, if indeed she was a mortal at all, and not a spring goddess in person.

The girl opened her eyes wide at this, and protested vehemently that she was no heathen goddess. Then, more diffidently, she begged them to show her the way to the harbor. She was surprised that the road back seemed so long. Her two guides had taken a detour, in order that they should not have to part from her too soon. On the way, they discovered that the enchanting creature was named Petronilla, and that she had decked herself so beautifully for her father's festive reception. With a shy side glance at the young man on her right, she added proudly: "My father is God's messenger. Whoever believes with him and is baptized, will be richly rewarded in Heaven, for the day of the righteous is at hand. There will be a new heaven and earth," she said. "None of your poets will harm you any more. They will not be able to destroy your souls."

The youths could not understand such strange talk from a girl's mouth; they asked so many questions that it became difficult to answer them all, and she was glad when the harbor came in sight again.

After some trouble, Joanna had managed to lead the laden donkey down the gangplank and onto the quay, while her husband was just emerging from the tavern, supporting the happily smiling captain. The captain quickly came to himself in the fresh air, and bawled to a couple of his sailors: "This man here—you know him?—he's my friend, my best friend! Don't kill him. My orders are canceled.

"You know," he explained to Peter, "I was going to have you done away with, because my crew wouldn't have respected me any more if you could sail the ship better than I could. But I am an honest man—you have taught me your trick and we are friends now and if you like I will listen to what you have to say, not only about what you call cross-sailing, but about that other cross as well."

At that moment, with a jingle of harness, the mule coach arrived from Rome, and Junius Bassus alighted. The arch-enemy of the capital had returned sooner than expected, and in very high spirits. His lawyer had informed him that despite heavy taxation, his fortune had doubled itself in a few years. Yes, since his slaves had adhered to the new faith, his estate had prospered as never before. He was obliged to admit that no one stole, none were lazy. If he had been angry at first that they had come to him in a deputation to ask for one free day a week, he had soon realized the diligence with which they tried to make up for the few lost hours. In their endeavor to do their best in everything, they missed not one of the almond-white, slightly resinous-tasting nuts in his mighty pine forests. In this happy mood of his, he learned that despite the unusually severe winter weather, his rich cargo had arrived undamaged. And more yet. His captain beamingly reported that, thanks to the seamanlike skill of a Palestinian fisherman, he would be able to undertake many voyages even in the dead months when other ships and sailors remained idle in the ports.

Years later, Junius Bassus would laughingly recall his arrival in Pisa: "Out of the tavern came a gray-beared worthy, and my old skipper as drunk as a donkey. By the gangplank, there was a handsome woman with a real donkey, and from between the houses, my nephew and his friend came in sight with a sweet little girl, both of them mooning around her like a couple of donkeys themselves. A real *gesta asinorum*. Quite unforgettable!"

THEY had been journeying for several days now on the Via Aurelia, along the coast of the Tyrrhenian Sea, whose fresh salt breezes the strangers from Lake Genesareth sniffed with pleasure. To their left the mountains were showing green, and all around lay well-cultivated land. To their right was the sea, of ever-intensifying blue. They traveled on through the ancient Etruscan towns of Populonia, Cosa, Tarquinia, and Centumcellae, greeted everywhere by cheering crowds in gala dress, honored and feted, bombarded with questions and with invitations to remain.

Jewish communities of the Diaspora had come from afar,

to hear of the Messiah whom they had been expecting for centuries. Slaves who had begged themselves off for the day, poor mountain peasants, shepherds and fishermen, joined the throng. Rumors had gone ahead of the visitors. The oldest one was said to be a man of mysterious powers, skilled in all kinds of strange arts. Of course, sorcery was punishable by death, but the Emperor Claudius had granted quite exceptional privileges to the Jews; throughout the Empire they were allowed to observe unhindered the customs of their forefathers, though the monarch warned them not to be contemptuous of the customs of other people.

How surprised the crowds were, when the expected visitors arrived at last. The rattle of the wheels of two large coaches was heard approaching along the paving stones of the Aurelian Way. Two slim riders headed the procession; the swarthy one appeared to belong to some foreign squadron, while the other, the fair-haired one, wore a toga with the broad purple stripe of senatorial rank. When the coach stopped, he checked his impatiently prancing horse at the coach window, from which a beautiful girl's face was peeping inquisitively as she listened to his words with a smile. At each halt, a powerful big-boned man, very simply dressed in linen, climbed down from the second coach. Large dark eyes looked out of his bold seafarer's face. It was not easy to endure his gaze. His beard was gray, and the tuft of curly hair over his forehead was only a little darker. With a firm tread he walked over to the crowd at the road's edge, as if it were not they who had been waiting for him, but he himself who could not wait to hear what was in the heart of the timid house slave, the flea-bitten swineherd, the old mountain peasant or the dismounted young horseman. Whatever was said, he listened as if just those faltering words were of the greatest importance to him. Every single sorrow was his own, and at that moment his greatest concern. The unbaptized stood hesitantly before him, the already baptized looked him blissfully in the face. Even frivolous youngsters who had only come there to laugh and jeer were surprised at his questions, for he seemed to read their innermost desires in their eyes. Long after Peter left them, they still gazed silently after him. They were curiously lighthearted, and many were smiling to themselves, for a strange man had spoken a few words, but words of such love as nobody had used to any of them, young or old, since their earliest childhood.

Peter was almost at the end of the line of people, when a stocky Etruscan, whose sly face with its pointed nose hardly seemed to fit his sturdy body, began excitedly complaining about the college of the priests of Apollo in Veii. "Since time immemorial my family, the Tarchnas of Caere—the last of the Roman kings was a great-great-uncle of mine—have worshiped the god of this town. A lovely Etruscan god! Real warrior's muscles—and calves, ha! the calves on him! Strong to trample all his enemies. A bold nose, like my grandfather's and my father's and mine, a hero's nose! He brought us happiness and joy. But for them, the priests, he is not good enough. He is grinning, they say; only his mouth laughs but his eyes just stare. May he forgive such an outrage! They bought a new god, a cheap Greek one from a Roman slave workshop. Wholesale. A little lad that our old god of Veii could have blown over. But our old family god, for whom we used to pay out a lot of money in sacrifices in the days when Rome was still a village, they put him in a vault like a dead god with other dead gods."

Bewildered, those already baptized heard the Etruscan scream in fury: "Do you nod? You think I am right, is it not so? And you know, I said to the priests, I do not trust this new god of yours. They pull a long face now, when the white bull-calf they used to get from me every year does not arrive. And a monthly present of money on top of it—finished! They would like to get the old god out again now, but too late! Pulling him off his pedestal, without any respect at all, they broke his feet off, and a patched-up god, you know, is not for me. A god is a god and dead is dead. I am looking for a new one now. I have heard a lot of good things about your God. Because people are flocking to him in crowds, the priests in Veii are worried. So they bought new gods. But I am going over to your God. What does he cost?"

Peter held out his right hand to the excited little man and said smilingly: "The priests were right to bury the dead god; they could have put away the newly bought ones with him. The images in your temples have never lived. If your forefathers were well-to-do, that may have been due to their honesty, or perhaps to their might. The painted manikin with clay feet had nothing to do with it; like all your other gods, he is only a phantom of the underworld. . . ."

"A black Orcus?" cried the Etruscan. "This powerful God of yours—what sacrifices . . . ?"

"He does not want your sacrifice. Go to the elders of our community and you will learn that our sacrifice, at our love feasts, appears no more than a piece of bread and a sip of wine. But of course, you must first understand the secret of the bread and wine. As soon as you have grasped it, God is within you. But first you must be a new man, free from all your old dead gods that even your own priests are beginning to bury. Then you will see a new earth and heaven. The deeper your belief, the happier you will be."

Stylus and wax tablet in hand, the Etruscan interrupted the fisherman. "I want to show you in writing what I have been spending on offerings to the gods. I do not skimp, if I get satisfaction."

A few of the baptized laughed, but Peter reproached them. "It is nothing to laugh at, when gods die." And he soothed the offended Etruscan, who had thrust his nose haughtily in the air, with: "Keep your bull-calves and your gifts of money. All you have left over, give to the poor." With these words, Peter turned to an old woman who had thrown herself on her knees before him. She was begrimed with dirt, but Peter took her arm and lifted her heartily to her feet. "I am only a man. Kneel to God, not to me. What is your request?"

The careworn, white-haired woman could not speak for sobbing, and as the fisherman fondled her head she raised her eyelids and her dim eyes at the same time, so that the whites showed, giving the appearance of some ghastly agony. Her shriek pierced the marrow of all who heard it: "My son! My son! He was poor and a slave. His father was poorer still, for he could work no more and lay sick to death. Everyone told my boy to take a sacrifice to the great mother of the gods, Isis, in Rome, and she would help. A night, a day and a night again he ran gasping there and back. His master had him whipped for being absent. He had taken all he possessed to the goddess, but the priests only laughed. He had to sacrifice at least a wether. Where are we to get a wether from? Barely a few hens and a goat are left to us. So in his desperation and his filial love, my boy stole a wether and drove it to Rome. Not for himself, by all the mighty gods, only for the goddess. But halfway there, they caught him." Again she shrieked in her boundless despair. "And they crucified him like a thief. The offended goddess let his sick old father die, and while he was breathing his last, his son was hanging on the cross for hours and hours, till the next day they broke his bones with wooden mallets and threw him, dying, into the boneyard. Master, is that just? Did ever a mother suffer like me over so good a son?"

The disgrace of her son's death lay like a pestilence on the unfortunate woman, and all the others drew back timidly from her. But Peter bent down and put his arms about her. "You ask, who has suffered so? The one I acclaim suffered more than your son, for there was not even the shadow of a wrong deed, and yet he came to take all your suffering upon himself. Your son was guilty according to the laws of man. But the Son of Man hung innocent on the cross. And what mother has suffered more terribly than you? His mother. From the ancient prophecies she knew what awaited her son. Every glance of this wonderful child was joy and sorrow at once, till she stood beneath the cross. For hours she watched her beloved son suffer. She fainted away when a soldier pierced her son's left side with his spear, and blood and water flowed out —the sign of death. Our belief demands testimony till death. Our handsome young Stephen was stoned to death, the first of them. James, my boyhood friend, was beheaded. They chained me in prison too. Only on the way to the place of execution were the chains to be struck off. I was already suffering the torment of work uncompleted, of parting from my family, but an angel led me out of prison, past the guards. Now I have been spared for your sakes. I have been sent to bring comfort to you and everyone. If you believe in Jesus, you will live forever, not in the want and sickness of your earthly life, but in Him, with Him, through Him."

The old woman began to weep. She tried to smile through

her tears, but then in grief she stammered: "Will my son be allowed to be with your God when he does not even know him? His master had him crucified like a thief...."

"Who was his master?"

Trembling, she pointed to the little Etruscan, who was already preparing to defend his rights as a master against the thieving of his slaves, when precisely at that moment, on a farm some way inland, a cock crowed.

Startled, Joanna and Petronilla looked at Peter. They knew that every cockcrow was like a physical pain to him. On that account they had been delighted to be going to Rome, for they had heard that in the maze of houses in the gigantic city, no poultry were to be found. Peter had fallen silent, deep in thought. To disturb the laws was no task of his. He had always preached to the slaves that they must respectfully obey their masters, even the wicked ones.... The crucified slave had not only offended against Roman law, but also against the seventh commandment of Moses in order to keep the first one.

Then a kindly smile spread over his bearded face. He turned to the Etruscan, who had just been calculating how much cheaper the new faith was. But would the new god pay back promptly, and in full? Peter's next words came as a slight disappointment to him, though as some comfort to his conscience. This new god did not do things quite so cheaply as he had thought. Peter asked him if he was prepared to offer a cheaper sacrifice in place of the bull-calf.

"You mean, a pig, a sheep?"

"A wether, like the one the priests of Isis demanded. Like the one your slave stole and you took back; a wether like the one you nearly lost."

Half out of eagerness, half out of caution, he had been about to offer the traditional pig-sheep-bull sacrifice. Now, delighted that nothing more than a wether was involved, he said: "A wether? Just one? Where would your god like it?"

"Give it to the dead thief's mother."

"But your god will not have any of it then, not even you...." He thought of the feasts enjoyed by the pagan priests. Was Peter going to resign his share?

"We will have your good deed, and we will redeem the

crucified slave from his guilt. For then he will not have stolen the sheep and his honor is restored. But you will have been merciful, and will have repaid evil with good, the evil that he only did out of love for his father. And thus you will have earned God's blessing. And you"—he took the grateful, sobbing woman by the shoulder—"go with your master there to the elders of our community, and learn to love one another. And all the sorrow you have borne so hard, and that you will still have to bear, for a mother's heart never heals, hoard it as a wondrous treasure. And when you close your eyes on this world, and waken again in another, more beautiful, in God's eternity, you will be asked what claim you have to everlasting happiness. And all your sorrow and hunger, your trouble with your husband and that far greater grief over your son, you will be able to display like a precious jewel. The angels will bow before you. They will lead you into that shining realm of light, into the arms of those you loved, into the arms of God. And He and you and your joy will be everlasting."

Peter had spoken very quietly and peacefully, but all around held their breath, all listened, none dared move. And when he walked on, they felt grateful and purified, and none of them had any desire that did not seem paltry compared with such great glory.

SOME three hours before day, the coaches and horsemen had set out from Lorium, the last stopping place before Rome. The wheels rattled monotonously over the dark-gray paving stones of the Via Aurelia, uphill, downhill, towards their destination. Wrapped in their thick fur cloaks, Flaccus and his friend rode ahead. The longer the journey lasted, the more reserved the Egyptian had grown. His companion hardly noticed this, for he was too taken with the beautiful girl, so unlike the young Roman women he was used to. Each day he had grown more and more enchanted with her gentle, open nature, though Petronilla, with her varied experiences, seemed strangely mature and superior to the young men. The very thing that, planned on a large scale, comprised her father's lifework, was happening between these two youngsters as spon-

taneously as the blossoming of the spring: East and West were
being bound together in love.

The pain of being too late in everything, of being the last-
born of a dynasty outstripped and forgotten, lay heavy on
Ptolemy's heart. Like happiness, fortune, everything else, this
young girl flew past him too, towards his friend, and nothing
was left but envy, jealousy and bitterness.

Rome, the dangerous city, seemed to lurk in wait for his
arrival like a murderer eager for hire. Already he could discern in the half-light the great figures on the milestones.
Shorter and shorter grew the distance to the Forum, the "Navel
of the World." The prince of royal blood would arrive there
as outrider to a humble man bringing nothing with him but
the Word. Peter had landed with an ass, but now he was
accompanied by a young Roman of senatorial rank and a
prince of the same age, and riding in a coach, with his wife
and daughter following in an even finer vehicle behind.

In Pisa, Junius Bassus had expressed his thanks to Peter for
saving his cargo, instructing his captain, and not least for the
good and efficient conduct of his servants. He had been astonished at their festivities. They had not prepared a sumptuous meal like greedy starvelings set on enjoying a licentious
holiday. Instead, tasty fish from the Arno had comprised the
main course, for it had been Friday, and a fast day.

All this was very much after the heart of the honest land-
owner, and he begged Peter to tell him more about his God
and his faith. They had sat long together. The apostle talked,
his host drank, till at last he stretched out his arm and, with
a warm handshake, said: "Even if I have not understood
everything you have said—and some of these things come hard
to a faithful servant of the old gods—I know one thing: You
have made more of these people here than ever laws or priesthood did. For that I owe you many thanks and, I must confess, a lot of money. I would have liked you to stay longer
here." Smiling, he wiped his lips and looked across at Petronilla. "To see such a delightful child about me warms even
an old heart like mine. But you say you must go to Rome. I
would like to show my gratitude." So Junius Bassus had generously placed his carriage at Peter's disposal, and to Joanna

and her daughter, he lent the carriage that had once belonged to his dead wife. Everything was quickly got ready, the mules were brought, the two young men provided with mounts, and a messenger sent on ahead to prepare the patrician's house in Rome for all the guests.

The travelers had reached the boundary of the capital. Cheerfully Flaccus cried: "We will slacken down to walking pace just once more, up this hill. Janiculum lies ahead of us, and behind it Rome and the house. May the destination reward the journey!"

The guards on the Porta Aurelia, with their wearisome questions, were behind them now. Between high garden walls, the road curved gently downhill towards the spacious rock terraces that jut out of the Janiculum, affording a view over the Eternal City. The young horseman signaled for them to stop. Slipping from the saddle, he hurried to help the passengers out of their carriages, so that they could stretch their limbs after the long journey, and could see the capital of the world at their feet in the morning sunlight, nestling in the surrounding hills like a great bowl of golden glory.

Smiling, Flaccus recited the lines of Horace:

> "O Sunlight!
> Under your eye there is nothing greater
> Than this my Rome!"

The guests from Palestine followed him to the lower slope, blinded by the morning light that shone back from the pale-yellow travertine stone of the grand buildings which the young nobleman proudly pointed out. Marble on marble rose the temples and palaces with their gilded beams. There stood the ancient fortress of the Capitol and the gigantic statue of Jupiter, built of the metal from trophies of war. How small Jerusalem seemed, how modest its holy buildings, compared with such splendor. Colonnades enclosed the evergreen lawns of the Field of Mars. Crowned with its cupola, the Pantheon rose above the thermal springs of Agrippa. Nearer the beholders stood the theater of Pompeius, in which Julius Caesar fell under the daggers of his assassins.

214

When the young Roman looked round, to savor the impression which the greatness of his city had made upon Peter, he found him apart from the others, on a stone bench in front of a little temple which was scarcely more than a niche for the statue of a pagan god. The fisherman was gazing in some surprise at the image of Proteus Claviger, a bearded man with a pair of keys in his hand. "My keys?" He felt sand under his feet; picked up a handful and let it run through his fingers, beautiful, glittering, golden sand, covering the terrace. A premonition of his fate overcame him: Peter on the golden mountain.

Disappointed, Flaccus turned silently to his companions and pointed to an open door, from which servants were coming to welcome their guests. Down a shady avenue of dark evergreen oaks, they came to a handsome villa nestling comfortably against the hillside and affording a peaceful view over the huge, restless city. In Pisa, Peter and his family had stayed with a freed slave, and had only entered the rich man's house for the feast; but now the three pilgrims found themselves surrounded with elegance and luxury.

Flaccus was one day to live with his bride on that charming estate on the Janiculum. Sedulously he roused Petronilla's curiosity, led her over one marble threshold after another, and was delighted at her admiration for the luxurious furniture and the wall paintings depicting the stern life of craftsmen and tradesmen as some delightful children's game.

At her husband's request, Joanna had gone to look for the young couple; and now, Peter, strangely inattentive to everything around him, sat on his bench, staring into infinity. Abstractedly, he took from his sleeve a handful of roasted wheatears and a few dried figs which were his frugal morning meal.

Ptolemy began to take his leave. "Simon Peter, it was clever of you to keep your arrival in Rome a secret. If your followers had come rushing out here to greet you, they might have trampled the walls down. But now that you are going to install yourself in the palace, they will be inclined to draw back in awe of such a noble messenger of God. And so you will be given the opportunity to rest and ponder over that contempt for worldly things which you preach to the poor. Already the wicked city has folded you in its flattering arms. You have no power over Rome, Rome has you in its power."

"Prince of Egypt, see that my ass is brought to me."

Ptolemy was about to protest that that was a slave's task, but curiosity made him obey. Before he returned, Joanna had emerged from the house with her daughter, followed by Flaccus, who came to invite the guests to the richly spread table. The fisherman stood up. "It is time for work. Thank you for escorting us. Go back quickly with the carriages. You know how much your uncle's kindness eased my service to the crowds along the way. May the Lord bless the noble Junius Bassus, and lead him soon to us!"

Flaccus was about to demur, but before he could do so, the steward was seen coming down the avenue with two men, one of whom wore the uniform of the Roman fire watch. He took his companion by the arm and hurried forward. The other, dressed in foreign style, appeared to have come from abroad. He was carrying a satchel full of papyri. As he caught sight of the fisherman, he let his bag fall to the ground and ran to him: "Simon Peter!"

"Mark! At last!" He embraced him. The beloved companion of his first evangelical mission to Joppa and Caesarea had come by land along the Via Egnatia, with news from home. Several days before, he had heard in Rome that the apostle was expected, and he had made his way here, with the help of the fire watch, the *vigiles*—amongst whom he found many fellow believers—to greet him on his arrival.

The good members of the fire watch had not said a word to anyone else. They were weary of the old gods, whose fanatical followers gave them endless trouble with street rioting and the like. They had decided for the Crucified One, for on earth he had been as poor as themselves, and he had promised wonderful things for the day when they would lay aside their ropes and buckets at last, and need keep no more night watch, and could sleep without having to waken again in their wretched underground barracks, when they would be nobler than the noble, richer than the rich, awakened from the darkness of their duty to the day of everlasting bliss.

Mark was beaming as he looked round. "What an honor for folk like us, to be able to walk in and out of such a place!" But immediately he fell silent, for to his alarm he saw the veins on Peter's forehead standing out with rage. Like Ezekiel on the endless plain of bleached bones, he stormed: "Is that the news you bring, that the rich are awaiting us?"

"The host of the poor who hope for the Kingdom of God is far greater."

As Ptolemy returned with a slave leading the ass, he heard Flaccus agitatedly implore the fisherman not to scorn his uncle's hospitality in such an offhand way.

"You do not know what poverty is in Rome! The starving, verminous poor live in holes whose length and breadth you could span with your arms. They rot in cellars among the rats and garbage, or pine away up on the top floor of some ghastly tenement, and if a fire breaks out they burn to death because the *vigiles* cannot reach them through the flames. Gaping cracks in the walls are artfully smeared over. The lying caretakers assure you that you will rest soundly, while the rafters creak and threaten to collapse over your very couch. You get no sleep, for you hear your neighbors sneezing, coughing, snoring, scolding, quarreling, through the thin walls. The basements are haunts of vice and harlotry. If a woman is in labor, next morning you find a dying scrap of humanity at your door, for it is the parents' right to kill or abandon a newborn child. That is the Rome of the poor!"

"That is my Rome!" cried Peter, immovable, though Joanna too began to beg desperately for her child's sake. "Mark, what did Matthew Levi write down of our Master's words about the Baptist? 'What did you all come here to see? A man dressed in soft garments?'" He took the ass's halter rope from the slave. Petronilla fell sobbing into her father's arms.

Fondly, Peter stroked his daughter's hair, and sliding his hand down her tear-stained cheeks and under her chin, he raised her troubled face to his for a farewell kiss.

At that moment when the Egyptian prince thought he was wavering, a flock of hens came through a gap in the laurel hedge, into the avenue, five white hens, and in front of them, proudly ruffling his feathers, a cock. He drew himself up as if in defense of his hens, as the steward tried vainly to chase them away.

The cock looked at Peter, and Peter looked at the cock with a painful smile. Then he freed himself fondly but firmly from his daughter's arms. "You need not remind me by crowing," he murmured to the cock. He gave the ass a gentle slap on the rump, uttered a "God bless you," and turned towards the gate. Followed by Mark and the fire watcher, he walked along the street, through the maze of alleys towards the mighty task of the conquest of Rome. He hurried down the hill to the poorest of the poor, and he came empty-handed.

RUEFULLY, Mark reported that at home the apostles were becoming increasingly isolated. Some of the more fickle followers had gone over to Herod Agrippa. The community was threatened by dissension. Meanwhile, Saul of Tarsus and Barnabas, Mark's uncle, had set out to convert the whole of Asia Minor. And what they were attempting in the East, was that not Peter's task in the West? He was eagerly awaited in the capital. Even the highest of the priests of Isis, a dangerous enemy or a powerful friend, wanted Peter to visit him.

But first of all, Peter was to go to the Office for the Registration of Gods, otherwise he would be brought there by force and would be liable to punishment. The *vigiles,* Mark's kindly hosts, were charged with seeing that Peter appeared.

Their barracks were near the bank of the Tiber, at the Aurelian bridge. Inside, it smelled of food and sweat. A number of bunks, rough-hewn stools and tables were ranged along the walls, which were covered with scribbled notices.

Peter was to lodge in the commander's room. The commander, an elderly, heavily built war veteran, was able, as captain of the fire watch, to give free rein to his old fancy for disciplined service, good-natured complaints, and stern commands. He extended a cordial hand to Peter. "Welcome! Your lieutenant Mark has been staying with us for a few days. A fine persevering fellow, though a bit too much of a townsman. But you are from a different workshop. That's what I call a real barrel chest!"

Peter gazed round the room in astonishment. Everywhere about the walls, owls and bats were nailed between wolves' heads and antlers. On the old soldier's wrist a number of little amulets hung from a bronze bracelet. They jingled as he pointed to a couch, to the left of the door. "You should be satisfied with that bunk, because you will be getting up right foot first every morning. That is how I began every campaign. I am glad to have you with us, for they tell me you have mysterious powers at your command. Disobedient men fall dead with fright at your word, so I hear; and prison and fetters could not hold you, you were so strong. Tell me, is it possible to ward off the eye of an envious man? I know you swear by a new god, but beware of the old gods, especially of Pallor and Livor, the pale Begrudger and the leaden-colored Ill-wisher. They are a torment here on the right bank of the Tiber." He fumbled for one of his amulets and kissed it fervently. "You come from foreign parts, so you probably don't know much about these matters of belief. But you don't want to be cleverer than the Emperor Augustus, do you? Because he believed an oracle, he had to do everything in reverse. He had to put on his right shoe first, for it had been prophesied that when he put his left shoe on his right foot, he would die."

"Poor emperor," said Peter sympathetically.

"You will have to start out early tomorrow morning. They are strict at the Registry of Gods. I will send a man with you who knows his way about. And to show that I wish you well, I'm giving you these amber beads. They help against sore throats, and should be handy if you find your mouth drying up when they interrogate you."

NEXT morning, they went first to the Office for the Registration of Persons, where the newcomer's name had to be entered on the records. There Peter received two clay discs which he turned over and over in wonderment, until Mark explained that one was for admission to the circus, while the other was a voucher for free bread. Now their path ran uphill, along the Via Sacra towards the Temple of Jupiter Capitolinus, opposite which the Registry of Gods was situated.

219

The fire watcher had warned them to be cautious, and he quietly went in front. At the end of a narrow corridor on the ground floor, a door stood open. The shoptalk of idle officials reached them.

"It is disgraceful how incompetent the gods are!" complained an unctuous voice. "If the sacrifices are in vain, who gets the blame? We, of course. The dissatisfied worshiper goes to some new foreign god, to Serapis or Isis, and then the priests of our native gods hold us responsible for the fact that the gift offerings don't arrive."

"Shall I be frank?" interjected a nasal voice. "We should put a stop to all these new-fangled foreign gods."

"Who would have the courage to do it, apart from you?" mocked a shrill peevish voice.

The nasal one agreed. "Rome's heroes flog the conquered armies through our streets, but the gods of the defeated—nobody wants to fall out with them. We have to register them. They get looked after by the state, even if nobody is left alive who believes in them."

"You never can tell," warned the embittered voice, and the unctuous one agreed: "Were you ever stuck in a swamp in some German forest? Did you ever look on helplessly while a green meadow swallowed up a rider who was unsuspectingly trying to cross it—horse and man? Not a living enemy for leagues around. You learn to be damned careful not to annoy any of the gods!"

"People should agree on one god," decided the nasal one.

"And dismiss us?" protested the unctuous one. "The high priest of Isis tries to do that quite openly. He calls his goddess the unified figure of all gods and goddesses. But who would trust that Egyptian? He has already been banished once for pimping."

"I don't know—the Judaeans have a very practical arrangement—one god and that's that."

"According to our information, it is not quite so. Only the older ones say that. The younger ones insist that their god had a son who is one with the father and a spirit of both. How and why, I have no idea."

"It is difficult for us up here," complained the bad-tempered one, "high above the everyday affairs of law courts and oratory, triumphs and business deals. From having nothing to do one turns to thinking, and in the end one has thought everything to pieces."

The haughty nasal voice said in a melancholy tone: "Haven't we all the gods here in our files? And when is a god going to enter this room at last?"

As a thoughtful silence fell at this remark, the fire watcher plucked up courage and knocked at the door. Someone called listlessly, "Come in!" Annoyed at the interruption, two of the officials strode pompously to the door of the next room, as the others entered. One, a corpulent man, carried a bowl of olives and a slice of bread, while the other had a half-peeled fig in his hand. They were leaving the youngest of them, a man of senatorial rank by the border of his toga, to deal with this affair, and gave only a fleeting glance to the newcomers as they retired. No doubt that foreign-looking fellow was the one who had been summoned?

As Romans they were accustomed to observing, from the busts and statues of the famous, what was most characteristic in a man, and they hardly gave the humble fire watcher a second look. Their quick glance took in Mark as an honest, and for Rome a rather overidealistic, youngster, but Peter's head they remembered ever after. His blunt features seemed to have been hewn out of grained stone with mighty hammer blows. His beard sprouted from jaws firm-set by years of struggle with the reefing of sails in hard weather and the hauling of heavy nets. His gray hair was as dense as his beard, as his unruly forelock, and his tufted brows. The sturdy laborer had been trying to build up in his mind a whole world, a new earth, whose outlines he guessed at, but which was not yet complete. The expression in his eyes went to the hearts of even the haughty officials: an infinite kindness, a deep understanding of distress, and an awareness of the bliss of a love that demands nothing for itself, but merely gives and consoles and strengthens and is ready to sacrifice itself. His glance was on the lookout for souls, while Mark's roamed in wonder over the high shelves with round metal bins ranged along them, full of papyrus scrolls, each marked with numbers and letters, and in many cases with the names of gods. Through the open window, Peter and Mark could see the temple entrance opposite. The smoke of incense clouded the noble statue in which, for eight hundred years past, the growing might of Rome had honored its own embodiment. Against such might, against Jupiter Capitolinus, stood Simon son of Jonah, a man, and alone.

At present, the Fisher of Men could say nothing that spoke to the heart. He was hemmed in with bureaucratic formalities, and obliged to answer endless questions about his birth and place of origin, the whither and whence and the purpose of his journey. No digressions were permitted. Where he wanted to speak of his vocation, his questioner was only concerned with his profession. Instead of putting down "Messenger of God," he wrote "Fisherman."

The conversation which ensued was halting, for though the fisherman had understood both Greek and Latin well for some time now, he anxiously took advantage of Mark's greater education, since every word might be of the greatest consequence. The young official began by warning them that Claudius, the emperor and god, had exercised unusual mildness towards their compatriots, though their belief—or unbelief, as some might call it—bordered closely on treason. Did not their priests refuse to allow offerings to be made to the divine Caesar Augustus in the Temple at Jerusalem? Did they not shrink from setting his sublime likeness in that same Temple? Rome was keeping a sharp eye on the Jews, particularly on their funeral brotherhoods, so that—to quote his instruction—"no proscribed group should meet together under any pretext. Any contravention of this will be severely punished. Strangers from Palestine are bringing a spiritual pestilence with them that threatens to infect the whole world." His voice took on a metallic tone.

Mark protested that they sought to have no connection with the Jewish communities, nor had they any secret plans. "Render to Caesar what is Caesar's, is what Jesus's followers believe."

"You incite the poor with your teacher's words: Woe to the rich!"

222

To which Peter replied: "Does it not make you happy that you only need sacrifice your riches to enjoy supreme bliss, in all eternity?"

Back came the mocking answer: "Because I am the overfed son of a rich father, do you have to curse me?"

"I came to bless, not to curse."

"Your belief threatens the unity of the Empire."

"We do not live for earthly things. And if all souls are as one, what can man put asunder?"

"The masses are as shapeless as clay. First a mighty hand has to make them men worthy of the name."

With a smile Peter answered: "When God created the world, He made man in his own image."

Shaking his head, the young man got up and went to the window. He looked down the road past the temple, towards the Forum. His lip curled in scorn. "Do you mean to say that the rabble down there, one and all of them, resemble the Highest Being? That screaming, raving, cringing, menacing lot, lying and cheating and acting like wolves to each other? Runaway slaves, broken-down gladiators, shifty customers of all kinds, peasants who live with sheep and hens under the same thatch, thieves, robbers, assassins waiting for hire—all gods?" He laughed aloud, though it annoyed him that such a crowd as he saw should be coming up the Via Sacra at this hour, filling the usually deserted street below.

Peter answered: "Can you tell who among them may receive the call? In our country, many passed by a poor carpenter's mate, and some took him for a criminal and nailed him to the cross. Only we knew that he was the Son of God."

"One of those down there a god? A god who has to die?"

"So that we all might live forever."

"Do you think anyone down there would be tempted to prolong his miserable existence into eternity?"

At a gesture from the official, the fire watcher went out, not without an anxious glance at Peter. For a moment he hesitated, considering whether he should stay. With a heavy heart he descended the stairs, and found it impossible to get out of the building, so dense was the crowd which spread up and down the street and into the hall of the temple itself, the people turning their backs on Jupiter and staring up at the office window in strange silence.

Peter answered slowly and thoughtfully: "A few weeks ago I landed at Pisa and set out for Rome. Along the Via Aurelia, the crowds were lined up shoulder to shoulder, a multitude believing in God and eternal life. Come with us and see for yourself how belief in the Crucified One is growing daily in this city. We have not messengers enough to preach the truth. If you do not believe what I say—is it not the greatest miracle that a poor murdered man of a hated people, abandoned by his own faithful followers—and I am accusing myself now!—who suffered the basest indignities and died the most shameful death, because he knew that he is the Son of God and King of the World—is it not miracle enough that his name now goes from mouth to mouth so that even you know of him too?"

"Have you considered our faith in the Emperor? On a marvellous edifice of human might, human skill, human duty, he is throned as a god. He is the State, and the State is the world, and each of us is set in his place for the good of the whole."

"And yet—" Peter answered softly but weightily, for he was conscious of the danger, not to himself (he did not care about that) but to his work, "and yet this edifice in which you serve is a beehive of ceaseless toil, a structure of harshness and severity. You kill and kill without pity, you slaughter your slaves, your starvelings, your children, your wounded gladiators and injured charioteers—even your emperor-god Caligula you killed. Did you never receive a grateful look or bestow a gift that made you happy? Don't you long for some great kindness that waits for you with open arms and takes you to its heart into an eternity where no worldly arm nor envy nor murder nor sorrow can reach? Lay aside the pride of your garment and be good, nothing but good!" He pointed to the innumerable scrolls. "They say that every god in your vast empire is registered here. I call on them all, whatever their name may be, wherever they are enthroned—in all their might let them rise against me in battle array as high and wide as the sky itself, and I will deny them, pity them, destroy them. Jesus said: 'Wherever only two are brought together in my name'—like Mark and me here—'I am always in the midst of you.' At your request, we two have come here. God is in us, he is called Wonderful, Counselor, Mighty God, Eternal Father, Prince of Peace. One of you said: 'You have registered all the gods here, but no god ever entered this place.'" He stopped, made the sign of the cross, and put his arm round Mark's shoulder, and concluded quite softly: "God has come to you. He is here."

It was noon. The two other Romans who had entered cautiously, hearing these last words, were terrified at this monstrous challenge to all their gods. Nothing stirred. A great silence spread on angel's wings over house and hall, temple and hill, over the city swarming with people. Even the mightiest of Rome's gods did not dare to release any lighting, any thunderbolt, as Peter said: "Your own gods, poor demons, bow in silent adoration before the Almighty. They know that Jesus is All and One. You wanted to punish me, but I came to you in love, to bring you a blessing. I thank you for summoning us, so that God at last could enter into this office of the gods. Peace be with you."

As he fell silent in the silence of the world about him, the great crowd below grew anxious for him. A tremendous sigh from thousands of oppressed hearts rose trembling into the quiet room, then all at once, as with one mouth, the multitude cried: "Simon Petrus! Petrus! Ave!"

PRINCE PTOLEMY's sad dark eyes had too long been accustomed to the noble slender columns of the Roman temples, those polished heirs of Greek perfection. For all his Egyptian upbringing, he found the painted pillars of the sanctuary of Isis heavy and oppressive, standing as they did so thickly massed that it was hardly possible to obtain a clear view down the aisles; and a terrifying view it would have been, in any case, arousing a fear that in the sleepy monotony of shrill flutes and whirring sistra, the horrible man-headed lions and the giant human figures with their merciless, threatening falcon and ibis heads, might step down among the bald priests and the garlanded temple prostitutes.

The prince hated the embarrassment that always overcame him in the Iseum; for all that, it would have been beautiful to become a falcon, and a falcon-god moreover! But the Romans had chained his hands, and Peter had clipped his wings.

Doors opened, doors shut. In the mysterious green light, the High Priest of Isis rose to his feet. His illustrious head shone in all its baldness like a timeless masterpiece in green slate, the long, narrow, well-bred face of one to whom nothing human was strange, and who exercised his mastery over men by virtue of his knowledge. His face revealed a curious balance between the bestial and the spiritual. Ptolemy felt repelled by the arching wrinkles that stretched up from the corners of the priest's mouth, faintly twitching from time to time in secret irony. His eyes had seen so much, both of physical and mystical ecstasy. Wisdom and intellect shone from his features, while the crow's-feet at his temples betrayed him as an old man nearing the end of his time.

Eventually the green face broke the silence: "King Falcon in the egg! You come too late and too soon! Too late, because Simon Peter is preaching already; too soon, because he has not yet dared to appear before me."

Ptolemy could not restrain a smile at the haughtiness of these last words, but a cryptic remark took him by surprise: "The Judaean is doing himself much harm." At a gesture from the High Priest, one of his servants answered the prince's questioning look from the green shadows. He began as if he were reading a hero-epic:

"The Forum Romanum lay empty in the heat of high noon. Every idler had drifted homewards, every court had pronounced sentence, every shop was closed. Everyone who had anything to eat was eating, everyone was a welcome guest who had gossip or news or flattery. And then, between arches and halls, statues and pillars, basilicas and temples, the sewers spewed forth the dregs of mankind, everything that Rome could not and would not digest."

Another interposed, his voice trembling with fear: "Wedged among the festering, slavering, garlic-reeking masses—their sweat stinking through their garments and onto mine—I was swept by the multitude filling the Forum away up the road to the very summit, to the Capitoline Temple. They were expecting Peter, they shouted for Peter, they demanded Peter. 'Peter!' they howled. They seized him, lifted him, bore him along. All who were in their way they shoved aside with blows. He was everyman's man and the liberator of all. They greeted him with hoarse shouts of joy."

Anxiously, the first one continued: "Around the Emperor, before the palace, the guards sprang to arms, set arrow to bow and stone to catapult. Doors slammed and were bolted, heavy beams laid across them; the trembling hands could not find the grooves quickly enough."

As if he were experiencing over again his own terror, the rioting of the multitude, and the merciless testing of the apostle, he went on: "On their sweating shoulders they swung Peter high up to the rostrum, among the trophies of land and sea victories, between the statues of the mighty leaders of the people, onto the tribune of Julius Caesar. Now before Caesar himself stood Simon son of Jonah, the man from the Galilean sea—poor before the masses of the poor. . . ."

His voice failed him, and his colleague tremblingly repeated the wild challenge of the multitude: " 'We are the persecuted, we are the tortured, we are those crucified for a whim, the lowest of the low—over us, the cruel she-wolf and the whelps of the she-wolf. Rotten, rotten at the root is the tree under which she suckled them. But the tree that bears no fruit will be hewn down and thrust into the fire! May your Lord God wither the tree and cause the fruit to perish! We are all with you, the chosen of your God who came to the poorest of the poor. We have gathered from all the four quarters of the world, from sky's edge to sky's edge, for the Last Judgment!' "

That cry from a hundred thousand throats still seemed to quiver in the marrow of the two reporters. They had not noticed the prince among the enormous throng in the Forum Romanum. They knew nothing of his feelings, compounded of love and hatred, towards Peter, which had urged him in the wake of the Messenger of the Lord right to the very

227

tribune. But now he could no longer control himself, for he lived through those terrible moments again with the narrators, helpless among the helpless, a rebel among rebels, and knowing better than any that the State, like an executioner, was already raising the ax to strike off every head with a single blow.

Ptolemy, standing in the mob, had sensed the terror of the lonely man on the speaker's tribune, knowing how bitter it must be for him to realize that false prophets had distorted the words of the Lord into a doctrine aimed at overthrowing the State. Had unexpected victory beckoned to the chief apostle on the Forum there? Or were merely Peter's weaknesses again being put cruelly to the test? Now that he had raised his banner over a world of suffering, was that not the realization of his young manhood's wish to have at his back an invincible army of believers? But the Kingdom was to have been a Kingdom of Love, whereas here all was vengefulness, greed and the lust to kill. Would he, Ptolemy, have been able to resist, if such a mighty host of desperate men, matching in numbers even the Emperor's own guard, had called on him to be their leader?

On the tribune of Julius Caesar stood a man as poor as those around him, a man living even more frugally than they, a man with nothing but a Word and a pitying love for his neighbor, but a man who was now called on to show himself inexorable. He stood alone against the bloody cravings of a whole city of misery. He had to take from them what is the wishful dream of every beggar, and to give them instead what Jesus had provided: "No worldly happiness on earth, but in the afterworld—everything."

The priests of Isis were never to forgive the prince for his refutation of their carefully staged account, their proof of the miscarriage of Peter's plans and the foundering of his faith. Calmly, proudly, noble as the tallest of his ancestors' pyramids in the desert, Ptolemy spoke like a true son of kings: "In our sacred hieroglyphics, there is but one symbol for 'Justice,' and that same symbol means 'Truth.' On the Forum, the rabble threatened to tear Peter to pieces, like mad dogs.

His 'No' was his death. And now, you faithful recounters of that noonday moment: Truth! Justice! —What did Peter do?"

Hesitantly, they both confessed that he had merely asked them to pray with him, to repeat his prayer, word for word.

"But what he said, and the manner in which they repeated it, was the greatest miracle I ever saw," said Ptolemy. "I have seen him heal physical suffering. But here he was healing souls. His God had taught him the words, and many already knew them. To others, they were new, and newest of all was the ardent understanding of the poor man on the tribune of the mighty, fighting for his life and for his faith. For his prayer was a prayer for them all. Like him, they had been searching all their wretched lives for a kingdom of kindness and justice, for a Will, to obey which is happiness. Peter had shared all their suffering and more besides. He forgave us, and we all answered that we forgave him, even if all his love spared us not a drop of sweat, not a blow with the whip, not the smallest disappointment, even if his God brought us not peace but the sword; and that, for many of us, was bound to mean the sword of the executioner.

"For the first time they understood, and I understood, sentence by sentence, plea by plea. 'Our Father,' they cried and many of them had never known a father worthy of the name. But from the sound of Peter's voice they realized what and who their Father is. They bowed their heads and they who had dreamed of wresting power from Caesar himself yielded to the might of the Almighty: 'Thy will be done'—even on the earth soaked with their sweat and stained with their blood. Humbly, they begged for their daily bread, and the next thing they asked was something tremendous: 'Forgive us our sins,' all the sins of those born in iniquity, living in iniquity, and condemned to iniquity. But then came the greatest moment of all. The guards must have heard it, perhaps the Emperor himself, when the hundreds of thousands gathered there wholeheartedly forgave all those who had sinned against them. On that account the new God was merciful to the misfortunate. He would lead them away from the temptation to seize power and to do evil. They saw in astonishment that even Peter was begging his God not to lead him into temptation. And his temptation had been great!"

IN THE Roman settlements, emissaries of the priests of Isis incited the orthodox Jews and superstitious pagans against Peter's new communities. Already there were rumors of impending famine, of grain fleets run aground—the start of the old gods' judgment.

Whenever Jews and Jewish Christians began to quarrel—and it happened all too often—the pagan rabble were lying in wait ready to strike, to raid and plunder. How the merchants and dealers, the money-changers and cookshop owners lamented! The fire watch had to be in so many places to protect them, that their seven regiments threatened to be too few. As usual, the worst areas were those on the farther bank of the Tiber where, among the teeming Jewish population, intolerant Pharisees were calling down God's wrath on their heretical brothers, to the malicious delight of the Romans.

One evening some hundreds of fanatical Palestinians had gathered in front of the fire-watch barracks, wildly shouting for Peter to be handed over to them. They would not disperse until two of their number had convinced themselves that he really was not hidden inside. When the apostle came home, late that night, the good fire chief had to ask him to look for some other lodging. It was with heavy heart that he watched him go, for Peter was always in good humor, despite his indifference to the old gods and the old customs, and to the evil eye itself. In the face of his rough seafarer's jokes, the worst omens lost their power. The centurion began to be ashamed of his amulets, and inclined more and more to Peter's faith.

Peter and Mark moved to the Aventine, where lay the house and workshop of the tent-cloth maker Aquila, a compatriot of theirs who lived on the northern slope of the long hill with his wife Prisca. When they married, Prisca's mistress, the good lady Priscilla, wife of the Senator Quintus Cornelius Pudens, had given her her freedom and a handsome dowry. Mark knew that this house with its sparkling cleanliness was right after the

apostle's heart. It contained nothing unnecessary. The craftsman's belief allowed of no pictures; a cross was the only
ornament.

Taciturn and reflective as Master Aquila was by nature,
he liked to spend his leisure hours in his wife's company.
On fine evenings she would accompany him up to the jasmine
arbor at the top of the slope behind their house, which afforded a wonderful view over the noblest of Rome's seven
hills. His silence was a prayer of thanks. He had tried to put
his feelings into simple words for his guests, Peter and Mark,
on the previous Sunday, when he had asked them to his house
after the love feast of the recently formed Aventinian community.

"This is my very own view of the city, Simon Peter. Up
there on the Palatine are the most resplendent of mortal men,
whose power is so absolute that they believe themselves to
be gods. Down there in the valley between Aventine and Palatine is the gigantic playground of all that is evil in the Roman
soul: the Circus Maximus. Cruelty, trickery, force, above and
below."

Aquila had traveled widely about the Mediterranean. His
guests were surpised to hear that he had worked in the same
shop as Saul of Tarsus, far away in Saul's home town. He
had wanted to learn tent-weaving as the tribes in Arabia
Petraea practice it in their endless wandering. Such tents were
impermeable and everlasting.

He told them: "You in Jerusalem had sent him home. Being
avoided by Jew and Christian alike, he had to work hard to
earn his bread. He was burning with the desire to proclaim
his knowledge of God to mankind. I was one of his first pupils,
though he was still worried whether you would let him do
as he wished. Day after day he put himself to the test. He
was sure of his mission, for Jesus had revealed himself to him.
He was my guide and teacher, and it happened that the others
listened also, and all unawares they became his first Chosen
Ones, his group, his *ecclesia,* as he called us, the Church of
Tarsus. Quite a number of us were pagans. The wise Stoic
Athenodorus, Augustus's teacher, and one of the great men
of the Emperor's court, the poet Seneca, were among his audi-

231

ence. Allow me to quote a saying of his, which I never tire of: 'Live with men as if God saw you; speak with God as if men were listening.' Is he not already one of us?"

Peter shook his head. "But you think that Saul was one of us?"

"To him, you were the great ones, the important ones. He had come to you to redeem himself for his complicity in Stephen's death. And how grateful he was that he was allowed to see you, that you agreed with his belief that faith and trust are more than law. To see all his converts united in one church over the whole world, that was his desire; and he always cited you pillars of the original community."

THE Aventine community, which was growing in numbers and importance through Peter's presence among them, had just ended another love feast. Now the members were quietly resting on the benches at the top of the slope. They looked down and saw far below them the circus filling with spectators; for the games were due to start at dusk. To avoid the discomfort of the hot sun, the Praetor Cornelius Pudens had arranged for the contests to take place at nighttime.

A little embarrassed, Prisca explained: "My former master is inclining more and more to the true faith, but his high position obliges him to arrange the games here. His wife often complained to me how difficult it is for them to free themselves from the fetters of heathen custom. But she and her daughters are growing into the faith."

"And still they will be following behind the puppet-gods in the procession this evening, because it is reckoned to be an honor," said Aquila ironically.

Mark suddenly became attentive. In alarm, he thought: How can I get Peter away from here? If he could guess what was awaiting him! The young man had been so preoccupied with his many duties that he had given no thought to the spectacle which was shortly to take place just below them. Cornelius Pudens, in his capacity of Praetor, would lead the festive procession that was to move from the Capitol down to the gigantic arena. Petronilla had been chosen, along with

232

his own children, to follow in a festive chariot. Flaccus had implored her not to refuse such a high honor.

Mark knew of these arrangements, and he also knew that such a godly man as Peter would see nothing in it but heathen idolatry. What would confront him now was the very thing that grieved him about so many candidates for baptism. Listening to them, he found that, next to their daily bread, what they considered most essential were the cruel games in honor of their gods. From Aquila's garden, the apostle would see the triumph of the demons, and his own child in the midst of it all!

Below him, on either side of the valley which had been made into a huge racecourse between the Palatine and the Aventine, thousands of eager spectators were already gathered on the packed terraces. They were impatiently waiting for the ceremonial procession that marked the start of the festival, and the moment when the four-horse chariots would drive onto the track and they would be allowed to rave and rejoice. As was customary, before the races and the fights the gods were to be carried in front of the ceremonial procession of gladiators, then the priests would line them along the wall in the middle of the arena, so that they too could watch from their exalted thrones.

The polished marble walls of the Emperor's palace opposite were still lit by the glow of the setting sun, but twilight had already descended on the foot of the valley, from whence rose the mighty muffled roar of the conversation, banter, laughter and quarreling of a lively southern crowd.

Mark pressed more and more urgently for them to leave. He constantly brought new arguments to bear. The priests, Narcissus, Linus and Anaclete, must be waiting on the Tiber bank for their promised interview. Ptolemy had warned them that the priests of Isis were gathering all sorts of evidence to shake the converts' belief in Jesus's apostles. If Peter were seen there as a spectator at a heathen festival, what an uproar that would create!

But today the usually restless apostle seemed tired. Was it the long-feared collapse of his native strength? It had been useless to remind him that he must take care of himself, that he should not indiscriminately listen to, teach, test, initiate every unworthy individual who came his way, as if all the angels were rejoicing over the penitent sinner. He shared with each one the sorrows of his life, as if he himself had hated and loved, slandered and murdered, and must now repent. He reached into their shame and burdened his head and heart with the refuse of human misery. If his mission was to preach to everyone, then he must be everyone. It was his duty to search for the last lost drachma.

Furthermore, he exhausted himself by his style of preaching Jesus's life and sorrows, which overwhelmed his audience like a holy tempest. It was a gripping and frightening thing, to see his eyes opening wider and wider as he relived those three tremendous years with the Redeemer, three years of deadly peril, of fighting unarmed against enemies, enemies, enemies, who became more numerous all the while. At last came the grievous yearning of the Thursday before Easter, and the desperate remorse of Good Friday. All his listeners longed with him to be able to see the Lord's hands, emaciated with suffering, trembling in loving self-sacrifice, hands that healed, hands that caressed children, hands that comforted. Hands that had shaken him into wakefulness in vain on the Mount of Olives.

Mark, so much younger than he, had more than once fallen asleep of an evening over his writing, and Peter had wakened him gently as if he were still conscious of his guilt, saying: "Lie down and rest, my son."

This quiet Sunday evening the apostle sat leaning back on the garden bench, relaxed and happy. In the deep shadows about his face it was not possible to tell whether his eyes were fixed on something down below, or merely dreaming in the twilight, oblivious of the vast swarm of people in the valley.

Night was falling now, and suddenly a swarm of torch-bearers mounted the steps leading from the palace to the Imperial box, making the arena shine as if the sun rose. Torch upon torch led the royal couple, Claudius and Messalina, who stood out against the golden background of the guards' armor.

Hoarse with excitement and contempt, Aquila growled:

"The Emperor and his Babylonish whore! To think that Romans could be so silent!"

The thousands below them lay quiet as death. Only the cicadas were heard.

Unexpectedly, cheering broke out. The enormous crowd stirred and grew excited, for far along the dark valley of the Velabrum, points of flickering flame could be seen, falling into line for the torchlight procession. In the reddish gleam the faces of the torchbearers glowed like little red moons as they slowly began to approach. The leaders had already reached the racetrack, and still the end of the procession could not be seen. They split to right and left and marching along the mighty wall of the arena itself, they formed a triumphal lane to illuminate the procession. At the same time gigantic pitch flares were lighted along the tops of the outer walls.

Breathlessly Prisca whispered: "My master!" She had discerned the Praetor Quintus Cornelius Pudens in his purple toga interwoven with gold. A chariot drawn by four white horses, whose flowing manes and tails were also decked with gold, bore him onto the racetrack. He stood proudly leaning on his scepter. Above his head wavered the gilded oak-leaf crown, held up by a slave, as a sign that he was the *triumphator* of the festival. The erect images of the gods, made by a Greek sculptor, followed on gigantic trolleys. The stiff images swayed and staggered in step with those who drew them along.

Anxiously Mark threw a sidelong glance at Peter. The sight of these images—Jupiter and Juno, Apollo and Diana, Venus and Bacchus—had roused him out of his repose. He was just about to turn away in disgust, when a sudden burst of cheering from the spectators made him look again.

A wide carriage made of mother-of-pearl shells artfully joined together, and drawn by gold-harnessed mules, was pulled out onto the track, preceded by young knights on thoroughbred horses. A gentle moonlike light shone from the carriage, from which the Praetor's daughters, dressed in expensive white stuffs from the Far East, were strewing roses out of silver baskets. Dominating the charming group was a slender girl with a wreath of white roses in her dark hair, and enormous wings of snowy swan feathers on her shoulders,

235

like the angel of the Annunciation. Enraptured, Prisca whispered: "How beautiful..."

Peter looked down more intently, for he had recognized one of the horsemen as Flaccus, and another, on a prancing white Arab, as Prince Ptolemy. And now the group came nearer, into the bright light, and the enormous crowd burst into a roar of wonder and delight. They sprang to their feet and stormily clapped their hands, and in time to the clapping, thousands of throats acclaimed the goddess of victory.

Startled, Prisca fumbled for her husband's strong arm. Mark knit his brows and closed his eyes in pain. Peter recognized his daughter, his daughter in the midst of the heathen.

Till that moment, the unsuspecting Petronilla had been enjoying as a delightful mummery her strange expensive clothes, the magic of her wings, the torchlight procession, the gay company of the young knights and the enchanting proximity of her beloved. She had felt as if she were hovering blissfully over the whole scene like an angel from heaven. As the applause rolled down from the highest benches and broke all round the arena like a sea of enthusiasm, the girl only felt delighted at the success of her own grace, enlivened by the joy she shared in common with her friends, and heightened by the pride which her fleeting glances read in Flaccus's eyes.

But suddenly, out of the turbulent roar and the storm of clapping, she distinguished the syllables, the words they were rhythmically repeating: *"Nike! Nike!"*

All Rome had understood Cornelius Pudens' allusion. Everyone had recognized in the winged maiden the ancient goddess of victory, the Victoria, who had for centuries sanctified the sessions chamber of the Senate. With insane joy, they snatched at this opportunity for a demonstration in favor of the old republican freedom, with its elected representatives of the conquering people, whose symbol was the winged goddess, the senators' protectress. From their benches, from those of the knights, and from the lowest to the highest terraces, roared the wild battle cry of Latin warriors: "Victoria! Victoria!" It was a unanimous protest against the tyranny of

236

Claudius. The cheering was for Rome, for Rome's future, its glory and greatness.

Even Aquila leaned far over the balustrade and grimly joined in. Let Claudius the god listen to this!

But Peter was only looking at the winged girl, and he saw the swan pinions flutter as if an arrow had struck her. Petronilla seemed to sway, she threatened to fall. All at once she had realized what she must seem to be to the satanic Roman crowd, not an angel of the Lord but a heathen deity, the blasphemy incarnate of the living God.

The daughters of Pudens were dismayed to see her so disturbed, and Flaccus even more. He knew how strictly the pagan religious ceremonial had to be observed at the games. Even the slightest deviation would throw the superstitious crowd into a frenzy of fear of the vengeance of the gods. The festival would have to be broken off, and only after consulting every oracle would they dare to consider repeating it. The crowd, deprived of their spectacle, would be so furious, they would hardly know how to get their revenge. Alarmed for his beloved, he shouted to her through the tumult: "Don't move! Else we shall fall victims to their fury, yourself and your father with you!"

That the danger was all the greater on account of the insult to the Emperor, Petronilla did not guess. In her distraction the lights seemed to spin round her like fiery whirlpools.

Quietly she began to pray: "Father in Heaven! Forgive my vanity. How could I guess they would acclaim me as a heathen goddess. Lord! The temptation to seem beautiful in the eyes of my beloved was too great. Is it a sin that I was happy at his pleasure? Let me atone alone, and punish none of those I love."

High above her, where the green of the Aventine gardens made a dark frame for the cheering crowd, without her suspecting it, her father stood. He ran his hand over his forehead and eyes, and suddenly he began to beat his breast. Dismayed, Mark, Prisca and Aquila saw the mighty messenger, the Rock on whom Jesus meant to build his Church, begin desperately to accuse himself: "I have been weak once again, Lord! Once? A dozen times! And now you punish me through my own

237

flesh and blood. I wanted to serve you without rest, without feasting, the shepherd of your growing flock. Meanwhile my wife and child have become tainted. Forgive me that I rested too soon, that I grew tired. I cast my net among the heathen, and my own family slipped through the meshes. I will bring you others, and when you ask me, I will be deep in shame, for what is mine is no longer yours. At your last supper you proudly said: 'Those whom you gave me, none of them have gone astray.' Let me redeem my child, and punish us all here, and not in the hereafter!"

IN STREETS and alleys, markets and squares, along the tenement passages, in the palaces of noblemen and the fire watchers' barracks, around the cookshops and taverns, in the Forum, in the priestly colleges, the law courts, the Senate, in the Imperial Court, and outside the Porta Capena, the rumor ran upstairs and downstairs, from window to window, from door to door: "Misfortune has befallen the miracle-man! He who could preach so eloquently is dumb. The old gods have punished him. No, his own God, because his daughter mocked him as a heathen goddess!"

Everyone who could, hurried to the Aventine. The sympathizers, the merely curious, the zealots, the fanatics, all flocked in a mass towards the southeast of Rome. Soon the steep paths were so packed with crowds that the air was full of the cries of half-fainting women and lost children. As if some tremendous spectacle was about to take place, fresh crowds surged up the slope above the Circus Maximus. As it was now impossible to move between the garden walls and the houses, the multitude filled the enormous arena without regard to rank or worth. All eyes were turned to Aquila's garden and house.

The imperial guard had great difficulty in making way through the crowd for Scribonius Largus, the imperial physician, whom Cornelius Pudens had summoned. The surgeon was accompanied by a group of his pupils, of whom one was allowed to let blood, another to deaden pain by administering mandragora, while there were medically trained slaves to tend to eyes and throat. Prisca had recognized the physician immediately as a frequent guest at Cornelius's house. She knew his name and rank, and knew also that as Claudius's physician alone, he earned 250,000 sesterces a year, and though she shrank at the thought of a heathen examining the apostle's daughter, she greeted him respectfully and led him to the sick girl.

Peter, sitting locked in his room, his clenched fists pressing into his knees, was racked with sorrow for his child. He knew that great decisions confronted him. Had he the right to forgive those who had so wantonly involved his daughter in their heathen masquerade—or had she taken part of her own free will?

He recalled how the night before he had gone down in silence, and had himself taken off the wings and the expensive dress. He had wrapped his child in his own overgarment, and with his enormous strength had carried the girl past the rearing chariot teams, out of the Circus through the quiet night lanes up to Aquila's house. She lay lifeless when he carefully set her on the bed. In the sultry south wind, the sweat had been streaming down his face. His wide eyes blazed in the flicker of the little oil lamps, while Joanna knelt and laid her ear to her child's heart. "She is alive..." she whispered. With wet cloths which Prisca brought she tried to bring the unconscious girl to her senses. When she loosened her light garment, the girl's body was revealed in its tender beauty, but strangely limp, as if the muscles along her right side had dissolved. At last she succeeded in rousing the girl from her deep sleep. But she could only open her left eye. She still seemed to be seeing terrible things. Slowly she recognized her sobbing mother. With an obvious effort, she raised her left hand a little and gently stroked Joanna's tear-stained cheek. But when she tried to lift her right arm to embrace the kneeling woman, she cried aloud, and took hold of her right hand with her left, but it was unable to move of its own. Terrified, the girl realized that her limbs were without feeling. With an enormous effort of will, she tried to become mistress of her body again, but she remained paralyzed and lay as if she had been felled, till with a sigh of exhaustion even her good eye closed, and she resigned herself to her fate.

On her knees, Joanna crept to Peter: "Simon, I cannot understand this dreadful thing. When a cripple lay by the wayside and called to our Master, Jesus said: 'Stand up! Your sins are forgiven.' But what sin can this pure child have committed? Was it so sinful, that my child and I lived in a more beautiful house than you, where the air was purer? Should we have sheltered with you in the fire barracks? You who have healed so many, heal my child for me, your child!"

The burly man fell to his knees, leaned heavily on his daughter's bed, gazed long at her, and humbly kissed the hem of her garment. Then he got up slowly and with difficulty, and stood silent, his eyes closed. He gave his child one more dolorous look, then went to his room.

WHILE Peter was struggling with his conscience in the loneliness of his room, the imperial physician had arrived. The despairing Joanna, still greatly upset that the father who could have helped so much had left his child to languish, put all her hopes on the stranger, not realizing that his self-assured and dignified manner effected half the cure for many of his patients.

His eager pupils stood round in a half circle, while he began his examination and, at the same time, gave them a learned discourse. Joanna was unable to answer many of his questions. She could not say how her daughter had fallen so dangerously ill. She could assure him that her child had never suffered from epilepsy. For that illness, Scribonius mentioned in an aside, physicians were using human blood nowadays, to be taken while warm—for preference, gladiator's blood while it was still flowing. The limp condition of her paralyzed limbs reminded him of similar cases in which he thought the patient's nerves were the cause of the trouble. For such cases, there was no quick cure.

Petronilla raised her left eyelid and stared in astonishment at the stranger by her bed. Now that he was touching her left side also, she was aware of the examination. The great physician leaned over her and tried to raise her right eyelid.

240

He spoke soothingly to her, and sought to find out what had caused the paralysis. As she could not speak, he asked her to answer with her good eyelid: If she closed it twice, that meant "yes"; if thrice, "no." To the question: Was it caused by shock? Petronilla closed her eye twice. The doctor thought it might be worth trying the power of saliva, which was efficacious in certain infectious illnesses. In his opinion the girl should be brought to the sacred region of Puteoli, to have her complaint treated with mud baths.

Tears ran down Joanna's cheeks. The disappointment was too great. Involuntarily her glance wandered towards the door of the room in which her husband had locked himself. She saw Flaccus forcing his way through the crowd, accompanied by Mark, both of them gasping for breath. Everyone was silent now, and she heard him knock at the apostle's door, and cry out desperately: "Simon Peter, you who call the keys your own, to bind and to loosen, unlock the curse that has stricken your daughter! Why do you let the innocent suffer?"

At his cry of distracted love, the women burst into loud weeping, and those standing near fell on their knees and cried louder and louder still: "Heal her!"

As Flaccus went on shouting and hammering at the door as if his life were at stake, his cries echoed up and down the street, all across the Aventine. There was none who was not stirred, none who did not join in the thundering cry of "Peter! Heal her!" To Peter, listening, the sound of Joanna's voice was the most painful of all. He tore the door open so violently that the handle came away in his fist. He let it fall carelessly to the ground, and saw before him a sea of faces along the passage and in the front garden, through the gate and under the tree shadows of the lane, the despairing faces of his followers. He looked through the door opposite, at the physician in his richly bordered toga by his daughter's bedside, with his slaves and students around him. He saw Flaccus on his knees before him.

Again and again the cry of the multitude rang in his ears: "Heal her! Heal her! Heal her!"

His great chest heaved as if he were drawing breath to shout the same cry, louder than all of them, to the Lord.

It seemed to him he was no longer merely himself, it was as if every man's thought and will were centered in him. Currents of love and countercurrents of hatred, longing and pain, faith and doubt, raged against each other in this inner world of his. Right, Truth, God must surely prevail—only, what was Right?

Could he, would he be allowed to fail? What they were all shouting for, was that God's will too? Dare he let his fatherly love rebel against the love of God, the love that called his Son home to Him only after the cruelest martyrdom? Must he sacrifice his daughter as God the Father sacrificed God the Son?

In the midst of his indecision, a voice came to him over the heads of the crowd, a furious voice whose Latin had a guttural Syrian burr. Someone had clambered up the slope above the terraces of the Circus Maximus, and was shouting despite the protests of the citizens who tried to silence him with cries of: "Onesimus! The chief of the cutpurses and the runaway slaves! Get back where you belong!" But they fell quiet before the bloody vengefulness of his cry.

"Simon Peter! You tried to beguile us into love, when hatred is the order of the day. And now it is having its revenge, that love you preached and now deny!"

Peter looked around him. No fists were clenched, no hand raised in his defense. Everyone was listening. Did Onesimus speak for them all? Did they sneer with him: "Love your neighbor as yourself, provided he is rich; feed the poor with words until they starve their way into everlasting bliss!"

The ragged horde screamed their applause and again the voice of Onesimus shrilled: "Simon Peter, do you still dare to pretend to be God's word? Have yourself nailed on the cross first, then you will see what Christ wants. He has crucified your child on your own teaching, so that you may see where you have fallen short. Who sent you out among the rich? Jesus? Never! His orders were: Go in the squares and alleyways. Bring me the poor, the crippled, all those dulled by suffering and infirmity. Run out along every road and call them in from the hedgerows so that they fill my house. But those you bring in are the senators and knights, the princes. All

242

Rome knows it. But we want a Jesus who calls for the sword. Who brings fire and intends it to burn. When we pray, there are sparks before our eyes with hunger, our teeth are chattering for fear one of our children is just dying of hunger or our wives are selling themselves in the darkness under the colonnades for the bit of bread that means salvation. If you do not bring us a Saviour from such misery, do not tell us that our misery is grace! Set us free, we who are stricken like your own child! Here we are, God's lost sons, thousands of us, ready to take you and God at your word, and to keep you to your own pledge of love!

"Hurl the cross at the world, that enormous cross from which all our blood is dripping! Strike with its crossbeam like an ax and fell the power of evil, and then your child will be your child again, and all of us, all your children!"

Peter knew that every miracle had happened when his faith stood firm. What stirred his innermost feelings now was the knowledge that Jesus had never wrought a miracle for himself; dare he work one now for his most dear, for his child, and in the last resort, for himself?

With a pensive shake of his head, the master-physician had just declared that such a serious illness in one so young would require very lengthy treatment. Peter stood beside him. Flaccus was the only one to raise his voice in the silence: "Can your God do nothing to make her well?"

Peter replied: "He alone knows the why and the purpose...."

"How can those outside believe in his justice?"

The young knight fell silent, for Peter had turned his eyes upon him, and his look seemed to take in far more than his poor self. In Peter's expression there was something great, something exalted, and though the impatience of thousands of overwrought people was centered upon him, something sublimely patient. He summoned all his compassion for mankind, all his paternal love, for a deed that was at once salvation and attestation, self-denial and glorification.

His prayer was too great, too deep for him to express in words. Once again the cry of the masses reached them, and again they all joined in, except Scribonius Largus, who smiled in embarrassment, thinking that the cry was meant for him. He heard Peter saying to Flaccus, with a catch in his voice: "My son, a father who sees his child suffer may tear his garment and beat his breast, because he gave the child life but not happiness." Then he bent over Petronilla's bed and looked at her intently. He whispered: "Not for us, Lord, not for us . . ." He drew a deep breath and stood up to his full height, took a few paces back and said in a calm and powerful voice: "Get down from your bed, my child, with the help of none but Jesus, and come with me."

A roar burst from above. The sultry southerly breeze gave way to a fresh north wind with a scent of mountain meadows. The sun broke through and the sky became blue and radiant.

With her left hand, the sick girl fumbled at her dress, which the physician had undone in order to examine her. She drew the garment over her gently curved and heaving breast. Her right arm, just now paralyzed and seemingly lifeless, seemed to swell with new strength, and became her support. Before the astonished onlookers, the girl stood up. For a moment she seemed to sway, but then she stood firm. Her narrow feet walked more and more quickly across the tiled floor. The women burst into tears, the men stood as if bewitched. The youngsters lifted their hands to support and protect the girl who was so miraculously gliding towards them.

As if she had risen from a long rest, Petronilla almost danced in front of her father along the passage. She did not notice whether the gravel hurt her tender feet. She stood unsupported in front of the stone bench, beside Peter who had not dared to touch her. High above the Circus Maximus, as if on a platform, her slender figure shone against the dark laurel bushes.

The crowd burst into a joyous roar, as if the Palatine and the Aventine were thundering against each other.

Somebody struck up a hymn of praise, and others joined in. Those who did not know the words sang the tune. The hymn which the Christians had learned for their high feasts, the Magnificat of the Redeemer's mother, echoed over the valley. Petronilla threw her arms round her father's neck. None realized better than she what an honor it was, to be greeted with this song of the humble maid on whom God bestowed his grace.

She whispered: "Father, dear father. Now all the cheering for that heathen goddess of victory is atoned for. You have been victorious in me. We have been permitted to glorify Jesus through a miracle!"

Peter gently bent over his daughter and kissed the joyous tears from her lashes. He lifted her high above the stone balustrade so that she stood out against the clean-swept sky. As she had seen her father do many times before, she raised her right hand and while the wide-eyed people sank to their knees, with all the gratitude of her heart and the strength of her healed arm, she made them the sign of a mighty cross.

For a moment, the vast crowd stared at her in silence, then suddenly all over the valley, they began stamping, cheering, and waving their kerchiefs.

THE weather and the miracle seemed to have brought new promise to Peter's followers. A cool breeze blew the sultriness out of the rooms, out of the city, out of mind and soul. In the gardens between the white palaces, the lawns grew green again, while above the ancient oak woods the dark leaves rustled, and the tall slender pines swayed their gilded tops in the scented wind.

Mark and the two presbyters Linus and Anaclete were accompanying Peter to his home on the Aventine that evening. In the growing darkness, they were discussing the still more miraculous consequences of the miraculous healing of Petronilla.

There had been an enormous rush of new candidates for baptism. The two presbyters complained that they could not find enough new teachers, they had to establish new communities, find new meeting places. How was one to prune these wildly growing vines, so as to keep the vineyards of the Lord in proper order? Despite all their efforts, they did not succeed in making the fisherman aware that the time had come to

245

knot his mighty net for fear the captive world should slip out again; the sure and firm edifice was still lacking.

With a furtive side glance, Mark noticed how tired and downcast his beloved master looked, and in no wise happy at his enormous catch. He had not made a single answer to all their complaints that a staff, a whole administration, was now necessary to deal merely with the visits, to arrange appointments for interviews, and to answer the many questions and demands for the establishment of new officers. The ignorant, the overeager had to be put on the right road. Dangerous weeds of error, of untidy thought, of peculiar custom, were beginning to spread. Of course, just a few words from the Fisher of Men would be sufficient to settle those dissensions, to steady those ambitions, to stifle those errors with ridicule.

"The moment you come into a meeting place," said the disciple admiringly, "where there has just been a clash of opinion, and those with grievances are complaining, everything is quiet. They fall on their knees. You are the one who accompanied Jesus everywhere. There you are, as if you had all their souls in your hands and held them out to the Lord. . . .

"As soon as you start to speak, whether the community is assembled in a quiet garden or deep underground where the eternal sleepers lie row on row, bricked into the soft stone, to me it is always as if I were hearing your sermons for the first time. The presbyters and the elders stammer some embarrassed words of greeting, the deacons stumble over each other in their hurry to invite you to eat; but you do not hear them. The holy storm of your sermon lifts even the dullest and most self-centered out of their everyday life, and makes them forget all their ugly plans, their malice, their envy, their strange fancies. For a brief span of time they are worthy of the blessing you bestow, before you leave them once more. Jesus called you his Rock, and you continue to roll like one. Alone, how shall I, how shall any of us answer those endless questions? To whom shall the ignorant and the inconstant cry, when you are no longer among them? Yours is the Word."

"Here you are, Simon Peter!" a cheerful boy's voice called

out of the darkness. It was Clemens, the son of the noble Faustinus, a regular guest at Aquila's home, who had impatiently hurried out to meet them. He had news for them. The Emperor Claudius had sailed for Britain early that morning to take over supreme command. Also his father had received letters from Antioch. "They say King Herod Agrippa has died unexpectedly."

"His reign was a short one!" cried Mark, and folded his hands. "The execution of James is atoned for; your chains are atoned for, Peter."

"Everything goes in our favor," cried Clemens jubilantly, and he tossed his untidy forelock back off his forehead. "More and more are coming to us across the sea, soon the whole earth will not be able to hold us."

"I beg you, to whom Jesus entrusted his mission, to be our shepherd and the bishop of our souls." There was a ring of entreaty in Anaclete's voice.

Peter's glance roamed from one to the other. "What else? Year in, year out I have been wandering up and down the streets, up and down the stairways, from soul to soul. Tell me, how many are there who do not know me face to face? There is no Jewish Christian, no heathen Christian my hands have not blessed, these hands that touched Jesus...."

Linus the presbyter began to speak. "We have to kneel before you in admiration of your work. No gratitude is great enough. Only people like us who think we are doing well if we gather a mere handful of believers round us from just a few blocks of houses, are able to begin to appreciate how heavy is your task of teaching, advising, encouraging, comforting...."

Peter smiled ruefully and growled: "Are you going to hurt me so grievously, that you praise me so?"

"I am talking of our pain, our grief. We do not accuse, we lament." A conciliatory smile played about the lips of the Etruscan.

The little group had reached the top of the Aventine, and arrived at Aquila's garden gate. Aquila was waiting to lead them respectfully to their communal supper, which was spread on an expensive, newly bought table of citrus wood. He had purchased it out of the money received for the Emperor's new campaign tent, which, he was delighted to say, had turned out a great success, his masterpiece, in fact, well able to withstand the notorious rainstorms of the enemy country. Aquila, faithful soul, had thought it proper to use the proceeds to furnish a room in a fitting manner for the love feasts. Today's was to be in the nature of a preliminary celebration, intended to make Peter favorably inclined towards Mark's work, the Evangelium, which Mark felt now ready to be entrusted to all Christians. It was to be read out so that Peter might approve it, and the deacons and young Clemens could satisfy themselves that it was clear and comprehensible. Everyone knew that the fisherman was by no means happy about such records of Jesus's life; and for that, the distrust of a man who can neither read nor write was to blame. The faith of the Jews had become rigid through being set down in writing by the scribes. The Christian faith was a thing living in the mouths of those who had seen and loved Jesus and had heard his words.

A premonition of what was afoot had so disturbed the apostle that he hardly returned Aquila's greeting and peremptorily demanded to know the grounds of Linus's complaint. Linus replied: "The good of all souls is concerned. How are we to lead them on the right road? They are calling to you from all sides; you require to be everywhere at once. So any day it may happen that you leave us all here. And what then? You are the Rock, you bear the Church of Rome on your shoulders. Believers are streaming to us, but what believers! They crowd together in the forecourts, eager for baptism, impatient to learn. We cannot find words enough to curb their errors. They are fearful of the wrath of God's justice. But they only see you occasionally; us, they see day by day. You bring the words as Jesus spoke them, but us they dare to defy. Make us your dogs to guard the flock."

Mark made bold to agree. "We will all be your officials, your Senate."

"Are you all like us twelve apostles?" cried Peter angrily. "Are you all greedy for some high position in the Kingdom of the King of the Jews?"

248

But Linus persisted: "I will not enter this room until you do justice, not to me, but to my work. Give us men to lead and teach and to regulate our customs, men who know the road and the goal. I ask for no name or title, but you may call them presbyter or elder or bishop."

"I am the bishop!"

"You are our happiness. But it may happen that here a community becomes devoted almost entirely to communal prayer till the old folk fall asleep and the young are in agonies of impatience, and there a community becomes dominated by one who wants only to listen to himself, and like some mystagogue of the Great Mother, recites dreadful accounts of the end of the world, and forgets the resurrection. To your words they add inventions of their own. What they have heard you say they twist and distort. And you must not forget how the heathen priests are raging against us. They are starving, because everyone is turning to us. We must be prepared for arrest, trial, danger, because we do not sacrifice to the divine Claudius. Informers are reporting of us that we do not pray 'Kyrie Kaisar,' but 'Kyrie Eleison' is our battle cry. They call it treason. We must not become weak. Every one of us needs a weapon, we need the Word."

AFTER praying fervently, Peter reclined at the table with his companions. The deacons Alexander, Maternus, and Rufus had joined them, as had Aquila and his wife Prisca, Joanna and Petronilla. The meal was simple, though richly served, and the conversation was growing more and more heated. Each of them had disturbing things to report about the pagan converts attracted by the mysterious miracle. Assassins were coming to get their knives blessed before the next crime. Legionaries had demanded that their weapons be blessed before setting out for Britain. They eagerly sought images of Jesus, images of the Almighty, images of Peter. Already the dealers were selling little bearded stone dolls inscribed *Apostle* instead of *Jupiter*. Onesimus was inveigling others into demanding another miracle of feeding the multitudes, which

249

he had heard of back in Syria, before he had run away from his master.

Petronilla listened with growing anxiety, and she saw her father raise himself up on his couch and say in a terrible voice: "Am I to regret that miracle?"

Mark, who had loved the girl as a sister since her childhood, noticed her terror. She was staring with mournful eyes into the darkness. He caught her whisper: "And I did so want to live."

"Turn them away!" the fisherman's voice thundered through the room, as if he were shouting above the storm tide. "Teach the unworthy that our faith is the realization of death here, and of life hereafter."

What Linus had begged for they all implored with one voice: "They need the Word, the Word! They cannot read it or hear it often enough, the word made flesh—Jesus!"

Now his host handed him a beautiful cup, which the apostle raised heavenwards, the wine offering, and the aromatic bread offering which Peter blessed and took. He spread his arms in prayer: "Lord, why did you not wash my hands and my head, as I begged you? You promised to pray for me when Satan should try to sift me like wheat. Pray for me now! Pray for me! I must strengthen my brothers, as you commanded me."

The room and its occupants seemed to fade away before his eyes. One by one, the faces seemed to change. He was sitting once again with his brother Andrew, the sons of Zebedee, all the Twelve, at the supper table in the house of Mark's mother. He rose, broke the bread and blessed it piece by piece, and as he went from one guest to the next, he repeated the Lord's words whose fearful prophetic sense was now beginning to show itself: "This is my body which is given for you. In your memory, Lord Jesus, I do this." Each one fell on his knees and lifted his face to Peter as he proffered the bread, himself the sacrifice and the redeemer.

Anaclete, the Greek, had closed his eyes blissfully, aware of the one perfection, the God who became man and who had entrusted the key of the eternal Kingdom to him who was at that moment offering him bread and wine. The anxiety had disappeared from Linus's face also. No demon would dare approach the holy community here, for God the Son was amongst them.

With mounting emotion the apostle bent over the kneeling company. He had reached those who were closest to him. Aquila took the bread like a well-earned reward, Prisca in deep veneration. Joanna's happiness was almost too great, now that she believed, now that she knew they were all safe in the peace of God. At every repetition of Peter's gift of grace, she recalled Christ's Calvary, which she had once witnessed through bloody tears, as a terrible road to God's most sublime glory. But before Petronilla's glance, so full of heroic resignation, her father's hand began to tremble. She experienced his every emotion, his sorrow and his happiness. Beside her kneeled Mark. At every breath he seemed to be groaning and yearning for grace, for the grace to be allowed to give himself for everyone in all eternity.

As Peter knelt to partake of the body and blood of the Redeemer, with a superhuman resolve, he offered himself as a sacrifice, his will and his conviction. He stood up and drew Mark up with him. "I am only a fisherman, and not learned like Saul of Tarsus, who from being Jesus's deadliest enemy has become his best interpreter. But I learned to follow a higher impulse, the breath of the Holy Ghost. Yet, 'the Spirit bloweth where it listeth,' as John said often enough. And you, who are lying in wait for my words, mark this: The secrets are not for every man's ears. All of you, do you think I did not see through your conspiracy? Everyone for Mark, all against me. You wanted to snare the Lord with letters, to nail him to your parchment. So let us hear what you have written down. If it was everything, you would have to write till the end of the world, and with your last words the heavens would open and the Almighty would come in a cloud to judge the living and the dead. God forgive me that I yield, and may the curse light on my head, not on your souls. I tell you, a blessing lies on the Word, but a curse lies on words. In the Word is meaning and spirit and love, but they will tear the Word into words, piecemeal! And you, see that you have finished reading before the cock crows twice."

THE little group around Peter were never to forget those three hours during which they listened to Mark in the warm, quiet September night under the glitter of the autumn stars. The eleven of them sat on Aquila's semicircular garden bench, facing the reader. The master of the house had a three-legged table set before him, a new bronze table that shone like gold in the lamplight. Beside the table squatted a slave, who changed and filled the oil lamps. He was not alone. The other house slaves had learned, through stray scraps of conversation, what was taking place that evening. A silent audience crouched in the still shadows of the trees, behind the low hedges, to hear about the life of the man who had suffered so much for their sake.

Mark had not yet begun to read. The warm red light of the three little oil lamps shone from below on his cheeks, picking out the dark shadows set by his determination, on his excited eyes, and his mouth which now and then trembled with emotion.

Petronilla sat on soft cushions at her father's feet. She looked uneasily at the faithful friend of her childhood, feeling somehow estranged from him as he sat there silhouetted in the lamplight against the enormous night-dark walls of the imperial palace and the starry sky. She was quite unaware that someone in the darkness of the garden was following her every glance lovingly and jealously. A kindhearted old servant of Prisca's, who was fond of the handsome young couple, and was looking forward to shedding a few tears at their wedding, had told Flaccus of Mark's secret. At the same time, Ptolemy had been informed of what was happening, by a tent-weaver slave to whom he slipped a little canteen brandy now and then. So the two friends were crouched in their hiding places, quite near each other without knowing it.

Before Mark began, Peter made his last attempt at resistance: "Why go to all that trouble? Matthew Levi has written down everything Jesus said."

"And I, what Jesus did."

Again the apostle warned him: "Are you sure we are not sinning against the Holy Ghost? God lives in the spoken word. I hold onto him as I always see him before me, as I hear him speak in my memory. In writings you do not find what is, only what was. Is it not dead, what Mark holds rolled up in his parchment there? The rabble will fall on it and twist it and read all kinds of subtle meanings into it and hold to it that they are right. They will break each other's heads over an iota. They will hate each other for his love's sake. Let Jesus's being and his will blossom from the heart; only fear writes things down."

"Then forgive us our fear," begged Linus. And Maternus knelt before the apostle. "We promise not to leave the Word rolled up. It shall be inscribed on living hearts."

Deeply moved, the fisherman stroked the head of the humble Maternus, and called on Mark to begin.

Mark's voice had a solemn yet uneasy ring as he recited the facts set down without artifice, and with not a word too many.

"The beginning of the gospel of Jesus Christ, the Son of God."

Then followed, like a challenge to mankind, Isaiah's mighty lines about the messenger and forerunner, the voice in the wilderness. Peter's companions listened, fascinated. John had hardly announced the coming of the One who was mightier than he, when only a hundred words or so further on, Jesus of Nazareth stood before their rapt attention, and a voice sounded from heaven: "This is my only-begotten Son, in whom I am well pleased."

Joanna looked at Peter, full of nostalgia, as the account turned to the Galilean sea. He and Andrew were the two first-called, and with them their boyhood friends, James and John. Believers were swarming to them, but hatred, calumny and persecution lurked around them. The listeners shuddered as if behind the dark hedges the spies and eavesdroppers of the High Court were crouched, and Herod's Syrian troops, and John's executioner with his uplifted sword, as if the cohorts of the Sebastenes were in wait for them, and the governor's legionaries, shield to shield, javelin to javelin. Menacingly, their enemies gathered. Subtle questions concealed the dangers of treason and blasphemy. Herod would not be dissuaded that Jesus was the resurrected Baptist. Priests and Pharisees pressed Pilate to act. So the Son of Man journeyed on—hated and persecuted, rejected by his neighbors, misunderstood by his disciples, without rest, without thanks, without shelter, poor as a beggar, and yet hailed by the young as King of the Jews—until that night on the Mount of Olives.

The listeners shuddered with fear, for Judas the traitor never sleeps. At last the horror of the scourging, the carrying of the cross and the execution was over. Easter Sunday had dawned. Broken with unutterable sorow, the women came to the grave. They heard the young man say out of the darkness: "He is risen." They trembled so that they could not speak. "Tell Peter and the disciples that Jesus has gone ahead of them to Galilee." Then Mary Magdalene had caught sight of him, and two of his followers saw him as they traveled the countryside, then all eleven. And now the great command was heard: "Go out into the world and proclaim the good tidings to all creation. Whoever believes and is baptized, shall be saved; but whoever does not believe shall be condemned."

The listeners had no idea how many hours had passed. They had not grown tired. Without noticing, they folded their hands as Mark read the last words about the Ascension, and ended: "And they went out and preached everywhere; the Lord was working with them, and he confirmed the word by the miracles that followed."

Before Peter could master his emotions, the others had sprung to their feet and gone to Mark. Anaclete put his arms about him, Linus was clasping his right hand, the boy Clemens had thrown himself at his feet and was embracing his knees, while Rufus, Maternus and Alexander were patting his arm, his shoulder, his left hand, so proud they were of him. From the women's eyes, happiness shone through the tears; and as a mark of respect and a reward, Aquila ordered a golden cup to be set before him, and said softly: "Keep this and may you often say a blessing over it."

The apostle had heard his name mentioned repeatedly.

The Lord had always taken him with him. He had visited his house and healed his mother-in-law. And now Peter came to Mark with such a wild look in his eye that Mark tried hurriedly to roll up his parchment for fear it should be snatched from him. Peter's reproach rang out: "You spared me, you tried to hide what I was really like, how weak, how lacking in insight! Do you think Matthew will keep secret what you have concealed?" He demanded that the praise which Jesus had bestowed on him at Caesarea Philippi, when Peter had been the first to shout: "You are the Christ!" should be struck out. "And there is no need to keep saying all the time that I am the Rock on which the Lord would build his Church. And do not forget how childish I was when I wanted to build three huts for the three Mighty Ones, Jesus, Moses and Elias, so that I could live alongside them. And too much honor is done to me, just because I was permitted to find the double-drachma and pay for Jesus and myself. Think over these matters before you let the scroll out of your hands."

Petronilla watched her father absently fingering the scrolls. She was sad that he had not allowed any mention of the thrice-repeated command to care for the Lord's flock. Peter wrested bitter confessions from himself: that he had been furious with the sons of Zebedee because they wanted to sit on the right and left of Jesus's throne; that to establish his claim to eternal award, he had complained that he and the others had renounced all their worldly possessions.

Obediently, Mark entered everything, and sadly struck out much that he had compiled so laboriously and had so proudly set down. He did so only because he hoped at last to be able to make his work available to everyone. The Holy Scriptures of the new faith should be like the Books of Moses, every word unalterable through the ages. "And what is the book to be called?" he asked in a faltering voice. Anaclete cried: "The Memoirs of Simon Peter!"

The apostle streched out his arms as if to ward off a tempter. Was his whole life merely a parable? Did not death creep in the wake of those very incidents that were praised as his miracles? Hananiah and Sapphira, and the guards of the prison he was freed from, all had to die. If these writings were to go out into the world under his name, would he not be to blame if unlearned and capricious men distorted the words, would he not be guilty of their ruin?

Mark glanced timidly from one to the other, near to tears. He looked at Petronilla and was aware of her beauty as she stood in the red gleam of the lamps against the starry sky. Did the light flicker or was she trembling? Her father's struggle with his conscience was a torture to her. To see him so weak and undecided before so many people seemed to take away some of his sanctity. She knew how he suffered because the greater part of those who streamed in for baptism were far removed from holy thoughts, a depraved city rabble with no desire for learning nor for purification, but merely hoping superstitiously to gain some advantage. It was these wretches, with their lust for miracles, who would snatch at Mark's life-work. She felt him looking anxiously at her, and she lowered her eyes and sighed. She was just hoping desperately that Flaccus would not visit them that evening, when he stepped out of the darkness, and so, to their mutual astonishment, did Ptolemy. Each of them was carrying a scroll in his hand. Hastily they engaged the presbyter in conversation.

Linus called to the apostle: "We cannot wait any longer. There are others already trying to exploit the curiosity of the mob. Here are two candidates for baptism whom you have not yet found worthy of admission into the community. They are impatient to enter into the spirit of Jesus's words. Each of them has got hold of a different book, one called 'The Gospel of the Hebrews,' the other 'The Gospel of the Egyptians.' Now they have been listening to Mark, and are astonished to see how misleading and full of errors their books are."

Presbyter and deacons compared the writings, reading a little here, a little there, and then called on Peter to testify to the truth of Mark's account.

Sadly Joanna watched her beloved daughter fold her hands. Petronilla was looking only at her father. She hardly dared to turn her head as Flaccus came to her and whispered: "I see you are suffering. Let me take your pain on myself!" She swayed, and quickly but gently he reached out and supported her. He led her away from the others, to a stone bench in the shadows.

"Do not be sad," she said softly and tenderly. "You make my heart too heavy. What is this body of mine? You lost me once already, when I lay paralyzed with shock, and the cleverest doctor in Rome had given me up."

"But God gave you back to us," entreated the young man.

"When I lay for hours on my sickbed, with no power over my limbs, I lived my whole life over again. I sat, a tiny creature, on my mother's lap, or on the big donkey saddle, always traveling with my father and mother. He whom they call the Son of Man held me on his knees and I was allowed to thrust my little hands into his silky beard. How long a year was, then! The more one grows up, the quicker time seems to shrink together. Can it be that I did not know you then? For I have only been myself since I was obliged to love you."

"Obliged to love me?"

A kind, devoted smile lit up the girl's dark eyes. "Yes, like any of those girls waiting at the window bars in the street in case the one they long for passes by, or laughing and talking louder at the well, as soon as they know their loved one is near. Did no one ever teach you those lines from the Song of Songs? 'They set me up as a keeper of the vines, but my own vineyard I have not cared for.'"

"You never spoke in this fashion before."

"The most modest girl is not able to be mistress of her thoughts. . . ."

"Your father must let us marry."

"No. He cannot. Onesimus has reminded him of his duty, and me of mine, in a terrible way. We come of poor folk, and to poor folk we are sent out. Blessed are the poor, for theirs is the Kingdom of God. Blessed are they that weep now, for they shall rejoice. . . . No, Flaccus. I know a saying of the Son of Man that fits us well: 'The children of these times marry and are given in marriage but those who are deemed worthy to share in everlasting bliss and the resurrection from the dead, neither marry nor are given in marriage. Neither can they die any more, since they are like the angels, and are God's children, being the offspring of the resurrection.

257

God is not the God of the dead, but of the living.' But we, Flaccus," and her voice sounded strange, as if caught between sobbing and rejoicing, "we will live forever, will live in Him for all eternity. Would you renounce such happiness? Be strong, and we shall see each other again and celebrate our eternal marriage in Heaven."

An anguished cry from Peter made her start up. She looked at him as he sat with the others, comparing Mark's testament with the false ones. The apostle was staring into the night, lamenting: "Are they already rising, the false prophets? Are teachers of heresy among us already? Book against book, letter against letter! Curses will be pronounced for the sake of a mere word; blood will flow, pyres will blaze, wars rage from one land to another, battled for the Word against the Word. The Book is death!"

Mark and his listeners stood transfixed with fear. Such anguish left them defenseless. Petronilla had closed her eyes and she pressed Flaccus's soldierly hand. "Be strong," she whispered, and he did not know whether she was reassuring herself or him. Then she began to speak aloud, and her voice carried far beyond its usual strength: "When I was a child, I was frightened by the old legend that a virgin had been walled up alive in the foundations of the Temple on Moriah, and under every tower of the fortress of Antonia, so that her purity could serve as a bulwark. Do not weaken, father, and let me not weaken either! Show all men that God's justice works miracles that seem cruel to those without knowledge. Work a stern miracle on me now! Teach the multitude that the love of the Lord must endure sorrow or it is not worthy of the name. Do not weep for me. I shall not be lost; I shall have merely gone on ahead. Like you, father, I see the Earthly rebelling against the Divine. Are you already lining up for the march towards martyrdom? Priest after priest—Peter, Linus, Anaclete, and an endless column behind them—men, women, children, coming as pilgrims from every quarter of the world. On the far side of the Tiber they burn like torches. Their bloody bones crack between the teeth of lions and tigers. But I will embrace the knees of the Almighty. Give me strength, Jesus, to fly down to my suffering loved ones.

Mother, I will be the dark cloud of smoke that deadens your pain. Father, I will tear the heavens asunder for you so that you do not feel the nails in your hands and feet. I will lead hosts of angels to meet you, so that you will no longer hear the roaring of beasts above their hymns. Do not let me grow old, father! Do not let me fade! Leave me forever as I am! Farewell, my dear, dear father! Farewell, my kindest mother! Farewell, my Flaccus!

"Lord of the World, take me, an eternal bride immured in the ivory tower of Mark's gospel. Take me to you, if that is your holy will. I will go back to my bed of pain and sickness, to be a witness for Jesus, for your holy office, father, a witness for Mark's work. No earthly riches nor earthly happiness can outweigh the grace our Master promised. Tell Onesimus I am taking all my riches with me, the saying written down by Mark: 'Everything is possible to the one who believes.' Redemption is what Mark recorded, and it shall be poured out over land and sea. Lord, thy will be done...."

The slaves had lit all the lamps in trembling haste, and they illuminated the face of the beautiful girl who had dedicated herself to martyrdom through the power of her own love.

She embraced her father, who silently pressed her to his breast. She embraced her mother, who could not speak for trembling. All shyness gone, she embraced her beloved Flaccus, who did not dare to touch her, and received her chaste kiss like a sacred eucharist.

Then Petronilla went into the house. Sobbing servants lit her way. With soft prayers on their trembling lips, the rest followed her to her room, and watched her stretch herself out, and saw the powerful fisherman, shaken with sobs, raise his hands, and the girl's lovely body stiffen into the image of a saint.

In the morning, bewildered heathen priests hurried through the streets of the city, lamenting that the stone goddess Roma had been weeping all night long.

ROME was a city of resplendent funerals. Yet even Rome had never seen such a vast burial procession as this one, when a prince, a youth of senatorial rank, and Mark and the deacons Rufus, Maternus and Alexander carried the bier containing the shrouded remains of the girl Petronilla out of Aquila's house.

Their way lay far over the Velabrum, up the Vicus Longus, and all the while, others were constantly asking to be allowed to carry the coffin for a few steps at least. So the bier was lifted from shoulder to shoulder and borne from the Alta Semita highway along the ancient Etruscan salt route, and out through the Porta Salaria. A vast crowd surged after it.

Ahead and alongside the bier, boys were swinging censers, and choirs of children sang plaintive songs of farewell. All Rome followed the bier along the streets, pressing forward to see the miracle-worker who only seemed to have tested his powers on his child in order to let her perish later. In thick white mourning veils, the wife of the senator Pudens and her daughters were awaiting the corpse at its last resting place. On her country estate, Priscilla had underground tombs cut in the soft tufa, for the benefit of the believers. There, the dead girl was set down on a great heap of roses, in a marble sarcophagus. For hours the mourners passed by to look for the last time on the veiled face that seemed to be asleep with a barely perceptible smile, a sad smile of resignation and promise.

Timidly, respectfully, they looked at Peter in his inscrutable sternness. The faithful were aware that Joanna had parted from her husband without a word, and had gone to live on the country estate of Cornelius Pudens, in a little house near her daughter's resting place.

Only to God had Peter confessed how greatly he suffered. To mortals his sermons rang as indomitable as a funeral bell. All Christianity must be action—charity towards others, self-denial, every gaze fixed firmly on the Hereafter, as if earthly existence were only misfortune and trial; the more merciless, the greater the reward. Flaccus and Ptolemy afforded examples of this: Both left the scene of their keenest, most painful memories, Flaccus to seek the way to himself and to his dead sweetheart on the frontier wall of Germania; the prince, to return to his homeland, and in its most desolate region, in

260

the Thebaid desert, to renounce all that he had learned for the sake of a God whose highest honors are gained through love and death. He took nothing with him but a copy of Mark's gospel.

PETER's severity dismayed those who had not courage enough to acknowledge the saying of the Son of Man: "Renounce yourself. Take up your cross. He who is ashamed of me and of my Word among this people of adulterers and sinners, the Son of Man shall also be ashamed of him, when he comes in the glory of his Father with the holy angels."

Many who had been ready for baptism were full of anxiety. Instead of comfort, they were confronted with terror, stars that fell from heaven, the sun and moon eclipsed.

Even Linus and Anaclete breathed easier when the ten disciples in Jerusalem asked Peter to hurry back to them, because Saul of Tarsus had announced his arrival. Message after message had come from Antiochia complaining that this new missionary, the pupil of Gamaliel, was destroying the holy order. Indiscriminately, Saul was taking heathens and the sons of heathens into the community of the saints. "Till now the sublime symbol of the covenant between our forefathers and the Creator—circumcision—was the condition of baptism. But this wicked innovator declares: 'To be at one with the Almighty, his grace suffices; nothing else is necessary.' "

After his long absence, Peter strode excitedly up the ancient streets towards his beloved brethren. Not to be alone any more, he thought. To feel again the strength of a common front of resolution, and himself the first and mightiest among them, the one empowered to make decisions as the Shepherd of the Lord. He hurried on.

That was a memorable meeting, when the Twelve gathered round the supper table, the eleven companions of Jesus and the one who was later to be called "the people's apostle." They were to decide in which direction to steer for thousands of years to come. In his speech of welcome, Jacob mentioned their longing, which was at the same time a fear of the end of the world and a rejoicing at the sight of the Judge in the clouds of heaven. He closed with the warning of the Son of Man: "Watch therefore! For you do not know when the master of the house will come, whether in the evening, or at midnight, at cockcrow, or in the morning. Let him not find you asleep when he unexpectedly stands amongst you. I tell you, watch!"

Then the Zealot spoke. The ancient dread of the Psalmist's threats trembled in his reference to Israel who would not obey. Saul wanted to lead the fight for freedom, freedom from the burden of such trifles as were no longer worthy of the name of Law, but the Tsaddik drew himself up to protest: "What do you know of the words of the Lord which we have heard with our own ears? He said himself, he came to fulfill the Law."

"He has fulfilled it!" cried Saul.

"But there remains one thing which you always dispute," Jacob insisted. "The highest of all the commands in the fifth book of Moses: 'You shall love the Lord your God with all your heart and with all your soul and with all your might.'"

Here Peter intervened, for the conversion of the heathen was a matter which concerned him too. His voice was strong and stern, and none of them dared to interrupt: "At the same time, Jesus recalled a saying of his Father's to Moses: 'You shall love your neighbor as yourself.'"

There were tears in Saul's eyes, as he said quietly and sadly: "Will you call everyone your neighbor but me?"

Until then, John, the Master's favorite disciple, had been silent. Still handsome and youthful-looking, he was gazing into space as if he saw again the tremendous experiences he was recounting. Now sentence after sentence came from his lips as if from the stars in the night sky. He spoke of Jesus on the Mount of Olives. No man ever told so movingly of the road to Christ's last agony. Again, he comforted their hearts with the words: "As my Father loved me, so have I loved you. Abide in my love. If you keep my commandments, you shall remain in my love; as I have kept my Father's law, and abide in his love. This is my commandment, that you love one another, as I have loved you."

Peter stood up, and he stood like a Rock. The grace of God

filled his heart, filled his breast, and he cried: "Has not Jesus fulfilled every prophecy? You know it, but this people here know it less than anyone. Saul and I come from cities whose people it is impossible to count. Against them, what is this little mountain town of Jerusalem with its handful of inhabitants? Any cripple or blind man I heal here counts for far, far more, because everyone knows him. But there, what is all Jerusalem to the Romans? In that Babylon, every one of the countless houses, story on story, is like a clenched fist mercilessly gripping the fate of men and crushing them together until they perish. There, hell begins this side of the grave. I have wandered alive through hell upon hell. If you had been with me on my travels, pity would have gnawed your hearts and you would have blushed to oppose me. Most of them do not seek the Saviour, but Jesus died for everyone on earth, whether he wanted it or not. We have no right to close the gates of heaven on anyone, even the farthest from God, if he is truly impelled to believe. The Lord gave me the key, and I will use it, will use it with you, brother Saul."

Tears came to Peter's eyes as the eloquent, learned Saul of Tarsus, the brilliant pupil of Gamaliel, stammered in a faltering voice: "O fortunate men! You heard Christ's every word, and I should not boast because of the revelations vouchsafed to me from the Highest. But believe me, I heard his words of comfort: 'My grace is sufficient for you, for my power is made perfect in the weak.' "

Peter bent over to Thaddeus and whispered to him. Thaddeus shyly fumbled in his leather wallet and drew out a fine silk kerchief, barely two spans wide. He spread it and held it up so that it hid his face. All twelve stared silently at Veronica's kerchief, which he always carried with him, jealously hidden from the gaze of the ungodly.

Saul had heard the voice of the Son of Man on the way to Damascus. Now he looked Jesus in the face. He fell on his knees. "Jesus." He wept before the bloody and ineffably sad face. "Not for myself, but everything for you, every step, every word. . . ."

Deeply moved, Peter and John bent over the kneeling man. It had been a long time since Peter had relaxed his stern expression. Now he whispered to Saul: "Just as you said: My power is made perfect in the weak." He joined the hands of their former persecutor with those of Jacob. With his wide eyes fixed on the bloodstained image of Christ, he said: "Three times you commanded me: 'Be my shepherd.' You gave me power to bind and to loosen. You said: 'Go out and teach *all* peoples, baptize them in the name of the Father, the Son and the Holy Ghost. I will be with you day by day until the end of eternity.' "

THREE years had passed since Mark had left Rome and the chief apostle, whose first companion, interpreter and secretary he had been. He had gone to join Saul, for he had been unable to overcome his sorrow at Petronilla's death. Perhaps he was the only one to understand Peter's acceptance of her sacrifice, but her unaverted fate had caused him too much suffering.

After her death, he had gone at first to Antioch, to Luke, who was also gathering facts about the life and sayings of Jesus. With him, he accompanied Saul on his journey to Cyprus, the home of his uncle Barnabas. Here they met with an unexpected triumph, for in the midst of their missionary work the Proconsul Sergius Paulus summoned before him the man from Tarsus and his companions. The Roman was no stranger to the teachings of the unseen God, for he had heard of the new faith from one of his servants, a Jew named Bar Jesus, and despite all the protests of that Old Testament zealot, he wanted to hear more about the miracle-man from Nazareth. So Saul talked, and it came to a violent quarrel between himself and Bar Jesus, and eventually he struck his adversary blind, declaring him a son of the devil. The witnesses were terrified. Deeply moved, the Proconsul had himself baptized, and in his great joy, Saul changed his Hebrew name for that of his Roman convert and from then on he was called Paul.

But when Paul returned to the mainland of Asia Minor, and prepared to set out through Pamphylia, across Perga to Lycaonia, Mark's heart grew heavy. He carried his work, his gospel, with him, for though many copies were already going from hand to hand, he was still improving it according to his

264

uncle's memory, and the account of the physician Luke. Could he expose his manuscript to the dangers of a journey through regions notorious for robbers and pirates?

So it happened that he parted with the man for whose sake he had left Peter, and went back to Jerusalem. Even there he found the situation insupportable. The disturbances in Palestine were growing increasingly dangerous, and the punishment threatened by Jesus seemed to be drawing nearer and nearer. The Feast of the Passover, the most sacred festival for the original community, was at hand. Resolved to allow no disturbances, the Roman prefect, Ventidius Cumanus, posted troops all round the Temple, for the nationalist zealots, the knifemen, were harrying more cruelly than ever those who did not profess the faith of Moses. But all his precautions were in vain; the festival ended in a ghastly massacre. Legionaries stormed the Temple and drove the crowds out of the sanctuary with naked weapons. Ten thousand Jews were trampled in their wild flight. From every house came the lament for the dead.

The circle of apostles in Jerusalem took this profanation of the place where Jesus had preached as an insult to themselves. They became more bitter than ever against the heathen world, whether the unclean were baptized or not. Only those who had made the Old Testament their own, they said, were able to comprehend Jesus. Mark was entrusted with the task of warning Peter in Antioch that messengers were on the way, to demand the strictest adherence to the Law.

Before the splendor of the house in which the bishop lived, Mark hesitated. He gazed uneasily round the garden full of exotic plants. Oddly enough, the door was open, guarded only by a mosaic picture of a snarling dog. The bronze door of a marble-tiled vestibule was also ajar, and Mark could see into the sumptuous rooms on either side. In the dining room, whose colonnades gave out onto the garden, stood handsomely carved tables, but no couches or chairs.

Feeling at a loss, Mark strayed farther into the garden, which had been allowed to run wild, until he came to an old rough brick structure, perhaps the hut of one of the garden slaves. The rusty hinges on the crooked jamb had not supported a door for a long time. Now that Mark had come out of the rays of the southern sun into the deep cool shade, a shiver ran over his perspiring skin. Gradually, he made out some wooden shelves against the wall, once used for baskets and tools, no doubt, and a bench, a table, a bedstead. Through the narrow horizontal window slits streamed sharply delineated beams of golden-white sunlight, and in their light he saw Peter's face lifted towards him. His expression was so stern, his serious eyes seemed to bore so deeply into the disciple's conscience that Mark fell on his knees and sobbed: "Forgive me."

As heavily as if he bore the burden of the world's sorrows on his powerful shoulders, Peter got up and went to the kneeling man. With a kindly hand he raised Mark's averted face. "Forgive you, when for years you deserted me in my bitterest loneliness? You chose between Saul and me. Your heart had long since forsaken me because I did not save my child. Or what you would call 'saving' her. You had no pity for me, only for the man of Tarsus, is it not so?"

Mark admitted it with a sigh.

"Of course, Saul deserved your pity. Through years of toil he wrested soul after soul from heathendom. Out of the poorest of the poor he built up a Church. For their sake he, the scholar, was ridiculed by a crowd who think in Greek and fancy themselves to be powerful in the spirit. I was called on for help, I, the rough fisherman. Without grammar or rhetoric, they all run to me because, as you wrote in that book of yours, the miracles come with me. But I chided the sinners with Saul's own words: 'Christ sent me out not to baptize, but to preach the gospel.' How I wish Saul were here! These immature and overripe brethren of ours would confuse the Lord God himself with their wrangling."

Saul was near at hand, Mark hastened to tell him. Would Peter not leave the management of affairs in Antioch to him? The Roman community was imploring the Rock to return. Letter after complaining letter was arriving. Simon the Magus was leading the weak into the abyss. Linus had sent one of the Magus's works, "The Great Interpretation." Mark had not dared to read out this mystical monstrosity.

266

Since the Magus was barred from godliness, he had to make a god of himself. He was the Great One, the Universal Providence in its earthly form. With all his mystification, he appeared to the Samaritans as the Heavenly Father, to the Jews as the Crucified One, to the pagans as the exhalation of the Holy Ghost. He gave it out that he had divine power at his disposal in the form of an angel. His companion, he said, was that same Helen for whose sake the Trojan War was fought, she was the lost sheep of the Good Shepherd. Simon Magus had in fact taken her from an Alexandrian brothel as one practiced in magical arts. As he with her, every man might embrace every woman, for where a man sowed was of little importance, but the fact that he sowed was the highest and holiest thing. All Rome was flocking to him.

Mark felt himself suddenly lifted up from the ground to Peter's side. The fisherman put his muscular arm around the disciple's shoulder and together they began to walk up and down the dark shadowy avenue of oaks.

"I know now," declared Mark, "how near I am to you once more. Your work and my work, who knows what threatens them both? There is unrest in Jerusalem, unrest here. I was in the Basilica of Theophiles, and have just come from the former synagogue by the Singon. Both the heathen Christians and the Jewish Christians feel the want of you bitterly. Today is that spring day again when once the boys of Israel spread their garments in the way when Jesus came riding by. They waved palm branches at him. 'Hosanna!' they shouted. 'Blessed is He who comes in the name of the Lord.'"

"We thought it was a coronation procession, and it was the beginning of his march towards death. Am I not also a king here? An Antiochus incarnate? Everywhere my subjects await my coming."

"It is precisely those whom you reproach who feel the most aggrieved. They wanted to surprise you with new splendor, all in your honor! The singing of the Antiochian choirs is renowned. Till now they sang for heathen gods. Now for the first time they wanted to greet you at the love feast with the wonderful sound of their altos and basses. They sang your own texts. But you were not there. When I asked where you were, the elders said bitterly: 'With his compatriots, the heretical Jews in their church by the Singon.' Yet I did not find you there. Had the poor fellows known you were here on your own, it would have been a comfort to them."

Sandal soles grated on the gravel. The two turned anxiously. They saw a group of men approaching, their faces familiar, yet strangely reserved and forbidding, their eyes downcast as if they feared their courage might desert them. Their pace grew slower. They were judges who feared their own office.

Mark whispered: "I meant to warn you. Too late now. But these are not all. Paul is going to demand his flock from you too."

Simon Peter straightened up to his full height. "All the flocks are mine and the gates of Hell will have no power over them." But as he began to recognize face after face among those who were approaching, the apostle was overcome with emotion. His memory went back to the days when he had experienced happiness without parallel in the company of these very believers. They were all numbered among the disciples, some of them from Lake Genesareth. The resurrected Jesus had walked among them. Peter's eyes grew moist as he greeted one after another by name. They saw to their delight that they had remained unforgotten for half a lifetime.

"Joseph! So we meet again! Still inseparable from your friend Micha? And you twins, Thomas and Elieser, can I still tell you apart? And the Temple priests! I greet you as messengers of God the Father in his Son. And all four of you here, Phineas, Eleazar, Elias and Benjamin. Is your mother, Sephora, living still? And Rubilus and Sechariah, as builders, what do you think of our churches here? Don't they rejoice your hearts?"

The apostle noticed a little man standing behind the corpulent Zephaniah from Jericho. "Zaccai!" he cried. "You old archsinner and chief taxgatherer! Still no bigger? You would not climb any sycamores for my sake, as you once did for Jesus. I nearly overlooked you!"

With the heartiness of his welcome, he made them forget that they had come to reproach, to warn, to threaten him.

Happily they crowded round the man of whom they had at first been so frightened, till he suddenly shook them off with quite disconcerting vehemence. "You are fine messengers for Jacob! Do not pretend that you came here to embrace me and give me brotherly kisses. Hatred of the heathens drove you here. And it is not only the heathens that you hate, but the heathen Christians as well. Am I right?"

Their embarrassed silence was answer enough. He waited a moment, to see if any would attempt to speak, then he led the way to a shadowy clearing among the thick shrubbery and brushwood. There, he indicated they should sit down on a semicircular stone seat, large enough for the twelve of them. They were so frightened that they all crowded together at one end.

The apostle gazed at this huddle of opposition with a pitying smile, while he drew back a few paces. Should he not make it clear to them that they were trying to remain merely a miserable Jewish sect? "Was it for the sake of a few Jewish heretics like you," he began, "likely to be hounded and stoned out of the Temple at any moment, that Christ became man? You, rolled up in the Torah as you are, do you not remember the mighty psalm of the Messiah: 'All the kings of the earth shall worship him and all peoples shall be his servants'? Are you still trying to cower in the shadow of the Temple?" He called to Mark: "You wrote down what Jesus said when we were admiring the Temple: 'What stones! What a building!' And he answered: 'There shall not be left here one stone upon another, that shall not be thrown down. You shall see the Son of Man approaching on the clouds in all his might and glory; he will send out his angels to all four corners of the earth.' But first the Gospel must be preached to all peoples—to all peoples! What do you know of this work among the heathen?" Peter threw himself down on the stone bench, and, breathing heavily, he stared towards where the sun was shining through the shadow of the leaves. At the end of the avenue, he perceived a tall, elegant figure coming towards him. The apostle stretched out both arms in greeting. He recognized the pale face shining like that of an ivory Zeus above the impressive bushy beard.

"Barnabas!" cried the old fisherman, no longer the grave

269

bishop, the severe shepherd of souls. As if he stood laughing in a fair wind aboard his boat, he asked: "Have the Lycaonians let you down off your pedestal in their heathen temple again, you, Zeus, father of the gods, and Saul, the Hermes?"

The emissaries stared at Peter in astonishment, and then at Barnabas, who blushingly replied: "How can you jest at our shame? They took us for their gods. . . ."

The apostle drew Barnabas to him on the bench, and laid a comforting arm about his shoulder. "Tell these Jerusalem stay-at-homes what it means to travel about in the world, always faced with the choice of being stoned by the Jews or killed by the heathen. Just because you cured a cripple in Lystra, they all began to rejoice: 'The gods have taken human shape and have blessed us with their presence!' Was it not so?"

"Indeed it was. The priests of Zeus came with bulls and garlands. They had been preaching about their gods for years, and dusting them off and touching up their colors, and there never came life to the stones or the metal; they had never set eyes on one of their gods. And now they believed no less than two had come down. We tore our garments in despair at their crazy delusions."

The emissaries from Jerusalem beat their breasts and their foreheads to hear how the Jews made use of the disappointment of the heathens to incite them so that at last the populace had fallen on Paul, and stoned him.

Timidly the little taxgatherer Zaccai had crept to Barnabas and was stroking his hand, while Peter embraced him. "Perhaps it is our lot, to be taken for gods one moment and for criminals the next."

"But we did not give up. With all those who were brave enough among the disciples in Lystra—and there were many of them—we gathered around Paul. The Lord gave him back his strength, and he got to his feet, wearing his rags and blood and dirt as if they were the festive garments of his creed, and encouraged the newly won souls to persevere like us."

Peter put his two hands on Barnabas's shoulders and looked him severely and searchingly in the face. "Can one give encouragement without the blessing of the Law? Barnabas, is it not our hell on earth, always to know what should be, and always to see what is?"

Barnabas's voice faltered, and he looked like a Zeus near to tears. Peter continued: "We here know ourselves to be one, and we feel the more powerful, the more we are of the same blood and the same customs. But go to Rome, go anywhere in the streets of the heathen, and the more your own kind are about you, the more lost you will feel yourself to be. Each is against everyone there."

"And so it is on all sides," groaned Barnabas. "Who would not feel pity for them? The boundless pity of Jesus."

But the Rock beat his breast with his clenched fist. "And yet they in Jerusalem are right, and I too; unclean are all the heathen, in thought and deed! Every one of their festivals is a defilement. How are we to teach them to honor their bodies as temples of the Lord? Or to realize that love between bride and bridegroom is God's grace, that marriage is a sacrament? What can we do against idolatry when this city employs two hundred decurions just to arrange heathen festivals and sacrifices? Does it not grieve the heart that we expose the holy scriptures of the ancient covenant as a doctrine for the infidel, and what we worship is trembling, bare and naked before the eyes of the libertine? I cannot, I cannot go on!"

"Do not cast pearls before swine!" cried the men from Jerusalem, but Peter continued: "But the angels gave me my orders, when they let down that vast cloth from heaven, full of all the vermin and the quadrupeds of the earth, the waters and the sky. Their cry still thunders in my ear: 'Up, Peter! Kill and eat! What God has declared pure, you shall not call impure!'" As if he were angrily turning from them, Peter went quickly back to the house and into the garden room with its stone tables. The others followed timorously.

Empty as the bishop's palace seemed, to care for Peter was a matter to which the Antiochians attended with special devotion. If he lived frugally, and slept in the garden slave's hut, nevertheless there were certain pious souls who looked after his wants, more or less unseen. Spinsters and widows, till then objects of mockery for both Jews and heathens, had found that Christianity allowed them to fill their empty and wasted

271

lives with sacred duties. Though they shyly avoided him, they were always secretly at hand. Smiling, they whisked here and there through the deserted rooms in his wake, allowed no dust to settle, and knew exactly what to set before him, though he had little relish for anything. So the twelve men from Jerusalem were surprised to find, in that hitherto empty dining room, that the table was laid ready for them. Modest dishes were set in each place, and in Peter's place was a basket of white bread and a great cup of dark wine. There seemed something unreal about this meal, served by invisible hands. Were silent listeners huddled behind the drawn curtains at the doorway?

The men gathered round Peter, who took a piece of bread in his hand and seemed to gaze at it apologetically. "Must I not help? What do you know of the agony of the heathen soul? Because Augustus brought peace after the long terror of the civil wars, they put up monuments to him. In Halicarnassus and elsewhere I have seen their eternal longing carved in stone. In the inscriptions they call the emperor 'saviour,' not knowing that the true Saviour has been born already. What is heresy with them is faith with us."

Sadly the apostle murmured to himself: "Of course they tremble when I tell them to their face of their vices and transgressions. But they don't want to upset their father Peter, they try to keep secret their frivolous pleasures, so that he does not fly into a rage because they have eaten the flesh of a beast of sacrifice consecrated by a heathen priest, or because they have taken part in a mystery. They hang their heads and blush for shame. Yes, I belong to all of you, and to all of them. I am a Jew, but almost a heathen too; and I want to be a Christian, a Christian above all Christians. My work is not yet finished. And I have to be hard, terribly hard, cruel out of love, lest he should ask again: 'Peter, do you love me?' Lord, let me grow in my work, let me grow heavenwards to thee!"

But who was this, striding so impetuously that his cloak billowed out like a sail behind him? His face was as pale as a leper's, his beard and hair were unkempt, the hair already thinning at his high temples. There was a gleam of accusation in his small eyes.

"Peter!" he called from a distance. "You are not treading in the strait path of the gospel. If you, as a Jew, live as the heathen do, and not according to Jewish custom, why do you compel the heathen-Christians to live like the Jews? We are Jews by birth, and not of sinful heathen parents, yet we know that man is not justified by the Law of Moses, but only by faith in Jesus Christ."

The men from Jerusalem had been cowering before Peter's solemn words, but now they rose up together in protest. They had recognized the speaker as Saul, who had discarded his Jewish name to take on a heathen one. But he cut them short before they had uttered a word. "We accepted the faith in Jesus Christ so that we might come to righteousness through that faith, and not through what the Pharisees call 'the works of the Law.' Is God only the God of the Jews and not of the heathens? What are the wretched works of man against the power of faith? There is no difference. If we are justified by the Law alone, then Christ has died in vain!"

It was on the tip of Mark's tongue to cry: "There is more at stake than you realize! Paul, you bequeathed to us this huge community in Antioch, when you left. But to keep such inexperienced believers pure for God, in the face of all the perils and temptations of this sinful city, is far beyond human power!" But when he timidly looked at Peter, he saw him draw himself up, and heard him say softly: "Jesus, I love you. . . ." and softer still: "Lord, you know I love you." And almost inaudibly: "Master, you who know everything, know how much I love you. . . ."

Paul had heard the words also. When his eyes met Peter's, the impetuous speaker seemed to falter for he divined the reproach in Peter's gaze, that tremendous reproach that had felled him to the ground on the road to Damascus: "Saul, why do you persecute me?"

He saw the fisherman take up the basket of bread, and make the sign of the cross over it. Then he took a piece of the fragrant white loaf, held it up, and muttered an ardent prayer. Slowly and heavily he walked along the rows of kneeling figures, those from Jerusalem as well as those from Antioch, and set piece by piece in their mouths. Paul was worried whether Peter would return to him, to offer him the bread too. Though the chief apostle had at first only asked a blessing in a whisper, he stopped before his accuser for a solemn grace according to their custom in the room of the Last Supper. He held in his sorrow as a rider reins in his horse. Over his shoulder, he said to Phineas, who had once been a priest in the Temple of David: "Recite the lesson that we twelve apostles determined on at table before we went up with Jesus to the Mount of Olives."

Eagerly, Phineas intoned: "Gather together to break bread and give thanks, after you have confessed your sins so that your offering is worthy. For the Lord said: Let a worthy sacrifice be offered up to me, for I am a mighty king and my name will be honored among the peoples."

"Mark, you wrote down the words and deeds of our Master, let us hear how it happened, which we celebrate in his memory now and henceforth."

Standing before his two great masters, the disciple blushed. He was tempted to repeat the words according to Matthew, who says that Jesus gave the bread to his twelve disciples, among whom the man from Tarsus was not included. But in the kindness of his heart, he kept to his own work: "And as they were eating, Jesus took the bread, and when he had blessed it, he broke it and gave it to them, and said: Take it, this is my body. . . ."

No one knew better than Paul about the two accounts. Painfully conscious that he was not reckoned among the Twelve, he closed his eyes and sighed with relief as he knelt. The chosen keeper of the keys was uttering the eternal words of comfort: "We thank you, Father, for the sacred vine of David your servant, of whom we know through Jesus, your son. Honor to you in all eternity!" And over the morsels of bread: "We thank you, Father, for the life and the understanding, about which we know through Jesus, your son. As this bread grew as wheat scattered about the hillsides and yet became one, so may your Church be gathered together from the ends of the earth, into your kingdom, for yours is the honor and the power through Jesus Christ in all eternity."

Humbly, Paul took the bread from the man whose feet the Son of Man had washed. He gratefully whispered to the apostle: "I have been crucified with Christ, and so I no longer live, but Christ lives in me."

And for these words of atonement, Peter stretched out a brotherly hand to the kneeling man and drew him up.

BAREFOOT, his sandals tied to his pilgrim staff, Peter trod the gray basalt slabs of the Via Flaminia. Tired as he was, his calloused soles did not feel the heat of the road. His heart was heavy with concern for the Roman Christians, who had anxiously called to him for help. Though he was in a hurry to reach the city and to enter it unrecognized, he turned off eastward along the ancient salt route of the Etruscans. Downhill, uphill he walked out of the valley of the rushing Aniene, between the rough-hewn stone walls of lonely gardens. On either side, the tops of the dense dark evergreen oaks hung like heavy clouds over the landscape.

With the deepening twilight, a strange melancholy joy rose in the traveler, and a painful nostalgia. The country estate of Priscilla, the senator's wife, must be near at hand, he thought, and that maze of underground passages where Petronilla slept. Before him, between the walls and the gardens, the stars seemed to be dancing in a ring near the ground, and singing as they danced. It was the light shining through the horn sides of cheap lanterns and the songs came from a small group of wine-happy revelers who had emerged from the shadows of the dark brushwood, and were traveling along the Via Salaria back to the city.

With his last strength, the weary traveler lengthened his stride and soon arrived at a doorway in the wall, whose door was just slowly closing. Peter hurled himself against it and almost fell, so easily it gave. The strong arms of a couple of men caught him as he stumbled through. One of them, tall and lean, shone his lantern on the intruder's face, and said with a cackling laugh: "Are you in such a hurry to get here?"

The other, a short, stout man, said cheerfully: "Let's hope you have not come to the wrong inn!"

Their lanterns and mattocks showed that they were *fossores,* who dug the niches, deep down in the passages of the catacombs, for the burial of dead Christians.

"They kept us long enough with their love feast, that lot up there, singing as they march, all of a stagger." The laugh rang out again.

His stout workmate brooded: "That rabble has no idea of God's gospel. The grave is hardly walled up before they're changing the funeral meal into a banquet, the libation into an orgy. I begrudge them every grave niche. Heathens like them ought to be cremated. I was baptized by a hand that touched the hand of the Son of God, and I'm ashamed of them."

"Don't boast just because Simon Peter took you into the community."

"Of course, they all run after Simon Magus now, his devilish namesake. They are all beside themselves with wonder at his conjuring tricks. The stupid lot get all kinds of sinful ideas from him."

By now, the two gravediggers and Peter had reached a clearing under the tall pines. The entrance door leading into the depths of the earth was still open. Clay lamps were glimmering in a quiet stone passageway, pointing the way rather than illuminating it. Their light hardly extended more than a few handsbreadths over the scarred brown tufa arches and the walls in which, here and there, a rectangle the length of a man had been hewn out, ready for a corpse to be set in behind a thin marble or brick tablet. On the grave-tablets, a name or a last salutation was scratched, a pair of doves or a fish. The very poor and unlettered pressed an amulet, a toy, or sometimes merely a button into the soft surface of the stone.

The gravediggers led their guest into a subterranean room not far from the entrance, with stone seats ranged along the walls. On the tables lay the remains of a love feast, the dregs of wine still in the earthenware cups.

Not to offend the gravediggers, the apostle drank their health, but before doing so, he took up a piece of the fragrant

276

wheat bread, blessed and broke it. The two *fossores* stared in
astonishment and reverently took the proferred bread. Their
astonishment grew as the stranger blessed the wine also, and
offered it to them to drink before he set it to his own lips.

"I have the feeling I know you," stammered the stout grave-
digger. "I've only seen that done once before, the way you
bless and divide the bread. Are you by chance one of the holy
twelve in Jerusalem?"

The apostle stared before him without speaking, for he
wanted to make his stand against Simon the Magus un-
heralded. "Your heart is not upright before God. You have
no part in this teaching," he had told Simon of Gitton, back
in Samaria. Because he took money for his favors? Were not
he and Paul, and the priests and deacons kept by their communities? But still, divine grace was not to be withheld from
any, no matter how poor.

His silence troubled the gravediggers. Was this one of the
Magus's followers, sitting opposite them here?

Then the cackling laugh rang out again. "You should have
heard them at their love feast. They nearly came to blows.
They were calling each other out for Samaritans and Galileans.
The Gittonites were crowing that Simon Peter had not been
able to keep his own daughter alive."

The unknown apostle nodded thoughtfully. "Yet Simon of
Gitton always runs away from Simon of Galilee, as if he did
not trust his own miracles. Of course when Simon they call
the Rock works a miracle, it is likely to be one of punishment and death."

"What we think is: Just a few more years, perhaps only
months or weeks, and they will all be silent. They will belong
to our great quiet community then, however wildly they have
quarreled with each other in their lifetime."

"What do the likes of us understand of the Magus's talk?
And if we Romans can't find our way, how can a poor devil
like you, who have traveled in from the provinces?"

Peter smiled to himself. Once he had set out to burden
himself with a world of belief. Here in Rome he had, as it
were, straddled the hills, to sow with a mighty swing of the
arm. Thousands flocked to him. To thousands he came as a

saviour. And now? Such a short time had passed and everything lay in ruins. An enemy had deprived him of the fruit of his labor. He was the guest of gravediggers. They spoke of the Magus's magic arts, his vices, and his crafty indulgent smile at everyone's sins and failings. The man with the cackling laugh said: "The more believers there are, the more they split up, away from each other. Everyone clings to his own opinion, certain it's the only right one. Instead of loving one another, they hate the sight of one another."

"And you?" asked Peter.

"We stay with the quieter brethren, the good and holy ones. The two of us, we remain true to God and to each other. Whoever comes to us, has peace."

Except me, thought the traveler. "May my blessing bring you everlasting salvation. For you, living here in the darkness, a great light will shine. But I must go out into the daylight, back to the black sheep and the goats, I must bind and loosen, and hurtle down like an avalanche on the evildoers. Give me a bag of straw, so that I may sleep the night, and show me the way to the daughter of Simon Peter."

His stout host assured him he was welcome to a bed in their hut at the entrance, seeing that he was with them in the faith. He could not mistake Petronilla's grave. If he counted a hundred steps straight ahead, he would find an *arcosolium*, a beautiful painted arch, with a marble sarcophagus below it, covered in flowers. Dozens of lamps were burning around it. The young believers made pilgrimages here in honor of Petronilla. All Rome vied to show their love for the innocent girl. All quarrels were silenced at her grave.

Before the tomb of his beloved child, the apostle sank to his knees. The warm ruddy glow from many lamps lay quietly over the underground chapel between hanging garlands of flowers, which spread everywhere a perfume of roses. The painting in the niche seemed to grow out of the hundred-petaled flowers. In the center stood a slender youth with a kid on his shoulder, and beside him, six on one side, six on the other, splendidly dressed men of various ages. In the place of honor on the right, with a bunch of keys in his hand—was that Peter? A dying flame began to flicker, and in the play of light and shade, the silent group seemed to become strangely alive, and to rise and greet him.

Here lay his child; here he sought strength and love, he, the deserted apostle whom no one welcomed save two grave-diggers.

ANYONE nearing the Forum that day could hear from afar the stirring, terrifying roar of the crowd. They whispered and shouted to each other in expectation of something never before experienced. The impatient pressed forward with curses, jostling one another amid a rain of insults. Peter was so tightly packed into the crowd of Christians, Jews and heathens, that his sweat mingled with theirs. All were on edge, their hearts full of mingled fear and glee. Was the Magus going to give the proof of his divine power?

A group wreathed in clouds of incense was making its way up the Palatine Hill at a ceremonious pace. Through the scented mist showed purple, gold, and the outlandish silken garments in which the Magus's followers decked themselves.

A few hisses, a few pleas for silence, and the great crowd fell quiet and stared up, their emotions almost unbearably tense. As the torchbearers at the head of the procession mounted the hill, their monotonous hymn sounded more like humming than singing. Under a canopy, two glittering, golden figures walked with measured step. They were Simon and Helena.

Already the procession had reached the summit of the Palatine Hill. The couple beneath the canopy walked slower and slower, the nearer they approached the orators' platform, whose marble balustrade rose high above the Forum and the countless upturned faces. To the apostle, all the ado about the magician seemed blasphemy, the smoke clouds of a circus juggler, and he clenched his fists in fury.

With those around him, he was swept along between the law courts, the pedestals of statues and memorial pillars, the booths and taverns, right up to the steps of the Dioscuran Temple. Beside him the smoke rose more and more thickly from the altar of Vesta, whose fire was being furiously prodded

279

by the angry priestesses. For the heathens of the old stamp were in an uproar. In the curia of the Senate, a number of senators had gathered and were standing on the steps as they used in the mighty days of old. A few bold grayheads among them, with vehement and magistral gestures, reviled the authorities for their weakness, and ordered the lictors to make use of their axes and their bundles of rods; the penalty for sorcery was death. But others, younger and softer men, begged them to consider whether one was not dealing with an unknown god. Reliable witnesses had reported that in Ariccia, this magician had caused a pillar of fire to appear and to wander about among the crowd, who dispersed screaming in all directions. Even the Jews with their rigid sects, worshipers of a crucified slave, the most inflexible people in the world in matters of faith, were beginning to waver.

Such things Peter heard in whispers. He stood on the edge of the temple colonnade. Below him, the poor folk were surging forward, all of them ready to believe whatever they were told. Here and there, the onlookers were discussing whether one could trust the new wonder-worker. Were the clever ones themselves sure? What a fuss they had made a few years since, when that other Simon, the one they called Peter, had drawn Jews and heathens after him. And yet his miraculous powers had failed before his own daughter, and he had slunk back home in shame. Everybody had followed him for a while. But who remained now? Only the old priest Narcissus and a few matrons. They locked themselves away and prayed night and day for their God to send them a mighty messenger from the east, Saul, Paul, or some such person.

Meanwhile the procession above had disappeared between the hedges and behind the balustrades. And immediately a loud clamor arose to the south. Many of the onlookers recognized Marcellus, one of the noblest senators, in whose house the Magus was staying. A bearded and deformed artisan whose garlic breath stank in the apostle's nostrils, said: "A mighty patron! Who would be wiser than Marcellus?"

A half-blind old man began to wail: "All his charity turns to blasphemy. He has poor Christians flogged from his threshold, and calls the emissaries of the Jerusalem apostles impostors."

"Simon Magus has taught him something better!" cried the deformed one. A fat old hawker-woman furiously shouted him down: "I tell you, there is someone here who will bring him to order. Someone who can deal with kings, with bloody Herod, even. With just a look he can fell you to the ground and you are as dead as a rat!"

"Are you trying to frighten me with Simon Peter? You make me laugh!"

Now on all sides, imperious cries were heard. Young men from the sorcerer's following were elbowing their way through the crowd, shouting, "Come, give, give!" Others came after them, boys and girls, distinguished middle-aged men, some of them wearing the senatorial toga. No one was allowed to think himself too lowly or too high, each and every one of the Magus's followers had to beg for their master. On the crest of the hill, the torchbearers had lined up behind him and raised their torches high. The collectors began to jingle their moneybags and copper vessels: "All of you, give as much as you can or you will have no share in the heavenly grace. To him who gives shall be given." Gold, silver and copper rolled into the proffered moneybags. Rumors had gone round that, provided the money offering was sufficient, not only the Magus but all his believers too would be raised up to heaven. But this time, the collection was not enough to insure the journey to the other world. Only the sorcerer himself seemed to have purchased grace. Simon the Magus was about to demonstrate, before his bemused followers down below, how he could raise himself up from the ground in a mystical act of levitation.

As the apostle stared up, doubts assailed him like snapping dogs. "If God allows grace to be bought like this, then why did I cross the sea? They want Paul here; what would he do in my place? Would they not kill me, if I were to spoil this miracle?" He remembered the two mighty ones who had stood beside the mightiest of all, and how he had seen them hovering weightless in the air, in that sunrise on Mount Tabor. And now, perplexed, he rubbed his eyes, for he thought he saw the Magus rising up from the ground. With all the strength of his lungs he cried to his stern God of old: "Lord, thy will be done!"

A scream rose from thousands of throats, for high above them, the Magus, who had raised himself for a moment just a few ells above the marble balustrade, suddenly plunged in terror over the railing and into the abyss.

In panic fear the crowd gave way before the weight of the falling man. But above their clamor Peter's voice rose once more. All his anger had turned to pity, and in an appeal for help he cried: "Jesus!" and threw himself on his knees so violently that the hard stone gave way. An iron founder could have cast the knees of a giant from the hollows Peter made.

As the apostle gazed around, master of himself once more, the space about the Dioscuran Temple was empty. On the gray, blood-spattered basalt stones, the man who had tried to be a god lay senseless. The Vestals, women trained in the healing arts, swarmed out of their temple in triumph at the vindication of their goddess. She had had her revenge. The scavengers could bear this bloody bundle away.

But the apostle's interceding cry had given the Magus a last respite and a chance to repent. In astonishment, the white circle of priestesses bent over him, felt him with their expert hands, and discovered him to be alive. His right leg, however, was broken in three places.

The crowd had recovered from their fright and now they surged back, full of rage at being cheated of their spectacle and of their money. They began to chase the Magus's followers, who scattered on all sides. Then they went looking for the body of the impostor who had hawked God's grace as if it were the salt fish of his native land. They stopped in front of the atrium of Vesta, and saw to their surprise that the Magus had after all not been dashed to pieces. What power of miracle had saved him from destruction? They gathered in a wide circle about the Vestals, who were washing his wounds, and the gray-bearded man.

So quiet was the hot sunlit square that the low whisper of "Peter" reached everyone's ear. A man, Ariston by name, who had always believed only in him, had guessed that the apostle's power lay behind the miracle, and had hurried to the spot.

The Romans looked at him in amazement as, trembling, and in a voice that threatened to fail, he told them that Simon—not the Magus but the true Simon, the messenger of Jesus Christ—had crossed the sea to expose the sorcerer's cursed trickery, and to restore the Kingdom of God. Yet even his punishment was a thing of grace, for the Magus had not met with the instant death that he deserved.

Peter was so absorbed in his own emotions at the pitiful sight of the fallen sorcerer that he noticed nothing else. Only when Ariston and a number of others surged forward to kiss the hem of his garment, while the Vestals stared in astonishment, only then did he look up and try to fend them off. Now everyone was for him. His believers surrounded him joyfully. Strong hands reached for him and lifted him carefully on the men's shoulders. Proudly they carried him like a victor. The procession marched along the ancient Via Sacra, the street of triumphant conquerors. Singing, singing multitudes joined them.

It was late at night before Helena, with two of her old slaves, dared to set out in search of the Magus. They laid him on a stretcher, shaking with fever, confused words issuing from his bloodless lips. In his delirium he saw the face of Simon Peter terribly close to his eyes, as the last of his followers carried him to Ariccia. But the rumor of his fall hurried after him, and he had to flee farther and farther towards his homeland. They only got as far as Anxur. There his wounds became gangrened. His death was lingering and painful. He had time to repent. His last word was a word of hope: "Peter."

THE Roman sun went down in the red-gold glow of enormous flags of light. Westward over the darkening rooftops, a world seemed to be on fire. Below, on the house walls, countless little lanterns before the niches of the household gods shone like stars. Boys with torches led a small group of strangely dressed men up the Esquiline towards the estate of Quintus Cornelius Pudens. None dared disturb the powerful man with the shaggy forelock, who walked on with downcast eyes, deep in thought. Timidly, the gray-haired priests and young deacons followed at a distance. No one else was abroad in the evening gloom; no one saw their clothes soiled with the dust of the roads, spattered with filth, the heads and hands of many of them hastily bandaged. Some of their wounds were still oozing blood, but they bore the marks of the persecution with pride.

For days, riotous crowds, many from the other side of the Tiber, had been waylaying Christians, looting their houses, and breaking into their churches to defile and lay waste to them. The persecution stemmed from the rabbis, but had soon become a public festival. New reports of atrocities were coming in all the time, new calls for help, and here and there men were being beaten or stoned to death. The heathen mob sided now with the Christians, now with the Jews, themselves incited by rumors of the anger of their gods. Everyone who killed a Christian believed that he was performing a service for his god.

For all that, the swarm of heathen candidates for baptism grew. They crowded before the booksellers' pillars, to see whether the gospel of Jesus Christ was available again. Aristocratic ladies, borne along in litters, had their slaves halt and hand in to them the newest scriptures.

But in the poorest streets the manhunts went on, over stacks of fruit and vegetables, of cheeses and smoked goods. The barber stools on the pavements were overturned. Murderous gangs chased their bloody fugitives into the cookshops. Lamentation on lamentation arose till finally the Emperor Claudius lost his patience. He tried to end all the uproar at one blow. The bridges over the Tiber were sealed off with iron chains. The Germanic cavalry squadrons took to the saddle.

It was not the first time that Aquila had barricaded his house on the Aventine. He and his family were all the more terrified when Simon Peter was suddenly summoned in the twilight, to the Senator Cornelius. All the Christians trusted his wife Priscilla, but throughout the years he had remained the distinguished and unapproachable Stoic, too much a dignitary of Rome, the master city of the world, ever to show any understanding of the hereafter.

In spite of the danger, in spite of their fear of the strangely empty streets, some of the faithful insisted on accompanying Peter over the Caelian Hill to the Esquiline. Cornelius's torch-bearers led the way through alleys between tall, dilapidated tenements, and then they entered the district of the garden estates of noble patricians, well-guarded, and screened from the road by high park walls. One of the torchbearers rapped with the door knocker, and as he did so the Christians crowded round Peter and tried to bar his way. But he took his leave with a blessing and told them to take the shortest route home. The door closed behind him. His companions heard a plashing of water as it ran into a silver basin, probably for foot-washing. Steps echoed along the narrow house passage, then all was still, for Peter had followed the torchbearers through the atrium into the garden court.

Darkness was falling peacefully about him over the laurel hedges and the rose-tinted oleanders, which were slowly losing their color in the night. The smooth-raked gravel was empty, and empty the colonnades with their curtained doorway. The water from a softly bubbling spring ran down in marble gutters beside the elegant steps. Beyond the spring, the little ruddy flames of a bronze candelabrum shone on two cushioned thrones, beside which stood small, onyx-topped tables, set with silver bowls of fruit and cups of wine.

Invisible hands drew a curtain aside. With the heedless stride of a man accustomed to seeing everyone respectfully make way for him, the senator came towards the apostle. Peter's sharp seaman's eyes recognized him despite the long years that had elapsed since their last meeting. He observed that the masterful Roman was much balder, and his features had grown sharper. The serious, impassive face with its narrow curved nose came closer, and to Peter's surprise, the patrician greeted him, a member of a despised outlandish race, with the brotherly kiss of the nobility. With a gesture that was rather a command than an invitation, he bade Peter take a seat. Smiling wearily, he excused the pictures on the back and arms of the curule chairs: "I hope you will take it as an honor, and not as an insult, that the ivory reliefs show the tasks performed for the good of mankind by the son of our

285

highest deity—Hercules. Wherever I have traveled, the people have always believed that only the son of the Highest can help mankind."

At the senator's invitation, the apostle took one of the enormous strawberries that ripen all the year round in the green sunny crater of Lake Nemi. Cornelius had reached for one of the flat bowls of golden wine, but he drew back his hand. Peter noticed the Roman's polite embarrassment over the matter of the libation. According to his belief, he should sprinkle a few drops of wine on the ground, as an expiatory offering to the gods of the underworld. The Fisher of Men took up his cup, made the sign of the cross over it and said quietly: "Allow me to bless you and your house in the name of the All-Highest." But before the senator could drink with him, he tipped out a little wine on the gravel, in the form of a cross. "And may this consecrated wine banish the dark powers that threaten your life."

Cornelius raised his eyebrows. "Mine? I thought your life was in danger."

Abruptly, with a bull-like movement, Peter thrust his shaggy forelock down towards his host. "He stands and feeds his flock in the strength of the Lord. . . ." The senator remembered hearing these words once before, in a prayer of his wife's. Now he became aware that the conversation ahead of them was going to be no easy matter. Both of them were accustomed to give their thoughts a clear and final shape, the one in determining what was just, the other as a teacher of his flock, whose sentences none of them might twist. The senator relied entirely on earthly matters; he knew the consequences of human action, saw the fates at work, heard the clash of the shears of Atropos. The apostle recognized in earthly things, whether affecting him or others, only the Idea, the Way, the Goal.

The world, which seemed everything to Cornelius, seemed unreal to Peter. The one lived in reality, the other in the Faith. Between the two men on their thrones lay the threshold between one era and the next.

IT BEGAN with a misunderstanding. The Roman guessed that uppermost in his guest's mind was his urge for self-preservation, in order to continue his work; Peter thought he had been summoned there out of some desperate longing for salvation.

"I wanted," Cornelius began, "to warn you that you will have to vindicate yourself and your cause before the Emperor Claudius, for your life is at stake." He paused to observe the effect of his words, but the apostle was only concerned with the soul confronting him, which he had hoped was his already. There had been other Corneliuses who were of importance. A Cornelius had uttered the humble words: "Lord, I am not worthy. . . ." A Cornelius had fallen on his knees at Caesarea, and Peter, shocked, had raised him up again with the fond admonition: "I am only a man!" And now, must Simon Peter himself be scourged, crowned with thorns, stained with blood and spat upon, so that this Cornelius might say, as Pilate did, "Behold, a man"?

A fanfare startled the senator to his feet, though not his guest. Cornelius signaled him to remain silent. It was the trumpet call of the Emperor's German household cavalry. Outside, the horseshoes of a whole squadron clattered on the paving stones, near at hand and all too clearly. Then they trotted by. Even the Roman seemed to sigh with relief as he said: "I have saved you from death in the streets. But if Claudius's lictors find you here, then nothing can save either of us."

"Save me? From prison? Angels took me out of prison. Execution? The guards to whom I was chained were executed. Your Rome? What is left of it? Empty graves, helmets without heads, armor with no heart inside."

"You think we are standing like hollow statues? While you are marching from all sides—the multitudes, the poor, the believers in the cross and in your God, who only considers great the one who is least of all? From all sides your followers are creeping together. In the East as in the West, they are worshiping the Invisible One."

Peter's eyes lit up. "From whence did you derive such knowledge?"

287

"The Emperor summoned a special meeting of the Senate. Perhaps you know that I am one of the two secretaries who sit beside the Emperor. From all sides, the governors reported the most disturbing growth in your numbers. No land is without you, no people, no town. Soon there will be no village without Christians."

Peter leaned back in his chair. As if from some subterranean source he felt the power of the multitudes of his faith surging through him. Like a prayer of thanksgiving he murmured to himself: "When the Son of Man shall come in his glory and all the angels with him, then he shall mount his throne and all peoples will gather round him."

"We have investigated your conspiracy. Such a powerful community of like-minded people must be led and mastered like a state within a state."

"If we are of one mind, do we need anyone to command us?"

"The Senate found no proof of any conspiracy. From my wife I know that you gather in groups of Chosen Ones—of Churches, as you call it. But one thing the Senate knows, the Emperor knows, and that is that you are master of them all, lord of a universal kingdom."

From the Emperor's fear, the apostle could judge the gigantic growth of his work. Cornelius misinterpreted his guest's silence. His voice had an edge to it: "You feel we have seen through you? Tell the truth! I know from Priscilla that lying is forbidden to you. Your speech must be: Yes, yes or No, no."

Smiling, Peter answered: "You have taught me the extent of my power."

"The sinister Pallas, Claudius's freedman, the most powerful man in the empire, has made accusations against you. He never demeans himself to address a word to anyone lower than the Emperor. He gives his orders only in writing. No one is richer than he, no one crueler. A year ago, we were the breathless onlookers at the spectacle, the deadly contest, between Pallas and Messalina. The Empress fell as his victim. So beware!"

"Our weapon is love."

An uncertain smile contorted the Roman's face. "Love? With bloodhounds like Pallas, like Narcissus? With a tyrant like Claudius? With the Senate over you like a court of execution? With the law..."

"We know only one Law: You shall love the Lord your God with all your heart and with all your soul and with all your might, and you shall love your neighbor as yourself."

Cornelius laughed. "To love the Parthians and the Germans, your Judaean knife-carriers, the Pamphylian pirates, the criminals of Subura, the Roman mob, is that not suicide?"

"It must be so."

The statesman thumped with his clenched fist on the arm of his ivory chair. "You are dangerous. The multitudes swarm to you, the rabble of the city. You paralyze our power over the people, over the world. Such a faith is the most murderous threat to our might. You are guilty of a crime that carries the penalty of death!"

The shepherd of the world drew himself up to his full height. "And if you nailed us to a hundred thousand crosses, we would still pray as we bled like the dying Son of God: Lord, forgive them, for they know not what they are doing. With this love, with this faith in God's love, we shall rise and live forever through the ages."

The senator would not have been a Roman, bound by an ancient fear of the gods, and to whom everything incomprehensible was demonic, if he had not felt the supernatural greatness of such fervor. Carefully picking his words, the wise administrator of Roman law pronounced sentence on the past as on the future, a sentence on mankind: "Hatred and greed and envy are all that holds our empire together. The best among us have long guessed what you say: Virtue is all. If you teach that to those whom we are subduing with such relentless severity—who knows for how long?—the nameless, the starving, those who have nothing else but Rome and are nothing else but Romans, if you teach the non-Romans of the earth your new Law, so that they demand higher things than this world is able to give, then you are the future master over all earthly things, for they do not count any more."

Had the Messiah's promise come true? That the faithful should be enthroned not merely over the twelve tribes but over the whole world! Peter closed his eyes before the sublime prospect. But then he heard terrible news. "The Senate has pronounced sentence and the Emperor has just made it public. All Jews, and you among them, are banished from Rome, from the Alps to the southern tip of Sicily. Within twelve hours you must be on your way and you may take no more possessions than each of you can carry. For, incited by the Chrestus, your stiff-necked behavior constitutes rebellion. Those who do not obey will be put to death."

The apostle opened his eyes wide. He bent over, searching for Cornelius's glance. In the sultry night wind from the south, his body was still wet with the sweat of his feverish exaltation at his vision of victory over the world. "Chrestus?" he stammered.

"So the accusers name the unknown god. I presume they have parodied the name which my wife and children pronounce as a prayer."

"Driven from Rome? The Jews? Whether baptized or not?"

Darkly, emphatically Cornelius repeated: "You too, Peter. So—to the sorrow of myself and my family—your empire falls!" He was astonished to see his guest rise slowly to his feet. Instead of the lowering sultry night sky he seemed to see another world of shining glory. Like a song of rejoicing he cried: "Master of this house! Judge and executioner in the name of worldly power! All my love, all my gratitude is yours!"

"Did you understand the meaning of my words? At this moment, those like you are being driven out of Rome as beggars. The authorities are swinging their rods, the fasces of punishment, and whipping the Jews, man, woman and child, out of the land. They will perish on the roads, whether they hate Jesus or are hated for his sake."

"And only those from Judah!" cried the Rock. "Now all the baptized thousands may live in peace, who come from elsewhere and cling to the true faith, the faith of love, within Rome's walls!"

"You are no doubt thinking that an emperor drove your people out once before, the merciless Tiberius. You are remembering that these obdurate and persistent people came back again. Expulsion and return, again and again. . . ."

"Only Jesus's work remains and will flourish unimpaired,

more peaceful than ever. I am prepared to journey out and
die on the way. So you send us out again, Son of Man, again
your word applies: Take no gold nor silver nor copper in
your girdle, nor any wallet, only one garment, no sandals,
and no staff! But on your travels, tell it out that the Kingdom
of Heaven is at hand! Now do you believe, noble Cornelius,
you who must remain under the bloody fist of a Claudius, a
Pallas, an Agrippina, now do you believe that you are more
in need of consolation than I?"

Deeply stirred, the Roman rose and embraced the stranger
who had suddenly become so dear and familiar to him. "Go
with my blessing. I will cherish and honor this ivory throne
of yours. And if you return, I will believe in your might, and
will believe that love is more powerful than the power of
my ancient Rome, and that you are the lord of a new and
mightier Rome, the Rome of love."

UNDER the autumn stars, a sailing ship was scudding before
the wind. The masts swayed and dipped gently, regularly,
over the long swell. Up in the crow's-nest a feeble lantern
swung in the darkness like a rocking star. It was late at night,
and only the officer, the steersman and the watch were on
deck. The rest were below in their bunks, tormented by the
heat, amid the smell of tar, fish and salt water. Alone, Peter
was sitting wide awake on a coil of rope, in the bow of the
ship. He did not hear the regular breathing of Joanna, who
was accompanying him after many years of separation, he did
not hear the hum of the wind in the rigging nor the constant
regular surge of the sea, nor the creaking of the ship's planks.
His thoughts were turned on himself.

After witnessing the unspeakable suffering of all those suddenly uprooted people, their trembling hope that the order
might be rescinded, he felt himself vindicated by the fact that
he too was taking part in a journey into poverty and death.
The imperial command drove him, as a Jew, back to the Jews
again, though no one hated him more than his own compatriots. To the fury of the priesthood and the Pharisees was
now added the thirst for vengeance of all those driven out

by the cavalry squadrons. Mobs had gathered to despoil the outcasts, to break into their homes almost before they had left them, and to carry off or destroy the unfortunate Jews' belongings before their very eyes. The rich had been fore-warned in time, no doubt by senators who were either friendly or indebted to them, and they had been able to escape with gold or jewelry, after hastily transferring their property to helpful Romans. But all the poor folk, of whom there were so many, stumbled on and on, sore-footed, their last few possessions in a bundle over their shoulder, hungry and thirsty, and still not allowing themselves to accept anything from the unclean heathen. Many fell by the way, or watched their exhausted children die. The others dragged on, their numbers dwindling, towards their ancient homeland.

Those who were Christians had to thank the love of their pagan coreligionists for the fact that they were able to sail to the Holy Land in fast ships. Aquila and Prisca had fled to Corinth, where the tentmaker owned a workshop. But Peter reflected sadly that he would have to sit inactive again in the room of the Last Supper. Involuntarily he cried aloud: "Loafing, I call it! And what was the good, Jesus! What was the good of ever sending us out!" He was again the hotspur of old.

Joanna started from her sleep. Sorry to have awakened her, he clumsily stroked her hair. For the first time, after days of silence, she spoke: "Why did you come back to Rome, you Rock of misfortune? You remind me always of the curse: 'You shall be hated of all peoples....'"

Sorrowfully he gazed into her eyes. "More than ever do Isaiah's words apply to me: 'Look at the rock out of which they are hewn.' Every single one of them is hewn out of me, and each time with pain...."

"To think that I have only bitter sayings for you from the mouth of the God of Love. They are with me always: Brother shall deliver brother unto death and the father—the father his child."

She could not have cut him more cruelly. The old man's gaze lost itself in the night.

"Today I could still have been praying at my Petronilla's grave, and gone on until they bury me by her, till she is one with me again. But you had to come back to Rome and your first road ..."

"...led to my daughter's grave."

Joanna started with surprise. "And I did not see you?"

"I came at nightfall, along the Via Salaria. Gravediggers took me in."

"With death as your companion. This time it cost Simon the Magus his life."

"Do you defend him?"

"I only know that Christ gives life, eternal life and life on earth."

Peter sighed. "Is your hatred for me as steadfast as once, for nearly a lifetime, your love was? Do you not know what I am going to? From the king to the lowest Temple servant, from the governor to the most despised soldier, from the high priest to the most carefully hidden knifeman, they are all waiting to plant the death thrust between my ribs."

Joanna threw herself forward and embraced his knees. Once again everything was as it had been in the days of their youth: lurking death, constant danger, soldiers, murderers, judges, hangmen. Again, fear gripped her by the throat as it had at Capernaum, at Bethsaida when she had clung trembling to her mother. The steady implacable wind was driving them with taut sails straight towards the murderous hail of stones, right into the midst of the outstretched spears. At the end of their journey rose the blood-crusted gallows on Golgotha.

"Simon," groaned the desperate woman, "why do you travel towards your death? Why not make yourself safe with Aquila and Prisca in Corinth? Why not seek refuge with the community in Antioch? Why do you let yourself down like Daniel into the lions' den?"

"Have I not that death-miracle to atone for? Lord, for whose return they wait in Jerusalem, you have given me the charge and the grace. I ask for no reward for leaving everything behind—my home, my land, my child."

Dark clouds fluttered like a shroud across the sky, and here and there a star loomed like a veiled candle. Joanna's eyes widened in a Golgotha terror. "Will they not all beset you on Moriah, that unyielding Jacob and those with him? And Paul

293

of Tarsus will call you to task again, because you did not check the Emperor with a miracle. The flock is scattered, the Shepherd slain."

"They will stand small before me, for I bring great news. Even Cornelius the senator despairs of Rome, the mighty empire that stretches to the bounds of the earth. It must pass away, because no one believes in it any more. The Senate knows, for the governors have reported, how numerous we are on every hand. The invincible legion of Christ! The Kingdom over the whole world in heaven and on earth!

"Jesus has to draw mankind to him. He imposes no Ten Commandments on us now, only the single commandment to love, and the Kingdom will come to us. No more enmity, no more hatred. Then the angel guarding Paradise will dip his flaming sword in the stream that is called oblivion. The way to God will be open."

Joanna looked at Peter timidly, but in admiration.

"I will cry out and call to each and every one, to my people, to all people to the confines of the world. A trumpet call will storm through the marrow of their bones, a call to battle against all that is base and sinful and abhorrent to God!"

Joanna began softly to pray: "Our Father, for how many centuries of centuries must Simon be on the way towards his goal?"

Now that the imperial order of banishment had driven the Jews home, the hunted sons of the twelve tribes in the Dispersion came swarming back to Jerusalem, whether they believed in Jesus or Moses. The Temple was too small. The city was surrounded by encampments as during the most radiant Easter days. As the deacons gazed southeastward from the Temple battlements, over the approaching crowds of Christian believers, they had the impression that the steep rock falling away below them was the side of a heavenly ship, and that they were drifting from one angelic choir to another. Songs rose up to them from thousands of throats, psalms in ancient Hebrew, Aramaic chants, Greek hymns, languages that none of them had heard before. Cries rang out: "Peter is here! Paul is coming! Believers are raining down on us like manna!"

At Paul's request, the Roman governor had handed over the unfinished theater to the Christians, for their gathering. In the Tyropöon valley, where the rock of Golgotha slopes down, Agrippa had started building this theater for the Roman troops. It was nearly finished by now. Rows of seats had been hewn in the mountain slope, in a bold semicircle swinging wider and wider. But the wall at the back of the stage, the "scene," was unadorned by any idols. Of course, the building was consecrated, for every play, however frivolous, was considered as a sacrifice to Dionysus. But the king had drawn back before the threat of the high priests' curse; the marble-decorated scene and its side walls remained incomplete, their niches and balconies empty.

Paul had guaranteed there would be no disorder, and the cunning governor had agreed to their using the theater, for in the event of trouble he had all these deportees from Rome right under his mailed fist. Before daybreak, the legionaries had already taken up their positions around the theater. Past their spears and shields came the disciples, priests, deacons and elders from Syria, Cilicia and Cappadocia, from Pisidia, Phrygia and Galatia, from Bithynia, and from the distant Black Sea shore of the Paphlagonians. Crete, Cyprus and Achaia sent their holiest men. Thessalonians and Illyrians arrived. More and more arrivals in strange costumes, yellow, brown, black men from Asia, Africa and Europe, proud dignitaries in purple-edged Roman togas from Spain, Gaul, Italy and Greece filled the gigantic theater. Peter had summoned Christians from the remotest regions, and they had come with eternity and immortality in their hearts.

The constantly growing crowd was already beginning to spill over the rising semicircular rows of benches like a vessel full to the brim. The only unoccupied seats were the marble thrones of honor down below by the "orchestra," where the chorus usually stood. There was a feeling of tension in the air, for the Jewish Christians from Jerusalem itself found all the benches occupied by delegates from former pagan districts and had to crowd on the terraces or between the seats, all the more irritated to find themselves so obviously in the minority.

On the raised platform of the stage were gathered the community deacons. From the top rows, they looked tiny and rather frightened before all those thousands of intently staring faces. They had sent one of the elders, the Archdeacon Nicholas, hastily to the twelve apostles, for it was high time to begin. Some of the apostles asked indignantly why Paul had brought so many delegates with him, but the old archdeacon had chuckled happily, for all his troubles about looking after the community in this famine year had been lifted from his shoulders, despite the enormous influx of believers. "It is a blessing to us he did bring so many! The promise he gave as Saul, he has kept as Paul. The Christians from the heathen lands brought with them blessings of goods and food far beyond their own needs."

As Peter entered the theater past the spears of the legionaries, the gigantic door in the center of the scene opened before him. He walked onto the stage and saw reared up before him a huge wall, terrace upon terrace, face upon face, tens of thousands of pairs of eyes, all turned towards him.

Around him, everyone fell silent, and the silence spread in increasing circles, like the noiseless waves that ripple towards the margins of a well when a stone is dropped.

Peter raised his arms heavenward so suddenly that many winced with fear. He who only a little while before had brought down Simon the Magus seemed to them to grow to enormous stature, as if the bull-horned Moses were standing before his guilt-laden people. At his enormous gesture, the air rushed fresh and vivifying into his lungs, and his heart swelled with joy to see his growing church there before him. Let them quarrel, let them doubt, let them err, they were his. As if to cut through the midst, with one thrust downwards, one thrust from left to right, his sword arm made the sign of the cross over them all.

Gravely, and in some embarrassment, the crowd crossed themselves, with anxious glances at the keeper of the keys of heaven. Out of the side streets, new arrivals were still streaming in, packing the semicircular space in front of the stage to an alarming extent. They did not dare to utter a word, but stared timorously at the powerful man who, accustomed to speaking in enormous meeting places in Rome, began the Lord's Prayer. The faithful repeated it, plea by plea. The rhythm of the prayer was matched by the rhythm of their hearts. Shepherd and flock were one.

The Amen died away. Already, barely a score of years after the Saviour's death on the cross, there was a danger of the Chosen falling away. In the course of that day, the sea of opinions, the storm of convictions was to toss the ship of the Fisher of Men in all directions. Already he could hear the elder Tebuitis's denunciations: Jacob and his brother were trying to establish a dynasty of the house of the Nazarene. A tattered philosopher from the top row of seats interrupted. He was an Ionian, concerned about the improbability of a God taking on the burden of human sorrow. Jesus was probably a mere symbol. The Jerusalem deacons angrily demanded whether he thought a symbol could die; could blood and water flow from a symbol? And in the midst of their outraged cries came a yell from a lean fanatic, who tore his garment and beat his hairy breast with his fist as he screamed: "I am a sinner and you do not help me! God cursed us when he drove us out of Paradise. You are trying to hide that from us. But we know of our misfortune from the holy scriptures of the Jews!"

From the groups of Jewish Christians who had been unable to find seats came wild shouts: "Our holy books are profaned! The ignorant have soiled them with their unclean hands, their unclean minds!" Another besought Jacob: "Tell them to hold their tongues. Shout in their faces that faith without works is a dead thing, as you wrote to us!" In wild confusion the crowd began to cry all their faintheartedness, their doubts, their dogmatism and their ignorance. Up and down the rows they shouted, screamed, howled furious questions to each other: "Why is the evil within us, why does the Lord scourge us with sorrow and death?"

The Bishop of Jerusalem came to Peter's side and implored them: "Brothers, do not set yourselves up as teachers. Do you not know that teachers have to submit to a more severe judgment; for as a tiny flame may set a forest on fire, so a man's tongue is a firebrand that kindles a whole world of mischief."

But from the mouth of a Syrian, a flaming hatred was directed on him, and in his fury that so many Jewish Christians demanded that the baptized should first become Jews, the Syrian invoked a saying of Jesus.

"The Pharisees have sat in the chair of Moses the lawgiver. They lay heavy burdens on the shoulders of mankind, but they do not stir a finger themselves. Has not the Lord himself declared: Punishment for all their crimes shall fall upon these people?"

Tears rolled down Jacob's cheeks. "Do not insult the race to whom you owe your salvation! From the blood of its greatest kings was born Jesus of Nazareth. Remember! The judgment is merciless on those who are themselves unmerciful." A storm of howling broke loose. "He is threatening us!"

Paul could no longer restrain himself. When he saw the Rock rear up so mightily before him, the thought entered his mind that Peter had the power of life and death over him; he remembered the fate of Simon the Magus. Yet he climbed up on his seat, supported by Luke and Mark, and overtowered those around him, only a little lower than Peter and Jacob. Some of the Jewish Christian outcasts from Rome turned to him, and a few ventured the ironic cry of "Hermes! Hermes!" But he silenced them with a look.

In his enthusiasm the words streamed from his heart, and with the warm glow of his powerful oratory he painted a picture of distant and populous cities, and described how he and Barnabas had appeared within their confines, and rejoiced at the rush of converts. The synagogues and market places were too small. In his footsteps, new communities sprang up. "And what is Jewry to all these? What do the godly folk of distant countries care about the bloodstained history of the Jordan lands? They want to live free in the word and the will of the Lord."

His fiery speech raged on: "Let the rabbis look to their Old Testament, and we will present our counterevidence when they reproach us with falsifying the prophecies! Let the realm of the Emperor become the realm of God! The saying of Isaiah is apt: 'I will send out to the heathen those who are saved, and they will proclaim my glory to the heathen, said the Lord.' Jesus was the grain of wheat who died from the disbelief of the Jews and who will bring forth rich fruit from the faith of the heathen!"

Jacob leaped to his feet and interrupted the speaker. "A commandment is a commandment and Law is Law. Jesus maintained that too."

". . . and he upbraided those like me, as Pharisees—for I was one then—as whited sepulchers. How I hated him for that! Until he blinded me in order to enlighten me. Then I was freed from the fear of every little offense—one step too much on the Sabbath, a hand-washing forgotten. Now I know: The Lord is God, and where the Lord God is, is freedom! And all of us from whose eyes the veil is lifted are mirrors of the glory of the Lord!" A great burst of cheering came from the Christians of Asia and Achaia.

Protesting wildly, the baptized Jews were about to storm forward against this man who had committed a heresy against the law of Moses, but some pointed uneasily at Peter, who appeared to have risen to a superhuman stature; something enormous seemed to be opening out before his eyes. To the onlookers, it was as if he was there, yet not there.

But the man from Tarsus realized what was happening. That which he himself kept secret from men, uncertain whether it was real or a dream, he guessed was being experienced now by Peter. He whispered to himself, as if in prayer: "So—just so—it happened to me in Christ—whether in my body or outside of my body, I do not know, but God knows. I was hurled up to the third heaven—and I know—this Paul here—this ego of mine—whether in my body or far from my body I am not sure, but God knows—was led up into Paradise and heard words that no one has been permitted to repeat. . . ."

The silenced crowd hardly dared to breathe in their tense expectation of a new Whitsun miracle. The chief apostle stood high above them all in his mighty faith. No one dared say or do anything against him. They all knew him to be lord over life and death, and now he perceived tremendous visions surging towards him in his ecstasy. Some power from above set everything dancing and whirling around him in ever-rising circles of light that became smaller and smaller till they were barely visible in the sunlit splendor of the sky. Then the whole theater rang as if golden strings were stretched from star to star, and angels were harping immortal melodies upon them. The dawn of future centuries shone before them.

Peter felt as if he were one with the growing rock under him, and he himself were the living Rock of God which bore the everlasting Church, and which held up to his Maker all that mankind would create in the future of beauty, of greatness, of immortality. Domes sprouted from the palms of his hands, the echoing halls of the basilicas, the stone forests of Gothic cathedrals, until—prophetic vision!—his own gigantic mausoleum began to arch above him as a new firmament, a new heaven over a new earth, the cupola of Saint Peter's in Rome. Silver fanfares blared for victory, and the Hallelujah of the choirs rejoiced: *"Tu es Petrus!"*

The spectators sighed with relief when they saw the ecstatic smile that lit up his face. Now they knew he had not come to punish but to bless. "Brothers," he cried, "you know that in the early days, God decided that the heathen should hear the words of the Gospel from my mouth, and should become believers. And God, who knows the hearts of men, testified for them, in that he gave them the Holy Ghost as he did to us. He did not differentiate between them and us, for through the faith he made their hearts clean. Then why do you try to challenge the Lord, and to set a yoke upon the necks of the disciples that neither our fathers nor we have had the strength to bear? No, through the grace of our Lord Jesus, we trust in our salvation as you do also."

The multitude hung on his words. Here and there the elders and bishops exchanged radiant glances of joy. Suddenly there was a stir, an agitation among the crush of Jewish Christians between the benches and on the terraces right down to the orchestra. In silent fear they were hurrying out through all the exits, draining away like sand in an hourglass. And where they had just been threatening, demanding, accusing, suddenly heavily armed legionaries stood, with sword and shield and spear. A warrior, Rome incarnate, entered with a light clatter, his plumed helmet visored as if for battle, so that it looked like a tragic mask. Over his armored shoulder he wore a general's scarlet cloak. With his hand on his broad-sword, he stood like the figure of death itself.

But Jacob stepped forward, quite unperturbed. "Men! Brothers! Hear me. Simon Peter has shown you how God had wished from early times to win from the heathen a people of his own name." He repeated solemn words of the prophet Amos. Only one thing was demanded from them, that they should abstain from defiling themselves in the abject service of the demons, abstain from consorting with temple prosti-tutes, abstain from eating the flesh of strangled animals, and from drinking blood.

In their thousands, the heathen Christians rose from their benches to applaud the apostles, who confessed with deep emotion that they had never imagined such a mighty world of faith. Paul had joined them, and the enraptured onlookers saw that the holy band of twelve was complete again. While those above were exchanging the kiss of brotherhood, the enraged Tebuitis, seeing the armored figure with the closed visor had turned to go, shouted up to them maliciously: "Simon Peter, do you believe you are really called to be ruler of the earth above Rome, and mightier than the Emperor Claudius? If so, then carry on the banner to the final victory over the world that does not yet believe in Jesus Christ!"

Sure enough, the warrior's attention was caught, and he turned again to listen.

"Yes," replied Peter, "I see the Kingdom which you ask for so impatiently. The Kingdom is God's and must be ours. The Kingdom is within us, and it is boundless. It has been from the beginning, but we have to complete it. We must not weaken...."

Tebuitis climbed up on his seat. In hellish derision the sharp-nosed old man bent his arms into wing stumps and blazed out a yelling cockcrow which the theater amplified so enormously that the mocker himself was frightened. The priests crossed themselves against such devilry; the youngsters threatened to hurl themselves on the old man, so that his companions, some of them ashamed, others alarmed, reached for their clubs. The apostle hid his face in his hands and groped for words. At last he let his arms fall and said, smiling through his tears: "I thank you, brother, for showing me my weakness in believing we were already on the way to purification, we were already to be considered virtuous. You are right. We shall have to work for centuries in order to be worthy of the Kingdom of God. Perhaps when our grandchildren say complacently: "Now we are Christians," perhaps then the princes of the world will raise their scepters and will be crueler than the cruelest beast of prey, more godless than the Dead Sea. The Satan of Satans will blush with shame and envy at their deeds. The cocks crow without cease. Jesus must be born again, year after year, for us and in us. With your bitter reminder, you have shown me the Kingdom of God. What is the Rome of the visible world against the inner Rome? All power is damnation, save only one—the power of love. Let love be master of the world, and Jesus is here!" Peter fell on his knees and prayed in the words that Jesus spoke on the way to Golgotha: "Father, the hour has come. Glorify your son, that your Son may glorify you: even as you gave him authority over all flesh, to all that you gave him he shall give eternal life."

All fell on their knees like Peter. All prayed like him. The soldier took off his helmet, and wondered what had come over him.

"AND they went forth and preached everywhere. . . ." These few words of Mark's gospel concealed a tremendous mission, a ceaseless toil. For Peter, more than thirty years of wandering, of searching for truth, of caring for souls, of comforting, of fishing for men.

The people of the heathen world had nothing but their life, to which they clung with all the roots of their heart. But every hour faded in the shadow of impending death, which they feared beyond measure, for then they sank without hope into nothingness, a handful of ashes and burnt-out bones. Not to lose a moment of this short span of existence, was all their care. As a reminder, they set skeletons in mosaic on their thresholds. Skeletons embossed in silver grinned from cups and spoons. The Romans no longer believed in their gods, they merely feared them. In many of them a remnant of paternal love towards their children still flickered. But despite the penalties and taxes imposed on childlessness, many renounced even that happiness, in order to spare their sons and daughters their own misfortune—the rich out of fear of assassination and lurking greed, the poor out of their inescapable daily fear of starvation, and their nightly fear of fire or the collapse of their dwelling. Their ancestors had created a mighty Rome, but they had undone it. The State weighed heavily on them all, for it took their last coin, and in exchange it doled out bread and a few scanty pleasures. They were a generation that had lost everything, even their future.

Then Peter came with his cry of *"Sursum corda!"* "Lift up your hearts!" Like Paul in the East, he traveled along the western highways of the empire, till the priests, the deacons, and, not least, the family of Cornelius implored him to return to the capital of the world, to his ivory throne. Each time he returned, Quintus Cornelius received him more cordially.

This time, however, he had been annoyed when he heard that after long travels, the apostle had again reached Rome, for he had not come to occupy his ivory throne with the deeds of Hercules upon it, but was living in the Subura, among the poorest of the rabble, in one of the many forlorn and dilapidated tenements. Today, Cornelius was on his way to call Peter to account, to ask why the man to whom he had offered the world was hiding like a coward and a weakling.

From the Vicus Patricius, the quiet noble street between high-walled gardens, the forerunners of the two resplendent litters—for the senator was accompanied by his wife—turned off into the tenement quarter of the Fagu valley and the Subura. Here the senses were assailed by the smell and din of bustling crowds. The stale reek of oil from the cookshops clung nauseously to the tongue. From dark caverns of brick, on all sides, came the scream of files and saws, and the pounding of hammers. Money-changers clattered their copper coins. From the windows, angry women screamed down to their children.

Regardless of all this, the gigantic Numidians pushed their way through the crowded alleys. It was afternoon already.

Only after nightfall would the roads be free for vehicles. But at present the narrow defiles between the towering houses could hardly contain the enormous throng. Fortunately they soon found the house they were looking for. Pouring with sweat, their brows puckered, Cornelius's slaves set down the two litters, and lined up on either side to keep back the press of curious onlookers, while the man in the broad-edged toga and his gentle wife entered the house.

Two linkboys scuttled along in the wake of one of the Numidians, who laboriously groped his way up the steep stairs, to light the way for the master. The senator's heart was pounding with the unwonted exertion. The stench took his breath away. On the first landing, Cornelius started back at a sudden groaning, as if he had trodden on someone lying there. Unbidden, a hoarse voice embarked on a recital of misfortune.

On the next landing a woman, leaning against a half-open door, accosted the Numidian with an obscene joke. But when the senator suddenly stood before her in the dim light of the horn lantern, she pressed her slack body against him. When she caught sight of Priscilla, she hid herself with an embarrassed laugh. The stairway was darker still. The strangers heard agonized coughing through the thin staircase walls.

Wretch after miserable wretch begged from them, the higher they went. When they had climbed more than a hundred stairs, the aging senator became so exhausted that he had to calm his heart by resting. Priscilla anxiously lifted her arms as if, frail as she was, she could support her burly husband. Already, the Numidian slave had knocked on a trap door, in the rhythm of a quail's call. The door was opened. They stepped onto an open roof terrace at the end of which were a few rooms. Leaning on the parapet, Simon Peter's mighty silhouette rose dark against the golden light of the setting autumn sun. The Numidian hurried to the apostle and was about to fall on his knees, but Peter took the slave fondly in his arms and kissed his ebony-black face. He turned to his master and mistress, and saw the love and reproach in their sunset-gilded faces.

The noble Roman had never experienced such embarrassment as he felt before the man who had greeted his slave with a kiss, as Roman aristocrats were wont to greet each other. Was it merely his lack of breath that made his question sound so uneasy: "You greeted my slave . . . ?"

"With the holy kiss," said Peter.

"And do you not reckon me as one of yours?"

The apostle opened his arms and held the senator to his breast, so close that Cornelius could not see the dark pain in Peter's eyes that betrayed his certain knowledge of impending misfortune, a look so profound, so full of sympathy, that Priscilla almost screamed with fear. Jesus's faithful companion had learned too much about human sickness not to know that the racing, irregular beat of Cornelius's heart was a sign of approaching death. Mark, who respectfully stood a little distance off, was no less disturbed at Peter's expression. With the Numidian, he pushed forward a broad heavy bench that stood against the parapet. There the couple sat down, and the Negro arranged warm wraps about them, for the October evening air was cool.

With a curious haste, as if he were afraid he would not be able to say everything, the senator began to speak of his life-long wish to be able to penetrate to the very boundaries of knowledge; the Eleusinian mysteries and the horrors of the cult of Isis—of them, nothing remained. He told them of his friend Seneca, who betrayed his own wisdom for the sake of an outward show of honors. At the end of all his striving he was left hopeless, confronted with a great void.

Peter spoke to him comfortingly: "Trust against trust! Everything that is true in the world belongs to us, to the Christians, and you too, for you are an upright man. And like the upright among the peoples of the world, you seek the way to God. When you have found that, you will never be alone. Give yourself to me, give yourself to us and to the Almighty, whose great power of love flows through us and makes us flourish and grow up to him in his everlasting light. Does not Priscilla, do not I carry your image everywhere, even where you are not? Do you not live in us? So the love of God carries us within itself, and God forgets nothing and nobody. Leave everything and come with us. Listen to the saying of Jesus:

'Everyone that has left his house, his brothers and sisters, father and mother, children or lands for my sake, shall receive a hundredfold and shall inherit eternal life.' "

Suddenly a piercing ululation, resembling the cry with which Bedouin women urge on their camels, rose out of the walled abyss of the alley below, and the crack of whips, wild howls and the cries of people as they fled. Almost at the same moment a furious altercation broke out. Peter's guests sprang to their feet and looked anxiously towards the parapet, over which Mark and the Numidian were already leaning. Giant Sudanese, with only leopard skins about their hips, were quarreling with Cornelius's Numidians, for not removing their litter quickly enough from the tenement entrance.

Mark heard the Negro beside him utter a suppressed cry of fear and saw the whites of his eyes bulging out of his black face in alarm. His thick lips faltered the name "Narcissus," and again "Narcissus," almost inaudibly. Mark no longer feared for himself, only for Peter and the house of Cornelius, as he leaned far over and watched the slaves of Claudius's powerful freedman, his Lord High Chamberlain, help their master out of his litter. Two gigantic Negroes knelt and clasped each other's hands crosswise, to form a seat to carry their master up the stairs.

The uproar in the street had been followed by a deathly quiet, during which the little group on the roof terrace stared at the trap door, until the heavy planks slowly and soundlessly rose. On naked, noiseless feet, one after another, the leopard men came hastily towards them, saluted them as if ironically with their hippopotamus-hide whips, and surrounded their purple-clad master as he slid down from his seat.

To show the senator and his wife and the much-admired priest of the mysterious foreign god how little he thought of their dignity, Narcissus greeted first the Numidian slave, deriving malicious pleasure from his terror. "A giant, a god almost, and frightened of me? As if a more benevolent man could be found at the Emperor's court! My dear fellow, I am like you and yet I am one of the highest in the land. I was down, down, far lower than you, I suppose, and now I am next in rank to the God-Emperor himself! No one was less than I. After the Emperor Claudius, no one is greater than I. I have undergone every experience from the bottom to the top, so I am everyone, I think all their thoughts, their desires are my desires."

The freedman had often enough gloated over his victims' terror, but under the senator's incorruptible gaze, he felt on the hand he stretched out in an involuntarily defensive gesture, an icy exhalation from the corpses of those he had murdered. Narcissus recovered himself, went across to the senator, and embraced him with the patrician kiss. Rigid as iron, Cornelius submitted to his salute. In growing fear, the freedman stumbled across to Simon Peter. Was he, whom the cowardly majority of the senators had honored with the title of Quaestor, after the murder of Messalina, was he to demean himself by bestowing the aristocratic Roman kiss on this Asiatic? Suddenly he yelled: "Did not his imperial majesty forbid any assembly, when he allowed you and your partisans of Chrestus to return to grace?"

"So you say," the apostle answered, with calm dignity.

"And what is this here?" cried Narcissus furiously.

"I see no assembly, unless you are counting your own slaves."

"The penalty for sorcery is death!"

"All eternity is ours," said Peter, and his voice seemed to shower down from the countless stars of the southern night.

"Eternity—so you say." Against his will, Narcissus forced himself to ask: "They say your Chrestus was master over life and death. You are supposed to have brought men from life to death—" Grinning maliciously, he had to add: "I can do that myself." But immediately he went on seriously: "—but also from death back to life. Is that true? Is it true that your Chrestus rose from the dead?"

"It is as you say."

"Tell me about immortality. It is urgent. What does it cost to be immortal?" he begged the magician from the East.

The answer was a single word: "Faith."

He did not know what to make of that. "One of your crowd taught me your secret. What you say is not enough. What you believe is: Faith apart from works is dead."

Peter had to smile. "I am delighted that you know the

right road. Good. Wash yourself clean. We call it the baptism of John."

"I, wash myself? You, baptize me?"

"He who taught you, did he find you clean? Are you clean?"

"Nobody ever dared call me unclean!"

Then it was as if the storm of the Last Judgment broke from the apostle's lips. Terrified, Mark and Priscilla crossed themselves in the darkness. Like thunder from Sinai his voice boomed forth and must surely have made itself heard down below in deserted Subura. "I see the place of the Lord's chastisement! Darkness is about you already. The somber-winged angel hosts are casting their shadows over this doomed land. Red glowing cavities appear in the rocks, abysses that no eye can fathom. Around us, hanging by their tongues, are those who scorned the path of righteousness. Below them burn the agonizing fires and there is a mighty sea of reeking, boiling mud in which men are writhing in unspeakable agony, souls who perverted the truth. But murderers and their accomplices will be cast by the dark angels into abysses full of great coils of cold snakes. There they are inflamed from the bites of the poisonous fangs till they writhe in agony. Around them the souls of those they murdered are arrayed, crying: "God, how just is your judgment!" The slanderers stand before God, waist-deep in flames, scourged by evil demons. From rocks glowing like still-molten lava, their tongues bitten through, they hurtle headfirst into the depths. You will be hunted through all the fires of darkness. They will beat you with burning staves. All of them will inflict as much pain on your tortured soul as you ever did to them."

At that moment, close at hand and far in the distance, military trumpets sounded the alarm call of the Praetorian Guard. The signal blared from the Palatine, up from the Forum, from far away on the Capitol and the Aventine, from the Janiculum and the Caelius. Trumpeters blew the strident call from the Viminal, and along the Subura came the staccato clatter of running men in armor.

Quintus Cornelius gently disengaged himself from his wife's embrace and entrusted her to the support of the Numidian, while he stepped in front of Peter and Narcissus, swiftly as a fencer on the attack. He was obliged to close his eyes for a moment, for with a stab of pain his heart warned him against such haste. He drew a deep breath. "You were not in the Senate, Narcissus. Do you not know what happened today at Sineussa?" The freedman made a startled gesture, but the senator continued: "Weary from his bath, our Emperor was reclining at the meal table. His eyes were heavy from the wine he had drunk. The Empress had ordered mushrooms, his favorite dish. He did not see clearly whether his eunuch Halotus fulfilled his duty as taster. Hardly had he eaten, than he seemed to fall into a weakness. The God-Emperor suddenly vomited and voided at once. Was the murderous attempt going to fail, after all? His physician Stertinius Xenophon, Claudius's friend and even more the friend of Prince Nero, thrust a feather into his throat as if to ease the vomiting. If this feather was poisoned, the poison was powerful. The Senate has adjourned for the summoning of witnesses."

In his alarm, Narcissus once again turned back to Peter. He wanted to make him realize that he, Narcissus, saw through him. The freedman told Peter to his face that he was intent on treason, that he had built up a state within the state and above the state, a most grave danger to the Empire. Soon there would not be a place in the settled world where secret meetings were not taking place. All the conspiratorial bands were strictly organized. From bishop down to doorkeeper, each had his allotted task. Every group had its own little senate, in the meeting of its elders. They maintained guardians of the poor who went from house to house, gathering the havenots, the poor and wretched into a vast army of malcontents with nothing to lose, and ready for any desperate act. They made themselves known to each other by secret signs; they practiced mysterious rites in underground rooms full of corpses.

Narcissus was overcome with rage when the apostle did not answer. Craftily, he tried with flattery and temptation: "But look, I am just, and I know the good side too. Masculine discipline and the dignity of woman are more prevalent among your people than anywhere else. You all help each other. The slightest failing is rigorously punished. Now listen: Your

309

hour has come. I can win over the army commanders for you, who are at this moment swarming to protect the State. The Empire is without an emperor. Britannicus is a boy; Nero, who wants to wrest the empire from him, is little older. Fourteen, seventeen years old; but on the frontiers of the Empire the Parthians are threatening, and the Germans to the north. Yours is the Kingdom of the Universe. Take Rome with it."

Startled, Cornelius looked at the apostle. He had offered him the curule throne in his own household, but in vain; and now the sinister and treacherous Narcissus was trying to bribe him with the imperial wreath of Claudius. Was the very thing the senator had hoped for, that universal Kingdom of purity and human nobility, to arise as a means whereby Narcissus could satisfy his boundless ambitions? Were the timbers of martyrdom on which men nailed a God to become the crosses on which all mankind was crucified? Peter too had to compose himself before he answered. Had he been right to refuse the throne in Cornelius's house, when even his enemy offered him the mastery over Rome? For the sake of his believers, did he still dare to hesitate? To the astonishment of the onlookers, the fisherman fell on his knees and cried to God: "Lead us not into temptation but deliver us from evil."

The senator's heart beat more painfully than ever. Then from the steps below the trap door he saw the gold helmet of an officer of the imperial guard appear. It was his son Sextus Cornelius Pudens. Spear after spear, the praetorians followed him, more and more, a whole century of them. They drove the leopard men into a whining knot and, seizing Narcissus, they violently clapped handcuffs and fetters on him. He implored Peter to work a miracle, to rescue him. He offered his whole fortune, four hundred million sesterces, but the soldiers dragged him down all the two hundred stairs to his execution.

The senator, the only one to realize fully the danger they had all been in, clutched at his heart with a suppressed groan. He would have fallen had not Peter sprung up and caught him and held him firmly in his strong arms. With the faithful Numidian, he laid him down on the bench. Under his head, which had fallen back helplessly, Mark thrust his cloak;

then he turned to support Priscilla, who was trying not to realize the dreadful thing that was happening. She saw soldiers with torches step silently to right and left of the bench on which the senator, with closed eyes, was breathing his last. His wife and son groped towards him, and tried to kiss his face, to lift him and hold him, but his limbs were moist with an icy sweat. Desperately, his son lifted the dying man's eyelids and saw his last loving look slowly fading away.

They listened in vain for his heartbeats. Sextus plucked a feather from the crest of his helmet and held it to his father's lips. No breath stirred the delicate down. Nothing was to be heard save the slight crackle of the torches, which were burning low, and the disconsolate weeping of the widow.

Then Sextus Cornelius lifted his moist eyes to Peter and begged him: "You whom they call the Rock. I know that when someone passes away who has not been received into your community like my mother, my sisters, my sons and daughters, it may happen that you baptize a living person above the dead one, so that both may share in the grace of the life everlasting. Let us find our father again; you know there was no fault in him."

Peter asked him whether, after such a long hesitation, his wish to become a Christian was strong. The soldier replied: "I had sworn the oath of allegiance, the sacramentum, to Caesar. But Caesar is gone. I swear my new oath to the invisible God."

PETER's life was approaching its sixtieth year when he entrusted the care of the Eternal City to Linus, the descendant of Etruscan kings. He himself set out on a great journey of visitation. Already in many places dangerous innovations were trying to establish themselves. Heresies were beginning to flicker like will-o'-the-wisps here and there. Thinkers and sciolists were trying to interpolate their own thoughts into the sayings of Jesus. Over and again, heathens were detected trying to smuggle in superstitious customs dear to them from childhood. The task before him resembled the great imperial tours of Augustus and Hadrian, it was a journey for the foundation of God's universal empire.

So once more he took leave of Joanna; he with great things before him, realizing the dangers, but impelled by a mighty urge: she, to pray for him at her daughter's grave during the lonely hours.

Peter and Mark left Rome secretly. Though it was already autumn, the sun shone hot at midday as they sat down under the shade of a spreading golden-green pine tree beside the Via Appia, to eat a snack consisting of a few olives and a piece of bread. Countless men, horses, wagons passed by them, long trains of pack mules, laden high on the way to the city, and returning even more rapidly, with empty saddles. On high, massive-wheeled carts, protected from the sun under colored parasols, vine-growing peasants from the Alban hills lolled among piles of wineskins. Little trotting donkeys carried, besides their masters, oil jars of reddish earthenware. Leaning on the forepart of his two-wheeled chariot, almost suspended over the narrow driving ledge, a sunburnt half-naked young peasant stood like a Homeric warrior, urging his jingling three-horse team homeward.

The chariots of the imperial express mail pushed all other vehicles aside. A column of soldiers marched by. Horsemen and travelers passed them.

"They press on as if death were sitting on the neck of each of them, and he was hurrying to some pleasure or other, a meeting, a meal, if only an execution breakfast. Mark, I wonder if you feel as I do the joy of being free to go out to God, to throw all his affairs up to him, and yourself as well! Just stay where you are, my ivory throne, and let them complain to you!"

"But what they ask, they ask out of a deep need," Mark objected.

Peter looked at him wide-eyed, and asked with a painful smile: "And I, whom can I ask?"

Mark was startled. The apostle's strong hand had always been decisive, and after any hard-fought spiritual battle, his impetuosity had always been succeeded by a great calm, but now he betrayed how heavily his position as arbiter weighed

312

upon him. "I suppose you think I should be ashamed of my weakness? No. I would be weaker if I let myself be stupefied by the monotony of those audience days in Rome. I must find God again, must find myself. In Rome? Instead of everything becoming more holy there, it merely becomes more human."

Peter laughed and went on: "Now I am leaving them time to turn the love-commandment over and over in their minds. Now they will not be able to make a slave of me with their everlasting requests for rules and regulations. If you make a law, you are the slave of that law, for you must hold to it, must be merciless, must kill for it. The mighty men of Rome, the Cornelians and Narcissus, who knew all about how to enslave the peoples of the world, threw it in my face that we were creating post after post, and prescribing duties for a multitude of people—teachers, prophets, priests, bishops, councils of elders, deacons, even widows. Cornelius wanted to make a statesman of me, Narcissus, a traitor to the Empire. Were they not right, the two of them?" He laughed outright. "All we lack is an army with weapons, to set out to kill for Jesus, to plunder and to rape. Did not my very presence there offend against the word of Jesus? We are not to have ourselves called teacher or father. 'You are all brothers,' he warned us, 'only one is your Father, the one in heaven, and only one is your leader, Christ!'"

The couple had been paying no attention to the passers-by, and neither Peter nor his disciple had noticed two simply dressed men who, deep in conversation, had left the road and were walking up the gently sloping meadow, to wait in the shade of the pines for the arrival of a vehicle. At present they were hidden from view by a tombstone. They heard Peter loudly speaking of Jesus, and then a younger voice, Mark's voice, saying: "How can you talk of weakness?"

"I wonder. Is it weakness, when I want to have no more to do with all this mummery of government, all these affairs of rank and grade and honors, among people who should all be equal?" Again he laughed heartily. "I don't want to be an emperor, like Claudius, so that they can write lampoons about me when I die."

Half shocked, half amused, the two Romans exchanged glances. Who was speaking so openly of that dangerous secret, of Seneca's mocking lines about the deification of the poisoned emperor, in which he described him as appearing before the gods as a hollow pumpkin? Miserable new god! The lampoon was both treason and blasphemy, a tardy revenge for the eight years' exile which the poet had to spend in Corsica. By writing his pamphlet he made amends for the fulsome funeral oration which Nero had ordered him to prepare. Everyone who knew his secret constituted a threat of death for Seneca.

For that reason, the two men came up to confront the speaker. Mark immediately recognized one of them who, despite his simple attire and his unkempt hair and beard, had the air of a great lord. It was the famous Seneca himself. His companion seemed no less noble, though his toga bore no purple edge. He had just observed that their vehicle had arrived, a peasant cart containing two mattresses, some rolled-up blankets and a couple of valises. In his cool, condescending fashion, the worthy Caesonius had fallen in with his friend Seneca's whim, to travel to Rome without baggage, unknown, and without any of the appurtenances of courtly life. At his gesture, the peasant driver reined in, the servants jumped down and quickly carried mats under the pines for them to lie upon, spread a cloth between them, and laid out wooden plates with dried figs, slices of bread, and some heavy green grapes. From his wineskin, the cupbearer filled two wooden beakers.

The poet had recognized Peter as a member of his friend Cornelius's household, and he embarked on a conversation about religion with him. Meanwhile, Caesonius was inquiring after the carriages of the two men, whom he took to be priests. He was surprised to find that they were traveling without companions or luggage.

Peter and Mark had pointed silently to their little bundles, which contained the bare necessities.

"That is what I call traveling light," cried the astonished Seneca. His companion remarked that the Roman calendar with its hundred and nine feast days in the year demanded a great many sacred implements.

Offended at such a comparison with pagan practices, the apostle answered brusquely: "With your priests, the services to their various gods are merely services to themselves. Your sacrifices are only licensed trading with the gods: I give to you so that you give to me."

The poet's mind rejected anything so prosaic. As he had just been trying to explain to his friend on their lonely walk, he had invented his own god. And just as he had thought up his god, so his god thought up the whole world. "My own life is just a pure and beautiful figment of the god's imagination!" On the other hand, Caesonius viewed the customary sacrifices as an expression of a noble way of life and of traditional duty. And he answered: "What is God, or the gods, to me? All my life I have dispensed power, over life and death, over the good and the bad. If there were a God, I would invite him to sit up in court with me, and he would have to commit suicide before he could bring himself to confess that he was the creator of such specimens. Your life, a thought of some god's?" He stopped and looked at Seneca. "Are we capable even of recognizing good, let alone doing it? Is not logic missing in all our experience? Can there be anything more wretched than the distribution of power on earth? I honor God by denying him."

Shaking his head, Peter turned to him. "Our earthly existence is only the workshop of the soul, a testing through deeds. I do not doubt that you have both reflected deeply about goodness. But the time has come for you to consider others. To do good to others is to do good to oneself, to do good to God. We all must work in active love, then the glory of ultimate perfection will be imparted to you, in that bliss which is granted by the sacred contemplation of the true God. Through this contemplation, the great, the ever-lasting peace will be yours, and the reward of happiness."

The two Romans were not quite sure whether the words of this Asiatic were to be taken as an insult or not. Even the philosopher was unable to calm his disquiet. His deepest longing was to live in peace, and at ease with himself. But here he was, the tutor of an emperor, being lectured to like any schoolboy. Seneca smoothed his ruffled hair. Despite himself, he felt a strange impulse to confess to Peter everything about his existence that did not correspond to Aristotle's teachings. His lampooning of the dead cuckold was mere weakness, cowardice, and it was out of cowardice that he had accepted the post of tutor to Nero and pretended to be guiding him, who was already impatiently trying out every conceivable vice.

Astonished, the two Romans saw Peter raise his arms heavenwards. In the vast noonday stillness of the hot, desolate Ager Romana, a great peace seemed to spread. Like Mark, the slaves had also raised their arms. Had they fallen victim to the new doctrine already? Listening to their prayer, Seneca involuntarily raised his hands too, and even Caesonius overcame his reluctance, and, not liking to leave his friend alone among strangers and servants, he tactfully adopted the same posture. They heard Peter say: "Lord Jesus, the end of the world is near! Besides their cleverness, give to these well-disposed here the power of prayer. Yours is the power to forgive pride and cowardice before the mighty ones of the earth. When they speak, may it be God's word they utter. When they serve, may it be in the strength you give them, so that the glory may be God's through Jesus Christ, for his is the power and the majesty for ever and ever, Amen."

The Romans had never felt so lighthearted and free. It was as if they had cast off all the things the stranger had spoken of so boldly, and were purged from sin. As the servants shyly drew back, Peter murmured softly: "I bow before your greatness of soul. God grant that I may one day stand before him with your pride. What can I, a simple fisherman, teach you, who bear within you the wisdom of two races, the knowledge of the Greeks and the justice of the Romans? You are like beautiful idols, and now I am daring to breathe life into you, for true faith is more than complacently being at ease with oneself. We must fight, fight with ourselves, fight with the world for the completion of everything. Let once all mankind be as one, full of charity in thought and deed, in prayer and sacrifice, then Jesus's work is completed. Then let the day of judgment come. In his name I call on you to do your duty, your duty to yourselves, and to Rome, and to the Kingdom."

Caesonius had been staring at the two strangers. Now he asked: "You men without a burden, will you soon be at your destination?"

"We do not know."

"Is it far?"

"It is everywhere."

"Will you be long on the way?"

"Maybe until the end of time."

"And whom do you seek?"

"Everyone."

"Who will protect you?"

"God."

PETER traveled through Sicily and North Africa, Spain and Gaul, and even distant Britain. He ventured across the Rhine into the trackless forests and on the way back through Gaul he made his way from community to community on both sides of the Alps.

Difficult as it was to find their way into the minds and hearts of the many peoples, the two travelers were astonished how rapidly the gospel had spread, and how it had gone ahead of them right up to the confines of the Roman Empire and beyond. In his letter to the Romans, Paul had just announced his arrival and he jubilantly declared: "Your faith is proclaimed throughout the whole world."

Peter brought order to the sacred customs and divine teachings. Childish superstitions he checked with implacable sternness, so as to impress the true Word on his helpless flock. He was deeply grateful that Roman warriors, Roman laws, the Roman language had traveled ahead of them everywhere. The mighty traffic of Roman government reached everywhere, too. Messages from the capital, news from all parts of the Empire followed them, and ever more urgently, the requests to come home.

Thrice-fearful news made them decide to return: Paul had

been recognized by an Asiatic Jew in Jerusalem; he had been maltreated and thrown out of the Temple. Only the Lex Valeria, which forbade the punishment of a Roman citizen who had not been condemned by the Roman people, had saved his life. Still in danger of being handed over to the Sanhedrin by the Procurator, Porcius Festus, he had appealed to the Emperor. In the custody of a Roman captain he was to be brought from Lycia to Rome. A large grain ship from Alexandria was willing to risk the winter journey to Italy. Instead of lying-up in Crete, as Paul had advised, the captain had ordered the anchor weighed. Heavy storms had overtaken the ship off the heights of Melita, and she disappeared. Of the six hundred men on board, there was no news.

Florianus, the young officer of the imperial guard who had arrived at Lauriacum with official dispatches, was startled to see how deeply the news dismayed Peter. He hardly dared to report the second dreadful item. "Porcius Festus is dead also...."

"How the Judaeans will run wild, when they do not feel his firm hand any longer!"

"Before two years were past, he died. His successor is already announced: Albinus...."

Peter sighed with relief: "A good name. The husband of a Christian."

Florianus drew a deep breath before saying sadly: "Too late. The High Priest Hananiah ben Hananiah was beside himself with rage because a caravan arrived with gifts from distant communities, intended only for our folk in Jerusalem. The Temple got nothing. Festus was dead, Albinus still far away, so Hananiah had the godliest member of the community —Jacob the Tsaddik—dragged before the Sanhedrin. Even the Pharisees were aghast. But the high priest put on his sacred garments and sentenced the Tsaddik, who had never broken one of the commandments, either of Moses or of Christ, to death by stoning."

Peter had become fearful to see. He visualized to himself the horrible scene as he, a helpless onlooker, stood at the foot of the Mount of Olives, and watched the godliest of the Twelve being pushed up to the battlement of the Temple, high above

318

the Kedron valley. "I hear you praying louder, louder. Master of your own fear, you are singing: Hosanna to the Son of David!"

With profound grief, Florianus said softly: "They thrust Jacob down. Flakes of his congealed blood stuck to the Temple wall. The weeping brethren bore the body to the grave."

A premonition of the third item of disastrous news made the apostle falter: "And the rest of the brethren?"

"One against the other, all was war and murder this side of the Jordan. The community fled till they found refuge in Pella, in the East Jordan country, in a heathen town where no Judaean sets foot."

Mark, trembling, looked humbly up at Peter. He could hardly realize the monstrous news: The power of the earthly Jerusalem at an end, the original community uprooted, Paul's Asia without a teacher and leader. Rome remained, the word and will of Peter, his vast responsibility before God as shepherd of the whole world for centuries to come.

As THE traveler comes down from the north towards Rome, the Tiber valley opens up before him on his last day's journeying, between rocky, sparsely vegetated hills and the two riverside roads, the Via Flaminia and the Via Salaria. The valley is white with gravel, and in places it is an hour's march wide, in other places only a quarter of that distance. Along the foot of the valley on calm days the river runs narrow and muddy, as treacherous as it is peaceful-looking. It meanders along as if it never filled the valley with its wildly foaming, swirling flood, though in fact this happens several times a year in the storms and rains. Just here and there a dead tree trunk cast up on the hot dry pebbles betrays its malice.

The last post station before the capital was called "The Red Rock." Only some five-and-twenty miles separated the traveler from the golden milestone at the "Navel of the World" in the Forum Romanum. Novatus Cornelius, Sextus's youngest son, had given the order that they were to change horses here for the last time on their hurried journey to the capital, and after the seemingly endless ride, he had dismounted and was impatiently walking up and down to stretch his legs. At increasingly short intervals, he would look out for Peter and Mark, who had wanted to go a stretch on foot, so as to breathe the cooler air of evening, after the hot, stuffy, odorous confinement behind the leather curtains of their traveling cart.

Whatever happened, they must not arrive too late! The churches of Rome were clamoring for Peter. The Cornelian had traveled as far as the "town of the sacred shields," to Lauriacum, where the shields of the Roman legionaries were forged out of northern iron. Here, the apostle had wanted to rest.

The clatter of hoofs caught Novatus's ear. His brother Timotheus came along the Flaminian road from Rome. He slid from the saddle and embraced Novatus. Then he saw Peter and Mark approaching. The young man's eyes were moist. "At last my prayer has been answered. Day after day I rode here in vain." Obeying his orders, the drivers and grooms hurried to get the traveling carts under way. As the Fisher of Men paused deep in thought by the step of the cart, his gaze turned southward where the glittering metal statue of Jupiter Optimus Maximus stood out against the sky on the top of Capitol Hill, and Mark and the Cornelians were caught by the joyous look of victory in his eyes. He said: "Add the strength of your young manhood to my old age! I know my last road. Death will travel hourly before me, beside me, behind me. But the nameless legions of God are on my side: the poor, the sick, the cripples, the aged, the widows, and the servants of the great."

Timotheus glanced sidelong at his brother, who had so urgently summoned the apostle home. Danger threatened them all, and particularly, Claudia, the wife of Sextus Cornelius Pudens whom Nero had posted to Lusitania, on the ocean coast, virtually banishing him.

The two youngsters hesitated, but their older friend Florianus, who had already mounted, signed angrily to them that it was time to speak. In the evening light, the young horseman seemed surrounded with magnificence. Was it that the bright medals on his leather jerkin mirrored the setting sun, or did the radiance proceed from him, the warrior? From his fair hair—his helmet was already hanging from the pommel of his saddle—to his long-toed feet, his young body was springing with strength and the urge to live a thousand lives at once. With a resolute look in his bold blue eyes, he rode over to Peter. "Will you forgive me, who have brought you so much bad news, if I now tell you of a grave danger ahead?"

"I will, and I bless you."

"Timotheus knows that the prefect Vipsanius Agrippa is secretly watching the house of Cornelius, in order to abduct Sextus's wife, Claudia. Now, the prefect hates you more than anyone." Florianus laughed bitterly. "His mistresses have left him, one after the other, to follow you. He is staking everything on winning over the Emperor to expel the Christians again. Through the mouth of Poppaea, your enemies from Judaea are agitating against you. Nero is dependent on this ambitious God-fearer through all his senses. She refuses herself to him if he does not carry out her wishes."

Timotheus whispered shyly: "As you enter the city—forgive me for not warning you straightaway—Vipsanius will try to have you clapped in chains by the guard at the gate. You must not be recognized as Simon Peter. As we are your property, so ... for him ... you must be ours."

The apostle looked up, and understood that he would have to make his entry into Rome in the guise of a Cornelian slave. He said with a smile: "You will have to estimate one-eighth of my value for the tax. But what is a fisherman, over sixty years old, worth on the slave market, between friends?" Kindly, humbly, he bowed before his new master. "I have so often told our brothers who are servants: Slaves, be respectful and obedient to your masters, not only the good and gentle ones, but also," and he smiled at the youngsters, "the bad ones too. I will be the servant of the servants of God."

Now Timotheus burst in: "Rejoice! Heartening news has just reached Rome from Puteoli. Paul, whom we thought drowned, is alive! After being miraculously saved from shipwreck he reached land, and will be arriving tomorrow morning. Great crowds will be going to meet him. My brother and I are riding out tonight."

The apostle offered a joyous prayer of thanksgiving, but

321

it pained Mark to think that Paul would be entering Rome as a Roman citizen, while Peter came in as a slave. When Florianus had announced all his dreadful news at Lauriacum —Paul drowned, Jacob murdered, the rest of the twelve refugees on the far side of the Jordan—the disciple had thought that Peter was at the pinnacle of his earthly power. But now the man who had written the letter to the Galatians was traveling towards Rome. Involuntarily he hazarded the question: "Will Paul still have a heart for the work, or for you?" But from the depths of his astonishing memory, the Fisher of Men drew the words Paul had written to the Corinthians: "And if I know all mysteries and all knowledge, and if I have all faith, but I have not love, I am nothing."

They lay down side by side in the traveling cart. They heard whipcracks, and the rolling of the wheels on the huge basalt slabs of the Via Flaminia. Mark sighed: "If only you were not on your way towards the city of demons."

"They are waiting for me. The demons as well."

As the Cornelians rode along, they noticed that all the roads and streets were deserted whereas usually at this time they were packed with vehicles waiting to get into the city, many of whose streets and alleys were closed to traffic during the day. The little houses and gardens by the bridge entrance could no longer be seen in the darkness. Normally, they led a gay life of an evening, with wine, music, and Iberian dancing girls, but now they seemed dead. Even over towards Rome, the road could hardly be made out in the darkness. They had a strange feeling of concealed life all about them, as if a horde of men were holding their breath in some dark hiding place.

Timotheus remarked to his brother, in an undertone, how dead the streets had seemed as he rode out of the city. "The shopkeepers were shutting their shops and barricading them. The children were being anxiously called in from play. Here and there, gangs of suspicious-looking hooligans were prowling about."

Suddenly Novatus's horse reared. Timotheus's horse would have bolted had not someone seized the bridle in the dark.

The mules drawing the wagons were halted too. The drivers had raised their whips to strike out, but a low call, probably a password, caused them to be still. When Florianus went to draw his sword, one of his soldiers, who seemed to be in the know, warned him: "They are not after our lives. They are after more. They are Onesimus's men."

Out of the darkness, the travelers heard a warning voice: "There are so many of us, any resistance is useless. We are not out for robbery. Otherwise you would be sounding your death rattle already. We are looking for the only man who would dare to travel into the city today—Peter."

Novatus was about to deny any knowledge of him, but out of the darkness came the voice that no one forgot, once they had heard it: "Who is it that looks for me?"

"The future masters of the world: the dispossessed."

Peter seemed to be smiling as he asked: "Are you so many? Who robbed you?"

"The rich and the mighty."

There was no doubt in the reply: "Those unfortunates?"

"Who is more unfortunate than we?"

"Those you have named. They tremble before you, before each other, before emperors, freedmen, before their demons. And why should they not tremble? No drink without poison, no night without dagger, nobody who might not conspire against them. Fortunate is he who has nothing to call his own."

"You say that, who walk on marble in the Cornelian mansion, and take your ease on an ivory throne!"

"Ever since I received it as a present, I have never sat on it. It is a symbol of high dignity; to become worthy of it, I have been traveling from country to country for years."

"Why do you not say: a symbol of world mastery? Why do you hesitate?"

"You are so many, what good is a poor old fisherman to you?"

The speaker's voice sounded harsh in the dark, sultry night: "He who sent you out used to teach about a scabby beggar who lay at the reveler's door. Angels took poor Lazarus into paradise."

Mark had followed Peter out of the cart. He knew how dangerous the city rabble could be if they thought someone was mocking them, and that even the Emperor Claudius, at the Circus, if ever he risked a joke, always addressed the masses only as "Most worthy gentlemen." The disciple was startled at the apostle's grim humor: "And you wanted to change places with the reveler in hell? You want to renounce your certain claim to a place at the Lord's table and to enjoy the happiness of so glutting yourself with imperial splendor that Roman knights will tickle your throat with a poisoned peacock feather, and senators will hold out silver vessels to catch your spew?"

Sullen murmurs threatened out of the night. "We came to Jesus because he was poor like us. I tremble for fear of being recognized because my master would have me crucified. I fled here out of longing for freedom. How often the word of Jesus was my last consolation when I was wandering about with no shelter. I was a Son of Man too, then, who had nowhere to lay his head, though the foxes have holes and the birds their nests."

"I could embrace you, my son, for being so well acquainted with the word of the Lord."

"Your Paul was always in and out of my master's house in Colossae. And were you not the guest of the rich Philemon too? We all know about your righteousness and we value it highly. Before you, Judas's rope broke because he had thirty pieces of silver too many. Before you a man fell dead because he did not give up all his money to the community, and his wife died too because she knew about the fraud. Your word felled the sorcerer. Help us to wipe out our exploiters!"

"God judged them!" The rage of the one-time partisan fighter Simon Peter broke out. "No curse of death or psalm of hatred ever passed my lips. The lame I healed, the dead I awakened— do you know nothing of them? You are not worthy of any miracle if you set wrong against wrong. You are calling down judgment on yourselves!"

"Are you threatening us? Not them?"

"Not I—God!"

"He who banished the rich from the Kingdom of Heaven?"

"And do you want to enrich yourselves for your own journey into hell?"

Mark and the Cornelians could feel the fury of the speaker in the darkness. Once again he begged: "We are all standing under the cross. For the sake of our freedom, save us!"

"Are you servants of the rich not freer than those wretched people the impoverished patricians, than the plebeians who starve without the crumbs from the rich man's table? The men of property are the ones who must care for you."

"Just a few, like the Cornelians. The rest grow fat on our sweat. We work, they enjoy themselves. Our daughters are their whores, our sons are misused by them. The slaves on the country estates are still worse off, who have to toil in chains, of no more worth than stalk or sheaf, ox or sow, sold at any time to the highest bidder. Look across on the slope of the Esquiline. Down there, hundreds of the likes of us writhe and gasp till they smash our shinbones with clubs, so that the strongest of us perish of gangrene, a meal for the vultures and ravens."

"Who would dare to maltreat a slave? They tremble before you."

"Try being a slave like us!"

"I am one," said Peter humbly.

"Don't mock us!"

"You are mistaken. I gave up my freedom and am reckoned among the Cornelian slaves. If I were recognized, I would have to die on the cross like you, as Jesus foretold of me."

The other stood silent and thoughtful, and then he replied with the same calm dignity: "We welcome you as one of us. No one will betray you."

Peter walked over to the man in the dark, the rebel who was liable by Roman law to the death penalty, and groped for his shoulder and embraced him. He could not distinguish his features, but he felt his brotherly kiss heartily returned. Reproachfully he asked: "For what purpose did you all come together?"

"For a surprise attack. The fire watch, the praetorians and the German bodyguards have their hands full. They are all scuffling with the wild crowds in the Forum and on the Palatine."

"Has civil war broken out?"

325

"The crowds are furious at the unjust charges against our Empress Octavia, whom Nero has tried to have executed out of his lust for Poppaea. Rioters have already overturned the marble statutes of Poppaea, and have garlanded those of the Empress. But Nero turned his men loose among the masses with whips. Stand up against him! Be our master or, as Paul says, our fellow servant. The State will be ours. Away with all those who exploit us!"

"Am I to be your bailiff?" roared Peter. "A fine State that would be! For thirty years I have been shouting in the ears of the rich: 'See that you do not incur the death sentence of the Holy Ghost. To God, nothing is great, save guilt and injustice. The price of power is death. Revenge will be on your heels, terror will be your tyrant. In order not to lie murdered in your own blood, you must murder and murder, until at last you are killing each other!'

"I will gladly lead you to power in all eternity. But then you will not be ransomed from your slavery by any earthly means, but with the blood of Jesus. I call to the Christians among you as free men, free to decide, but not as liars whose freedom is but a cloak for your wickedness. God's goodness is entrusted to each of you through God's greatness. It is written: You shall be holy as I am holy. —So let everyone set to work on himself! Let every one of you come with me, to me. Together we will work the miracle of life, of your eternal life.

"But do not keep me now. I have to confront the prince of the world. It is not I who will judge him, sentence him, execute him. Nero will sentence himself. But follow me, and if it is to the cross then you shall be with me in Paradise, the poorest first. So live with me, then, as if you were already good and full of love for each other like God's angels, like our dear brother Paul, like Jesus. To serve God is to rule. So be yourselves at last, as God created you in his own image."

EARLY the next morning a young Egyptian slave girl had bent over Claudia's slender toes, tinting her oval nails a tender pink, and polishing them till they decorated her narrow feet like semiprecious stones. Colored stuffs lay on a marble table

326

by the beautiful wife of Sextus Cornelius. She compared them, chose a piece here, a piece there, and with her elegant scissors cut them into apparently quite arbitrary shapes. She took small pieces, large pieces, curious zigzag shapes, and sewed them, sometimes beside each other, sometimes on top of each other, on a length of heavy material. She seemed absent-minded and perturbed. Now and again she unpicked, sought, sewed again. She seemed to be impatiently awaiting a guest, but no question came from her lips.

But when she looked up from her task again, she saw with surprise that the curtain at the entrance to the hall had been drawn aside.

"The illustrious Praefectus Vipsanius Agrippa of the Imperial Guard!" announced the nomenclator.

A resplendent figure stood before the startled woman. His breastplate and greaves were like golden ornaments rather than armor, his sword merely a sign of his rank. His helmet was a precious example of the metalworker's art. He gave off a light odor of leather, maleness and thoroughbred horses. His bronze medals jangled on their golden chains.

His spies had told him that the two young Cornelians, Timotheus and Novatus, had ridden southward early that morning to bring home a number of Christians, including an elderly Oriental. Realizing that Claudia, whom he so hotly desired, would be alone, he had set out for her house. And now he stood like a weasel in a dovecote.

He began by speaking with hypocritical regret of how disagreeable his duties often were. He had not mentioned Peter's name yet, but the astute woman understood whom he meant when he spoke of the godless traitors to the State, the enemies of order, who in their secret hatred of mankind gathered in underground tombs under the shameful sign of the cross, in the hope of inciting the slaves. Their hordes had risen on behalf of the traitress Octavia, against Poppaea. The runaway slaves, under the leadership of a certain Onesimus, had organized themselves into a vast rebel army. Vipsanius Agrippa raised his clenched fist. "With this grip I will strangle their ringleader Peter and all who harbor him."

He was not to know that the hated preacher was standing

327

behind the curtain in the innermost part of the house, dressed in a slave smock and as an opponent all the more powerful for it. When Simon Peter heard his death sentence from Vipsanius Agrippa's mouth, he nearly called jubilantly: "Yes!" but his fears for the Cornelians restrained him. As he peered between the curtain and the pillar he saw Florianus on the threshold in the golden armor of the imperial guard. The young centurion was in command of the detachment of soldiers who had accompanied Vipsanius. After a hasty glance round the room, he came across to his chief to report that a vast crowd was moving straight towards the Esquiline from the Via Appia. "For all the dust and sweat of their long march they do not cease singing. Those who do not flee from them are joining them. Among them, in the very front of the crowd, is a Roman citizen, a small bowed old man, his right hand chained to a centurion's left."

Just as Vipsanius Agrippa, who had not quite grasped what was happening, was repeating these last words, Claudia sprang to her feet and unrolled her tapestry. With both hands she held it up. The astonished onlookers saw upon it, like the pattern repeated round an old Greek vase, an endless procession of men, women and children walking towards a shining sun whose bright golden rays fell on two men, both of divine stature and noble bearing, with the long beards of patriarchal wisdom. One was dressed in foreign clothes, the other wore the purple-edged Roman toga. Ecstatically she cried: "And so I have conjured you all here by my art and my love: Simon Peter and Paul of Tarsus. My faith has triumphed! With singing crowds you are coming to my aid. The prayer of my hands has become a triumphal procession. Allelujah!"

Those who still retained vestiges of pagan supersition held their breath in fear. The terrifying memories of Simon Peter's power over life and death came to their minds. Vipsanius's gestures seemed uneasy, as if he wanted to strike out but did not dare. In a hoarse parade-ground voice he put the question: "And who is hiding the ringleader, Peter, and his gang?"

Florianus tried to divert his fearsome commander with the news: "The crowd must be near by now . . ."

"Seal off the Vicus Patricius so that no one can enter it until we have ridden away."

"They will not give way. They cannot go back, for an enormous crowd is pressing them forward."

"Then form up and charge them!"

"If our cavalry were to butcher them till their arms were tired they could not make a way through a whole people; and a Roman citizen is marching in front of them."

"Do you mean we are trapped here?"

"I ordered the horses and cavalry as well as your litter into the yard beside the house here. A way to the Vicus Longus is still open . . ."

"That would look like flight," whispered the commander, pale with rage.

"Not if we ride off in time. The girths are tight."

Vipsanius turned to go; his lips, till now narrow and cruelly pressed together, slowly opened. "We will take hostages! Simon Peter! I know they have got him hidden here! They are all answerable for him. Even if we have to put the whole Cornelius family in the Mamertine jail!" Death seemed to be reaching out between the pillars with its bony hand. Suddenly the deep solemn voice of Peter was heard: "Do not be afraid. No hostage is necessary. The Rock is here, to whom Christ said: 'Follow in my steps.'"

Vipsanius saw a man, gray with age, and of powerful stature, clad in a short slave smock. He was so awe-inspiring that the Roman had to summon all his pride to master his fear of the old man's magic arts. At the same time as the apostle had made his appearance, a servant had entered from the other side. Terrified at the sight of Peter, for he thought his masters lost, he could hardly stammer out his news that an enormous crowd was approaching the house. He listened in silence as Claudia ordered him to put a purple garment on her guest Simon Peter. But the Rock paid no heed to his wretched clothes, nor to the men in golden armor. He blessed Claudia, who had stood up respectfully. For all his commander's fury, Florianus did not hesitate to draw himself up as if before the Emperor. The curtains were raised here and there. The Cornelian serv-

329

ants crowded in, fearful for Peter. If he was going out to die, they would all die with him!

But he stepped forward till he stood in a pillar of sunlight streaming down between the purple canopies like fire from heaven. Hot and golden in the June brightness, the sun gripped him like the hand of the Lord. He spread his arms to heaven in prayer, and in the face of the others' anxiety he uttered his command to be strong: *"Sursum corda!"* "Lift up your hearts!"

The servants hurled back the curtains from the entrance. In the long passageway to the street, and up and down the street itself, in all the roads leading from the south, stood the *ingens multitudo,* the huge throng of Roman Christians. At the head of the procession Vipsanius recognized the two young Cornelians, and before them a gray Roman, and at the same time the nomenclator announced: "The honorable citizen Paul of Tarsus."

Claudia's gaze wandered uneasily from the illuminated likeness on her embroidery to the old man himself, who by his toga shared in the worldly power of Rome. At every movement, his chains rattled lightly. His right wrist was handcuffed to the left wrist of a grizzled centurion of the First Ituraean Cohort, who had been entrusted to bring him before the law.

Peter was deeply moved at Paul's appearance. How he had aged! Imprisoned for years, for years separated from the many communities from the Black Sea to Illyria whose growth he had watched over so fervently, had he now become weary and exhausted? But the believers were crowding behind him in such numbers that the stone walls threatened to collapse, for the house, the street, the city, the whole earth was becoming too narrow, and among them Peter recognized more and more of his former companions, as if they had all set out together to conquer the visible world and God's heaven. He saw Linus the Etruscan, in a white cloak. There was Onesimus, the leader of the poor and destitute. And was that not the youngest of the twelve disciples behind him, his beloved Judas Thaddeus?

The man in the golden armor felt as if he were being mocked. What kind of war lords were these to fight against? One in a slave smock, the other chained like a tame beast.

330

With one stroke he could destroy the leaders of the rebellion. Yet all his clattering troops, his bold young officer, were of no avail. Peter heard the dreaded prefect say to the startled youngster: "Unless Nero stamps out Christianity within two years, he will have lived in vain."

Those who heard his threat glanced at Mark and Luke, who had gone across to Peter. They had written down the word of Jesus. It was traveling through the world, never to be overtaken, never to be stopped.

Closer and closer the crowd swarmed around Vipsanius. Now he could no longer have made a dagger thrust. He might have fought battles against the Parthians and Germans, but here he was faced by a more powerful enemy.

More and more people crowded into the room, and as the crowd grew, the Roman's fear grew with it. They were approaching by every street, as he knew. No power on earth could stop them. Then Simon Peter drew himself up. In his powerful voice he commanded: "In the name of Jesus Christ, kneel!"

As if a storm blew from his mouth over ripening grain, the crowd swayed and sank on their knees. The order passed from mouth to mouth, out over the Fagu valley and Subura and Argiletum, to the Velia and the slopes of the Palatine, and over the Merulana and along all the streets leading from the Via Appia to the house of the ivory throne. Christianity had obeyed.

Vipsanius stared into Peter's dark eyes, which seemed to draw the very soul out of him. Against his will, perhaps hardly realizing what he was doing, he destroyed his own golden glory as a warrior and sank to his knees with the rest.

No miracle could have stirred the Christians more than to hear in the devout stillness, the clatter of the golden greaves on the stone floor.

Last of all, the Rock of God knelt. Jubilantly his cry to the Almighty rang out: "We praise thee, God the Father."

The thousandfold echo of the response surged back: "Amen!" and again the cry: "We praise thee, Son, we praise thee, Word, we praise thee, Grace!"

"Amen."

331

For the first time, the Church's prayer of thanks, statement and response, was heard like God's thunder in the seats of the mighty on earth:

"We praise thee, Father, we thank thee, Son, we rejoice in thee, Holy Ghost enthroned in light!"

"We thank thee, we thank thee, we thank thee!"

"Let me cry our gratitude in prayer and song!"

"Let us cry it in a thousand words!"

"We prayed for salvation."

"Thou hast saved us."

"We trembled from the wounds deep in our hearts. Thou hadst wounded us; our wounds burned and were healed in the fires of happiness. Thine was the grace that led our dance. We harped, we played our flutes and pipes. We danced from clouds to stars, from planet to planet, around the throne of your might. Who did not dance did not perceive the flowers that blossomed there. I have no house on earth but all heaven's mansions are mine!"

"Amen!"

"I know no resting-place, yet there is no resting-place without me."

"Amen!"

"Let me be thy mirror, thy door and thy way. Thy suffering is my suffering, our sorrow is every man's sorrow. I am thy rest, rest in me. Who am I? Thou knowest, but I do not. That which I seem, I am not. That which I am, only thou perceivest."

"Teach us to suffer, then we shall not suffer."

"Say with me: Honor to thee, Father! Glory to thee, Word! Honor to thee, Holy Spirit! Behold, we are one and are thine. Thine on the way to thee. Thine on the way to perfection. And thou art the perfection. Thou art the fulfillment which we honor, O God!"

"Amen!"

The Rock rose as if wings bore him. They heard him speak out of his simple, deep wisdom: "I pray you, beloved, abstain from earthly desires which are the enemies of the soul. Stand up against those who oppose you but let your actions be honorable among those who are not yet of the faith. By your good works you may open their eyes. Be obedient to the laws of man, for the sake of our Lord, whether they are of the Emperor, as your supreme master, or of the governors he has appointed to administer justice. Honor those to whom honor is due. Love your brothers, fear God, do homage to the Emperor. But for us poor brothers of the poor, it is not seemly to dwell among marble pillars under purple canopies. We come to you as captives of the captives like our brother Paul, as slaves of the slaves like myself. We would live among the poorest of the poor, to suffer with them, to weep with them, to console them and to rejoice with them when they enter the everlasting light, the never-ending rest in God."

Simon went to Paul and embraced him, while the kneeling folk sprang to their feet and cheered. Then they heard Peter's powerful voice: "Up, and away! Let us be the last of your procession. Let us accompany our honored guest, the golden-armored friend of the noble Emperor back to his house!"

Vipsanius had risen to his feet. Benumbed by events which he could not understand, he looked around and saw Peter and Paul kiss the foreheads of the Cornelians as they stood together, and Claudia put her arms round the old men's shoulders in a sisterly embrace. The maids and manservants did the same. Only he stood apart, for the first time unsure whether for such kisses, such an abundance of love, such sublimity in the face of hatred and persecution, it was not perhaps worth renouncing the rigid old gods who now seemed to be wavering in the distance, as powerless and irresolute as himself.

The man in the golden armor was the last to walk out onto the Vicus Patricius, between the fisherman Peter and the citizen Paul. Behind him the cavalry formed up, and the litter was brought. Exhausted from all the humiliation and the superstitious fears he had experienced, he climbed into it without a word, without a greeting.

POPPAEA savored with malicious pleasure Vipsanius Agrippa's report as, stinging under the indignity he had suffered, he described to Nero with military brusqueness the events of the previous day. "What are we," he asked, "against the masses? Once they held up the invincible structure of republican Rome, when each one was a warrior, and all together they made a mighty and unconquerable army, led by the ablest of them, their elected leaders. But now the army is no longer the State, only its tool. Soon the mercenaries will feel their strength and seize power for themselves. Our hope still lies in Caesar Augustus's living law. But traitors are at work who honor a new law. Heretics and traitors are at work. On the mighty scales of fate you are throned on a golden balance. To counterbalance you, the whole of mankind is crowded on the other side, but they, your counterweight, are lessening. You threaten to sink deeper and deeper."

"Where can the masses be vanishing to, that lift and hold me? Wherever I show myself, whether as Pontifex Maximus, as victor in my chariot or as a singer with my harp, everyone cheers me."

Vipsanius interposed: "I would have taken a solemn oath that all love for god was love for Nero, but yesterday I saw the multitudes setting out for a new destination, towards a miracle."

"Miracles in Rome," said the Emperor sardonically, but his laughter died away at the thought that there were things he could not do, for all his godhead. "And whom do they chase after, who can perform these things?"

"Their slogan-shouters no longer cry 'Nero! Nero!' No, 'Peter!' they shout, and 'Paul!' They do not pray to the Emperor."

"You say this sorcerer, Paul, is in chains?"

"He appealed to your Imperial Majesty when they brought proceedings against him in Caesarea and Jerusalem."

Nero was silent for a long time. Poppaea could hardly wait for the end of this ominous silence. What did one more murder mean to him who had murdered his brother, his mother, his wife, and countless others? Murder was always a swift and final solution. At last he began: "You think I should sit in judgment on men who can perform the impossible?"

Cunningly, Agrippa persisted: "The two gang leaders are

dangerous men. Peter can do anything with a word, Paul survived a viper's bite and threw the snake into the fire. Caution is advisable. Order the trial of these two traitors, O Emperor. The one who would judge them is a weakling who clings to the law, Titus Flavius Sabinus. Let Paul not have appealed to his Emperor in vain. In this affair, the public welfare is at stake. You are greater than your sublime forebear Claudius, who so loved the office of judge. Now, it is for you, the highest law of all, to decide."

Nero was hardly listening. He had sprung up with the agility of the bold racing charioteer. "Miracles are a sign of divinity. It is my will to work miracles. Every pleasure will be a commonplace for mankind. It will be the triumph of this world over any other! I will shape the golden frame and in the midst of it will be my golden house, and in front of the house like a golden colossus, the statue to my immortality: Nero, the life-giving god and the prince of this world! Call Paul to the bar of judgment, summon Peter to the court!"

SINCE the Emperor's decision to try the two foreign wonderworkers himself, the autumn rainstorms had twice poured down on the morose and shivering city. From the sea, the gales drove the deluge inland, and its heavy drops rebounded more than hand-high from the basalt paving stones and flowed together in puddles that gurgled rapidly down through the stone gratings into the sewers. The streets were empty. The Romans cursed the rain, and stayed indoors, muffled and hoarse.

In such cold damp weather, however much the cavalrymen greased their weapons and armor, the red tinge of rust kept appearing. Now, they were sullenly riding through the rain towards the Tiber under the command of the centurion Florianus, to where Paul, the wandering preacher, was imprisoned in a disused silo opposite the Janiculum. The huge granary afforded room for the crowds who came to listen to him; he himself lodged in an adjoining room, where he earned his own keep and that of his guard by practicing his trade of tentmaker.

Accustomed to early-morning guard duty, the captain, Julius, had already heard the cavalrymen approaching, and had unlocked the gate for them. While he gently wakened Paul and set before him an earthenware cup of warm goat's milk, Florianus looked into the lower room. In front of the high window stood the loom at which the prisoner worked for several hours each day. Hanks of yarn were tidily arranged on the walls, and many were already worked into a great roll of finished material, that had to be firm and watertight so as to afford protection against sun and rain. A few clumsy folding stools, a table roughly put together from planks, with writing utensils and wax tablets, and a few cylindrical containers for papyrus scrolls, comprised the furniture. The young officer gazed reverently at Paul's work; here, every thought was a prayer.

It was some time before the old man woke fully and realized that the decision he had been awaiting for years was near at hand. Dare he hope for an acquittal? For the inexpressible joy of freedom regained? Oh, to be allowed to go out once more into the lands of the earth, to bring the new Word to new people! But he would need superhuman strength. For years the prosecutor Tertullus had been preparing his deadly case. Was Nero, so dependent on Poppaea, really going to act as judge?

The little glimmering oil lamps spreading their dim reddish light from a niche seemed to emphasize how dark and nocturnal it still was, and the impression of gloom was deepened by the monotonous splashing of rain in the deserted streets. Today no one would be there to take the prisoner's part. If the faithful knew he was in danger they would come in hordes; but he had sent out those closest to him, Luke the physician, Jesus Justus and Epaphras, to preach, to warn, to bless. He was left utterly alone.

Softly he prayed for strength, not for his own sake—he had so often been flogged, and once stoned, thrice suffered shipwreck, there was hardly a danger he had not endured. The breath of God would give him wings. He would begin coolly, objectively, would try to be composed and clear, understandable to everyone. But then, he feared, his thoughts would

336

become crowded, half-formed, he would surprise himself with the mighty torrent of his words, hardly comprehensible any more. He rose for the journey which might prove to be his last.

Florianus had brought two reliable mules with him, and these carried the ailing old man and his faithful guard along the bank of the Tiber. They turned off before the Aemilius Bridge and rode along the Velabrum. Pillar after pillar, temple by temple, shivered in the rain. The statues lined up in stony crowds. Little pools collected in the folds of their garments. Drops streamed from the noses of the generals and emperors, the goddesses and queens. A gray melancholy dawn slowly spread over the Forum but did not yet lighten the immense chamber where attendants and clerks were setting the tables in position. The party dismounted. Julius walked between the close array of soldiers, up to the judgment bar, with Paul always a chain's length from his side. Near them, Tertullus was agitatedly bent over his notes, constantly rearranging them on the table.

A word of command. Like a thunderclap came the salutation: "Ave Caesar!" Tall and plump, the Emperor stood in front of his throne. He blinked, and seemed relieved that wherever he looked, soldiers were standing. Negligently he sank down on the cushions while his favorites Sporus and Spicillus spread a soft white blanket about his feet.

The Emperor nearly fell asleep during the endless disquisition on Jewish law with which Tertullus bored him, though the Prosecutor had made a number of furious demands in respect of Paul, the violator of the sanctuary in Jerusalem. He called for his extradition, so that this misleader of the people might be brought to justice according to the ancient sacred laws of the Jews. His speech grew more and more violent; meanwhile, Nero never let the strange, mysterious old man out of his gaze. Under his garment he held the point of a coral talisman directed defensively towards the Oriental magician. Impatiently, his eyes strayed to Vipsanius Agrippa, who stood guard over him, in his greenish eyes a reproach that he should have to waste his precious time listening to such dogmatic nonsense.

At last it was the turn of the accused to speak. Against his

337

will, the pupil of Seneca, the well-schooled connoisseur of all the arts of oratory, found himself enjoying the clear, well-ordered, philosophical discourse of the insignificant-looking old man. He must guard against being captivated by the storm of inner passion which the speaker, at first sight so morose and unprepossessing, displayed. Here was someone daring to say to the most powerful of judges: "Neither pagan nor Jew can carry out the Law. The letter kills, the spirit gives life."

When Tertullus furiously accused him of blasphemy against both Emperor and God, Paul cried: "The Law depends entirely on love, love for God and love for your fellow men." The prosecutor roared: "Do you mock Moses and his ten commandments? I will have your head for that!"

PAUL had contrived to beat down Tertullus's fanatical ravings with his wisdom and clarity, but now Vipsanius Agrippa mockingly remarked: "They tell me a certain Saul of Tarsus—yourself, Paul—had one of the noblest of the followers of Chrestus put to death by stoning?"

"You were a witness of my entry into Rome. You saw how everyone greeted me, the Saul of old, with the sacred kiss. We do not repay evil with evil, for: Judgment is mine, said the Lord. He has judged me, too. His word dashed me to the ground on the road to Damascus, and struck me with blindness. But then he blessed me with the light of faith, and I recruited an army for God...."

Nero interposed: "Do you betray yourself at last? You spoke of an army."

The accused man merely smiled. "Caesar Imperator, I recruited, indeed we are still recruiting, soldiers not only in your dominions, but beyond the frontiers of Rome and throughout the whole world, for our orders are to exclude none who is prepared to fight for King Jesus. If you have a mind to serve him as a soldier, you will not regret it. Through his mercy the Lord may save even you, but not for your works, for then mercy would be no mercy at all."

Tertullus tore his robes in despair. "Do you blaspheme against him who was and is and will be? Do you not know of

God's last words through the mouth of Moses? Where is the mercy in them? 'When my hand reaches out in judgment, I will take revenge on my enemies; I will make my arrow drunk with blood and my sword shall be gorged on flesh!' "

Paul raised his right hand. "We carry no weapons. We bear the cross. It is invincible. Our faith is love, our love is action."

The Emperor observed, as did Florianus, that many of the Guard were pressing closer to the accused man. Were they of his faith too? And disloyal to their war lords? Did they aim to lift the traitor on their shoulders and march out with him? The Emperor felt suddenly faint. Tertullus was frantically thumbing through the Pentateuch in search of some wrathful utterance of the thundering Jahveh: "I will strike you with poverty and with a fire that will blind your eyes.... I will multiply your tribulations sevenfold and the heaven over your head shall be brass and the earth under you shall be iron!"

Suddenly, as if this merciless God was storming from Mount Sinai itself, a hitherto unheard voice was raised, a disturbing voice for many there in the hall. Beside the insignificant-looking prisoner, who was just considering his answer, stood a sturdy and stubborn seafaring man, whose youthful eyes belied his shaggy gray hair and beard. People streaming in after him had left the basilica doors open, and a keen north wind drove over the crowd, straight into the face of the shivering Emperor. Sharp as a sword, a ray of sunlight thrust down from above onto the brightly illumined head of the man before him, and Nero's breath failed for he knew without asking: This is Peter, who has power over life and death.

Peter's cry echoed from the ceiling beams like God's angry laughter. It was directed at Tertullus: "Recite your ten commandments!"

Blind with fury, the Judaean began to recite the inexorable decrees, each one but a short sentence, the foundation of all moral order, of all earthly welfare, preached for thousands of years, and broken, day by day, for just as long.

Many of the troops in the hall, whether God-fearers or baptized, had learned the Ten Commandments by heart, and they began slowly reciting them with him.

The shivering Emperor had been listening to God's angry

339

curses, and now, without realizing his own terrible action, Tertullus was condemning Nero ten times over.

By a glance into the eyes of the two men, Nero became uneasily aware that he could not have abused the name of the Creator more outrageously than by calling himself God. Now the commandments concerning offenses against his neighbors were being enumerated, concerning the mother whom instead of honoring, he had slain, and the prohibition of murder, which he had so many times defied, of adultery, of stealing, of bearing false witness, of his insatiable greed for other people's possessions, to which some of the best and noblest Romans had fallen victim. The Emperor sat trembling as if Rome was praying, the Temple speaking, the statues joining in with their brazen mouths, and he, the judge, was being judged. In a voice that seemed strange to himself, he asked Peter: "What if someone charges himself with breaking the commandments?"

"He must come before the holy community, and accuse himself, and confess his fault to all his brothers and sisters before God. He must be banished into the anteroom of the prayer chamber, to do penance in word and deed. If he is rich he must share all his possessions among the poor, and follow Jesus."

"And what if, by name and rank, he himself is the Law, the Law of all the peoples of the earth?" What impelled him to say things of which he himself was frightened?

Beside himself with terror, Tertullus clutched his table for support, for he realized that he had accused not Paul, but the Caesar Imperator of the Romans, of every crime in the world. Then he heard Peter's answer: "Everyone must show virtue, and in his virtue, knowledge; and in his knowledge, temperateness; and in his temperateness, constancy; in his constancy, godliness; in his godliness, his love for his fellows; and in his love, the love of God."

"Love! Love!" repeated the Emperor hoarsely. "And what if someone whose magical powers are proved, what if he gets up and prays to his God that . . . that he may destroy the Emperor?"

"None of us has ever uttered a prayer that was not love,

even love for our enemies, and for our enemies more than anyone else."

Nero's voice suddenly regained its old power, as if he were singing in the Theater of Pompeius before twelve thousand listeners. Triumphantly he asked: "And Simon the Sorcerer?"

"His deadly sins were put an end to. In the hour of his death pangs, God gave him time to repent."

Suspiciously the Emperor watched every move of Peter's, however slight, to see whether he might not fling himself on his knees again as he once did in the Forum, with such force that the basalt stones gave way. He began cunningly: "We have acquainted ourselves with your works, through an examination of the writings of your sect. We know that you have been reproached with weakness, with failing your Master and denying him. Had you been a diplomat, you would have allied yourself with Judas Iscariot. Your god would have come to terms with our gods. Then there would have been peace in Judaea. I would not have had to send my cleverest general across the sea with his legions, to wipe Jerusalem out of the memory of man, to destroy the Temple of your invisible god, to drive the plowshare through the foundations of all that your kings built, and scatter salt in the furrows. Now we are conquering your god!"

Tertullus listened in horror, and Peter was strangely moved. Once, full of admiration, he had remarked to Jesus on the Mount of Olives how mightily the building reared up on Moriah, and he had been told: "Not one stone will remain on another." And so the fate of Jerusalem, that slew its prophets, was being fulfilled. Triumphantly he replied to Caesar's sneer: "The Father lives in the Son."

The more defenseless he felt the two men, the more Nero's insolence grew. "I will prophesy what is awaiting you and your god—I, a priest and god myself!" He motioned, and beside him a wicker cage was placed, covered with a fine napkin. Paul was groping for Peter's hand, to press it gratefully for his help, when a strident cockcrow came from the cage. At a sign from the Emperor, the *haruspices* zealously lifted out of the wicker cage a splendid motley-feathered cock, who, with its hens, forecast good things or bad by the way it pecked

341

at its food or spurned it. Nero gripped the bird by its iridescent neck. At first it ruffled its feathers and vainly clawed with its spurs into the Emperor's merciless fist, but eventually it hung still, looking wickedly around, as if it too were bearing witness to every charge against the apostle. Peter turned his somber gaze, under the bushy brows, full on Nero, till the cheeks and forehead of the red-haired Emperor blushed deeply. Was this the moment when the deadly miracle-worker would fall to his knees with that stone-shattering force of his? Even the Emperor's clenched fists began to tremble. With a sudden double thrust of its claws the cock slipped out of Nero's hand, which was pouring with blood, and crouched ready for combat at Peter's feet. At this unexpected omen the pagan Romans turned pale. The *haruspices* trembled with fear at having to interpret it. But after momentarily drawing back, Nero recovered his voice and made his own interpretation: "You see, even the cock, the symbol of your weakness, cowers before me to do homage. And you, be wise! Save yourself and the body of Chrestus. My statesmanship, Rome's power, your magic, together we are invincible. But if you do not join with me, you will betray your god for the very last time. Be mine. Say yes."

"Will you not crow?" Peter coaxed the fowl with a kindly smile. "No? You do not need to warn me any more. Stay with me and you will be kept in honor, and not as a miserable altar offering. We will be together forever over the whole earth. You will be enthroned on the steeples, high above mankind, warning them in eternity: 'Man, be not weak!' "

As Peter, the oracle of a mighty future, bent down, the Emperor was overcome by fear, for the cock had turned from him and had wounded him with its spurs, whereas it stayed quietly by his opponent, a disastrous omen for the heathen. Even the mighty men about the throne stood paralyzed before this victory of supernatural power over worldly power.

Hoarsely, Nero threatened: "An emperor, Caligula, declared of mankind: 'If only they had one single throat to cut!' Beware, lest out of the cock's entrails . . . your neck and Paul's . . . one grip and . . ."

Sternly Peter interrupted him. He was standing erect again now, more master of the world than the shortsighted blinking emperor. "I am eternal life. You are death." His words had a menacing ring. "Ask the oracle: My faith brought dead men to life. We are not afraid of those who kill the body but cannot kill the soul. We who speak for Jesus here in front of you, are at this moment being spoken for by the Son of God in front of his Almighty Father in heaven. That which you put your trust in—the executioner's sword and the murderer's dagger—what can such things do against our faith? We are reborn to a living hope and we shall be like the angels of the Lord. Through faith and mercy we are stronger than Rome and its army and its emperor. Tell him, brother Paul, who it is that the poor Caesar Imperator is daring to resist!"

"Through one single God we are all baptized into one single body, with God the Son as our head!" rejoiced the old man at his side, and pressed more firmly the hand of Peter, his advocate.

The Emperor cried out: "The execution sword to Paul's neck, and you, Simon Peter the archmagician, we will break your bones on the cross. We will cut the head off the body of your Church! With your heads the head of this body will roll, the head of Chrestus will roll, whom you tried to make into a god despite his shameful death!"

"And who rises again, year by year till the end of time for us, in us, with us!" cried the apostles triumphantly.

"No!" roared Nero.

"You are the No that we deny, that God denies, unless you do penance and repent, repent, repent! Nail me to the cross! Keep me no longer in the flesh! If my weary feet, sore from so much wandering about the world, will carry me no further, I will crawl to the cross, to victory there. You may kill the body of Christ, but against the spirit of God you are powerless through all the centuries of centuries!"

Nero was shocked. A weaponless, defenseless man like Peter must know himself to be master of enormous magical powers, to oppose the Prince of the World to his very face, and to proclaim his transience in front of all the great officials and sworn soldiers about his throne! He closed his eyes at the thought of such temerity, and then his melancholy gaze wandered into infinity, gray, comfortless, godless.

Deathly silence fell on the court. Everyone held their breath. Caesar Imperator Augustus Lucius Domitius Nero still stood sublime before his men, though he was groping uncertainly for the arm of his throne. Before the courage of this man who had dared to enter the high priests' court with the death sentence hanging over his head, the Emperor lost his sense of power, and dared not pass sentence, but only thought how best he could make a dignified exit.

At his signal, Sporus handed him his lyre. To their astonishment, the two apostles saw the murderer take a deep breath, open his mouth wide, and begin to sing in a powerful voice that, deep down, was a cry of deathly fear. He sought once again to deny guilt and judgment and the afterworld, and it was to ease his own conscience that he sang Seneca's lines:

> "Death—and then nothing; death is a nothingness,
> being but the post that marks the last lap of the race.
> Do not hope, greedy one, and you, the fearful,
> do not tremble. After your death
> you will sink down into the unborn.
> Death is impartial, slaying the body,
> and the soul too he does not spare."

His favorites Sporus and Spicillus clapped with feigned enthusiasm, but contrary to custom, no one else moved, in the whole of the enormous courtroom. Nero had already turned and gone, as if he had only come there as a singer, and not as a judge.

Peter looked after him and his words reached the Emperor like a sob of pity. "Lord, forgive him. Does he know, unfortunate man, what he is doing?"

The Emperor left it to the Prefect Titus Flavius Sabinus to pronounce the findings of the court. The praetorians marched out. In the presence of the handful of believers, the judge acquitted the apostles. The attendants roughly hurried the Temple's bewildered and disconcerted advocate, Tertullus, out of the emptying courtroom, and locked it.

In their many-storied tenements, the poor people of Rome lived in constant fear. Not a creak of the wooden joists, not a rattle of plaster within the walls but made them start out of their sleep with terror. Was the roof falling in? Were they going to be buried under the debris of the falling plaster? Was that a voice screaming: "Fire"?

Whenever the Emperor was carried through the narrow streets, the praetorians were hardly able to make way for his litter. Alleys without light or air, crowded with overhanging stories; streets through whose garbage no one dared to wade. Stench everywhere. For long the Emperor had intended to build a new Rome, worthy of himself. He dreamed of an imperial city of gold and marble, yet knew that the old must be destroyed before the new could be begun. Artist and god, he rehearsed with the singer Terpnos a dramatic description of the burning of Troy.

One morning, from Aquila's garden on the Aventine, Peter observed a number of the Emperor's slaves setting fire to wooden stalls about the Circus Maximus below the Palatine. The flames quickly spread to the wooden seats. Showers of sparks rained down on the poor quarter beside the road to Ostia. On all sides arose cries of *"Vindex! Vindex!"*—the customary desperate cry for help and revenge. The bold *vigiles* were hurrying to the scene, but the Emperor's slaves impeded them, picked fights with them, and mocked and beat them.

The blaze licked up the slope towards the imperial palace. While the mounting rows of circus seats were nothing more than smouldering charcoal, the priceless magnolia trees on the hill of imperial glory were lighting up like torches in the darkness of the smoke. Black soot filled the air. Out of the rain of ashes came the howls and lamentations of the burned victims. Terrible reports followed on each other's heels: "The Temple of the Forum is burning! Everything round the Capitol is in flames! The relics of our ancestors are destroyed! The votive offerings of the generals, all the trophies are burnt! Woe upon Rome!"

Across the valley of Velabrum the fire hissed, crackled, roared up the fortress hill, where for five hundred years only the fires of sacrifice had burned.

345

The Praetorian Guard hurried from their barracks at the double, detailed to the various districts of the city. They themselves set fire to the houses of the very rich in order to plunder them. Criminals known to all, paid to applaud the Emperor at the Circus, pretended to be followers of the Chrestus. They carried crosses through the streets and threw them on the flames, they aped the singing of the choirs, and hindered anyone who tried to put out the fires. Buckets of water, laboriously dragged by sweating men, blinded by the smoke, with singed eyelashes and blistered fingers, were snatched by these criminals and emptied away. "The God Chrestus does not want this. The world must burn!"

The devastating fire lasted for six days. Hordes of fugitives fled out into the Campagna, carrying their boundless despair with them. They mourned and lamented, prayed and cursed, hungered and thirsted, sweltering by day and shivering by night. Weeks and months were to go by before children found their parents or parents their children. Many had lost everything. Reduced to beggary, they called on the gods for revenge.

Whom were they to blame? More and more of them sided with the Emperor. He had been one of the first to lose his home. He, who hitherto had done everything to help his people with food and games, now showed his true greatness. He hastily summoned troops from all over Italy. Tents were pitched, barracks built. He had corn distributed. Sailors off his battleships were called in to rescue the wailing victims from normally inaccessible places in the burning ruins. The praetorians were ordered to tear down buildings threatened by the flames, in order to create firebreaks.

Then, as the royal artist stood on the lookout tower of Maecenas, surveying the ruins of the Forum, a new blaze rose high in the distance behind the Viminal and Quirinal.

"The palace of the Praetorian Prefect Tigellinus is on fire!" Now there was no saving Rome's most luxurious quarter. Excitedly Nero reached for his costly new Ionian lyre and began to accompany himself on its ten strings.

> *"It seemed to me that they collapsed in flames,*
> *Ilion and my Troy, razed to the ground,"*

346

he sang in a husky, mournful voice, but the mob on the slope of the Esquiline whose wretched hovels were still standing, and who were watching the new outbreak in terror, heard him at first with astonishment, could not understand, thought themselves mocked, became so enraged that they lost all feeling of respect and fear, and furiously whistled and hissed at their singing emperor. His faithful companions with him on the terrace were terrified at first, but then they acted as if they could not see the devastation but only heard his song; they sobbed and rejoiced about him, lifted him on their shoulders and bore him down the steps to the guardroom, to safety, where they lay the pale, exhausted singer on a couch. His artistic pride was deeply wounded, but there he sat up and cried hoarsely to Vipsanius: "Tear down the Esquiline houses at the foot of the tower!" Then he smiled. "So that the fire will not spread."

Three days after the renewed outbreak, the fires were still not out. Then, under menacing swords and spears, a huge tidying-up process began. None of the homeless was permitted to be idle. Noble Romans who had never demeaned themselves with physical work, the parasitical retainers of impoverished patricians, louts who never did anything but stand at the head of the bread lines and the queues at the Circus entrance, were now forced to work under pain of death, and were mercilessly driven to clear away the rubble of the old Rome and to help build the new. The flats of swords slapped down on the naked backs of the idlers. All who did not wish to starve, cursed and lent a hand.

They had continuously to load rubble onto ships which carried it away to the mouth of the Tiber. Slowly the beautiful new residential areas rose, with the houses not too high, the streets wide and full of light and air. Each house was detached from its neighbor, and the lower stories built of noninflammable stone or brick. Only in the upper stories was it permissible to use wooden beams. Fire buckets and water barrels stood ready in every yard. Water was laid on to the dwellings and to each street corner, to quench the thirst of passers-by. Compensation and loans helped the builders.

For all that, the toil-weary Romans were full of complaints, and spoke longingly of their old narrow alleyways. "He exposes us to the wind and sun on these desolate squares," they grumbled. "Anyone who wants to stay in Rome has the privilege of pitching his tent ten or twelve miles out in the Campagna. Then, of a daytime, while we are slaving here, the thieves can sneak around and steal our compensation money and our wages!" "What took days to burn down, takes years to build up again!"

Already the pillars were being gilded at the entrance to Nero's "Golden House." It cost two-and-a-quarter million sesterces. The last remaining rich people trembled for their possessions, and for their lives, when they were invited to the magnificent gardens and palaces, for the imperial splendor was spread all over the Palatine, Esquiline and Caelius.

Now it was spring again, the first spring since the terrible alarms of July 19th, 64 A.D., the day when Rome began to burn, and Nero was suffering worse than ever before in all his eleven years' reign under the hatred of those whose happiness had been his aim. His joy in building had become a positive fury of impatience. "I have not enough time left!" he wailed. But hourly, the reports grew more ominous.

Again he tried to win love through murder. Among the sparsely raftered ruins, into the Emperor's new suburbs, and out to the tent and barrack encampments, guards detachments were sent with three-horse wagons, and dagger at throat they compelled people to confess whether they were Christians. All who confessed, all who were suspect, were herded together like cattle for slaughter, urged onto the wagons and driven into the city, load after load. In the theaters and circuses, they were penned up as conspirators and incendiaries responsible for the burning of Rome, and sentenced to death by the Emperor.

The Emperor's agents had anticipated mass escapes, but to their astonishment, no troops nor guards were required. The news had hardly penetrated through the city and into the villages, before the faithful assembled as if summoned by angels. They had put on their best garments. The girls and young women were garlanded with flowers. In vast singing crowds, the Christians made their way to the Golden House, and peacefully camped before it. Constantly, new processions arrived, new songs rose to God. As a greeting, they called to each other the petition they used at the beginning of many of their services. From his place, it was not *"Kyrie Kaisar!"* that Nero heard, but *"Christe eleison!—Kyrie eleison!"*

The terrible news of the persecution came immediately to Peter's ears. Full of fearful premonitions, he had dispatched his closest companions to distant communities several weeks before—Mark to Alexandria, Flavius Clemens to the Black Sea. With a few deacons, he had stayed behind alone. And now, through every window, over every wall, he heard of the horrors that were to take place on the dreadful day of the first Christian massacre. Since early morning, the heralds had been making their proclamations, to attract the Romans to the spectacle. Enormous crowds had set out from far across the Ager Romanus, over the dust and rubble of the even more desolate suburbs. From the houses of the untouched districts as well as from the newly built areas, they streamed towards the circuses, intent on vengeance, their mouths full of curses against the hated Christians.

Wherever they went, wherever they rested, they heard the malevolent heralds bawling: "All into the circus of our sublime Emperor, the god Nero! Those found guilty of the burning of Rome, the ones who hourly called the wrath of the gods down on our heads through their unbelief, the ones who started the fires and prevented them being put out, destroyed the temples, and laughed when your children were stifled in the smoke and your gray-headed parents fell with the burning beams into the fiery abyss and were burned to a cinder—today they are going to suffer their just punishment! A spectacle such as the world has never seen! Sensations without number! Christians will be nailed to crosses in the arena like the founder of their heresy. Berber lions, Indian tigers, Dacian bears, hundreds of them, have been starving for three days, and now they are going to be fed before your eyes on virgins and children, men and women, young and old, and all alive! Hear them crack the bones; see them lap up the blood! The

349

haters of mankind, the Christians, will be exterminated by our noble Emperor in his glory-wreath, by the god Nero, who gives you this spectacle of justice!"

Peter, Linus and Anaclete were standing on the Nero Bridge. None knew when fate might strike, but they were ready. Their intention was to join the terrible processions, to give heart to the victims. The faithful stood tightly packed along the road beside them, those not yet recognized and arrested. Their faces looked pale and worn. All through the night, many of them had gone to the prisons to snatch just a glimpse of their fathers, mothers, children, sweethearts, wives, to hear just once the voices that in a few hours would be silenced for ever. Others who had contrived to avoid the investigators and were hiding in the houses of friends, either alone or with their families, had tossed restlessly on their couches all night. Should they confess? Was it not their duty voluntarily to tread the road to death? What good was a life in constant fear, a life without the loved ones? Others had trembled, prayed, listened in the darkness, been terror-stricken over and again, rushed to the windows to peer through a crack in the shutters, or crept to the door to hear if all was still. When the door knocker sounded, they leaned against the walls as if paralyzed, not knowing who had come for them.

Earthenware counters had been distributed at the entrances to the huge Neronian circus that sprawled along the Via Aurelia. They were given to everyone, but not to the three waiting on the bridge, not to the apostle and his companions, who were to be his successors to the ivory throne as well as in martyrdom. They knew they were being watched. They had been insulted and threatened by the angry pagan relatives of fellow believers, but when one vengeful man had tried to maltreat them, he had quickly found himself pulled back and shoved away.

They had celebrated love feasts with the few who were at liberty and trusted themselves to come to divine service. They had reached consecrated bread through the prison bars, which threatened to become mere choked-down morsels of fear. But even the waverers, even the mourners, learned the ancient

350

song of victory from their resolute brothers. Nearer and nearer sounded the psalm as the procession of doomed men and women came out of the darkness of prison into the light, their last light. Now the words could be heard more clearly:

> *"God is our refuge and strength!*
> *The heathen raged, the kingdoms were moved;*
> *God uttered his voice, and the earth melted."*

Men of the fire watch walked in front, the brave *vigiles,* so many of whom had died in the fires. Full of rage against the incendiaries, they knew only too well how monstrously unjust were the charges against the Christians. The feared and celebrated high priest of Christ had lodged in one of their barracks on the far side of the Tiber, when he first came to Rome. As one of his first believers he had baptized their oldest captain.

Silently, taking short steps, the *vigiles* approached in two files across the street. They looked grimly ahead, for many of their comrades would be suffering today. They had recognized Simon Peter from afar, but they hardly dared to cast more than a furtive side glance in his direction, for fear of betraying him. Even these rough youngsters could read the deep emotion in his features. For the stern messenger of God, to whom power was given over life and death, who always demanded the utmost from himself, and was always troubled for fear he was too complacent, for him the burning of Rome had been a turning point.

In the chaos and misery of it all—the flames had hardly chased the victims out of their burning homes, the houses were scarcely empty—the most peaceful citizens had changed immediately into a fierce rapacious horde. They stormed into the deserted dwellings and cellars, looting and plundering, fighting each other. They gorged themselves and emptied the last wine pitchers, then they fell senseless and perished as the glowing beams collapsed.

Were Christians to be found among these victims of their own rapacity? Had Peter's followers stood the test that he had so often begged for, in agony at the unreliability of the baptized pagans, though Paul had defended them over and again? Or had they deserted him, as they did before in favor of Simon the Magus?

After the fire, a rumor had gone from mouth to mouth that not a Christian had been lost. Once again the onrush of new believers was excessive. Peter had sifted them severely, and he was even pleased when timidity and estrangement reappeared because the Christians had suddenly been accused of arson. He had hurried from one communion to another, full of furious love, to seize the overwordly ones by the nape of the neck and make them look up, blinded, to God. "To be ready is all. The end is near!"

Magnificently, they put him to shame. Handsome girls walked in front. He had placed the veil on them himself with the words: "Take the holy veil, my child. Wear it without stain before our Lord's judgment seat, before which every knee bows in the heavens, on earth and in the deep through all the ages, Amen."

Among the matrons he caught sight of Joanna. Tears ran down his cheeks and into his gray beard. So she was called on the way to the eternal home before him. To hearten and comfort her he called the name of the Lord over their heads.

Her dark questioning eyes were turned on him. Her look called to him, stronger than the loudest cry. Till then, he had left it to Nero's men to take him to martyrdom or not—Thy will be done, Lord!—but now he felt a burning urgency to march at the head of the death procession. His Church was great and invincible. It needed him no longer. It was his duty to die with his followers. Though he was standing there in the bright sunlight despite the entreaties of his deacons, nobody, save Joanna, had so much as glanced at him. Out of their touching loyalty, they did not want to betray him to the lictors. But as he suddenly made up his mind to join the procession, he found himself prevented by the spears of the legionaries who had been ordered to line the death route. Even his powerful seaman's hands could not push them aside. While he was still trying to break through, Vipsanius Agrippa suddenly stopped before him, tall on horseback, and cried loudly and mockingly: "Simon Peter! Your friend, our noble Caesar Imperator, has ordered me to watch over your well-being. I am answerable for your health with my life!"

Was it in order that the flock should lose faith in its shepherd? The apostle groaned in despair. Now that his work was completed, he found himself barred from the consolation of entering into everlasting peace.

With a sad heart, he looked after his flock as on the farther bank of the Tiber they trailed past the impressive graves of the Via Aemilia, towards God without him. Men of many races and tongues, whether slaves or freemen, held each other by the hand and sang in the language of Rome. And so the procession of martyrs started on its road through the centuries, the road that was never to end, with the cry of *"Christe eleison! Kyrie eleison!"*

The believers marched between the densely thronging pagans in the Imperial Gardens, past the huge white marble vases decorated with garlands and pleasant reliefs of dancing girls. As they slowly began to draw closer together, they went arm in arm. In the bright blue of the evening, iron crosses were already rearing up over the hedges to right and left. At their feet, brushwood was piled, and torchlights were darting about. Now here, now there, rough hands dragged a silent, defenseless being out of the Christian ranks, threw the tar-spattered *tunica molesta* over him and hoisted him up on one of the iron crosses. Already, the woodpiles were beginning to crackle, eager tongues of flame were licking the hanging garments, the tar caught fire, dark clouds rose up. In the smoke of the pyres, the singing died away.

The enormous crowd drifted past the living torches, along their road to eternity. Between darkness and firelight, before the apostle's eyes, the sacred host of martyrs became one whole, whose outlines were no longer discernible. As one single Church they bore their share of Jesus's suffering, themselves the redeemers of those not yet of their faith but who would now be following their example. Above the high outer walls of the Circus, they heard the roar of hungry lions and tigers, their appetite roused by the smell of the flesh of thousands

353

of men. The body of mankind, the body of Christ, was going to its death in immortality.

UNDER the protection of Nero's cowardice, the apostle did not go into hiding, but challenged the authorities, who staked everything on making the Christians suspicious of their leader. They tried to make him appear as the Emperor's decoy, so that anyone greeting him, anyone visiting him, risked death. Only a few of his closest intimates were left to him, with the intention that they should fall under the same suspicion. In this way, Nero hoped to shake the Christians' faith in their God and his messenger.

With the two young daughters of Cornelius, the Fisher of Men went to the places of execution, to gather up the victims' remains and bury them. Weeping, the tender girls tried to soak up the martyrs' blood with sponges, and to collect it in glass bottles as a treasure. They went unmolested, but warnings came from various sources that their arrest and execution was imminent. It was hoped that his followers' fears would eventually persuade Peter to take to flight. Then, far from the capital of the world, he could disappear in contempt and oblivion.

But Nero was being reproached by a master of elegant behavior and cultured taste, the brilliant literary satirist Petronius, who could not understand how the nose of a poet and the breath of a singer could bear the disgusting smell of burnt Christians. Nero was anxious to restore his reputation, and being no longer troubled by the rebellious Christians now that his Romans had quenched their thirst for revenge, he decided to travel to Hellas in the company of Sporus Sabina, to be present at the Neronian Games, which he had lavishly endowed as a gesture to the Greeks.

In Rome, the most bloodthirsty of his freedmen had assumed the mantle of power. The Praefectus Praetorio Hegoumenos Helius Caesarianus was even more cruel than his master; he was the man to deal with the death-dealer, the dreaded destroyer of Simon Magus. But Peter did not humble himself. His wise, statesmanlike letters were laid before the

354

astonished and enraged Helius. In them, despite his distress, like his crucified teacher before Pilate, Peter recognized the power of the State, provided that, in turn, it conformed to the order desired by God. Wherever Christians gathered to pray and to celebrate their love feasts, the doomed man's warning to the doomed was read aloud: "Be subject to every ordinance of man for the Lord's sake, whether to the emperor, as supreme; or to the governors as sent by him to punish the evildoers and to reward those who do well. For such is the will of God, that by good deeds you should hang a muzzle on the ignorance of foolish men; as free men, and not using your freedom as a cloak for wickedness, but as the subjects of God. Honor all men; love the brotherhood; fear God; honor the King."

Linus and the children of Pudens, more concerned for him than for their own lives, had ceaselessly reminded him that it was his duty, as the Rock, to maintain the Church of Christ. And at their secret meetings deep in the catacombs, the brethren listened to him with greater reverence than ever, as he affectionately warned and strengthened them. For with death facing his followers, his dreaded severity had been replaced by a paternal kindness, which seemed to embrace their hearts like God's own arm. The knowledge that the apostle was still alive was bound to give support and confidence to the whole Church.

At last, the old man had reluctantly given in, and as so often before, had set out on his travels through the city gate. Did he not think himself due for a rest now that his life's work was done? He had allowed himself no respite. On the move in all his waking hours, he had hurried from one person to another whom he believed to be in fear of death, to console them and give them heart. They would be gold, tested in the fire and ready to take up their eternal heritance. In all this toil, the old fetter-wounds on his ankles had broken out again. One of his young deacons had torn his tunic into strips to bandage the open sores. Then, by secret byways, they accompanied him to the southward road. They finally left him at dusk, at the fork of the Appian and Ardeatinian Way. Resting in the darkness, he found the heat oppressive. The last good wishes were still sounding in the distance. When he reluctantly arose, he no longer knew whether his direction lay to right or to left. But when the stars eventually shone through a rift in the grim sirocco clouds, he found that he had wandered too far eastward. His bandage had come undone and he nearly fell as he turned back. Impatiently, he ripped it off, for he found it impossible to tie in the darkness. Soon he found himself among a dense column of people. He could not see them, but he smelled the dust and sweat and the odor of their tormented bodies. The sad procession was coming from Rome and they dragged him along with them. In the silence, only their heavy breathing could be heard, and occasionally a groan or a muffled curse. Now and then, someone even wearier than he stumbled against the fisherman. None of those reeling along dared to rest, for they would not have found strength to get up again.

They were burnt-out citizens, making their way home to their tents far out in the Ager Romanus, after their day's stint of clearing rubble and rebuilding. There they would spend the night, staggering up again in the first gray light of morning to journey back to their work. They had nothing before their night-blind eyes but the endlessness of the way; they did not see the stars by night nor, by day, the blood-spattered veil of the poppies that spread over the plain. Affected by the misery around him, Peter was tormented more than ever by doubts as to the wisdom of leaving Rome. Was it not through weakness that he was wandering about here? With a bitter twitch of his bearded lips he consoled himself that so late at night and in this desert among the countless gravestones, no cock was likely to crow after him. But on this dead march through the night, suddenly red firelight shone from a tavern among the gravestones. Perhaps some thirsty man had thrust aside the ragged sacking over the entrance. And now for the first time Peter saw how many were walking with him. But immediately he staggered back, for he had nearly collided with the only person coming towards the sufferers.

This was a man bent under the yoke of his sorrows as if he bore every man's grief, so bent that the crossbeam on his shoulders barred the fisherman's path at eye level. It was some misfortunate on his way to execution. His outstretched arms

356

were lashed to the heavy beam. He was probably to be hoist on a cross, among the crucified slaves on the slope of the Esquiline, to linger on in agony and to die of thirst.

Peter was about to reach out and help when the cross-bearer looked up at him in the blood-red light, with his huge kindly eyes, and his mouth, on which a gentle, knowing smile of sympathy seemed not quite to have faded in spite of all his torment.

"Jesus!" Peter was about to exclaim, but he choked back the cry. Supposing that huge crowd recognized the persecuted Christ! Yet what could they do to him but execute him? Now the two men who came to redeem the world through their self-sacrifice, stood face to face, as once before. Then, the Messiah's most faithful follower had not wished to see his Master so humbled; he had not been able to forgive him for accepting a slave's death instead of summoning the twelve hosts of saving angels. He had thought Pilate's prisoner faithless, and for that reason he had abandoned him on his hardest road. What the women of Jerusalem had contrived, what John had brought about, he had been unable to do. He had sat alone and wept....

But this time he must not let him, whose wisdom and intentions he understood so well since the fiery tongues of Pentecost, bear his misfortunes alone. And in his eagerness to help, beside himself with love and grief, he stammered: "Master, where are you going?" And immediately he remembered: Peter! You asked that same terrified question once before in your life. "Master, where are you going?"—would Jesus answer once again: "Where I am going, you cannot follow now. But later you will tread the same road." Had the time come at last?

The Saviour looked at him with a dolorous smile in his eyes and murmured: "To Rome, to be crucified again...."

The light went out. In his fear, the disciple tried to lift the cross from the bowed shoulders and to take it on his own. But someone knocked against him in the darkness and those coming after stumbled over Peter and struck out at him with the fury of hungry, overworked men on their way home, so that he fell by the roadside.

Summoning all his strength, he picked himself up. He had

357

to follow Christ to Rome, to arrive there before him. Jesus, the honor of the cross is mine! Even if I have erred, I will make it good. In your boundless mercy you have shown me the way. For thirty-six years I have been on the way to you. Now I have found you at last. I glorified you and the Father; I brought forth fruit a thousandfold. A church of heroes, a church of martyrs! My church! I will carry it, carry it to you through martyrdom and the pangs of death.

The road lay empty before Peter. He did not walk, he ran all the way back, rejoicing over and again: "Will you lead me at last, as you said, where I do not want to go? But I wish to go, Lord. I wish to go!"

At dawn, Peter hammered at the door of the guardhouse at the foot of the Appian Way with his fisherman's fist. After endless waiting and hours of cross-examination, one of the guards was sent to Helius Caesarianus, for his orders. For a long time, Helius stared before him with a malicious smile. One year after this man's death, the old prophecy said, the Emperor would die. And then? He had heavy irons set on the apostle's ankles and wrists, and after only a few steps the old wounds began to smart again. Through streets piled with debris, past hollow-eyed ruins, the rough soldiers urged him across the Forum to Rome's most infamous prison, whose iron-studded door only opened for traitors when they were led out to their death. As the group went by the Curia of the Senate, the entrance to the source of highest justice lay cool in the early-morning shadows. The mighty green bronze door rose up like a wall, as if justice had locked itself in.

Furious at being disturbed so early, Martinianus the jailer opened the gates and admitted Peter and his escort into the Mamertine prison. He laughed grimly when he heard that the old man was a dangerous traitor. "Into the Tullianum with him, then!" he shouted and added sternly: "Say farewell to the light. You will not see it again until you are brought out to die." With a torch he lit the way down the steps into the underground vault.

"This way!" he shouted, and pushed the prisoner towards

358

a low pillar where he was to be chained. As the weary man could not find his way quickly enough in the darkness, the jailer hit him in the face with such wild fury that the falling man struck his temple against the stone, hard enough to crack his skull and set the blood streaming down his face. But in the torchlight they saw a strange sight. The apostle was supporting himself with one fettered hand against the wall from which he seemed to have recoiled, yet his face was unhurt. In amazement, the soldiers thrust their torches nearer; they stared at the jailer, the jailer at them, then all of them looked at the stone, on which, in the flickering light, Peter's profile was recognizable, with sharp black shadows, as if his face had been cast in the wall. Furtively they touched the mysterious hollow with their hairy hands. Their frightened glances strayed to the prisoner. The bewildered jailer was forced to realize that for all its unyielding hardness, the travertine stone was softer than his own heart. The stone had yielded, and now it retained the image of the holy man for all time.

The pagans shrank back in fear. The jailer was questioned whether the hollow had been in the stone previously. He could not remember. But the image in the rough stone incontestably resembled the new prisoner.

In his clumsy violence, Martinianus dashed his fist against the wall so as to destroy this monument to his heartlessness. His mouth distorted by pain, he groaned horribly and wiped off the welling blood from his hand on his rough smock. This time the stone had not yielded.

One of the soldiers took him by the arm and pulled him away, but he tore himself loose and, his jaw quivering, he looked back at the old man before whom the ancient wall had given way. As if he himself had been beaten he went away with the legionaries, licking blood off the back of his hand.

Though they had all left him, Peter knew he was not alone. Reverently, he touched the stone. The thought of his miraculous escape from a horrible injury gladdened him like some delightful promise. Smiling angels seemed to whisper words of comfort. "If only the Romans had known that they were marching out with sword and spear to prepare the way for the weaponless Christ! We have crossed all the frontiers and the territories between. You led us, and we followed. May your kingdom come!" Never before had he so ardently prayed the mighty prayer of hope, the Paternoster.

"You taught us: He who would save his life must lose it; whoever loses his life for my sake will find it again. Dare I ask as once before: See, we have left everything and followed you, and what is before us now? Today I can joyfully repeat what you once said: Truly, I say that you who have followed me, at the resurrection when the Son of Man sits on the throne of his glory, you also shall sit upon twelve thrones!"

The warders listened as his voice grew louder:

> *"The darkness overwhelms me*
> *And the light about me becomes night ...*
> *But even the darkness does not hide from me,*
> *And night shines like day*
> *And darkness and light are both alike."*

Processus had come to relieve the jailer Martinianus, but when he heard this song of triumph from the mouth of a man to whom the stones were cushions, he was seized with fear and would not venture into the depths of the prison. They stole down a few steps only, to listen to the prisoner. Both of them shivered in the icy prison air. Everything had become so deathly still that they did not dare to move. They felt insects scuttling over their bare feet, spiders, scorpions or cockroaches. They could hardly bear the desolate stink of dried excrement and urine. Here and there, they heard rats squeaking as they let themselves drop down through holes and landed with a light slap on the wet stones. Then a sudden thundering at the door above startled the warders. Only when they realized that the noise was made by spear hafts, and that new prisoners were being brought, did they hasten to unlock the door.

Martinianus did not venture any mockery this time, though the prisoner before him was a much smaller man than Peter, with an almost bald head and a sparse gray beard. Another of the Christian leaders, another victim for the darkest cell in the prison.

Torches around Peter. "You've got company!" shouted Martinianus from the upper floor.

Peter's eyes had first to become accustomed to the bright light of the torches, then he greeted the newcomer with outstretched arms, his chains rattling on his wrists. Paul of Tarsus stood in the red light before Peter. "O faithful one!" the chief apostle cried to him in greeting. They embraced each other, before the newcomer was chained up.

"I was in Iberia when I heard about the persecution. I came to you, to our people, straightaway. I would not leave you to face it alone."

Meanwhile, Martinianus had shown his mate the apostle's image in the hard stone, and had let him feel it. Yet even this miracle did not astonish them so much as the joyous sound of the two prisoners' voices, and the light in their eyes. They had never imagined so much happiness possible in this place of ultimate despair. Fearfully they listened, and heard strange things of a crucified man who rose from the grave. "He made it possible for us to be born again to an undying hope," Peter said joyfully, and Paul spoke eagerly of the day near at hand, when Christ would reshape their tired old limbs according to his own glorified body. The old man with the forelock knelt before his own image in the stone and said gratefully: "With my own head, did you set the seal on your work and mine, your Church, for all time to come? Let me offer you a glorious Rome, founded on the freedom of us earth-rooted folk, and on our sacred will to be yours, and to live here on earth as we hope to be allowed to live in heaven." The two wise apostles joined in a prayer of thanksgiving: "Your bread is scattered upon the hills. It will be gathered together into one Whole. So will your Church be embraced from all the ends of the earth as your Kingdom, for yours is the power and the glory. We thank you for your holy name, we thank you for the knowledge and the faith, we thank you for the immortality revealed to us through your son. To all mortals, you gave meat and drink, but to us, your believers, you gave the food of the spirit and life everlasting. Let your grace come, let the earth pass away."

The two warders, rough men, specially chosen to break the defiance of the worst criminals, thrust a torch in the ring on the wall, though the prisoners of the Mamertine jail were not entitled to any light; they brought them wine instead of water, and bread from their own loaves.

HELIUS Caesarianus long hesitated over carrying out the sentence which had been passed some time before by compliant judges. The fact that the two ringleaders of the proscribed Christian brotherhood had given themselves up, had to serve as proof of their guilt. Helius feared the miraculous powers of the two magicians. Every day the thresholds all through his house had to be sprinkled anew with sacrificial blood.

Then the infuriating news came to him that the doomed men in the dungeon were holding court like princes. Daily, it seemed, numbers of their followers were bribing their way into the prison. There were fresh rumors of miracles. In the ancient wall, a spring had gushed forth, whose crystal-clear water was caught in stone basins. Peter had used it to initiate his two jailers, through some mystical ceremony, into the secret Christian brotherhood.

During a wild orgy, Helius drank himself into a state of boldness. Late at night, he thickly ordered the two jailers Processus and Martinianus to be executed out of hand. At daybreak, Peter was to be crucified, Paul to be beheaded.

The dreaded jailers, hitherto by virtue of their trade more sure of their lives than any other Roman, could not realize at first that they were going to be executed but, heartened by the constant sight of the happiness of their two prisoners, they too showed themselves strong. Astonished, Peter and Paul saw the two men they had baptized coming solemnly down the steps, dressed in their best, accompanied by soldiers and lit by torches. They knelt before the apostles and bowed low. One after another, the apostles laid their hands on the tousled heads with a prayer that reminded them of the omnipotence of him they believed in, and at the happiness that

362

awaited them, a happiness bought with brief suffering. There was so much of grace and power in the clear voices of the old men that Martinianus and Processus looked up at them, their ugly faces transfigured by happiness. When the soldiers saw the deep effect of the comforting words, they fell with a clatter to their knees, as if at a word of command, and asked for the same powerful blessing. Then they formed up in line, and marched off smartly with the two men who, from being hangmen, were about to become martyrs.

It was dark again, and became darker still as the torch burned out in its holder on the wall, and no one looked to the prisoners in the Tullianum. The two apostles thought themselves deserted and forgotten, and called to each other in the darkness. Were they to be left here to die of hunger and thirst, like so many of their predecessors in this eternal night? Out of the tranquillity of his soul, Peter jokingly remarked that they were only fasting as was seemly before they came to the Lord's table. "I am grateful that you came to accompany me on the way home."

"Home. If we were free, where would we find a home?"

"Our home lies in eternity."

The spirit of the two men was stronger than the shivers that ran through their freezing bodies.

"You stood by me before the Emperor."

"How could I have left you alone?"

There was a little silence, then Peter said: "For years we have been taking into our lives every torment of body and soul so that we might be masters of every form of human distress, till our longing was everyone's longing, and our love was their love."

Paul agreed. "Who grieved and I not with him? Who suffered insults and I did not burn? Every day the multitude came to me with their burden of sorrows, I had the care of all my Churches on my hands—and what sufferings did I not bear?"

"Rejoice with me that we are on our last journey. You cannot imagine how magnificently our people crossed the Nero Bridge." Peter's voice faltered at the thought of the martyrs' torments. "We offered up a tremendous sacrifice of all tribes and nations. All these years I had not relaxed my severity towards our Roman community. I could not forget their desertion to Simon the Magus. But now it was one triumphal procession of loyalty and faith. A victory without weapons. It was a hard thing to watch them going to the sacrifice. Yet already sorrow was a sin, for I knew these were no dying people who went by, but people about to rise again!"

By the rattle of chains, Paul guessed that his brother in fate had sunk down on the stones. Full of pity, he crept gropingly toward him as far as his chain allowed.

"And I thought you hard as a rock, when your heart was full of sorrow and love." The man from Tarsus felt that even the worst news would come as a consolation to Peter, and he said: "Listen. They have pronounced sentence on us too. For me, the sword. For you, the cross."

"That is why Jesus said: 'Follow me!'" He had been about to say: "That is why I saw you, Son of Man, on the way to Rome to be crucified again. You came to suffer with me." But he refrained. He who, as a youngster, had felt his father bleeding to death against his heart, took care to spare his fellow sufferer. Had it not always been Paul's pride that, though he had never belonged to the Twelve, it was precisely he who had been the last one Jesus spoke to on the road to Damascus, long after his departure from his disciples? And yet after all, it was Peter who had been the very last to see the Son of Man, on the Appian Way, and had questioned him, and heard his voice say: "I am going to Rome, to be crucified once more."

"Crucified in me," whispered Peter to himself, and he smiled as the Son of Man had smiled so often over the great and small errors of his twelve messengers. He left Paul his pride, and reached out as far as he could, and though he could not press the other's hand, he contrived to stroke it. "Who could come before God with a lighter heart than we?"

Paul agreed: "Over and again we made up our differences: in Jerusalem, in Antioch, and again in Jerusalem. You were always the pillar of the Lord. The Master knew to whom he was entrusting the keys. Your name, and yours alone, issued from the angel's mouth when the women went to the tomb of the resurrected Jesus: 'Go, tell Peter.' What an honor. 'Tell Peter!'"

WITH a clatter of weapons all around them, as if precautions were being taken against some enormously powerful ruffians, the two apostles left the Mamertine prison on their last journey. Peter had hastily staggered to his feet and despite his heavy chains, raised his arms. "Gird me!" he cried impatiently to the soldiers. "It has been prophesied of me: 'Another will gird you and carry you where you would not wish to go.' But I do wish it!"

With their escort they clambered up the ladders and steps into the early light of a summer morning. As they went across the still-deserted Forum, the Fisher of Men intoned his prayer while the love of those who were at that moment on their knees before the Saviour, interceding on his behalf, seemed to shine hotly on his face. "Lord of Heaven, you know all I intended was honorable, yet everything always turned out differently from what I had reckoned or wished for—always, through your greatheartedness, more splendid, more victorious! And when I was traveling all the roads of the world you set before me an ever more wonderful goal. And now my body is going to attain to the highest honor of all: to be raised up on your cross." Softly, quite softly, he said with a painful smile: "And, Lord Jesus, you will surely not call me Satan again, even if I deserve it...." and more serenely still: "At least, not in the first joy of our meeting!"

On that June morning in the sixty-seventh year after Christ's birth, the eight hundred and twenty-first since the founding of the Eternal City, the streets of Rome were still portentously silent and deserted about the prison, when the officer ordered Paul to be taken along the Via Laurentina, and Peter to be escorted across the Field of Mars to the Nero Bridge. But all at once a vast crowd grew out of the soil of the endless maze of streets. Stone by stone took shape, human shape, as far as the Tiber sands. All Rome opened its eyes, its bright, brave eyes transfigured by welling tears, in a farewell glance of gratitude and devotion.

365

In its strange mighty silence, the usually so noisy city seemed to be holding its breath in terror at the monstrous event about to take place. The Emperor's bloody power had thought to murder Christianity. But that day, it seemed, Christian Rome had risen anew.

Tears came to the eyes of the stern, much-feared Fisher of Men; he had to support himself, in all his weight, on Paul as he whispered with trembling lips: "Look about you! They are more than ever. Our work is as immortal on earth as in eternity. Farewell, most fortunate Paul."

"Farewell, my happy Peter! Today we shall be before Jesus, with all our loved ones."

"At last I, the rolling stone, will find peace, will find time for my former companions on all the roads of my restless life."

Children tore themselves from the hands of parents who were too distressed to hold them back. Girls and boys strewed flowers in the apostles' way. Their self-sacrificing love was triumphing over the tyranny of worldly power. Thousands upon thousands of hands waved palm and olive branches. On all sides rose the longing cry: "Peter and Paul, bear us in mind!" The seeds of martyrdom were taking firm root. The Word lived on.

As Peter looked back once more, he saw a noble matron kneeling in front of Paul. Her companion removed the veil from the old woman's unseeing eyes and held it out to the apostle. A soldier tried to push them both away with the haft of his spear, but Paul seized the fine cloth, made the sign of the cross over it, and gently replaced the veil on the blind woman's helplessly smiling face. In her inexpressible joy, she cried out in a voice that was still clear, though slightly cracked with age: "I can see, Jesus! I see your princes of the Kingdom of Heaven!"

Astonished people surged forward, knelt down and prayed, happily or anxiously, while as Peter walked on, he murmured to himself: "Does one need a veil to behold the truth? O knowledge without learning, knowledge beyond reason, that accompanies us on our last journey!" And he marched on lighthearted, transfigured with joy after years of error, uncertainty, and of decisions too difficult to make. From all sides, the waiting crowds formed up as if in the rear of a festive procession, to provide a last escort for the mighty one who was hurrying into eternity. Quicker and more impatiently he stormed along, till the praetorians in the rear ranks had to break into a trot to keep up.

The cross lay huge on the golden sands in front of the executioners. While with a few hammer blows they struck the fetters off his sore limbs, Peter's eyes drank in the mighty city for the last time.

"Rome, my Rome!" cried Peter, before he stretched himself out on the narrow timbers, and it came to his mind that Paul's sword was more merciful than his cross with its lingering death. Bravely he spread his arms to his Lord, as wide as he could. Blow by blow, the executioners drove the rough nails through nerves and veins and splintering bones into the clamorous wood. The weight of the Rock tugged painfully at the wounds as the cross was raised. The executioners had wanted to crucify him upright, but for all the tearing agony, he ordered otherwise, and they bowed to his will.

"I want to be crucified head downwards! Lord, I am not worthy to be raised above the world like you. As you, Jesus, opened your arms to take all mankind to your heart, so I will open mine for you! I take the whole world on my shoulders and bear the burden of man's guilt, man's longing, I carry all man's works up to your grace and mercy. Your bleeding feet were turned earthwards, mine want to travel heavenwards, that for years have been on their way to you!"

Just as they succeeded in ramming the shorter end of the cross into the pit prepared for it, the fisherman raised his head, dark-red from the rush of blood, on his muscular neck and took at once farewell and possession of Rome, which he had purchased through his hard toil, his great sacrifice, his agonizing death. That day, he brought the capital of the world to his Master, and in it the whole world itself. With his last look, in which the pain turned to pride, to just pride at his bloody elevation to the Redeemer's death, he saw the light of eternity. His own work was completed. He had served, with the strength which only the Almighty can bestow. Sanctified by his tremendous mission, he uttered his last groaning, jubilant cry to heaven: "The whole inhabited world is in my net. The net was your Word. Thanks to your mercy, my weakness became strength and I myself your Rock. I am carrying my Church, I am carrying you, my God, into eternity. Amen!"

(1)